博士后文库

中国博士后科学基金资助出版

On Existence and Multiplicity of Solutions for Some Nonlinear Equations

(几类非线性偏微分方程解的存在性和多重性)

Lixia Wang (王丽霞)

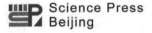

Science Press
Beijing

Responsible Editor: Qingjia Hu

ISBN 978-7-03-077454-5

《博士后文库》编委会名单

主　任　李静海

副主任　侯建国　李培林　夏文峰

秘书长　邱春雷

编　委　（按姓氏笔画排序）

王明政　王复明　王恩东　池　建　吴　军　何基报

何雅玲　沈大立　沈建忠　张　学　张建云　邵　峰

罗文光　房建成　袁亚湘　聂建国　高会军　龚旗煌

谢建新　魏后凯

《博士后文库》序言

　　1985 年, 在李政道先生的倡议和邓小平同志的亲自关怀下, 我国建立了博士后制度, 同时设立了博士后科学基金. 30 多年来, 在党和国家的高度重视下, 在社会各方面的关心和支持下, 博士后制度为我国培养了一大批青年高层次创新人才. 在这一过程中, 博士后科学基金发挥了不可替代的独特作用.

　　博士后科学基金是中国特色博士后制度的重要组成部分, 专门用于资助博士后研究人员开展创新探索. 博士后科学基金的资助, 对正处于独立科研生涯起步阶段的博士后研究人员来说, 适逢其时, 有利于培养他们独立的科研人格、在选题方面的竞争意识以及负责的精神, 是他们独立从事科研工作的 "第一桶金". 尽管博士后科学基金资助金额不大, 但对博士后青年创新人才的培养和激励作用不可估量. 四两拨千斤, 博士后科学基金有效地推动了博士后研究人员迅速成长为高水平的研究人才, "小基金发挥了大作用".

　　在博士后科学基金的资助下, 博士后研究人员的优秀学术成果不断涌现. 2013 年, 为提高博士后科学基金的资助效益, 中国博士后科学基金会联合科学出版社开展了博士后优秀学术专著出版资助工作, 通过专家评审遴选出优秀的博士后学术著作, 收入《博士后文库》, 由博士后科学基金资助、科学出版社出版. 我们希望, 借此打造专属于博士后学术创新的旗舰图书品牌, 激励博士后研究人员潜心科研, 扎实治学, 提升博士后优秀学术成果的社会影响力.

　　2015 年, 国务院办公厅印发了《关于改革完善博士后制度的意见》(国办发〔2015〕87 号), 将 "实施自然科学、人文社会科学优秀博士后论著出版支持计划" 作为 "十三五" 期间博士后工作的重要内容和提升博士后研究人员培养质量的重要手段, 这更加凸显了出版资助工作的意义. 我相信, 我们提供的这个出版资助平台将对博士后研究人员激发创新智慧、凝聚创新力量发挥独特的作用, 促使博士后研究人员的创新成果更好地服务于创新驱动发展战略和创新型国家的建设.

　　祝愿广大博士后研究人员在博士后科学基金的资助下早日成长为栋梁之才, 为实现中华民族伟大复兴的中国梦做出更大的贡献.

中国博士后科学基金会理事长

Preface

It is well known that nonlinear equations are important bridge connecting mathematical science with other natural and social sciences. Nonlinear equations, such as Schrödinger-Poisson equation, Klein-Gordon-Maxwell system, Kirchhoff equation, Hardy-Sobolev-Maz'ya equation and Choquard equation can well reflect the essential phenomena of certain practical problems in physics.

Schrödinger equation is a second-order partial differential equation established by combining the concept of material waves with wave equations. Poisson equation can be regarded as an incompressible fluid motion equation. The meaning of the equation is equivalent to the flow rate of liquid passing through any closed surface being equal to the total amount of liquid generated by the fluid sources contained within the surface. Schrödinger-Poisson equation comes from fields such as quantum electrodynamics and semiconductor theory, and is used to describe the motion laws of particles in space and time. When an electric field is generated during particle motion, a Poisson perturbation term is usually introduced, which adds interest to studying such problems.

The interaction between charged particles and the electromagnetic field generated by them can be described by the binary models of Klein-Gordon equation and Maxwell equation. The Klein-Gordon equation is the most fundamental equation in quantum field theory and relative quantum mechanics. It is the relativistic form of the Schrödinger equation, used to describe the relativistic motion equation of a free scalar field with spin 0. Under the framework of field theory, regularization quantization of free scalar fields can be achieved through the Klein-Gordon equation. Due to its ability to describe the kinetic energy of scalar particles, the Klein-Gordon equation is widely used in the field of high-energy physics and is known as one of the foundational equations of quantum field theory.

Kirchhoff equation is an extension of the classical D'Alembert's wave equation for free vibrations of elastic strings. Kirchhoff's model takes into account the changes in length of the string produced by transverse vibrations. M. Chipot and B. Lovat pointed out that Kirchhoff equation models several physical and biological systems.

Hardy-Sobolev-Maz'ya equation has been used to model some astrophysical phenomenon like stellar dynamics. It was proposed as for describing the dynamics of galaxies. Various equations similar to Hardy-Sobolev-Maz'ya equation have been proposed to model several phenomena of interest in astrophysics. Such as Eddingtons and Matukumas equations have attracted much interest in recent years. Various astrophysical models were introduced, including some generalizations of Matukumas equation.

Choquard equation was proposed by Choquard in 1976. It can be described as an approximation to Hartree-Fock theory of a one-component plasma. It was also proposed by Moroz, Penrose and Tod as a model for the self-gravitational collapse of a quantum mechanical wave function. In some context, Choquard equation is usually called the nonlinear Schrödinger-Newton equation.

In the past two decades, Schrödinger-Poisson equation, Klein-Gordon-Maxwell system, Kirchhoff equation, Hardy-Sobolev-Maz'ya equation and Choquard equation have been widely used in many physical problems. Many mathematicians are interested in them. This book intends to use variational methods to study the existence of solutions for several types of Schrödinger-Poisson equation, Klein-Gordon-Maxwell system, Kirchhoff equation, Hardy-Sobolev-Maz'ya equation and Choquard equation. The research on these types of problems is of great significance in both theoretical exploration and practical application.

The variational method can be traced back to the Euler era, and the development of critical point theory in the 1970s injected new vitality into this ancient method. Modern variational methods have become one of the most powerful tools in proving the existence of solutions to nonlinear problems. Variational methods have achieved many important research results in the periodic solutions of Hamiltonian systems, the multiplicity of homoclinic orbits, the multiplicity of solutions to boundary value problems of elliptic partial differential equations, the existence of solutions to nonlinear wave equations and nonlinear problems with nonlocal terms. At present, this method still plays a significant role in solving the problem of the existence of solutions to nonlinear equations, and its application is still an important research topic for researchers.

We mainly present our new results on these nonlinear equations: Schrödinger-Poisson equation, Klein-Gordon-Maxwell system, Kirchhoff equation, Hardy-Sobolev-Maz'ya equation and Choquard equation. We study the existence of solutions, the multiplicity of solutions and sign-changing solutions for these equations.

In Chapter 1, we study the following nonhomogeneous Schrödinger-Poisson equation

$$\begin{cases} -\Delta u + \lambda V(x)u + K(x)\phi u = f(x, u) + g(x), & x \in \mathbb{R}^3, \\ -\Delta \phi = K(x)u^2, & x \in \mathbb{R}^3, \end{cases}$$

where $\lambda > 0$ is a parameter. Under some suitable assumptions on V, K, f and g, the existence of multiple solutions is proved by using the Ekeland's Variational Principle and the Mountain Pass Theorem in critical point theory. In particular, the potential V is allowed to be sign-changing.

In Chapter 2 and Chapter 3, we study the nonhomogeneous Klein-Gordon-Maxwell system

$$\begin{cases} -\Delta u + \lambda V(x)u - K(x)(2\omega + \phi)\phi u = f(x,u) + h(x), & x \in \mathbb{R}^3, \\ \Delta \phi = K(x)(\omega + \phi)u^2, & x \in \mathbb{R}^3, \end{cases}$$

and the nonhomogeneous Klein-Gordon equation with Born-Infeld theory

$$\begin{cases} -\Delta u + V(x)u - (2\omega + \phi)\phi u = f(x,u) + h(x), & x \in \mathbb{R}^3, \\ \Delta \phi + \beta \Delta_4 \phi = 4\pi(\omega + \phi)u^2, & x \in \mathbb{R}^3, \end{cases}$$

where $\omega > 0$ is a constant. Under some assumptions on V, f and h, we obtain the existence of two solutions by the Mountain Pass Theorem and the Ekeland's variational principle in critical point theory.

Then we consider the existence of localized sign-changing solutions for semiclassical Kirchhoff equation

$$-\left(\varepsilon^2 a + \varepsilon b \int_{\mathbb{R}^3} |\nabla u|^2 dx\right)\Delta u + V(x)u = |u|^{p-2}u, \quad x \in \mathbb{R}^3, \ u \in H^1(\mathbb{R}^3)$$

in Chapter 4. Here $4 < p < 2^* = 6, \varepsilon > 0$ is a small parameter, $V(x)$ is a positive function and has a local minimum point P. When $\varepsilon \to 0$, by using a minimax characterization of higher dimensional symmetric linking structure via the symmetric mountain pass theorem, we obtain an infinite sequence of localized sign-changing solutions clustered at the point P.

In Chapter 5, on the existence of infinitely many sign-changing solutions, we also consider the following Hardy-Sobolev-Maz'ya equation

$$\begin{cases} -\Delta u = \mu |u|^{2^*-2}u + \dfrac{|u|^{2^*(t)-2}u}{|x|^t} + a(x)u, & \text{in } \Omega, \\ u = 0, & \text{on } \partial\Omega \end{cases}$$

in Chapter 5. Here $a(x)$ is a positive function, $\Omega \subset \mathbb{R}^N$ is bounded and $0 \in \partial\Omega$. We suppose $\mu \geqslant 0, N \geqslant 7, 0 < t < 2, 2^* = \dfrac{2N}{N-2}$ is the critical Sobolev exponent and $2^*(t) = \dfrac{2(N-t)}{N-2}$ is the critical Hardy-Sobolev exponent. By using a compactness result obtained in [209], we prove the existence of infinitely many sign-changing solutions by a combination of invariant sets method and Ljusternik-Schnirelman type minimax method.

We consider the existence of infinitely many sign-changing solutions for the following problem

$$
\begin{cases}
-\Delta u = \mu \dfrac{|u|^{2^*(t)-2}u}{|y|^t} + \dfrac{|u|^{2^*(s)-2}u}{|y|^s} + a(x)u, & \text{in } \Omega, \\
u = 0, & \text{on } \partial\Omega,
\end{cases}
$$

and

$$
\begin{cases}
-\Delta u = \mu |u|^{2^*-2}u + \dfrac{|u|^{2^*(t)-2}u}{|x|^t} + a(x)u, & \text{in } \Omega, \\
u = 0, & \text{on } \partial\Omega.
\end{cases}
$$

where $a(x) > 0$, $x = (y, z) \in \mathbb{R}^k \times \mathbb{R}^{N-k}, 2 \leqslant k < N$ and Ω is an open bounded domain in $\mathbb{R}^N$. Assume $2^*(l) = \dfrac{2(N-l)}{N-2}$ is the critical Hardy-Sobolev-Maz'ya exponents, where $l = s$ or t. By using a compactness result obtained in [79, 184], we prove the existence of infinitely many sign-changing solutions by a combination of invariant sets method and Ljusternik-Schnirelman type minimax method.

In Chapter 6, we consider the multiple solutions for the following nonhomogeneous Choquard equation

$$
-\Delta u + u = \left(\frac{1}{|x|^\alpha} * |u|^p \right) |u|^{p-2}u + h(x), \quad x \in \mathbb{R}^N,
$$

where $N \geqslant 3$, $0 < \alpha < N$ and $2 - \dfrac{\alpha}{N} < p \leqslant 2^*_\alpha = \dfrac{2N-\alpha}{N-2}$. Under some suitable assumptions on h, we obtain at least two solutions of these equations for the subcritical case $2 - \dfrac{\alpha}{N} < p < 2^*_\alpha$ and the critical case $2^*_\alpha = \dfrac{2N-\alpha}{N-2}$.

This monograph was compiled and completed by the author during her visit to the Chern Institute of Mathematics at Nankai University.

The author is partially supported by National Natural Science Foundation of China (11801400) and (11571187), Scientific Research Program of Tianjin Education Commission (2020KJ045 and 2023KJ216).

Lixia Wang

September, 2023

Contents

Chapter 1 Schrödinger-Poisson Equations

1.1 Schrödinger-Poisson equations with sign-changing potential

1.1.1 Introduction and main results

In this Chapter, we first consider the following Schrödinger-Poisson equations

$$(SP)_\lambda \begin{cases} -\Delta u + \lambda V(x)u + K(x)\phi u = f(x,u) + g(x), & x \in \mathbb{R}^3, \\ -\Delta\phi = K(x)u^2, & x \in \mathbb{R}^3, \end{cases}$$

where $\lambda \geqslant 1$ is a parameter, $V \in C(\mathbb{R}^3, \mathbb{R})$ and $f \in C(\mathbb{R}^3 \times \mathbb{R}, \mathbb{R})$. Under some suitable assumptions on V, K, f and g, the existence of multiple solutions is proved by using the Ekeland's Variational Principle and the Mountain Pass Theorem in critical point theory. In particular, the potential V is allowed to be sign-changing.

Such system $(SP)_\lambda$, also called Schrödinger-Maxwell equations, arises in an interesting physical context. In fact, according to a classical model, the interaction of a charged particle with an electromagnetic field can be described by coupling the nonlinear Schrödinger's and Poisson's equations (we refer readers to [23, 155] and the references therein for more details on the physical aspects). In particular, if we are looking for electrostatic-type solutions, we just have to solve system $(SP)_\lambda$.

Variational methods and critical point theory are powerful tools in studying nonlinear differential equations[140, 165, 200], and in particular Hamiltonian system in [167, 168], and also impulsive Hamiltonian systems[148]. In recent years, $(SP)_\lambda$ has been studied widely via modern variational methods under various hypotheses on the potential V and the nonlinear term f, see [11, 14, 23, 54, 75, 155, 185, 214] and the references therein. We recall some of them as follows.

The case of $g \equiv 0$, that is the homogeneous case, has been studied widely in [11, 69, 70, 74, 75, 113, 141, 155, 159] when V is a constant or radially symmetric, and in [185, 215] when V is not radially symmetric. Very recently, Azzollni and Pomponio in [14] proved the existence of a ground state solution for the following system

$$\begin{cases} -\Delta u + V(x)u + \phi(x)u = f(x,u), & x \in \mathbb{R}^3, \\ -\Delta\phi = u^2, & x \in \mathbb{R}^3, \end{cases} \tag{1.1}$$

with $f(x,u) = |u|^{p-2}u$ $(2 < p < 6)$ and non-constant potential V which may be unbounded below. When $V(x)$ and $f(x,u)$ are 1-periodic in each $x_i, i = 1, 2, 3$, Zhao et al.[214] obtained the existence of infinitely many geometrically distinct solutions by using the nonlinear superposition principle established in [1]. Zhao et al.[216] considered the existence of nontrivial solution and concentration results of $(SP)_\lambda$ provided that V satisfies:

(V_0) There is $b > 0$ such that meas$\{x \in \mathbb{R}^3 : V(x) \leqslant b\} < +\infty$, where meas denotes the Lebesgue measures;

(V_1) $V \in C(\mathbb{R}^3, \mathbb{R})$ and V is bounded below;

(V_2) $\Omega = \text{int} V^{-1}(0)$ is nonempty and has smooth boundary and $\bar{\Omega} = V^{-1}(0)$.

This kind of hypotheses was first introduced by Bartsch and Wang [18] in the study of a nonlinear Schrödinger equation and the potential $V(x)$ satisfying (V_0)—(V_2) is referred as the steep well potential.

Sun, Su and Zhao[170] got infinitely many solutions under suitable assumptions. Wu[202] studied the combined effect of concave and convex nonlinearities on the number of solutions for a semilinear elliptic equation. For more results on the effect of concave and convex terms of elliptic equations see [203, 204] and the reference therein. In 2014, Ye and Tang[212] studied the existence and multiplicity of solutions for homogeneous system of $(SP)_\lambda$ when the potential V may change sign and the nonlinear term f is superlinear or sublinear in u as $|u| \to \infty$. For the Schrödinger-Poisson system with sign-changing potential (see [171]) and sublinear Schrödinger-Poisson system (see [169]).

Next, we consider the nonhomogeneous case, that is $g \not\equiv 0$. The existence of radially symmetric solutions was obtained for above nonhomogeneous system with $\lambda \equiv 1$ and $K(x) \equiv 1$ in [159]. Chen and Tang[55] obtained two solutions for the nonhomogeneous system with $f(x, u)$ satisfying Amborosetti-Rabinowitz type condition and V being nonradially symmetric. In 2019, Wang and Ma[188] considered the nonhomogeneous Schrödinger-Poisson equation containing concave and convex terms. For more results on the nonhomogeneous case, see [81, 83, 112, 191, 192] and the reference therein.

Motivated by above works, in this section we consider system $(SP)_\lambda$ with more general potential $V(x), K(x)$ and $f(x, u)$. Under (V_0), (V_1) and some more generic 4-superlinear conditions on $f(x, u)$, we prove the existence of multiple solutions of problem $(SP)_\lambda$ when $\lambda > 0$ large by using variation method. Precisely, we make the following assumptions.

(f_1) $F(x, u) = \int_0^u f(x, s) ds \geqslant 0$ for all (x, u) and $f(x, u) = o(u)$ uniformly in x as $u \to 0$.

(f_2) $F(x, u)/u^4 \to +\infty$ as $|u| \to +\infty$ uniformly in x.

(f_3) $\mathcal{F}(x, u) := \frac{1}{4} f(x, u) u - F(x, u) \geqslant 0$ for all $(x, u) \in \mathbb{R}^3 \times \mathbb{R}$.

(f_4) There exist $a_1, L_1 > 0$ and $\tau \in (3/2, 2)$ such that

$$|f(x, u)|^\tau \leqslant a_1 \mathcal{F}(x, u)|u|^\tau, \quad \text{for all } x \in \mathbb{R}^3 \text{ and } |u| \geqslant L_1.$$

(K) $K(x) \geqslant 0 \in L^2(\mathbb{R}^3) \cup L^\infty(\mathbb{R}^3)$ is not identically zero for a.e. $x \in \mathbb{R}^3$.
(g) $g(x) \in L^2(\mathbb{R}^3)$ and $g(x) \geqslant 0$ for a.e. $x \in \mathbb{R}^3$.
Remark 1.1　It follows (f_2) and (f_4) that

$$|f(x, u)|^\tau \leqslant \frac{a_1}{4}|f(x, u)||u|^{\tau+1} \quad \text{for large } u.$$

Thus, by (f_1), for any $\varepsilon > 0$, there exists $C_\varepsilon > 0$ such that

$$|f(x, u)| \leqslant \varepsilon|u| + C_\varepsilon|u|^{p-1}, \quad \forall(x, u) \in \mathbb{R}^3 \times \mathbb{R} \tag{1.2}$$

and

$$|F(x, u)| \leqslant \varepsilon|u|^2 + C_\varepsilon|u|^p, \quad \forall(x, u) \in \mathbb{R}^3 \times \mathbb{R}, \tag{1.3}$$

where $p = 2\tau/(\tau - 1) \in (4, 2^*), 2^* = 6$ is the critical exponent for the Sobolev embedding in dimension 3.

Before stating our main results, we give several notations.

Let $H^1(\mathbb{R}^3)$ be the usual Sobolev space endowed with the standard product and norm

$$(u, v)_{H^1} = \int_{\mathbb{R}^3}(\nabla u \nabla v + uv)dx, \qquad \|u\|_{H^1}^2 = \int_{\mathbb{R}^3}(|\nabla u|^2 + |u|^2)dx.$$

$D^{1,2}(\mathbb{R}^3)$ is the completion of $C_0^\infty(\mathbb{R}^3)$ with respect to the norm

$$\|u\|_D^2 := \|u\|_{D^{1,2}(\mathbb{R}^3)}^2 = \int_{\mathbb{R}^3}|\nabla u|^2 dx.$$

For any $1 \leqslant s \leqslant +\infty$ and $\Omega \subset \mathbb{R}^3, L^s(\Omega)$ denotes a Lebesgue space; the norm in $L^s(\Omega)$ is denoted by $|u|_{s,\Omega}$, where Ω is a proper subset of $\mathbb{R}^3$, by $|\cdot|_s$ when $\Omega = \mathbb{R}^3$.

$\bar{S}$ is the best Sobolev constant for the Sobolev embedding $D^{1,2}(\mathbb{R}^3) \hookrightarrow L^6(\mathbb{R}^3)$, that is,

$$\bar{S} = \inf_{u \in H^1(\mathbb{R}^3) \setminus \{0\}} \frac{\|u\|_D}{|u|_6}.$$

For any $r > 0$ and $z \in \mathbb{R}^3, B_r(z)$ denotes the ball of radius r centered at z.

The letters c_0, d_i, C_0 will be used to denote various positive constants which may vary from line to line and are not essential to the problem. We denote "$\rightharpoonup$" weak convergence and by "$\rightarrow$" strong convergence. Also if we take a subsequence of a sequence $\{u_n\}$, we shall denote it again $\{u_n\}$. We use $o(1)$ to denote any quantity which tends to zero when $n \to \infty$.

Now we state our main results:

Theorem 1.1 *Assume that* (V_0), (V_1), (K), (g) *and* (f_1)—(f_4) *are satisfied. If* $V(x) < 0$ *for some* $x \in \mathbb{R}^3$, *then for each* $k \in \mathbb{N}$, *there exist* $\lambda_k > k$, $b_k > 0$ *and* $\eta_k > 0$ *such that problem* $(SP)_\lambda$ *has at least two nontrivial solutions for every* $\lambda = \lambda_k, |g|_2 \leqslant \eta_k$ *and* $|K|_2 < b_k (or \ |K|_\infty < b_k)$.

Theorem 1.2 *Assume that* (V_0), (V_1), (K), (g) *and* (f_1)—(f_4) *are satisfied. If* $V^{-1}(0)$ *has nonempty interior, then there exist* $\Lambda > 0, b_\lambda > 0$ *and* $\eta_\lambda > 0$ *such that problem* $(SP)_\lambda$ *has at least two nontrivial solutions for every* $\lambda > \Lambda, |g|_2 \leqslant \eta_\lambda$ *and* $|K|_2 < b_\lambda \ (or \ |K|_\infty < b_\lambda)$.

If $V \geqslant 0$, the restriction on the norm of K can be removed and we have the following theorem.

Theorem 1.3 *Assume that* $V \geqslant 0$, (V_0), (V_1), (K), (g) *and* (f_1)—(f_4) *are satisfied. If* $V^{-1}(0)$ *has nonempty interior* Ω, *then there exist* $\Lambda_* > 0$ *and* $\eta > 0$ *such that problem* $(SP)_\lambda$ *has at least two nontrivial solutions for every* $\lambda > \Lambda_*$ *and* $|g|_2 \leqslant \eta$.

To obtain our main results, we have to overcome several difficulties in using variational method. The main difficulty consists in the lack of compactness of the Sobolev embedding $H^1(\mathbb{R}^3)$ into $L^p(\mathbb{R}^3)$, $p \in (2,6)$. Since we assume that the potential is no radially symmetric, we cannot use the usual way to recover compactness, for example, restricting in the subspace $H_r^1(\mathbb{R}^3)$ of radially symmetric functions or using concentration compactness methods. To recover the compactness, we borrow some ideas used in [18, 82] and establish the parameter dependent compactness conditions. Let us point out that the adaptation of the ideas to the procedure of our problem is not trivial at all, because of the presence of the nonlocal term $K(x)\phi u$.

Remark 1.2 To the best of our knowledge, it seems that our theorems are the first results about the existence of multiple solutions for the nonhomogeneous Schrödinger-Poisson equations on $\mathbb{R}^3$ with sign-changing potential and general nonlinear term. Although the methods are used before, we need to study carefully some properties of the term $K(x)\phi u$ and the effect of the sign-changing potential V.

In Section 1.1.2, we will introduce the variational setting for the problem and establish the compactness conditions. In Section 1.1.3, we give the proofs of main results.

1.1.2   *Variational setting and compactness condition*

In this section, we give the variational setting of the problem $(SP)_\lambda$ and establish the compactness conditions.

Let $V(x) = V^+(x) - V^-(x)$, where $V^\pm(x) = \max\{\pm V(x), 0\}$. Let

$$E = \left\{ u \in H^1(\mathbb{R}^3) : \int_{\mathbb{R}^3} V^+(x) u^2 dx < \infty \right\}$$

be equipped with the inner product and norm

$$(u, v) = \int_{\mathbb{R}^3} (\nabla u \nabla v + V^+(x) u v) dx, \quad \|u\| = (u, u)^{1/2}.$$

For $\lambda > 0$, we also need the following inner product and norm

$$(u, v)_\lambda = \int_{\mathbb{R}^3} (\nabla u \nabla v + \lambda V^+(x) u v) dx, \quad \|u\|_\lambda = (u, u)_\lambda^{1/2}.$$

It is clear $\|u\| \leqslant \|u\|_\lambda$ for $\lambda \geqslant 1$. Set $E_\lambda = (E, \|\cdot\|_\lambda)$. It follows from (V_0), (V_1) and the Poincaré inequality that the embedding $E_\lambda \hookrightarrow H^1(\mathbb{R}^3)$ is continuous, and hence, for $s \in [2, 6]$, there exists $d_s > 0$(independent of $\lambda \geqslant 1$) such that

$$|u|_s \leqslant d_s \|u\|_\lambda, \quad \forall u \in E_\lambda. \tag{1.4}$$

Let

$$F_\lambda = \{u \in E_\lambda : \operatorname{supp} u \subset V^{-1}([0, \infty))\},$$

and $F_\lambda^\perp$ denote the orthogonal complement of F_λ in E_λ. Clearly, $F_\lambda = E_\lambda$ if $V \geqslant 0$, otherwise $F_\lambda^\perp \neq \{0\}$. Define

$$A_\lambda := -\Delta + \lambda V,$$

then A_λ is formally self-adjoint in $L^2(\mathbb{R}^3)$ and the associated bilinear form

$$a_\lambda(u, v) = \int_{\mathbb{R}^3} (\nabla u \nabla v + \lambda V(x) u v) dx$$

is continuous in E_λ. As in [82], for fixed $\lambda > 0$, we consider the eigenvalue problem

$$-\Delta u + \lambda V^+(x) u = \mu \lambda V^-(x) u, \quad u \in F_\lambda^\perp. \tag{1.5}$$

Since (V_0), (V_1) are satisfied, we see that the quadratic form $u \mapsto \int_{\mathbb{R}^3} \lambda V^-(x) u^2 dx$ is weakly continuous. Hence following Theorem 4.45 and Theorem 4.46 in [201], we deduce the following proposition, which is the spectral theorem for compact self-adjoint operators jointly with the Courant-Fischer minimax characterization of eigenvalues.

Proposition 1.1 *Assume that (V_0), (V_1) hold, then for any fixed $\lambda > 0$, problem (1.5) has a sequence of positive eigenvalues $\{\mu_j(\lambda)\}$, which may be characterized by*

$$\mu_j(\lambda) = \inf_{\dim M \geqslant j, M \subset F_\lambda^\perp} \sup \left\{ \|u\|_\lambda^2 : u \in M, \int_{\mathbb{R}^3} \lambda V^-(x) u^2 dx = 1 \right\}, \quad j = 1, 2, 3, \cdots.$$

Furthermore, $\mu_1(\lambda) \leqslant \mu_2(\lambda) \leqslant \cdots \leqslant \mu_j(\lambda) \to +\infty$ as $j \to +\infty$, and the corresponding eigenfunctions $\{e_j(\lambda)\}$, which may be be chosen so that $(e_i(\lambda), e_j(\lambda))_\lambda = \delta_{ij}$, are a basis of $F_\lambda^\perp$.

Now we give the properties for the eigenvalues $\{\mu_j(\lambda)\}$ defined above.

Proposition 1.2[82] *Assume that (V_0), (V_1) hold and $V^- \not\equiv 0$. Then, for each fixed $j \in \mathbb{N}$,*

(i) $\mu_j(\lambda) \to 0$ *as* $\lambda \to +\infty$;

(ii) $\mu_j(\lambda)$ *is a non-increasing continuous function of* λ.

Remark 1.3 By Proposition 1.2 (i), there exists a $\Lambda_0 > 0$ such that $\mu_1(\lambda) \leqslant 1$ for all $\lambda > \Lambda_0$.

Let

$$E_\lambda^- := \operatorname{span}\{e_j(\lambda) : \mu_j(\lambda) \leqslant 1\} \quad \text{and} \quad E_\lambda^+ := \operatorname{span}\{e_j(\lambda) : \mu_j(\lambda) > 1\}.$$

Then $E_\lambda = E_\lambda^- \oplus E_\lambda^+ \oplus F_\lambda$ is an orthogonal decomposition. The quadratic form a_λ is negative semidefinite on E_λ^-, positive definite on $E_\lambda^+ \oplus F_\lambda$ and it is easy to see that $a_\lambda(u, v) = 0$ if u, v are in different subspaces of the above decomposition of E_λ.

From Remark 1.3, we have that $\dim E_\lambda^- \geqslant 1$ when $\lambda > \Lambda_0$. Moreover, since $\mu_j(\lambda) \to +\infty$ as $j \to +\infty$, $\dim E_\lambda^- < +\infty$ for every fixed $\lambda > 0$.

It is well known that the problem $(SP)_\lambda$ can be reduced to a single equation with a nonlocal term (see [155]). In fact, for every $u \in E_\lambda$, the Lax-Milgram theorem implies that there exists a unique $\phi_u \in D^{1,2}(\mathbb{R}^3)$ such that

$$-\Delta \phi_u = K(x) u^2 \tag{1.6}$$

with

$$\phi_u(x) = \frac{1}{4\pi} \int_{\mathbb{R}^3} \frac{K(y) u^2(y)}{|x - y|} dy.$$

If $K \in L^\infty(\mathbb{R}^3)$, by (1.6), the Hölder inequality and the Sobolev inequality, we get

$$\|\phi_u\|_D^2 = \int_{\mathbb{R}^3} K(x) \phi_u u^2 dx \leqslant \bar{S}^{-2} d_{12/5}^4 |K|_\infty^2 \|u\|_\lambda^4.$$

Similarly, if $K \in L^2(\mathbb{R}^3)$,

$$\|\phi_u\|_D^2 = \int_{\mathbb{R}^3} K(x) \phi_u u^2 dx \leqslant \bar{S}^{-2} d_6^4 |K|_2^2 \|u\|_\lambda^4.$$

Thus, there exists a $C_0 > 0$, such that

$$\|\phi_u\|_D^2 = \int_{\mathbb{R}^3} K(x)\phi_u u^2 dx \leqslant C_0 \|u\|_\lambda^4, \quad \forall K \in L^2(\mathbb{R}^3) \cup L^\infty(\mathbb{R}^3). \tag{1.7}$$

Therefore, the problem $(SP)_\lambda$ can be reduced to the following equation:

$$-\Delta u + \lambda V(x)u + K(x)\phi_u(x)u = f(x,u) + g(x), \quad x \in \mathbb{R}^3.$$

By $(SP)_\lambda$ and the following Proposition 1.3, the functional $I_\lambda : E_\lambda \to \mathbb{R}$,

$$I_\lambda(u) = \frac{1}{2}\int_{\mathbb{R}^3} (|\nabla u|^2 + \lambda V(x)u^2)dx + \frac{1}{4}\int_{\mathbb{R}^3} K(x)\phi_u u^2 dx - \int_{\mathbb{R}^3} F(x,u)dx$$
$$- \int_{\mathbb{R}^3} g(x)u dx$$

is class of C^1 with derivative

$$\langle I_\lambda'(u), v\rangle = \int_{\mathbb{R}^3} (\nabla u \nabla v + \lambda V(x)uv + K(x)\phi_u uv - f(x,u)v - g(x)v)dx$$

for all $u, v \in E_\lambda$. It can be proved that $(u, \phi) \in E_\lambda \times D^{1,2}(\mathbb{R}^3)$ is a solution of the problem $(SP)_\lambda$ if and only if $u \in E_\lambda$ is a critical point of I_λ and $\phi = \phi_u$. We refer the readers to [23] and [75] for the details.

Set

$$N(u) = \int_{\mathbb{R}^3} K(x)\phi_u u^2 dx = \frac{1}{4\pi}\int\int_{\mathbb{R}^3 \times \mathbb{R}^3} \frac{K(x)K(y)u^2(x)u^2(y)}{|x-y|}dxdy.$$

Now we give some properties about the functional N and its derivative N' possess BL-splitting property, which is similar to Brezis-Lieb lemma[35].

Proposition 1.3[212, Lemma 2.1]   *Let $K \in L^\infty(\mathbb{R}^3) \cup L^2(\mathbb{R}^3)$. If $u_n \rightharpoonup u$ in $H^1(\mathbb{R}^3)$ and $u_n(x) \to u(x)$ a.e. $x \in \mathbb{R}^3$, then*

(i) $\phi_{u_n} \rightharpoonup \phi_u$ in $D^{1,2}(\mathbb{R}^3)$ and $N(u) \leqslant \liminf_{n\to\infty} N(u_n)$;

(ii) $N(u_n - u) = N(u_n) - N(u) + o(1)$;

(iii) $N'(u_n - u) = N'(u_n) - N'(u) + o(1)$ in $H^{-1}(\mathbb{R}^3)$.

Next, we investigate the compactness conditions for the functional I_λ. Recall that a C^1 functional J satisfies Cerami condition at level c $((C)_c$ condition for short) if any sequence $\{u_n\} \subset E$ such that $J(u_n) \to c$ and $(1 + \|u_n\|)J'(u_n) \to 0$ has a convergent subsequence; and such sequence is called a $(C)_c$ sequence.

We only consider the case $K \in L^\infty(\mathbb{R}^3)$, the other case $K \in L^2(\mathbb{R}^3)$ is similar.

Lemma 1.1   *Suppose that (V_0), (V_1), (K), (f_1)—(f_4) and (g) are satisfied. Then every $(C)_c$ sequence of I_λ is bounded in E_λ for each $c \in \mathbb{R}$.*

Proof. Let $\{u_n\} \subset E_\lambda$ be a $(C)_c$ sequence of I_λ. Arguing indirectly, we can assume that

$$I_\lambda(u_n) \to c, \quad (1 + \|u_n\|_\lambda)I'_\lambda(u_n) \to 0, \quad \|u_n\|_\lambda \to \infty \tag{1.8}$$

as $n \to \infty$ after passing to a subsequence. Take $w_n := u_n/\|u_n\|_\lambda$. Then $\|w_n\|_\lambda = 1$, $w_n \rightharpoonup w$ in E_λ and $w_n(x) \to w(x)$ a.e. $x \in \mathbb{R}^3$.

We first consider the case $w = 0$. Combining this with (1.8), (f_3) and the fact $w_n \to 0$ in $L^2(\{x \in \mathbb{R}^3 : V(x) < 0\})$, we have

$$
\begin{aligned}
o(1) &= \frac{1}{\|u_n\|_\lambda^2}\left(I_\lambda(u_n) - \frac{1}{4}\langle I'_\lambda(u_n), u_n\rangle\right) \\
&\geqslant \frac{1}{4}\|w_n\|_\lambda^2 - \frac{\lambda}{4}\int_{\mathbb{R}^3} V^-(x)w_n^2 dx + \frac{1}{\|u_n\|_\lambda^2}\int_{\mathbb{R}^3}\mathcal{F}(x, u_n)dx \\
&\quad - \frac{3}{4\|u_n\|_\lambda^2}\int_{\mathbb{R}^3} g(x)u_n dx \\
&\geqslant \frac{1}{4} - \frac{\lambda}{4}|V^-|_\infty\int_{\operatorname{supp}V^-} w_n^2 dx - \frac{3}{4}|g|_2 d_2\frac{1}{\|u_n\|_\lambda} \\
&= \frac{1}{4} + o(1),
\end{aligned}
$$

a contradiction.

If $w \neq 0$, then the set $\Omega_1 = \{x \in \mathbb{R}^3 : w(x) \neq 0\}$ has positive Lebesgue measure. For $x \in \Omega_1$, one has $|u_n(x)| \to \infty$ as $n \to \infty$, and then, by (f_2),

$$\frac{F(x, u_n(x))}{u_n^4(x)}w_n^4(x) \to +\infty \quad \text{as } n \to \infty,$$

which, jointly with Fatou's lemma, shows that

$$\int_{\Omega_1}\frac{F(x, u_n)}{u_n^4}w_n^4 dx \to +\infty \quad \text{as } n \to \infty. \tag{1.9}$$

We see from (f_1), (1.7), the first limit of (1.8), (1.9) and (g) that

$$\frac{C_0}{4} \geqslant \limsup_{n\to\infty}\int_{\mathbb{R}^3}\frac{F(x, u_n)}{\|u_n\|_\lambda^4}dx \geqslant \limsup_{n\to\infty}\int_{\Omega_1}\frac{F(x, u_n)}{u_n^4}w_n^4 dx = +\infty.$$

This is impossible.

Hence $\{u_n\}$ is bounded in E_λ. $\qquad\square$

Lemma 1.2 *Suppose that (V_0), (V_1), (K), (g) and (1.2) hold. If $u_n \rightharpoonup u$ in E_λ, $u_n(x) \to u(x)$ a.e. in $\mathbb{R}^3$, and we denote $w_n := u_n - u$, then*

$$I_\lambda(u_n) = I_\lambda(w_n) + I_\lambda(u) + o(1) \tag{1.10}$$

and

$$\langle I'_\lambda(u_n), \varphi \rangle = \langle I'_\lambda(w_n), \varphi \rangle + \langle I'_\lambda(u), \varphi \rangle - \int_{\mathbb{R}^3} g\varphi dx + o(1), \quad for \ all \ \varphi \in E_\lambda \quad (1.11)$$

as $n \to \infty$. *In particular, if* $I_\lambda(u_n) \to d$ *and* $I'_\lambda(u_n) \to 0$ *in* E^*_λ *(the dual space of* E_λ*), then* $I'_\lambda(u) = 0$ *and*

$$I_\lambda(w_n) \to d - I_\lambda(u),$$
$$\langle I'_\lambda(w_n), \varphi \rangle \to - \int_{\mathbb{R}^3} g\varphi dx, \quad for \ all \ \varphi \in E_\lambda \quad (1.12)$$

after passing to a subsequence.

Proof. Since $u_n \rightharpoonup u$ in E_λ, we have $(u_n - u, u)_\lambda \to 0$ as $n \to \infty$, which implies that

$$\|u_n\|^2_\lambda = (w_n + u, w_n + u)_\lambda = \|w_n\|^2_\lambda + \|u\|^2_\lambda + o(1). \quad (1.13)$$

By (V_0), $w_n \rightharpoonup 0$ and the Hölder inequality, we have

$$\left| \int_{\mathbb{R}^3} V^-(x)w_n u dx \right| = \left| \int_{\mathrm{supp}V^-} V^- w_n u dx \right| \leqslant |V^-|_\infty \left(\int_{\mathrm{supp}V^-} w_n^2 dx \right)^{1/2} |u|_2 \to 0$$

as $n \to \infty$. Thus

$$\int_{\mathbb{R}^3} V^-(x)u_n^2 dx = \int_{\mathbb{R}^3} V^-(x)w_n^2 dx + \int_{\mathbb{R}^3} V^-(x)u^2 dx + o(1).$$

Consequently, this together with Proposition 1.3 (ii) and (1.13), we obtain

$$\frac{1}{2}a_\lambda(u_n, u_n) + \frac{1}{4}N(u_n) = \left(\frac{1}{2}a_\lambda(w_n, w_n) + \frac{1}{4}N(w_n) \right) + \left(\frac{1}{2}a_\lambda(u, u) + \frac{1}{4}N(u) \right) + o(1).$$

Similarly, by Proposition 1.3 (iii), we have

$$a_\lambda(u_n, h) + \int_{\mathbb{R}^3} K(x)\phi_{u_n} u_n h dx$$
$$= \left(a_\lambda(w_n, h) + \int_{\mathbb{R}^3} K(x)\phi_{w_n} w_n h dx \right)$$
$$+ \left(a_\lambda(u, h) + \int_{\mathbb{R}^3} K(x)\phi_u u h dx \right) + o(1), \quad \forall h \in E_\lambda.$$

Since

$$\int_{\mathbb{R}^3} g(x)u_n dx = \int_{\mathbb{R}^3} g(x)w_n dx + \int_{\mathbb{R}^3} g(x)u dx,$$

therefore, to obtain (1.10) and (1.11), it suffices to check that

$$\int_{\mathbb{R}^3} (F(x, u_n) - F(x, w_n) - F(x, u))dx = o(1) \tag{1.14}$$

and

$$\sup_{\|h\|_\lambda = 1} \int_{\mathbb{R}^3} (f(x, u_n) - f(x, w_n) - f(x, u))h dx = o(1). \tag{1.15}$$

Here, we only prove (1.14), the verification of (1.15) is similar. Inspired by [3], we observe that

$$F(x, u_n) - F(x, u_n - u) = -\int_0^1 \left(\frac{d}{dt} F(x, u_n - tu)\right) dt = \int_0^1 f(x, u_n - tu)u dt.$$

and hence, by (1.2), we have

$$|F(x, u_n) - F(x, u_n - u)| \le \varepsilon_1 |u_n||u| + \varepsilon_1 |u|^2 + C_{\varepsilon_1}|u_n|^{p-1}|u| + C_{\varepsilon_1}|u|^p,$$

where $\varepsilon_1, C_{\varepsilon_1} > 0$ and $p \in (4, 6)$. Hence, for each $\varepsilon > 0$, and the Young inequality, we have

$$|F(x, u_n) - F(x, w_n) - F(x, u)| \le C[\varepsilon |u_n|^2 + C_\varepsilon |u|^2 + \varepsilon |u_n|^p + C_\varepsilon |u|^p].$$

Next, we consider the function g_n given by

$$g_n(x) := \max\left\{|F(x, u_n) - F(x, w_n) - F(x, u)| - C\varepsilon(|u_n|^2 + |u_n|^p), 0\right\}.$$

Then $0 \le g_n(x) \le CC_\varepsilon(|u|^2 + |u|^p) \in L^1(\mathbb{R}^3)$. Moreover, by the Lebesgue Dominated Convergence theorem,

$$\int_{\mathbb{R}^3} g_n(x)dx \to 0 \quad \text{as } n \to \infty, \tag{1.16}$$

since $u_n \to u$ a.e. in $\mathbb{R}^3$. By the definition of g_n, it follows that

$$|F(x, u_n) - F(x, w_n) - F(x, u)| \le g_n(x) + C\varepsilon(|u_n|^2 + |u_n|^p),$$

which, together with (1.16) and (1.4), shows that

$$|F(x, u_n) - F(x, w_n) - F(x, u)| \le C\varepsilon$$

for n sufficiently large. It implies that

$$\int_{\mathbb{R}^3} [F(x, u_n) - F(x, w_n) - F(x, u)]dx = o(1).$$

Next, we check that $I'_\lambda(u) = 0$. Indeed, for each $\psi \in C_0^\infty(\mathbb{R}^3)$, we have

$$(u_n - u, \psi)_\lambda \to 0 \quad \text{as } n \to \infty. \tag{1.17}$$

and

$$\left| \int_{\mathbb{R}^3} V^-(x)(u_n - u)\psi dx \right|$$

$$\leqslant |V^-|_\infty \left(\int_{\text{supp}\psi} (u_n - u)^2 dx \right)^{1/2} |\psi|_2 \to 0 \quad \text{as } n \to \infty, \tag{1.18}$$

since $u_n \to u$ in $L^2_{loc}(\mathbb{R}^3)$. By Proposition 1.3 (i), $u_n \rightharpoonup u$ in E_λ yields $\phi_{u_n} \rightharpoonup \phi_u$ in $D^{1,2}(\mathbb{R}^3)$. So

$$\phi_{u_n} \rightharpoonup \phi_u \text{ in } L^6(\mathbb{R}^3).$$

For every $\psi \in C_0^\infty(\mathbb{R}^3)$, by the Hölder inequality we obtain

$$\int_{\mathbb{R}^3} |K(x)u\psi|^{6/5} dx \leqslant |K|_\infty^{6/5} |\psi|_{12/5}^{6/5} |u|_{12/5}^{6/5},$$

that is, $K(x)u\psi \in L^{6/5}(\mathbb{R}^3)$, and hence

$$\int_{\mathbb{R}^3} K(x)(\phi_{u_n} - \phi_u)u\psi dx \to 0.$$

By $u_n \to u$ in $L^3_{loc}(\mathbb{R}^3)$ and the Hölder inequality, we have

$$\left| \int_{\mathbb{R}^3} K(x)\phi_{u_n}(u_n - u)\psi dx \right|$$

$$\leqslant |\psi|_2 |K|_\infty |\phi_{u_n}|_6 |u_n - u|_{3,\Omega_\psi}$$

$$\leqslant C|u_n - u|_{3,\Omega_\psi} \to 0 \quad \text{as } n \to \infty,$$

here Ω_ψ is the support set of ψ. Consequently,

$$\left| \int_{\mathbb{R}^3} [K(x)\phi_{u_n}u_n\psi - K(x)\phi_u u\psi] dx \right|$$

$$\leqslant \int_{\mathbb{R}^3} |K(x)\phi_{u_n}(u_n - u)\psi| dx + \int_{\mathbb{R}^3} |K(x)(\phi_{u_n} - \phi_u)u\psi| dx$$

$$= o(1). \tag{1.19}$$

Furthermore, by (1.2) and the dominated convergence theorem, we obtain

$$\int_{\mathbb{R}^3} [f(x, u_n) - f(x, u)]\psi dx = \int_{\Omega_\psi} [f(x, u_n) - f(x, u)]\psi dx = o(1).$$

Since $u_n \rightharpoonup u$ in $L^2(\mathbb{R}^3)$ and $g \in L^2(\mathbb{R}^3)$, we obtain

$$\int_{\mathbb{R}^3} g(u_n - u)dx = o(1).$$

This jointly with (1.17)—(1.19) and the Lebesgue Dominated Convergence theorem, shows that

$$\langle I_\lambda'(u), \psi \rangle = \lim_{n \to \infty} \langle I_\lambda'(u_n), \psi \rangle = 0, \quad \forall \psi \in C_0^\infty(\mathbb{R}^3).$$

Hence $I_\lambda'(u) = 0$. (1.12) follows from (1.10), (1.11) and Proposition 1.3(iii). The proof is complete.   □

Lemma 1.3   *Suppose $V \geqslant 0$, $(V_0), (V_1), (K), (g)$ and (f_1)—(f_4) hold. Then, for any $M > 0$, there is $\Lambda = \Lambda(M) > 0$ such that I_λ satisfies $(C)_c$ condition for all $c < M$ and $\lambda > \Lambda$.*

Proof.   Let $\{u_n\} \subset E_\lambda$ be a $(C)_c$ sequence with $c < M$. According to Lemma 1.1, $\{u_n\}$ is bounded in E_λ, and there exists C_λ such that $\|u_n\|_\lambda \leqslant C_\lambda$. Therefore, up to a subsequence, we can assume that

$$\begin{aligned}
&u_n \rightharpoonup u \text{ in } E_\lambda; \\
&u_n \to u \text{ in } L_{loc}^s(\mathbb{R}^3), \quad 2 \leqslant s < 2^*; \\
&u_n(x) \to u(x) \text{ a.e. } x \in \mathbb{R}^3.
\end{aligned} \tag{1.20}$$

Now we can prove that $u_n \to u$ in E_λ for $\lambda > 0$ large. Denote $w_n := u_n - u$, then $w_n \rightharpoonup 0$ in E_λ. By Lemma 1.2, we have $I_\lambda'(u) = 0$, and

$$I_\lambda(w_n) \to c - I_\lambda(u), \quad I_\lambda'(w_n) \to 0 \quad \text{as } n \to \infty. \tag{1.21}$$

Noting $V \geqslant 0$ and using (f_3), we have

$$\begin{aligned}
I_\lambda(u) &= I_\lambda(u) - \frac{1}{4}\langle I_\lambda'(u), u \rangle \\
&= \frac{1}{4}\|u\|_\lambda^2 + \int_{\mathbb{R}^3} \mathcal{F}(x,u)dx - \frac{3}{4}\int_{\mathbb{R}^3} gudx = \Phi_\lambda(u) - \frac{3}{4}\int_{\mathbb{R}^3} gudx,
\end{aligned}$$

here

$$\Phi_\lambda(u) = \frac{1}{4}\|u\|_\lambda^2 + \int_{\mathbb{R}^3} \mathcal{F}(x,u)dx \geqslant 0.$$

Again by (1.12) and (1.20), we obtain

$$\begin{aligned}
&\frac{1}{4}\|w_n\|_\lambda^2 + \int_{\mathbb{R}^3} \mathcal{F}(x,w_n)dx + o(1) \\
&= I_\lambda(w_n) - \frac{1}{4}\langle I_\lambda'(w_n), w_n \rangle
\end{aligned}$$

$$= c - I_\lambda(u) + \frac{1}{4} \int_{\mathbb{R}^3} g w_n dx + o(1)$$

$$= c - \left[\Phi_\lambda(u) - \frac{3}{4} \int_{\mathbb{R}^3} g u dx \right] + \frac{1}{4} \int_{\mathbb{R}^3} g w_n dx + o(1)$$

$$= c - \Phi_\lambda(u) + \frac{3}{4} \int_{\mathbb{R}^3} g u dx + o(1)$$

$$\leqslant M + \tilde{M} + o(1). \tag{1.22}$$

Here we use the fact $c < M$ and

$$\frac{3}{4} |g|_2 |u|_2 \leqslant \frac{3}{4} |g|_2 d_2 \|u\|_\lambda \leqslant \frac{3}{4} |g|_2 d_2 \liminf_{n\to\infty} \|u_n\|_\lambda \leqslant |g|_2 d_2 C \leqslant \tilde{M},$$

where $\tilde{M}$ is a positive constant independent of λ. Hence

$$\int_{\mathbb{R}^3} \mathcal{F}(x, w_n) dx \leqslant M + \tilde{M} + o(1). \tag{1.23}$$

Since $V(x) < b$ on a set of finite measure and $w_n \rightharpoonup 0$,

$$|w_n|_2^2 \leqslant \frac{1}{\lambda b} \int_{V \geqslant b} \lambda V^+(x) w_n^2 dx + \int_{V<b} w_n^2 dx \leqslant \frac{1}{\lambda b} \|w_n\|_\lambda^2 + o(1). \tag{1.24}$$

For $2 < s < 2^*$, by (1.24) and the Hölder and Sobolev inequality, we obtain

$$|w_n|_s^s = \int_{\mathbb{R}^3} |w_n|^s dx \leqslant \left(\int_{\mathbb{R}^3} |w_n|^2 dx \right)^{\frac{6-s}{4}} \left(\int_{\mathbb{R}^3} |w_n|^6 dx \right)^{\frac{s-2}{4}}$$

$$\leqslant \left[\frac{1}{\lambda b} \int_{\mathbb{R}^3} (|\nabla w_n|^2 + \lambda V^+ w_n^2) \, dx \right]^{\frac{6-s}{4}} \left(\bar{S}^{-6} \left[\int_{\mathbb{R}^3} |\nabla w_n|^2 dx \right]^3 \right)^{\frac{s-2}{4}} + o(1)$$

$$\leqslant \left(\frac{1}{\lambda b} \right)^{\frac{6-s}{4}} \bar{S}^{-\frac{3(s-2)}{2}} \|w_n\|_\lambda^s + o(1). \tag{1.25}$$

By (f_1), for any $\varepsilon > 0$, there exists $\delta = \delta(\varepsilon) > 0$ such that $|f(x,t)| \leqslant \varepsilon |t|$ for all $x \in \mathbb{R}^3$ and $|t| \leqslant \delta$, and (f_4) is satisfied for $|t| \geqslant \delta$ (with the same τ but possibly larger a_1). Hence we get

$$\int_{|w_n| \leqslant \delta} f(x, w_n) w_n dx \leqslant \varepsilon \int_{|w_n| \leqslant \delta} w_n^2 dx \leqslant \frac{\varepsilon}{\lambda b} \|w_n\|_\lambda^2 + o(1) \tag{1.26}$$

and

$$\int_{|w_n| \geqslant \delta} f(x, w_n) w_n dx \leqslant \left(\int_{|w_n| \geqslant \delta} |\frac{f(x, w_n)}{w_n}|^\tau dx \right)^{1/\tau} |w_n|_s^2$$

$$\leqslant \left(\int_{|w_n| \geqslant \delta} a_1 \mathcal{F}(x, w_n) dx \right)^{1/\tau} |w_n|_s^2$$

$$\leqslant [a_1(M + \tilde{M})]^{1/\tau} \bar{S}^{-\frac{3(2s-4)}{2s}} \left(\frac{1}{\lambda b} \right)^\theta \|w_n\|_\lambda^2 + o(1), \quad (1.27)$$

by (f_4), (1.23), (1.25) with $s = 2\tau/(\tau - 1)$ and the Hölder inequality, where

$$\theta = \frac{6 - s}{2s} > 0.$$

Since $u_n \rightharpoonup u$ in $L^2(\mathbb{R}^3)$ and $g \in L^2(\mathbb{R}^3)$, we have

$$\int_{\mathbb{R}^3} g(u_n - u) dx \to 0 \quad \text{as } n \to \infty. \qquad (1.28)$$

Therefore, by (1.26), (1.27) and (2.68) we have

$$o(1) = \langle I'_\lambda(w_n), w_n \rangle$$

$$\geqslant \|w_n\|_\lambda^2 - \int_{\mathbb{R}^3} f(x, w_n) w_n dx - \int_{\mathbb{R}^3} g w_n dx$$

$$\geqslant \left[1 - \frac{\varepsilon}{\lambda b} - [a_1(M + \tilde{M})]^{1/\tau} \bar{S}^{-\frac{3(2s-4)}{2s}} \left(\frac{1}{\lambda b} \right)^\theta \right] \|w_n\|_\lambda^2 + o(1). \qquad (1.29)$$

So there exists $\Lambda = \Lambda(M) > 0$ such that $w_n \to 0$ in E_λ when $\lambda > \Lambda$. Since $w_n = u_n - u$, it follows that $u_n \to u$ in E_λ. This completes the proof. $\qquad \square$

Lemma 1.4 Let $(V_0), (V_1), (K), (g)$ and (f_1)—(f_4) be satisfied. Let $\{u_n\}$ be a $(C)_c$ sequence of I_λ with level $c > 0$. Then for any $M > 0$, there is $\Lambda = \Lambda(M) > 0$ such that, up to a subsequence, $u_n \rightharpoonup u$ in E_λ with u being a nontrivial critical point of I_λ and satisfying $I_\lambda(u) \leqslant c$ for all $c < M$ and $\lambda > \Lambda$.

Proof. We modify the proof of Lemma 1.3. By Lemma 1.2, we obtain

$$I'_\lambda(u) = 0, \quad I_\lambda(w_n) \to c - I_\lambda(u), \quad I'_\lambda(w_n) \to 0 \quad \text{as } n \to \infty. \qquad (1.30)$$

However, since V is allowed to be sign-changing and the appearance of nonlinear term g, from

$$I_\lambda(u) = I_\lambda(u) - \frac{1}{4}\langle I'_\lambda(u), u \rangle$$

$$= \frac{1}{4}\|u\|_\lambda^2 - \frac{\lambda}{4} \int_{\mathbb{R}^3} V^-(x) u^2 dx + \int_{\mathbb{R}^3} \mathcal{F}(x, u) dx - \frac{3}{4} \int_{\mathbb{R}^3} g u dx,$$

we cannot deduce that $I_\lambda(u) \geqslant 0$. We consider two possibilities:

(i) $I_\lambda(u) < 0$;

(ii) $I_\lambda(u) \geqslant 0$.

If $I_\lambda(u) < 0$, then $u \neq 0$ and then u is nontrivial and the proof is done. If $I_\lambda(u) \geqslant 0$, following the argument in the proof of Lemma 1.3 step by step, we can get $u_n \to u$ in E_λ. In fact, by (V_0) and $w_n \to 0$ in $L^2(\{x \in \mathbb{R}^3 : V(x) < b\})$, we have

$$\left| \int_{\mathbb{R}^3} V^-(x) w_n^2(x) dx \right| \leqslant |V^-|_\infty \int_{\mathrm{supp} V^-} w_n^2 dx = o(1).$$

Combining this with (1.30), we have

$$\int_{\mathbb{R}^3} \mathcal{F}(x, w_n) dx$$

$$= I_\lambda(w_n) - \frac{1}{4}\langle I_\lambda'(w_n), w_n \rangle - \frac{1}{4}\|w_n\|_\lambda^2 + \frac{1}{4}\int_{\mathbb{R}^3} \lambda V^-(x) w_n^2 dx + \frac{3}{4}\int_{\mathbb{R}^3} g w_n dx$$

$$\leqslant c - I_\lambda(u) + o(1) \leqslant M + o(1).$$

It follows that (1.27)—(1.29) remain valid. Hence $u_n \to u$ in E_λ and $I_\lambda(u) = c(> 0)$. The proof is complete. $\qquad\square$

1.1.3   Proofs of main results

If V is sign-changing, we first verify that the functional I_λ have the linking geometry to apply the following linking theorem [154].

Proposition 1.4   *Let $E = E_1 \oplus E_2$ be a Banach space with $\dim E_2 < \infty, \Phi \in C^1(E, \mathbb{R}^3)$. If there exist $R > \rho > 0, \alpha > 0$ and $e_0 \in E_1$ such that*

$$\alpha := \inf \Phi(E_1 \cap S_\rho) > \sup \Phi(\partial Q),$$

where

$$S_\rho = \{u \in E : \|u\| = \rho\}, \quad Q = \{u = v + t e_0 : v \in E_2, t \geqslant 0, \|u\| \leqslant R\}.$$

Then Φ has a $(C)_c$ sequence with $c \in [\alpha, \sup \Phi(Q)]$.

In our context, we use Proposition 1.4 with $E_1 = E_\lambda^+ \oplus F_\lambda$ and $E_2 = E_\lambda^-$. By Proposition 1.2, $\mu_j(\lambda) \to 0$ as $\lambda \to \infty$ for every fixed j. By Remark 1.3, there is $\Lambda_0 > 0$ such that $E_\lambda^- \neq \varnothing$ and E_λ^- is finite dimensional for $\lambda > \Lambda_0$. Now we investigate the linking structure of the functional I_λ.

Lemma 1.5   *Suppose that $(V_0), (V_1), (K), (g)$ and (1.2) with $p \in (4, 2^*)$ are satisfied. Then, for each $\lambda > \Lambda_0$(is the constant given in Remark 1.2), there exist $\alpha_\lambda, \rho_\lambda$ and $\eta_\lambda > 0$ such that*

$$I_\lambda(u) \geqslant \alpha_\lambda \text{ for all } u \in E_\lambda^+ \oplus F_\lambda \text{ with } \|u\|_\lambda = \rho_\lambda \text{ and } |g|_2 < \eta_\lambda. \qquad (1.31)$$

Furthermore, if $V \geqslant 0$, we can choose $\alpha, \rho, \eta > 0$ independent of λ.

Proof. For any $u \in E_\lambda^+ \oplus F_\lambda$, writing $u = u_1 + u_2$ with $u_1 \in E_\lambda^+$ and $u_2 \in F_\lambda$. Clearly, $(u_1, u_2)_\lambda = 0$, and

$$\int_{\mathbb{R}^3} (|\nabla u|^2 + \lambda V(x)u^2)dx = \int_{\mathbb{R}^3} (|\nabla u_1|^2 + \lambda V(x)u_1^2)dx + \|u_2\|_\lambda^2. \tag{1.32}$$

By Proposition 1.1 we have $\mu_j(\lambda) \to +\infty$ as $j \to +\infty$ for each fixed $\lambda > \Lambda_0$. So there is a positive integer n_λ such that $\mu_j(\lambda) \leqslant 1$ for $j \leqslant n_\lambda$ and $\mu_j(\lambda) > 1$ for $j > n_\lambda + 1$. For $u_1 \in E_\lambda^+$, we set $u_1 = \sum\limits_{j=n_\lambda+1}^{\infty} \mu_j(\lambda)e_j(\lambda)$. Thus

$$\int_{\mathbb{R}^3} (|\nabla u_1|^2 + \lambda V(x)u_1^2)dx = \|u_1\|_\lambda^2 - \int_{\mathbb{R}^3} \lambda V^-(x)u_1^2 dx$$

$$\geqslant \left(1 - \frac{1}{\mu_{n_\lambda+1}(\lambda)}\right)\|u_1\|_\lambda^2. \tag{1.33}$$

Now, using (1.4), (1.32) and (1.33), we obtain

$$I_\lambda(u) \geqslant \frac{1}{2}\left(1 - \frac{1}{\mu_{n_\lambda+1}(\lambda)}\right)\|u\|_\lambda^2 - \varepsilon|u|_2^2 - C_\varepsilon|u|_p^p - |g|_2|u|_2$$

$$\geqslant \frac{1}{2}\left(1 - \frac{1}{\mu_{n_\lambda+1}(\lambda)}\right)\|u\|_\lambda^2 - \varepsilon d_2^2\|u\|_\lambda^2 - C_\varepsilon d_p^p\|u\|_\lambda^p - d_2|g|_2\|u\|_\lambda$$

$$\geqslant \|u\|_\lambda\left\{\left[\frac{1}{2}\left(1 - \frac{1}{\mu_{n_\lambda+1}(\lambda)}\right) - \varepsilon d_2^2\right]\|u\|_\lambda - C_\varepsilon d_p^p\|u\|_\lambda^{p-1} - d_2|g|_2\right\}.$$

Let

$$h(t) = \left[\frac{1}{2}(1 - \frac{1}{\mu_{n_\lambda+1}(\lambda)}) - \varepsilon d_2^2\right]t - C_\varepsilon d_p^p t^{p-1}, \quad \text{for } t > 0, p \in (4, 6),$$

there exists

$$\rho(\lambda) = \left[\frac{\frac{1}{2}\left(1 - \frac{1}{\mu_{n_\lambda+1}(\lambda)}\right) - \varepsilon d_2^2}{C_\varepsilon d_p^p(p - 1)}\right]^{\frac{1}{p-2}},$$

such that $\max\limits_{t \geqslant 0} h(t) = h(\rho(\lambda)) > 0$. It follows from above inequality,

$$I_\lambda(u)\,|_{\|u\|_\lambda = \rho(\lambda)} > 0, \quad \text{for all } |g|_2 < \eta_\lambda := \frac{h(\rho(\lambda))}{2d_2}.$$

Of course, $\rho(\lambda)$ can be chosen small enough, we can obtain the same result: there exists $\alpha_\lambda > 0$, such that $I_\lambda(u) \geqslant \alpha_\lambda$, here $\|u\|_\lambda = \rho_\lambda$.

If $V \geqslant 0$, since $E_\lambda = F_\lambda$, and

$$\int_{\mathbb{R}^3} (|\nabla u|^2 + \lambda V(x)u^2)dx = \|u\|_\lambda^2,$$

we can choose $\alpha, \rho, \eta > 0$ (independent of λ) such that (1.31) holds. □

Lemma 1.6 *Suppose that $(V_0), (V_1), (K), (g)$ and $(f_1), (f_2)$ are satisfied. Then, for any finite dimensional subspace $\tilde{E}_\lambda \subset E_\lambda$, there holds*

$$I_\lambda(u) \to -\infty \quad as \quad \|u\|_\lambda \to \infty, \ u \in \tilde{E}_\lambda.$$

Proof. Assuming the contrary, there is a sequence $(u_n) \subset \tilde{E}_\lambda$ with $\|u_n\|_\lambda \to \infty$ such that

$$-\infty < \inf_n I_\lambda(u_n). \tag{1.34}$$

Take $v_n := u_n/\|u_n\|_\lambda$. Since $\dim \tilde{E}_\lambda < +\infty$, there exists $v \in \tilde{E}_\lambda \setminus \{0\}$ such that

$$v_n \to v \quad \text{in} \quad \tilde{E}_\lambda, \qquad v_n(x) \to v(x) \ \text{a.e.} \ x \in \mathbb{R}^3$$

after passing to a subsequence. If $v(x) \neq 0$, then $|u_n(x)| \to +\infty$ as $n \to \infty$, and hence by (f_2),

$$\frac{F(x, u_n(x))}{u_n^4(x)} v_n^4(x) \to +\infty \quad \text{as } n \to \infty.$$

Combining this with (f_1), (1.7) and Fatou's lemma, we have

$$\frac{I_\lambda(u_n)}{\|u_n\|_\lambda^4} \leqslant \frac{1}{2\|u_n\|_\lambda^2} + \frac{C_0}{4} - \int_{\mathbb{R}^3} \frac{F(x, u_n)}{\|u_n\|_\lambda^4} dx - \int_{\mathbb{R}^3} g(x) \frac{u_n}{\|u_n\|_\lambda^4} dx$$

$$\leqslant \frac{1}{2\|u_n\|_\lambda^2} + \frac{C_0}{4} - \left(\int_{v=0} + \int_{v\neq 0} \right) \frac{F(x, u_n)}{u_n^4} v_n^4 dx + \frac{|g|_2 d_2}{\|u_n\|_\lambda^3}$$

$$\leqslant \frac{1}{2\|u_n\|_\lambda^2} + \frac{C_0}{4} - \int_{v\neq 0} \frac{F(x, u_n)}{u_n^4} v_n^4 dx + \frac{|g|_2 d_2}{\|u_n\|_\lambda^3}$$

$$\to -\infty,$$

a contradiction with (1.34). □

Lemma 1.7 *Suppose that $(V_0), (V_1), (K), (g)$ and $(f_1), (f_2)$ are satisfied. If $V(x) < 0$ for some x, then for each $k \in \mathbb{N}$, there exist $\lambda_k > k, w_k \in E_{\lambda_k}^+ \oplus F_{\lambda_k}, R_{\lambda_k} > \rho_{\lambda_k}$ (ρ_{λ_k} is the constant given in Lemma 1.5) and $\eta_k, b_k > 0$ such that, for $|g|_2 < \eta_k$ and $|K|_\infty < b_k$ (or $|K|_2 < b_k$),*
  (i) $\sup I_{\lambda_k}(\partial Q_k) \leqslant 0$;
  (ii) $\sup I_{\lambda_k}(Q_k)$ *is bounded above by a constant independent of λ_k,*
where $Q_k := \{u = v + tw_k : v \in E_{\lambda_k}^-, t \geqslant 0, \|u\|_{\lambda_k} \leqslant R_{\lambda_k}\}$.

Proof. We adapt an argument in [82]. For each $k \in \mathbb{N}$, since $\mu_j(k) \to +\infty$ as $j \to \infty$, there exists $j_k \in \mathbb{N}$ such that $\mu_{j_k}(k) > 1$. By Proposition 1.2, there is

$\lambda_k > k$ such that

$$1 < \mu_{j_k}(\lambda_k) < 1 + \frac{1}{\lambda_k}.$$

Taking $w_k := e_{j_k}(\lambda_k)$ be an eigenvalue of $\mu_{j_k}(\lambda_k)$, then $w_k \in E^+_{\lambda_k}$ as $\mu_{j_k}(\lambda_k) > 1$. Since $\dim E^-_{\lambda_k} \oplus \mathbb{R}w_k < +\infty$, it follows directly from Lemma 1.6 that (i) holds with $R_{\lambda_k} > 0$ large enough.

By (f_2), for each $\tilde{\eta} > |V^-|_\infty$, there is $r_{\tilde{\eta}} > 0$ such that

$$F(x,t) \geqslant \frac{1}{2}\tilde{\eta}t^2, \quad \text{if } |t| \geqslant r_{\tilde{\eta}}.$$

For $u = v + w \in E^-_{\lambda_k} \oplus \mathbb{R}w_k$, we obtain

$$\int_{\mathbb{R}^3} V^-(x)u^2 dx = \int_{\mathbb{R}^3} V^-(x)v^2 dx + \int_{\mathbb{R}^3} V^-(x)w^2 dx$$

by the orthogonality of $E^-_{\lambda_k}$ and $\mathbb{R}w_k$. Hence we get

$$\begin{aligned}
I_{\lambda_k}(u) \leqslant {}& \frac{1}{2}\int_{\mathbb{R}^3} \left(|\nabla w|^2 + \lambda_k V(x)w^2\right) dx + \frac{1}{4}\int_{\mathbb{R}^3} K(x)\phi_u u^2 dx \\
& - \int_{\mathrm{supp}V^-} F(x,u)dx - \int_{\mathbb{R}^3} gu\, dx \\
\leqslant {}& \frac{1}{2}[\mu_{j_k}(\lambda_k) - 1]\lambda_k \int_{\mathbb{R}^3} V^-(x)w^2 dx - \frac{1}{2}\int_{\mathrm{supp}V^-} \tilde{\eta}u^2 dx \\
& + \frac{1}{4}\bar{S}^{-2}d^4_{12/5}|K|^2_\infty\|u\|^4_{\lambda_k} + d_2|g|_2\|u\|_{\lambda_k} \\
& - \int_{\mathrm{supp}V^-,|u|\leqslant r_{\tilde{\eta}}} \left(F(x,u) - \frac{1}{2}\tilde{\eta}u^2\right) dx \\
\leqslant {}& \frac{1}{2}\int_{\mathbb{R}^3} V^-(x)w^2 dx - \frac{\tilde{\eta}}{2|V^-|_\infty}\int_{\mathbb{R}^3} V^-(x)w^2 dx + C_{\tilde{\eta}} + \frac{1}{4}\bar{S}^{-2}d^4_{12/5}|K|^2_\infty R^4_{\lambda_k} \\
& + d_2|g|_2 R_{\lambda_k} \\
\leqslant {}& C_{\tilde{\eta}} + 1
\end{aligned}$$

for $u = v + w \in E^-_{\lambda_k} \oplus \mathbb{R}w_k$ with $\|u\|_{\lambda_k} \leqslant R_{\lambda_k}$, $|K|_\infty < b_k := \bar{S}(d_{12/5}R_{\lambda_k})^{-2}$ and $|g|_2 < \eta_k := \dfrac{1}{2d_2 R_{\lambda_k}}$, where $C_{\tilde{\eta}}$ depends on $\tilde{\eta}$ but not λ. $\qquad\square$

Lemma 1.8 *Suppose that $(V_0), (V_1), (K), (g)$ and $(f_1), (f_2)$ are satisfied. If $\Omega := \mathrm{int}V^{-1}(0)$ is nonempty, then, for each $\lambda > \Lambda_0$ (is the constant given in Remark 1.2),*

there exist $w \in E_\lambda^+ \oplus F_\lambda, R_\lambda > 0, \eta_\lambda > 0$ *and* $b_\lambda > 0$ *such that for* $|g|_2 < \eta_\lambda, |K|_\infty <$
$b_\lambda (or |K|_2 < b_\lambda)$,

(i) $\sup I_\lambda(\partial Q) \leqslant 0$;

(ii) $\sup I_\lambda(Q)$ *is bounded above by a constant independent of* λ,

where $Q := \{u = v + tw : v \in E_\lambda^-, t \geqslant 0, \|u\|_\lambda \leqslant R_\lambda\}$.

Proof. Choose $e_0 \in C_0^\infty(\Omega) \setminus \{0\}$, then $e_0 \in F_\lambda$. By Lemma 1.6, there is $R_\lambda > 0$
large such that $I_\lambda(u) \leqslant 0$ where $u \in E_\lambda^- \oplus \mathbb{R}e_0$ and $\|u\|_\lambda \geqslant R_\lambda$.

For $u = v + w \in E_\lambda^- \oplus \mathbb{R}e_0$, we have

$$
\begin{aligned}
I_\lambda(u) &\leqslant \frac{1}{2} \int_{\mathbb{R}^3} |\nabla w|^2 dx + \frac{1}{4} \int_{\mathbb{R}^3} K(x)\phi_u u^2 dx - \int_\Omega F(x,u)dx - \int_{\mathbb{R}^3} gu dx \\
&\leqslant \frac{1}{2} \int_{\mathbb{R}^3} |\nabla w|^2 dx - \frac{\tilde{\eta}}{2} \int_\Omega u^2 dx - \int_{\Omega, |u| \leqslant r_{\tilde{\eta}}} \left(F(x,u) - \frac{\tilde{\eta}}{2} u^2 \right) dx \\
&\quad + \frac{1}{4} \bar{S}^{-2} d_{12/5}^4 |K|_\infty^2 \|u\|_\lambda^4 + |g|_2 d_2 \|u\|_\lambda \\
&\leqslant \frac{1}{2} \int_{\mathbb{R}^3} |\nabla w|^2 dx - \frac{\tilde{\eta}}{2} \int_\Omega u^2 dx + C_{\tilde{\eta}} \\
&\quad + \frac{1}{4} \bar{S}^{-2} d_{12/5}^4 |K|_\infty^2 \|u\|_\lambda^4 + |g|_2 d_2 \|u\|_\lambda.
\end{aligned}
\tag{1.35}
$$

Observing $w \in C_0^\infty(\Omega)$, we have

$$
\begin{aligned}
\int_{\mathbb{R}^3} |\nabla w|^2 dx &= \int_\Omega (-\Delta w) u dx \leqslant |\Delta w|_2 |u|_{2,\Omega} \leqslant c_0 |\nabla w|_2 |u|_{2,\Omega} \\
&\leqslant \frac{c_0^2}{2\tilde{\eta}} |\nabla w|_2^2 + \frac{\tilde{\eta}}{2} |u|_{2,\Omega}^2,
\end{aligned}
\tag{1.36}
$$

where c_0 is a constant depending on e_0. Choosing $\tilde{\eta} > c_0^2$, we have

$$
|\nabla w|_2^2 \leqslant \tilde{\eta} |u|_{2,\Omega}^2,
$$

and it follows from (1.35) that

$$
I_\lambda(u) \leqslant C_{\tilde{\eta}} + \frac{1}{4} \bar{S}^{-2} d_{12/5}^4 |K|_\infty^2 R_\lambda^4 + |g|_2 d_2 R_\lambda \leqslant C_{\tilde{\eta}} + 1,
$$

for all $u \in E_\lambda^- \oplus \mathbb{R}e_0$ with $\|u\|_\lambda \leqslant R_\lambda$ and $|K|_\infty < b_\lambda := \bar{S}(d_{12/5}R_\lambda)^{-2}$ and $|g|_2 <$
$\eta_\lambda := \dfrac{1}{2d_2 R_\lambda}$, where $C_{\tilde{\eta}}$ depends on $\tilde{\eta}$ but not λ. $\square$

Now we are in a position to prove our main results.

Proof of Theorem 1.1   The proof of this theorem is divided in two steps.

Step 1   There exists a function $u_\lambda \in E_\lambda$ such that $I_\lambda'(u_\lambda) = 0$ and $I_\lambda(u_\lambda) < 0$.

Since $g \in L^2(\mathbb{R}^3)$ and $g \geqslant 0 (\not\equiv 0)$, we can choose a function $\psi \in E_\lambda$ such that

$$\int_{\mathbb{R}^3} g(x)\psi(x)dx > 0.$$

Hence, we have

$$
\begin{aligned}
I(t\psi) &= \frac{t^2}{2}\|\psi\|_\lambda^2 - \frac{\lambda t^2}{2}\int_{\mathbb{R}^3} V^-(x)\psi^2 dx + \frac{t^4}{4}\int_{\mathbb{R}^3} K(x)\phi_\psi\psi^2 dx \\
&\quad - \int_{\mathbb{R}^3} F(x, t\psi)dx - t\int_{\mathbb{R}^3} g(x)\psi dx \\
&\leqslant \frac{t^2}{2}\|\psi\|_\lambda^2 + \frac{t^4}{4}C_0\|\psi\|_\lambda^4 - t\int_{\mathbb{R}^3} g(x)\psi dx \\
&< 0, \quad \text{for } t > 0 \text{ small enough.}
\end{aligned}
$$

Thus, there exists u_λ small enough such that $I_\lambda(u_\lambda) < 0$. By Lemma 1.5, we have

$$c_{0,\lambda} = \inf\{I_\lambda(u) : u \in \bar{B}_{\rho_\lambda}\} < 0,$$

where $\rho_\lambda > 0$ is given by Lemma 1.5, $B_{\rho_\lambda} = \{u \in E_\lambda : \|u\|_\lambda < \rho_\lambda\}$. By the Ekeland's Variational Principle, there exists a minimizing sequence $\{u_{n,\lambda}\} \subset \bar{B}_{\rho_\lambda}$ such that

$$c_{0,\lambda} \leqslant I_\lambda(u_{n,\lambda}) < c_{0,\lambda} + \frac{1}{n_\lambda}$$

and

$$I_\lambda(w_\lambda) \geqslant I_\lambda(u_{n,\lambda}) - \frac{1}{n_\lambda}\|w_\lambda - u_{n,\lambda}\|_\lambda,$$

for all $w_\lambda \in \bar{B}_{\rho_\lambda}$. Clearly, $\{u_{n,\lambda}\}$ is a bounded Palais-Smale sequence of I_λ. Then, by a standard procedure, Lemmas 1.2, 1.3 imply that there exists a function $u_\lambda \in E_\lambda$ such that $I_\lambda'(u_\lambda) = 0$ and $I_\lambda(u_\lambda) = c_{0,\lambda} < 0$.

If $V \geqslant 0$, we can get $\rho_\lambda, c_{0,\lambda}, u_{0,\lambda}$ are independent of λ.

Step 2   There exists a function $\tilde{u}_\lambda \in E_\lambda$ such that $I_\lambda'(\tilde{u}_\lambda) = 0$ and $I_\lambda(\tilde{u}_\lambda) > 0$.

It follows from Lemmas 1.5, 1.7 and Proposition 1.4 that, for each $k \in \mathbb{N}$, $\lambda = \lambda_k, |g|_2 < \eta_k$ and $0 < |K|_\infty < b_k$ (or $0 < |K|_2 < b_k$), I_{λ_k} has a $(C)_c$ sequence with $c \in [\alpha_{\lambda_k}, \sup I_{\lambda_k}(Q_k)]$. Setting $M := \sup I_{\lambda_k}(Q_k)$, then I_{λ_k} has a nontrivial critical point according to Lemmas 1.1, 1.4 and Proposition 1.4. That is, there exists a function $\tilde{u}_\lambda \in E_\lambda$ such that $I_\lambda'(\tilde{u}_\lambda) = 0$ and $I_\lambda(\tilde{u}_\lambda) = c \geqslant \alpha_{\lambda_k} > 0$. The proof is complete.   □

Proof of Theorem 1.2   The first solution is similar to the first solution of Theorem 1.1. The second solution follows from Lemmas 1.1, 1.4, 1.5, 1.8 and Proposition 1.4. The proof is complete.   □

Proof of Theorem 1.3   The proof of this theorem is divided in two steps.

Step 1   There exists a function $u_0 \in E_\lambda$ such that $I'_\lambda(u_0) = 0$ and $I_\lambda(u_0) < 0$.

In the proof of Theorem 1.1, we can choose $c_0 = c_{0,\lambda}, B_\rho = B_{\rho,\lambda}$, then by the Ekeland's Variational Principle, there exists a sequence $\{u_n\} \subset \bar{B}_\rho$ such that

$$c_0 \leqslant I_\lambda(u_n) < c_0 + \frac{1}{n}$$

and

$$I_\lambda(w) \geqslant I_\lambda(u_n) - \frac{1}{n}\|w - u_n\|_\lambda,$$

for all $w \in \bar{B}_\rho$. Then by a standard procedure, we can show that $\{u_n\}$ is a bounded Palais-Smale sequence of I_λ. Therefore Lemmas 1.3 and 1.2 imply that there exists a function $u_0 \in E_\lambda$ such that $I'_\lambda(u_0) = 0$ and $I_\lambda(u_0) = c_0 < 0$.

Step 2   There exists a function $\tilde{u}_\lambda \in E_\lambda$ such that $I'_\lambda(\tilde{u}_\lambda) = 0$ and $I_\lambda(\tilde{u}_\lambda) > 0$.

Since we suppose $V \geqslant 0$, the functional I_λ has mountain pass geometry and the existence of nontrivial solutions can be obtained by mountain pass theorem[154]. In fact, by Lemma 1.5, there exist constants $\alpha, \rho, \eta > 0$ (independent of λ) such that, for each $\lambda > \Lambda_0$,

$$I_\lambda(u) \geqslant \alpha \quad \text{for } u \in E_\lambda \text{ with } \|u\|_\lambda = \rho \text{ and } |g|_2 < \eta.$$

Take $e \in C_0^\infty(\Omega) \setminus \{0\}$, by $(f_1), (f_2)$ and Fatou's lemma, we get

$$\frac{I_\lambda(te)}{t^4} \leqslant \frac{1}{2t^2}\int_\Omega |\nabla e|^2 dx + \frac{1}{4}N(e) - \int_{\{x\in\Omega:e(x)\neq0\}} \frac{F(x,te)}{(te)^4}e^4 dx - t\int_\Omega ge dx \to -\infty$$

as $t \to +\infty$, which yields that $I_\lambda(te) < 0$ for $t > 0$ large. Clearly, there is $C_1 > 0$ (independent of λ) such that

$$c_\lambda := \inf_{\gamma\in\Gamma} \max_{t\in[0,1]} I_\lambda(\gamma(t)) \leqslant \sup_{t\geqslant0} I_\lambda(te_0) \leqslant C_1,$$

where $\Gamma = \{\gamma \in C([0,1], E_\lambda) : \gamma(0) = 0, \|\gamma(1)\|_\lambda \geqslant \rho, I_\lambda(\gamma(1)) < 0\}$. By Mountain Pass theorem and Lemma 1.3, we obtain a nontrivial critical point $\tilde{u}_\lambda$ of I_λ with $I_\lambda(\tilde{u}_\lambda) \in [\alpha, C_1]$ for λ large. The proof is complete.   □

1.2   Nonlinear Schrödinger-Poisson equations with sublinear case

1.2.1   Introduction and main results

The following Schrödinger-Poisson system

$$\begin{cases} -\Delta u + V(x)u + K(x)\phi(x)u = f(x, u) + g(x), & x \in \mathbb{R}^3, \\ -\Delta\phi = K(x)u^2, \quad \lim_{|x|\to+\infty} \phi(x) = 0, & x \in \mathbb{R}^3 \end{cases} \quad (1.37)$$

arises from several interesting physical contexts. It is well known that (1.37) has a strong physical meaning since it appears in quantum mechanics models (see [27, 123]) and in semiconductor theory (see [23, 129, 139, 155]). From the point view of quantum mechanics, the system (1.37) describes the mutual interactions of many particles[160]. Indeed, if the term $f(x,u)$ and $g(x)$ are replaced with 0, then problem (1.37) becomes the Schrödinger-Poisson system. In some recent works (see [11, 14, 17, 31, 49, 75, 98, 107, 169, 171, 198, 214]), different nonlinearities have added to Schrödinger-Poisson equation, giving rise to the so-called nonlinear Schrödinger-Poisson system. These nonlinear terms have been traditionally used in the Schrödinger equation to model the interaction among particles.

Many mathematicians have been devoted to the study of (1.37) with virous nonlinearities $f(x,u)$. We recall some of them as follows.

The case of $g \equiv 0$, that is the homogeneous case, has been studied widely in [10, 11, 69, 70, 74, 75, 113, 141, 155, 159, 185, 215]. In 2010, Cerami and Vaira[49] study system (1.1) in the case of $f(x,u) = a(x)|u|^{p-2}u$ with $4 < p < 6$ and $a(x) > 0$. In order to recover the compactness of the embedding of $H^1(\mathbb{R}^3)$ into the Lebesgue space $L^s(\mathbb{R}^3), s \in [2,6)$, they established a global compactness lemma. They proved the existence of positive ground state and bound state solutions without requiring any symmetry property on $a(x)$ and $K(x)$.

In 2012, Sun, Chen and Nieto[172] considered a more general case, that is, $f(x,u) = a(x)\tilde{f}(u)$ where $\tilde{f}$ was asymptotically linear at infinity, i.e., $\tilde{f}(s)/s \to c$ as $s \to +\infty$ with a suitable constant c. They established a compactness lemma different from that in [49] and proved the existence of ground state solutions. In [212], Ye and Tang studied the existence and multiplicity of solutions for homogeneous system of (1.37) when the potential V might change sign and the nonlinear term f was superlinear or sublinear in u as $|u| \to \infty$. For the Schrödinger-Poisson system with sign-changing potential, see [171, 202]. Huang, Rocha and Chen[107] studied the case that $f(x,u)$ was a combination of a superlinear term and a linear term. More precisely, $f(x,u) = k_1(x)|u|^{p-2}u + \mu h_1(x)u$, where $4 < p < 6$ and $\mu > 0, k_1 \in C(\mathbb{R}^3)$, k_1 changed sign in $\mathbb{R}^3$ and $\lim\limits_{|x|\to+\infty} k_1(x) = k_\infty < 0$. They proved the existence of at least two positive solutions in the case that $\mu > \mu_1$ and near μ_1, where μ_1 was the first eigenvalue of $-\Delta + id$ in $H^1(\mathbb{R}^3)$ and with weight function h_1. In [108, 109], the authors considered the critical case of $p = 6$; [157] studied the case of $p = 4$. Sun, Su and Zhao[172] got infinitely many solutions for (1.37), where the nonlinearity $f(x,u) = k_2(x)|u|^{q-2}u - h_2(x)|u|^{l-2}u, 1 < q < 2 < l < \infty$, i.e. the nonlinearity involving a combination of concave and convex terms. For more results on the effect of concave and convex terms of elliptic equations, see [203, 204] and the references therein.

Next, we consider the nonhomogeneous case of (1.37), that is $g \not\equiv 0$. The existence of radially symmetric solutions is obtained for above nonhomogeneous system in [159]. Chen and Tang[55] obtained two solutions for the nonhomogeneous system with $f(x, u)$ satisfying Amborosetti-Rabinowitz type condition and V being nonradially symmetric. In [81, 83], the system with asymptotically linear and 3-linear nonlinearity was considered. For more results on the nonhomogeneous case, see [112, 210] and the references therein.

Motivated by the works mentioned above, we handle the sublinear case, and hence make the following assumptions:

(V_1) $V(x) \in C(\mathbb{R}^3, \mathbb{R})$ satisfies $\inf_{x \in \mathbb{R}^3} V(x) = a_1 > 0$;

(V_2) for any $M > 0$, meas$\{x \in \mathbb{R}^3 : V(x) < M\} < +\infty$, where meas denotes the Lebesgue measures;

(K) $K(x) \in L^2(\mathbb{R}^3) \cup L^\infty(\mathbb{R}^3)$ and $K(x) \geqslant 0$ for all $x \in \mathbb{R}^3$;

(F) There exist constants $\sigma, \gamma \in (1, 2)$ and functions $A \in L^{2/(2-\sigma)}(\mathbb{R}^3, \mathbb{R}^+)$, $B \in L^{2/(2-\gamma)}(\mathbb{R}^3, \mathbb{R}^+)$ such that $|f(x, u)| \leqslant A(x)|u|^{\sigma-1} + B(x)|u|^{\gamma-1}$, $\forall(x, u) \in (\mathbb{R}^3, \mathbb{R})$;

(G) $g(x) \in L^2(\mathbb{R}^3)$ and $g(x) \geqslant 0$ for a.e. $x \in \mathbb{R}^3$.

Let

$$E_1 := \left\{ u \in H^1(\mathbb{R}^3) : \int_{\mathbb{R}^3} (|\nabla u|^2 + V(x)u^2) dx < \infty \right\}.$$

Then E_1 is a Hilbert space with the inner product

$$(u, v)_{E_1} = \int_{\mathbb{R}^3} (\nabla u \cdot \nabla v + V(x)uv) \, dx$$

and the norm

$$\|u\|_{E_1} = (u, u)_{E_1}^{1/2}.$$

Obviously, the embedding $E_1 \hookrightarrow L^s(\mathbb{R}^3)$ is continuous for any $s \in [2, 2^*]$. The norm on $L^s = L^s(\mathbb{R}^3)$ with $1 < s < \infty$ is given by $|u|_s^s = \int_{\mathbb{R}^3} |u|^s dx$.

Now we state our main result:

Theorem 1.4 (Sublinear)   *Assume that $(V_1), (V_2), (K), (F)$ and (G) are satisfied. Then problem (1.37) possesses at least one nontrival solution.*

Remark 1.4   It is not difficult to find function f satisfies our assumption (F). For example, let

$$f(x, u) = \begin{cases} |x|e^{-|x|^2} \left[\sigma|u|^{\sigma-2}u \sin^2\left(\dfrac{1}{|u|^\varrho}\right) - \varrho|u|^{\sigma-\varrho-2} \sin\left(\dfrac{2}{|u|^\varrho}\right) \right], & t \neq 0, \\ 0, & t = 0, \end{cases}$$

where $\varrho > 0$ small enough and $\sigma \in (1 + \varrho, 2)$.

Remark 1.5   The condition in (V_2), which implies the compactness of embedding of the working space E_1 and contains the coercivity condition: $V(x) \to \infty$ as $|x| \to \infty$, is first introduced by Bartsch and Wang in [18] to overcome the lack of compactness. We are not sure whether Theorem 1.4 hold without the condition (V_2).

Remark 1.6   To the best of our knowledge, it seems that Theorem 1.4 is the first result about the existence of solutions for the nonhomogeneous Schrödinger-Poisson equations with sublinear case.

1.2.2   Variation set and proofs of main results

We know that the embedding $E_1 \hookrightarrow L^s(\mathbb{R}^3)$ is continuous for any $s \in [2, 2^*]$. Furthermore, we have the following result:

Lemma 1.9[224, Lemma 3.4]   *Under assumption (V_1) and (V_2), the embedding $E_1 \hookrightarrow L^s(\mathbb{R}^3)$ is compact for any $s \in [2, 2^*)$.*

By Lemma 1.9, there exists $d_s > 0$ such that

$$|u|_s \leqslant d_s \|u\|_{E_1}, \quad \forall u \in E_1. \tag{1.38}$$

It is known that problem (1.37) can be reduced to a single equation with a nonlocal term, see [75]. In fact, for every $u \in E_1$, the Lax-Milgram theorem implies that there exists a unique $\phi_u \in D^{1,2}(\mathbb{R}^3)$ such that

$$-\Delta \phi_u = K(x)u^2 \tag{1.39}$$

with

$$\phi_u(x) = \frac{1}{4\pi} \int_{\mathbb{R}^3} \frac{K(y)u^2(y)}{|x-y|}\, dy.$$

If $K \in L^\infty(\mathbb{R}^3)$, by (1.39), the Hölder inequality and the Sobolev inequality, we get

$$\|\phi_u\|_D^2 = \int_{\mathbb{R}^3} K(x)\phi_u u^2 dx \leqslant \bar{S}^{-2} d_{12/5}^4 |K|_\infty^2 \|u\|_{E_1}^4.$$

Similarly, if $K \in L^2(\mathbb{R}^3)$,

$$\|\phi_u\|_D^2 = \int_{\mathbb{R}^3} K(x)\phi_u u^2 dx \leqslant \bar{S}^{-2} d_6^4 |K|_2^2 \|u\|_{E_1}^4.$$

Thus, there exists $C_0 > 0$ such that

$$\|\phi_u\|_D^2 = \int_{\mathbb{R}^3} K(x)\phi_u u^2 dx \leqslant C_0 \|u\|_{E_1}^4, \quad \forall K \in L^2(\mathbb{R}^3) \cup L^\infty(\mathbb{R}^3). \tag{1.40}$$

Now we consider the functional I on $(E_1, \|\cdot\|_{E_1})$,

$$I(u) = \frac{1}{2}\int_{\mathbb{R}^3}(|\nabla u|^2 + V(x)u^2)dx + \frac{1}{4}\int_{\mathbb{R}^3}K(x)\phi_u u^2 dx - \varphi(u) - \int_{\mathbb{R}^3}g(x)udx,$$

where $\varphi(u) = \displaystyle\int_{\mathbb{R}^3}F(x,u)dx$.

It follows from (F), we obtian

$$|F(x,u)| \leqslant A(x)|u|^\sigma + B(x)|u|^\gamma, \quad \forall(x,u) \in \mathbb{R}^3 \times \mathbb{R}, \tag{1.41}$$

which, together with (1.40) and the Hölder inequality, we have

$$\int_{\mathbb{R}^3}F(x,u)dx \leqslant \int_{\mathbb{R}^3}(A(x)|u|^\sigma + B(x)|u|^\gamma)dx$$

$$\leqslant |A|_{\frac{2}{2-\sigma}}|u|_2^\sigma + |B|_{\frac{2}{2-\gamma}}|u|_2^\gamma$$

$$\leqslant |A|_{\frac{2}{2-\sigma}}d_2^\sigma\|u\|_E^\sigma + |B|_{\frac{2}{2-\gamma}}d_2^\gamma\|u\|_E^\gamma$$

$$< +\infty. \tag{1.42}$$

Therefore, φ and I are well defined. In addition, we need the following lemmas.

Lemma 1.10[212, Lemma 4.1]   *Assume that* $(V_1), (V_2)$ *and* (F) *are satisfied and* $u_n \rightharpoonup u$ *in* E_1, *then*

$$f(x, u_n) \to f(x, u) \quad \text{in } L^2(\mathbb{R}^3).$$

Lemma 1.11[212, Lemma 4.2]   *Assume that* $(V_2), (K)$ *and* (F) *hold. Then* $\varphi \in C^1(E_1, \mathbb{R})$ *and* $\varphi' : E \to E^*$(*the dual space of* E_1) *is compact, and hence* $I \in C^1(E_1, \mathbb{R})$,

$$\langle\varphi'(u), v\rangle = \int_{\mathbb{R}^3}f(x,u)vdx,$$

$$\langle I'(u), v\rangle = \int_{\mathbb{R}^3}(\nabla u\nabla v + V(x)uv + K(x)\phi_u uv - f(x,u)v - g(x)v)dx, \tag{1.43}$$

for all $u, v \in E_1$. *Hence, if* $u \in E_1$ *is a critical point of* I, *then* $(u, \phi_u) \in E_1 \times D^{1,2}(\mathbb{R}^3)$ *is a solution of problem* (1.39).

We refer the readers to [23] and [75] for the details.

Now we give a proposition, which will be applied to prove Theorem 1.4. Recall that $I \in C^1(E_1, \mathbb{R})$ is said to satisfy the (PS) condition if any sequence $\{u_j\}_{j\in\mathbb{N}}$ is bounded and $I'(u_j) \to 0$ as $j \to +\infty$, possesses a convergent subsequence in E_1.

Proposition 1.5[140, 200]   *Let* E_1 *be a real Banach space and* $I \in C^1(E_1, \mathbb{R})$ *satisfy the* (PS) *condition. If* I *is bounded from below, then* $c = \inf_{E_1} I$ *is a critical value of* I.

Lemma 1.12 *Under the assumptions of Theorem 1.4, I is bounded from below and satisfies the (PS) condition.*

Proof. By $(K),(G)$ and (1.43), it follows from that

$$I(u) \geqslant \frac{1}{2}\|u\|_{E_1}^2 - |A|_{\frac{2}{2-\sigma}} d_2^\sigma \|u\|_{E_1}^\sigma - |B|_{\frac{2}{2-\gamma}} d_2^\gamma \|u\|_{E_1}^\gamma, \quad \forall u \in E_1.$$

Noting that $\sigma, \gamma \in (1,2)$, we have

$$I(u) \to +\infty \quad \text{as } \|u\|_{E_1} \to \infty. \tag{1.44}$$

Thus I is bounded from below.

Let $\{u_n\} \subset E_1$ be a (PS) sequence of I, i.e., $\{I(u_n)\}$ is bounded and $I'(u_n) \to 0$ as $n \to +\infty$. By (1.44), $\{u_n\}$ is bounded, and then $u_n \rightharpoonup u$ in E_1 for some $u \in E_1$. Recall that

$$(xy)^{1/2}(x+y) \leqslant x^2 + y^2, \quad \forall x, y \geqslant 0.$$

By $-\Delta \phi_u = K(x)u^2$ and the Höder inequality, we obtain

$$\int_{\mathbb{R}^3} K(x)(\phi_{u_n} u_n u + \phi_u u_n u)dx$$

$$\leqslant \left(\int_{\mathbb{R}^3} K(x)\phi_{u_n} u_n^2 dx\right)^{1/2} \left(\int_{\mathbb{R}^3} K(x)\phi_{u_n} u^2 dx\right)^{1/2}$$

$$+ \left(\int_{\mathbb{R}^3} K(x)\phi_u u_n^2 dx\right)^{1/2} \left(\int_{\mathbb{R}^3} K(x)\phi_{u_n} u^2 dx\right)^{1/2}$$

$$= \left(\int_{\mathbb{R}^3} \nabla\phi_{u_n} \cdot \nabla\phi_u dx\right)^{1/2} (\|\phi_{u_n}\|_D + \|\phi_u\|_D)$$

$$\leqslant \|\phi_{u_n}\|_D + \|\phi_u\|_D$$

$$= \int_{\mathbb{R}^3} K(x)(\phi_{u_n} u_n^2 + \phi_u u^2)dx,$$

which implies that

$$\int_{\mathbb{R}^3} K(x)(\phi_{u_n} u_n - \phi_u u)(u_n - u)dx \geqslant 0.$$

Since $u_n \rightharpoonup u$ in $L^2(\mathbb{R}^3)$ and $g \in L^2(\mathbb{R}^3)$, we obtain

$$\int_{\mathbb{R}^3} g(u_n - u)dx = o(1).$$

This jointly with Lemma 1.10, we have

$$\|u_n - u\|_{E_1}^2 = \langle I'(u_n) - I'(u), u_n - u\rangle - \int_{\mathbb{R}^3} K(x)\phi_{u_n} u_n - \phi_u u)(u_n - u)dx$$

$$+ \int_{\mathbb{R}^3} (f(x, u_n) - f(x, u)) dx$$

$$\leqslant \|I'(u_n)\|_{E^*} \|u_n - u\|_E - \langle I'(u), u_n - u \rangle$$

$$+ \left(\int_{\mathbb{R}^3} |f(x, u_n) - f(x, u)|^2 dx \right)^{1/2} \cdot |u_n - u|_2$$

$$\to 0,$$

That is, $u_n \to u$ as $n \to \infty$. Hence the (PS) condition holds. The proof is complete. □

Proof of Theorem 1.4   Theorem 1.4 hold directly by Lemma 1.12 and Proposition 1.5. The proof is complete.   □

1.3   Nonlinear term involving a combination of concave and convex terms

1.3.1   Existence of solution

Now we deal with the following nonhomogeneous Schrödinger-Poisson system

$$\begin{cases} -\Delta u + V(x)u + \phi(x)u = k(x)|u|^{q-2}u - h(x)|u|^{p-2}u + g(x), & x \in \mathbb{R}^3, \\ -\Delta\phi = u^2, \quad \lim_{|x| \to +\infty} \phi(x) = 0, & x \in \mathbb{R}^3, \end{cases} \quad (1.45)$$

where $1 < q < 2 < p < 4$, i.e. the nonlinearity of this problem may involve a combination of concave and convex terms.

We assume that $k(x)$ and $h(x)$ are measurable functions satisfying the following conditions:

(k) $k(x) \in L^{6/(6-q)}(\mathbb{R}^3) \cap L^\infty(\mathbb{R}^3)$ and $k(x) \geqslant 0$ is not identically zero for a.e. $x \in \mathbb{R}^3$;

(h) $h(x) \in L^\infty(\mathbb{R}^3)$ and $h(x) > 0$ for a.e. $x \in \mathbb{R}^3$.

Theorem 1.5   Let $1 < q < 2 < p < 4$, (V_1), (V_2), (k), (h) and (G) hold, then problem (1.45) admits at least one nontrivial solution.

Remark 1.7   In [159], the author obtained the existence of multiple radially symmetric solutions on $\mathbb{R}^3$ for (1.45). In our Theorem 1.5, we don't need the radially symmetric on the potential V, so we get the nonradially symmetrical solution for system (1.45) with the concave and convex nonlinearities.

Remark 1.8   In order to get our results, we have to solve some difficulties. The main difficulty is the loss of compactness of the Sobolev embedding $H^1(\mathbb{R}^3)$ into $L^s(\mathbb{R}^3)$, $s \in [2, 6]$ since this problem is set on $\mathbb{R}^3$. To recover the difficulty, some of the papers use the radially symmetric function space, which possesses compact embedding, see [163]. In this section, the integrability of k and the assumption

$1 < q < 2$ to ensure the space E_1 is compactly embedding in the weighted Lebesgue space (see the following Lemma 1.13).

It is known that problem (1.45) can be reduced to a single equation see [75]. In fact, for every $u \in E_1$, the Lax-Milgram theorem implies that there exists a unique $\phi_u \in D^{1,2}(\mathbb{R}^3)$ such that

$$-\Delta\phi_u = u^2, \quad u \in \mathbb{R}^3 \tag{1.46}$$

with

$$\phi_u(x) = \frac{1}{4\pi} \int_{\mathbb{R}^3} \frac{u^2(y)}{|x-y|} dy.$$

By (1.46), the Höder inequality and the Sobolev inequality, we get

$$\int_{\mathbb{R}^3} |\nabla\phi_u|^2 dx = \int_{\mathbb{R}^3} \phi_u u^2 dx \leqslant |u|_{12/5}^2 \|\phi_u\|_6 \leqslant C|u|_{12/5}^2 \|\phi_u\|_D,$$

then

$$\|\phi_u\|_D \leqslant C|u|_{12/5}^2,$$

and

$$\int_{\mathbb{R}^3} \phi_u u^2 dx \leqslant C|u|_{12/5}^4 \leqslant C\|u\|_{E_1}^4. \tag{1.47}$$

Therefore, the problem (1.45) can be reduced to the following equation:

$$-\Delta u + V(x)u + \phi_u u = k(x)|u|^{q-2}u - h(x)|u|^{p-2}u + g(x), \quad x \in \mathbb{R}^3.$$

We introduce the functional $J : E_1 \to \mathbb{R}$ defined by

$$J(u) = \frac{1}{2} \int_{\mathbb{R}^3} (|\nabla u|^2 + V(x)u^2)dx + \frac{1}{4}\int_{\mathbb{R}^3} \phi_u u^2 dx - \frac{1}{q}\int_{\mathbb{R}^3} k(x)|u|^q dx$$

$$+ \frac{1}{p}\int_{\mathbb{R}^3} h(x)|u|^p dx - \int_{\mathbb{R}^3} g(x)u dx. \tag{1.48}$$

By (1.47) and the conditions of Theorem 1.5, all the integrals in (1.48) are well-defined and in $C^1(E_1, \mathbb{R})$. Now, it is easy to verify that the weak solutions of (1.45) correspond to the critical points of $J : E_1 \to \mathbb{R}$ with derivative given by

$$\langle J'(u), v \rangle = \int_{\mathbb{R}^3} [\nabla u \nabla v + V(x)uv + \phi_u uv - k(x)|u|^{q-2}uv$$

$$+ h(x)|u|^{p-2}uv - g(x)v]dx.$$

Lemma 1.13 *Under the assumptions in Theorem 1.5, the functional J is coercive on E_1.*

Proof. By (k), we have

$$\int_{\mathbb{R}^3} k(x)|u|^q dx \leqslant |k|_{6/6-q} S^{-q/2} \|u\|_{E_1}^q. \tag{1.49}$$

For $\|u\|_{E_1}$ large enough, by (1.49) we obtain

$$J(u) = \frac{1}{2} \int_{\mathbb{R}^3} (|\nabla u|^2 + V(x)u^2)dx + \frac{1}{4} \int_{\mathbb{R}^3} \phi_u u^2 dx - \frac{1}{q} \int_{\mathbb{R}^3} k(x)|u|^q dx$$

$$\geqslant \frac{1}{2}\|u\|_{E_1}^2 - \frac{1}{q}|k|_{6/(6-q)} S^{-q/2}\|u\|_{E_1}^q - c|g|_2\|u\|_{E_1}$$

$$> \frac{1}{2}\|u\|_{E_1}^2 - c_1\|u\|_{E_1}^q - c|g|_2\|u\|_{E_1} \rightarrow +\infty,$$

since $1 < q < 2$. The proof is complete. $\qquad\square$

Lemma 1.14 *Assume that $(V_1), (V_2), (k), (h), (G)$ hold, and $\{u_n\} \subset E_1$ is a bounded (PS) sequence of J, then $\{u_n\}$ has a strongly convergent subsequence in E_1.*

Proof. Consider a sequence $\{u_n\}$ in E_1 which satisfies

$$J(u_n) \rightarrow c, \quad J'(u_n) \rightarrow 0, \quad \sup_n \|u_n\|_{E_1} < +\infty.$$

Going if necessary to a subsequence, we can assume that $u_n \rightharpoonup u$ in E_1. In view of Lemma 1.9, $u_n \rightarrow u$ in $L^s(\mathbb{R}^3)$ for any $s \in [2, 2^*)$. By the derivative of J, we easily obtain

$$\|u_n - u\|_{E_1}^2 = \langle J'(u_n) - J'(u), u_n - u \rangle + \int_{\mathbb{R}^3} k(x)(|u_n|^{q-1} - |u|^{q-1})(u_n - u)dx$$

$$- \int_{\mathbb{R}^3} h(x)(|u_n|^{p-1} - |u|^{p-1})(u_n - u)dx$$

$$- \int_{\mathbb{R}^3} (\phi_{u_n} u_n - \phi_u u)(u_n - u)dx.$$

It is clear that

$$\langle J'(u_n) - J'(u), u_n - u \rangle \rightarrow 0 \quad \text{as } n \rightarrow \infty. \tag{1.50}$$

By the Hölder inequality and the Sobolev inequality, we have

$$\left| \int_{\mathbb{R}^3} \phi_{u_n} u_n (u_n - u)dx \right| \leqslant |\phi_{u_n}|_6 |u_n|_{12/5} |u_n - u|_{12/5}$$

$$\leqslant C_1 \|\phi_{u_n}\|_D |u_n|_{12/5} |u_n - u|_{12/5}$$

$$\leqslant C_2 |u_n|_{12/5}^3 |u_n - u|_{12/5} \to 0,$$

since $u_n \to u$ in $L^s(\mathbb{R}^3)$ for any $s \in [2, 2^*)$. We obtain

$$\int_{\mathbb{R}^3} \phi_{u_n} u_n (u_n - u) dx \to 0 \quad \text{as } n \to \infty. \tag{1.51}$$

Similarly we can also obtain

$$\int_{\mathbb{R}^3} \phi_u u (u_n - u) dx \to 0 \quad \text{as } n \to \infty. \tag{1.52}$$

By $2 < p < 4$, (h) and the Hölder inequality, one has

$$\left| \int_{\mathbb{R}^3} h(x)(|u_n|^{p-1} - |u|^{p-1})(u_n - u) dx \right| \leqslant |h|_\infty (|u_n|_p^{p-1} + |u|_p^{p-1})|u_n - u|_p$$

$$\to 0 \quad \text{as } n \to \infty. \tag{1.53}$$

By $1 < q < 2$, (k) and the Hölder inequality, one has

$$\int_{\mathbb{R}^3} k(x)|u_n|^{q-1}(u_n - u) dx$$

$$= \int_{\mathbb{R}^3} k(x)^{\frac{q-1}{q}} k(x)^{\frac{1}{q}} |u_n|^{q-1}(u_n - u) dx$$

$$\leqslant |k|_\infty^{1-\frac{1}{q}} \left[\int_{\mathbb{R}^3} \left(k(x)^{\frac{1}{q}} |u_n|^{q-1} \right)^{\frac{6}{6-q}} dx \right]^{\frac{6-q}{6}} \left(\int_{\mathbb{R}^3} (u_n - u)^{\frac{6}{q}} dx \right)^{\frac{q}{6}}$$

$$\leqslant |k|_\infty^{1-\frac{1}{q}} \left(\int_{\mathbb{R}^3} k(x)^{\frac{6}{6-q}} dx \right)^{\frac{6-q}{6} \cdot \frac{1}{q}} \left(\int_{\mathbb{R}^3} |u_n|^{\frac{6q}{6-q}} dx \right)^{\frac{6-q}{6q}(q-1)} |u_n - u|_{\frac{6}{q}}$$

$$= |k|_\infty^{1-\frac{1}{q}} |k|_{\frac{6}{6-q}}^{\frac{1}{q}} |u_n|_{\frac{6q}{6-q}}^{q-1} |u_n - u|_{\frac{6}{q}} \to 0 \quad \text{as } n \to \infty, \tag{1.54}$$

since $3 < \dfrac{6}{q} < 6$, $u_n \to u$ in $L^s(\mathbb{R}^3)$ for any $s \in [2, 2^*)$.

Similarly, we also obtain

$$\int_{\mathbb{R}^3} k(x)|u|^{q-1}(u_n - u) dx \to 0 \quad \text{as } n \to \infty. \tag{1.55}$$

Therefore, by (1.51)—(1.55), we get $\|u_n - u\|_{E_1} \to 0$. The proof is complete. $\square$

Proof of Theorem 1.5   In view of Proposition 1.5 and Lemma 1.14, we only need to check that $\{u_n\}$ is bounded in E_1.

$$\tilde{c}_0 + 1 + \|u\|_{E_1} \geqslant J(u_n) - \frac{1}{4}\langle J'(u_n), u_n\rangle$$

$$= \frac{1}{4}\|u_n\|_{E_1}^2 + \left(\frac{1}{4} - \frac{1}{q}\right)\int_{\mathbb{R}^3} k(x)|u_n|^q dx + \left(\frac{1}{p} - \frac{1}{4}\right)\int_{\mathbb{R}^3} h(x)|u_n|^p dx$$

$$- \frac{3}{4}\int_{\mathbb{R}^3} g(x)u_n dx$$

$$\geqslant \frac{1}{4}\|u_n\|_{E_1}^2 + \left(\frac{1}{4} - \frac{1}{q}\right)|k|_{6/(6-q)}S^{-q/2}\|u\|_{E_1}^q - \frac{3}{4}|g|_2|u_n|_2,$$

for n large enough. Since $g \in L^2(\mathbb{R}^3)$, it follows from $1 < q < 2$ that $\{u_n\}$ is bounded in E_1. The proof is complete.   □

1.3.2   The multiplicity of solutions

In this section, we will consider the multiplicity solutions of the following nonhomogeneous Schrödinger-Poisson system:

$$\begin{cases} -\Delta u + V(x)u + \phi(x)u = -k(x)|u|^{q-2}u + h(x)|u|^{p-2}u + g(x), & x \in \mathbb{R}^3, \\ -\Delta\phi = u^2, \quad \lim\limits_{|x|\to+\infty} \phi(x) = 0, & x \in \mathbb{R}^3, \end{cases} \quad (1.56)$$

where $1 < q < 2, 4 < p < 6$, i.e. the nonlinearity of this problem may involve a combination of concave and convex terms. To our best knowledge, this is the first result on the existence of multiple solutions to problem (1.56).

We assume that $V(x), k(x), h(x)$ and $g(x)$ are measurable functions satisfying the following conditions:

(V_1) $V(x) \in C(\mathbb{R}^3, \mathbb{R})$ satisfies $\inf_{x \in \mathbb{R}^3} V(x) = a_1 > 0$.

(V_2) for any $M > 0$, $\text{meas}\{x \in \mathbb{R}^3 : V(x) < M\} < +\infty$, where meas denotes the Lebesgue measures.

(K) $k(x) \in L^{6/(6-q)}(\mathbb{R}^3) \cap L^\infty(\mathbb{R}^3)$ and $k(x) \geqslant 0$ is not identically zero for a.e. $x \in \mathbb{R}^3$.

(H) $h(x) \in L^\infty(\mathbb{R}^3)$ and $h(x) > 0$ for a.e. $x \in \mathbb{R}^3$.

(G_1) $g(x) \in L^2(\mathbb{R}^3)$ and $g(x) > 0$ for a.e. $x \in \mathbb{R}^3$.

Now we state our main result:

Theorem 1.6   Let $1 < q < 2, 4 < p < 6, (V_1), (V_2), (K), (H)$ and (G_1) hold, then there exists a constant $m_0 > 0$ such that problem (1.56) admits at least two different solutions $u_0, \tilde{u}_0$ in E_1 satisfying $I(u_0) < 0$ and $I(\tilde{u}_0) > 0$ if $\|g\|_2 < m_0$.

Remark 1.9   Salvatore[159] obtained the existence of multiple radially symmetric solutions on $\mathbb{R}^3$ for the homogeneous and the nonhomogeneous system (1.56). Since the potential V may be not radially symmetric in Theorem 1.6, we get the multiple nonradially symmetrical solutions for system (1.56) with the concave and convex nonlinearities.

Remark 1.10 Our proof is variational. The main difficulty is the loss of compactness of the Sobolev embedding $H^1(\mathbb{R}^3)$ into $L^s(\mathbb{R}^3)$, $s \in [2,6]$ since this problem is set on $\mathbb{R}^3$. To recover this difficulty, some of the papers use special function space, such as the radially symmetric function space, which possesses compact embedding, see [163]. In this section, the integrability of k and the main assumption $1 < q < 2$ to ensure the space E_1 is compactly embedding in the weighted Lebesgue space (see Lemma 1.15). Although the methods are used before, we need to study carefully some properties of the term $\phi(x)u$ and the effect of the sublinear therm.

Remark 1.11 To the best of our knowledge, it seems that Theorem 1.6 is the first result about the existence of multiple solutions for the nonhomogeneous Schrödinger-Poisson equations on $\mathbb{R}^3$ with concave and convex terms.

Then we give the variational setting of the problem. Problem (1.56) can be reduced to the following equation:

$$-\Delta u + V(x)u + \phi_u u = -k(x)|u|^{q-2}u + h(x)|u|^{p-2}u + g(x), \qquad x \in \mathbb{R}^3.$$

We will apply the variational methods to prove our theorem. We introduce the functional $I : E_1 \to \mathbb{R}$ defined by

$$I(u) = \frac{1}{2}\int_{\mathbb{R}^3}(|\nabla u|^2 + V(x)u^2)dx + \frac{1}{4}\int_{\mathbb{R}^3}\phi_u u^2 dx + \frac{1}{q}\int_{\mathbb{R}^3}k(x)|u|^q dx$$
$$- \frac{1}{p}\int_{\mathbb{R}^3}h(x)|u|^p dx - \int_{\mathbb{R}^3}g(x)u dx. \qquad (1.57)$$

By (1.38) and the conditions of Theorem 1.6, all the integrals in (1.57) are well-defined and in $C^1(E_1, \mathbb{R})$. Now, it is easy to verify that the weak solutions of (1.56) correspond to the critical points of $I : E_1 \to \mathbb{R}$ with derivative given by

$$\langle I'(u), v \rangle = \int_{\mathbb{R}^3}[\nabla u \nabla v + V(x)uv + \phi_u uv + k(x)|u|^{q-2}uv$$
$$- h(x)|u|^{p-2}uv - g(x)v]dx.$$

Lemma 1.15 Let $g \in L^2(\mathbb{R}^3)$. Suppose (V_1) and (V_2) hold. Then there exist some constants $\rho, \alpha, m_0 > 0$ such that $I(u)|_{\|u\|_{E_1}=\rho} \geq \alpha$ for all g satisfying

$$\|g\|_2 < m_0.$$

Proof. Since $\phi_u \geq 0, k(x) \geq 0$, using the Hölder inequality and $H^1(\mathbb{R}^3) \hookrightarrow L^s(\mathbb{R}^3), s \in [2,6]$,

$$I(u) \geqslant \frac{1}{2}\|u\|_{E_1}^2 - \frac{|h|_\infty}{p}\|u\|_p^p - \|g\|_{L^2}\|u\|_2$$

$$\geqslant \frac{1}{2}\|u\|_{E_1}^2 - a_2\|u\|_{E_1}^p - \frac{1}{\sqrt{a_1}}\|g\|_{L^2}\|u\|_{E_1}$$

$$= \|u\|_{E_1}\left(\frac{1}{2}\|u\|_{E_1} - a_2\|u\|_{E_1}^{p-1} - \frac{1}{\sqrt{a_1}}\|g\|_2\right),$$

where a_1 is a lower bound of the potential V from (V_1) and $a_2 > 0$ is a constant.

Setting

$$g(t) = \frac{1}{2}t - a_2 t^{p-1}, \quad t \geqslant 0,$$

we see that there exists a constant $\rho > 0$ such that $\max_{t \geqslant 0} g(t) = g(\rho) > 0$. Taking $m_0 := \frac{1}{2}\sqrt{a_1}g(\rho)$, then it follows that there exists a constant $\alpha > 0$ such that $I(u)|_{\|u\|_{E_1}=\rho} \geqslant \alpha$ for all g satisfying $\|g\|_2 < m_0$. The proof is complete. $\square$

Lemma 1.16   *Suppose that (V_1) and $1 < q < 2, 4 < p < 6$ hold, then there exists a function $v \in E_1$ with $\|v\|_{E_1} > \rho$ such that $I(v) < 0$, where ρ is given in Lemma 1.15.*

Proof. Since $1 < q < 2, 4 < p < 6$, $h(x) \geqslant 0$, we have

$$I(tu) = \frac{t^2}{2}\|u\|_{E_1}^2 + \frac{1}{4}\int_{\mathbb{R}^3}\phi_{tu}(tu)^2 dx + \frac{t^q}{q}\int_{\mathbb{R}^3}k(x)|u|^q dx$$

$$- \frac{t^p}{p}\int_{\mathbb{R}^3}h(x)|u|^p dx - t\int_{\mathbb{R}^3}g(x)u dx$$

$$\leqslant \frac{t^2}{2}\|u\|_{E_1}^2 + \frac{t^4}{4}\|u\|_{E_1}^4 + \frac{t^q}{q}\int_{\mathbb{R}^3}k(x)|u|^q dx$$

$$- \frac{t^p}{p}\int_{\mathbb{R}^3}h(x)|u|^p dx - t\int_{\mathbb{R}^3}g(x)u dx$$

$$\to -\infty \quad \text{as } t \to +\infty,$$

for $u \in E_1, u \neq 0$. The lemma is proved by taking $v = t_0 u$ with $t_0 > 0$ large enough and $u \neq 0$. The proof is complete. $\square$

Lemma 1.17   *Assume that $(V_1), (V_2), (K), (H), (G)$ hold, and $\{u_n\} \subset E_1$ is a bounded (PS) sequence of I, then $\{u_n\}$ has a strongly convergent subsequence in E_1.*

Proof. Consider a sequence $\{u_n\}$ in E_1 which satisfies

$$I(u_n) \to c, \quad I'(u_n) \to 0, \quad \sup_n \|u_n\|_{E_1} < +\infty.$$

Going if necessary to a subsequence, we can assume that $u_n \rightharpoonup u$ in E_1. In view of Lemma 1.15, $u_n \to u$ in $L^s(\mathbb{R}^3)$ for any $s \in [2, 2^*)$. By the derivative of I, we easily obtain

$$\|u_n - u\|_{E_1}^2 = \langle I'(u_n) - I'(u), u_n - u \rangle - \int_{\mathbb{R}^3} k(x)(|u_n|^{q-1} - |u|^{q-1})(u_n - u)dx$$

$$+ \int_{\mathbb{R}^3} h(x)(|u_n|^{p-1} - |u|^{p-1})(u_n - u)dx$$

$$- \int_{\mathbb{R}^3} (\phi_{u_n} u_n - \phi_u u)(u_n - u)dx.$$

It is clear that

$$\langle I'(u_n) - I'(u), u_n - u \rangle \to 0 \quad \text{as } n \to \infty. \tag{1.58}$$

By the Hölder inequality and the Sobolev inequality, we have

$$\left| \int_{\mathbb{R}^3} \phi_{u_n} u_n (u_n - u)dx \right| \leqslant \|\phi_{u_n}\|_6 \|u_n\|_{12/5} \|u_n - u\|_{12/5}$$

$$\leqslant C_1 \|\phi_{u_n}\|_D \|u_n\|_{12/5} \|u_n - u\|_{12/5}$$

$$\leqslant C_2 \|u_n\|_{12/5}^3 \|u_n - u\|_{12/5} \to 0,$$

since $u_n \to u$ in $L^s(\mathbb{R}^3)$ for any $s \in [2, 2^*)$. We obtain

$$\int_{\mathbb{R}^3} \phi_{u_n} u_n (u_n - u)dx \to 0 \quad \text{as } n \to \infty. \tag{1.59}$$

Similarly we can also obtain

$$\int_{\mathbb{R}^3} \phi_u u (u_n - u)dx \to 0 \quad \text{as } n \to \infty. \tag{1.60}$$

By $4 < p < 6$, (H) and the Hölder inequality, one has

$$\left| \int_{\mathbb{R}^3} h(x)(|u_n|^{p-1} - |u|^{p-1})(u_n - u)dx \right| \leqslant |h|_\infty (\|u_n\|_p^{p-1} + \|u\|_p^{p-1})\|u_n - u\|_p$$

$$\to 0 \quad \text{as } n \to \infty. \tag{1.61}$$

By $1 < q < 2$, (K) and the Hölder inequality, one has

$$\int_{\mathbb{R}^3} k(x)|u_n|^{q-1}(u_n - u)dx$$

$$= \int_{\mathbb{R}^3} k(x)^{\frac{q-1}{q}} k(x)^{\frac{1}{q}} |u_n|^{q-1}(u_n - u)dx$$

$$\leqslant |k|_\infty^{1-\frac{1}{q}} \left[\int_{\mathbb{R}^3} \left(k(x)^{\frac{1}{q}} |u_n|^{q-1} \right)^{\frac{6}{6-q}} dx \right]^{\frac{6-q}{6}} \left(\int_{\mathbb{R}^3} (u_n - u)^{\frac{6}{q}} dx \right)^{\frac{q}{6}}$$

$$\leqslant |k|_\infty^{1-\frac{1}{q}} \left(\int_{\mathbb{R}^3} k(x)^{\frac{6}{6-q}} dx \right)^{\frac{6-q}{6} \cdot \frac{1}{q}} \left(\int_{\mathbb{R}^3} |u_n|^{\frac{6q}{6-q}} dx \right)^{\frac{6-q}{6q}(q-1)} \|u_n - u\|_{\frac{6}{q}}$$

$$= |k|_\infty^{1-\frac{1}{q}} \|k(x)\|_{\frac{6}{6-q}}^{\frac{1}{q}} \|u_n\|_{\frac{6q}{6-q}}^{q-1} \|u_n - u\|_{\frac{6}{q}} \to 0 \quad \text{as } n \to \infty, \tag{1.62}$$

since $3 < \dfrac{6}{q} < 6$, $u_n \to u$ in $L^s(\mathbb{R}^3)$ for any $s \in [2, 2^*)$.

Similarly, we also obtain

$$\int_{\mathbb{R}^3} k(x)|u|^{q-1}(u_n - u)dx \to 0 \quad \text{as } n \to \infty. \tag{1.63}$$

Therefore, by (1.59)—(1.63), we get $\|u_n - u\|_{E_1} \to 0$. The proof is complete. $\square$

1.3.3   The proof of Theorem 1.6

The proof of this theorem is divided in two steps.

Step 1   There exists a function $u_0 \in E_1$ such that $I'(u_0) = 0$ and $I(u_0) < 0$.

Since $g \in L^2(\mathbb{R}^3)$ and $g > 0$, we can choose a function $\psi \in E_1$ such that

$$\int_{\mathbb{R}^3} g(x)\psi(x)dx > 0.$$

Hence, we have

$$I(t\psi) \leqslant \frac{1}{2}t^2\|\psi\|_{E_1}^2 + \frac{t^4}{4}\|\psi\|_{E_1}^4 + \frac{t^q}{q}\int_{\mathbb{R}^3} k(x)|\psi|^q dx$$

$$- \frac{t^p}{p}\int_{\mathbb{R}^3} h(x)|\psi|^p dx - t\int_{\mathbb{R}^3} g(x)\psi dx$$

$$< 0, \quad \text{for } t > 0 \text{ small enough.}$$

Thus, we obtain

$$c_0 = \inf\{I(u) : u \in \bar{B}_\rho\} < 0,$$

where $\rho > 0$ is given by Lemma 1.15, $B_\rho = \{u \in E_1 : \|u\|_{E_1} < \rho\}$. By the Ekeland's Variational Principle, there exists a sequence $\{u_n\} \subset \bar{B}_\rho$ such that

$$c_0 \leqslant I(u_n) < c_0 + \frac{1}{n}.$$

and

$$I(w) \geqslant I(u_n) - \frac{1}{n}\|w - u_n\|_{E_1},$$

for all $w \in \bar{B}_\rho$. Then by a standard procedure, we can show that $\{u_n\}$ is a bounded Palais-Smale sequence of I. Therefore Lemma 1.17 implies that there exists a function $u_0 \in E_1$ such that $I'(u_0) = 0$ and $I(u_0) = c_0 < 0$.

Step 2   There exists a function $\tilde{u}_0 \in E_1$ such that $I'(\tilde{u}_0) = 0$ and $I(\tilde{u}_0) > 0$.

From Lemmas 1.15, 1.16 and the Mountain Pass Theorem, there is a sequence $\{u_n\} \subset E_1$ such that

$$I(u_n) \to \tilde{c}_0 > 0, \quad \text{and} \quad I'(u_n) \to 0.$$

In view of Lemma 1.17, we only need to check that $\{u_n\}$ is bounded in E_1.

$$
\begin{aligned}
\tilde{c}_0 + 1 + \|u\|_{E_1} &\geqslant I(u_n) - \frac{1}{4}\langle I'(u_n), u_n \rangle \\
&= \frac{1}{4}\|u_n\|_E^2 + \left(\frac{1}{q} - \frac{1}{4}\right)\int_{\mathbb{R}^3} k(x)|u_n|^q dx + \left(\frac{1}{4} - \frac{1}{p}\right)\int_{\mathbb{R}^3} h(x)|u_n|^p dx \\
&\quad - \frac{3}{4}\int_{\mathbb{R}^3} g(x)u_n dx \\
&\geqslant \frac{1}{4}\|u_n\|_{E_1}^2 - \frac{3}{4}\|g\|_2\|u_n\|_2,
\end{aligned}
$$

for n large enough. Since $\|g\|_2 < m_0$, it follows from $1 < q < 2, 4 < p < 6$ that $\{u_n\}$ is bounded in E_1. The proof is complete. $\square$

Chapter 2 Klein-Gordon-Maxwell System

2.1 Two solutions for nonhomogeneous Klein-Gordon-Maxwell system

2.1.1 Introduction and main results

In this chapter, we study the following nonhomogeneous Klein-Gordon-Maxwell system

$$(KGM)_\lambda \begin{cases} -\Delta u + \lambda V(x)u - K(x)(2\omega + \phi)\phi u = f(x,u) + h(x), & x \in \mathbb{R}^3, \\ \Delta\phi = K(x)(\omega + \phi)u^2, & x \in \mathbb{R}^3, \end{cases}$$

where $\omega > 0$ is a constant and $\lambda \geqslant 1$ is a parameter, $V \in C(\mathbb{R}^3, \mathbb{R})$ and $f \in C(\mathbb{R}^3 \times \mathbb{R}, \mathbb{R})$. By using the Linking theorem and the Ekeland's Variational Principle in critical point theory, we obtain the multiple solutions for $(KGM)_\lambda$. Here, the potential V is allowed to be sign-changing.

It is well known that such system has been firstly studied by Benci and Fortunato[24] as a model which describes nonlinear Klein-Gordon fields in three dimensional space interacting with the electrostatic field. For more details on the physical aspects of the problem we refer the readers to see [25] and the references therein.

The case of $h \equiv 0$, that is the homogeneous case, has been widely studied in recent years. In 2002, Benci and Fortunato[25] considered the following Klein-Gordon-Maxwell system

$$\begin{cases} -\Delta u + [m^2 - (\omega + \phi)^2]\phi u = f(x,u), & x \in \mathbb{R}^3, \\ \Delta\phi = (\omega + \phi)u^2, & x \in \mathbb{R}^3, \end{cases} \tag{2.1}$$

for the pure power of nonlinearity, i.e., $f(x,u) = |u|^{q-2}u$, where ω and m are constants. By using a version of the Mountain Pass theorem, they proved that (2.1) has infinitely many radially symmetric solutions under $|m| > |\omega|$ and $4 < q < 6$. In [75], D'Aprile and Mugnai covered the case $2 < q < 4$ assuming $\sqrt{\dfrac{q-2}{2}}m > \omega > 0$. Later, the authors in [15] gave a small improvement with $2 < q < 4$. Azzollini and

Pomponio[14] obtained the existence of a ground state solution for (2.1) under one of the conditions

(i) $4 \leqslant q < 6$ and $m > \omega$;

(ii) $2 < q < 4$ and $m\sqrt{q-2} > \omega\sqrt{6-q}$.

Soon afterwards, it is improved by Wang[183]. Motivated by the methods of Benci and Fortunato, Cassani[47] considered (2.1) for the critical case by adding a lower order perturbation:

$$\begin{cases} -\Delta u + [m^2 - (\omega + \phi)^2]\phi u = \mu|u|^{q-2}u + |u|^{2^*-2}u, & x \in \mathbb{R}^3, \\ \Delta\phi = (\omega + \phi)u^2, & x \in \mathbb{R}^3, \end{cases} \quad (2.2)$$

where $\mu > 0$ and $2^* = 6$. He showed that (2.2) has at least a radially symmetric solution under one of the following conditions:

(i) $4 < q < 6, |m| > |\omega|$ and $\mu > 0$;

(ii) $q = 4, |m| > |\omega|$ and μ is sufficiently large.

It is improved by the result in [45] provided one of the following conditions is satisfied:

(i) $4 < q < 6, |m| > |\omega| > 0$ and $\mu > 0$;

(ii) $q = 4, |m| > |\omega| > 0$ and μ is sufficiently large;

(iii) $2 < q < 4, |m|\sqrt{\dfrac{q-2}{2}} > |\omega| > 0$ and μ is sufficiently large.

Subsequently, Wang[182] generalized the result of [45]. Recently, the authors in [46] proved the existence of positive ground state solutions for the problem (2.2) with a periodic potential V, that is,

$$\begin{cases} -\Delta u + V(x)u + [m^2 - (\omega + \phi)^2]\phi u = \mu|u|^{q-2}u + |u|^{2^*-2}u, & x \in \mathbb{R}^3, \\ \Delta\phi = (\omega + \phi)u^2, & x \in \mathbb{R}^3. \end{cases}$$

In [97], Georgiev and Visciglia introduced a system like homogeneous $(KGM)_\lambda$ with potentials and $\lambda = 1$, however they considered a small external Coulomb potential in the corresponding Lagrangian density. Cunha[73] considered the existence of positive ground state solutions for $(KGM)_\lambda$ with periodic potential $V(x)$. Other related results about homogeneous Klein-Gordon-Maxwell system can be found in [57, 74, 77, 78, 81, 118, 120, 132−134, 186, 187, 208] and other equations with sign-changing potential see [212].

Next, we consider the nonhomogeneous case, that is $h \neq 0$. In [59], Chen and Song proved that $(KGM)_\lambda$ $(\lambda = 1, K(x) \equiv 1)$ has two nontrivial solutions if $f(x,t)$ satisfies the local (AR) condition:

There exist $\mu > 2$ and $r_0 > 0$ such that $\mathcal{G}(x,t) := \dfrac{1}{\mu}f(x,t)t - F(x,t) \geqslant 0$ for every $x \in \mathbb{R}^3$ and $|t| \geqslant r_0$, where $F(x,t) = \int_0^t f(x,s)ds$.

Xu and Chen[207] studied the existence and multiplicity of solutions for system $(KGM)_\lambda$ for the pure power of nonlinearity with $f(x,u) = |u|^{q-2}u$ and $\lambda = 1, K(x) \equiv 1$. They also assumed that $V(x) \equiv 1$ and $h(x)$ is radially symmetric. Other related results about nonhomogeneous Klein-Gordon-Maxwell system can be found in [161, 188, 190−194].

Motivated by the above works, we consider system $(KGM)_\lambda$ with more general potential $V(x)$ and $f(x,u)$. Precisely, we make the following assumptions.

(V_0) There is $b > 0$ such that meas$\{x \in \mathbb{R}^3 : V(x) \leqslant b\} < +\infty$, where meas denotes the Lebesgue measures;

(V_1) $V \in C(\mathbb{R}^3, \mathbb{R})$ and V is bounded below;

(V_2) $\Omega = \text{int}V^{-1}(0)$ is nonempty and has smooth boundary and $\bar{\Omega} = V^{-1}(0)$.

This kind of hypotheses was first introduced by Bartsch and Wang[18] in the study of a nonlinear Schrödinger equation and the potential $V(x)$ satisfying (V_0)—(V_2) is referred as the steep well potential.

Under (V_0)—(V_1) and some more generic 4-superlinear conditions on the continues function $f(x,u)$, we prove the existence of multiple solutions of problem $(KGM)_\lambda$ when $\lambda > 0$ large by using the variation method.

(f_1) $F(x,u) = \int_0^u f(x,s)ds \geqslant 0$ for all (x,u) and $f(x,u) = o(u)$ uniformly in x as $u \to 0$;

(f_2) $F(x,u)/u^4 \to +\infty$ as $|u| \to +\infty$ uniformly in x;

(f_3) $\mathcal{F}(x,u) := \dfrac{1}{4}f(x,u)u - F(x,u) \geqslant 0$ for all $(x,u) \in \mathbb{R}^3 \times \mathbb{R}$;

(f_4) There exist $a_1, L_1 > 0$ and $\tau \in (3/2, 2)$ such that

$$|f(x,u)|^\tau \leqslant a_1 \mathcal{F}(x,u)|u|^\tau, \quad \text{for all } x \in \mathbb{R}^3 \text{ and } |u| \geqslant L_1;$$

(K) $K(x) \in L^3(\mathbb{R}^3) \cup L^\infty(\mathbb{R}^3)$ and $K(x) \geqslant 0$ is not identically zero for a.e. $x \in \mathbb{R}^3$;

(h) $h(x) \in L^2(\mathbb{R}^3)$ and $h(x) \geqslant 0$ for a.e. $x \in \mathbb{R}^3$.

Remark 2.1   It follows from (f_3) and (f_4) that

$$|f(x,u)|^\tau \leqslant \frac{a_1}{4}|f(x,u)||u|^{\tau+1}$$

for large u. Thus, by (f_1), for any $\varepsilon > 0$, there exists $C_\varepsilon > 0$ such that

$$|f(x,u)| \leqslant \varepsilon|u| + C_\varepsilon|u|^{q-1}, \quad \forall(x,u) \in \mathbb{R}^3 \times \mathbb{R} \tag{2.3}$$

and

$$|F(x,u)| \leqslant \varepsilon|u|^2 + C_\varepsilon|u|^q, \quad \forall(x,u) \in \mathbb{R}^3 \times \mathbb{R}, \tag{2.4}$$

where $q = 2\tau/(\tau - 1) \in (4, 2^*)$ and $2^* = 6$ is the critical exponent for the Sobolev embedding in dimension 3.

Remark 2.2 It is not difficult to find out functions f satisfying (f_1)—(f_4), for example,

$$f(x, t) = g(x)t^3 \left(2In(1 + t^2) + \frac{t^2}{1 + t^2} \right), \quad \forall (x, t) \in \mathbb{R}^3 \times \mathbb{R},$$

where g is a continuous bounded function with $\inf_{x \in \mathbb{R}^3} g(x) > 0$.

Before stating our main results, we give some notations.

For any $1 \leqslant s \leqslant +\infty$ and $\Omega \subset \mathbb{R}^3$, $L^s(\Omega)$ denotes a Lebesgue space; the norm in $L^s(\Omega)$ is denoted by $|u|_{s,\Omega}$, where Ω is a proper subset of $\mathbb{R}^3$, by $|\cdot|_s$ when $\Omega = \mathbb{R}^3$. Let $D^{1,2}(\mathbb{R}^3)$ be the completion of $C_0^\infty(\mathbb{R}^3)$ with respect to the norm

$$\|u\|_D^2 := \|u\|_{D^{1,2}(\mathbb{R}^3)}^2 = \int_{\mathbb{R}^3} |\nabla u|^2 dx.$$

$H^1(\mathbb{R}^3)$ is the usual Sobolev space endowed with the standard product and norm

$$(u, v)_{H^1} = \int_{\mathbb{R}^3} (\nabla u \nabla v + uv) dx, \quad \|u\|_{H^1}^2 = \int_{\mathbb{R}^3} (|\nabla u|^2 + |u|^2) dx.$$

$\bar{S}$ is the best Sobolev constant for the Sobolev embedding $D^{1,2}(\mathbb{R}^3) \hookrightarrow L^6(\mathbb{R}^3)$, that is,

$$\bar{S} = \inf_{u \in D^{1,2}(\mathbb{R}^3) \backslash \{0\}} \frac{\|u\|_D}{|u|_6}.$$

For any $r > 0$ and $z \in \mathbb{R}^3$, $B_r(z)$ denotes the ball of radius r centered at z.

Now we can state our main results.

Theorem 2.1 *Assume that (V_0), (V_1), (f_1)—(f_4), (K) and (h) are satisfied. If $V(x) < 0$ for some $x \in \mathbb{R}^3$, then for each $k \in \mathbb{N}$, there exist $\lambda_k > k, b_k > 0$ and $\eta_k > 0$ such that problem $(KGM)_\lambda$ has at least two nontrivial solutions for every $\lambda = \lambda_k, |K|_\infty < b_k (or |K|_3 < b_k)$ and $|h|_2 \leqslant \eta_k$.*

Theorem 2.2 *Assume that (V_0)—(V_2), (f_1)—(f_4), (K) and (h) are satisfied. If $V^{-1}(0)$ has nonempty interior, then there exist $\Lambda > 0, b_\lambda > 0$ and $\eta_\lambda > 0$ such that problem $(KGM)_\lambda$ has at least two nontrivial solutions for every $\lambda > \Lambda$, $|h|_2 \leqslant \eta_\lambda$ and $|K|_\infty < b_\lambda (or |K|_3 < b_\lambda)$.*

If $V \geqslant 0$, we remove the restriction of the norm of K and we have the following theorem.

Theorem 2.3 *Assume that $V \geqslant 0$, (V_0)—(V_2), (f_1)—(f_4), (K) and (h) are satisfied. If $V^{-1}(0)$ has nonempty interior Ω and $h \neq 0$, then there exist $\Lambda_* > 0$*

and $\eta > 0$ such that problem $(KGM)_\lambda$ has at least two nontrivial solutions for every $\lambda > \Lambda_*$ and $|h|_2 \leqslant \eta$.

To obtain our main results, we have to overcome some difficulties in using variational method. The main difficulty consists in the lack of compactness of the Sobolev embedding $H^1(\mathbb{R}^3)$ into $L^p(\mathbb{R}^3)$, $p \in (2,6)$. Since we assume that the potential is not radially symmetric, we cannot use the usual way to recover compactness, for example, restricting in the subspace $H_r^1(\mathbb{R}^3)$ of radially symmetric functions. To recover the compactness, we borrow some ideas used in [18,82] and establish the parameter dependent compactness conditions.

To the best of our knowledge, it seems that our theorems are the first results about the existence of multiple solutions for the nonhomogeneous Klein-Gordon-Maxwell equations on $\mathbb{R}^3$ with general nonlinear term and sign-changing potential. As it is pointed out in [73], many technical difficulties arise due to the presence of a nonlocal term ϕ, which is not homogeneous as it is in the Schrödinger-Poisson systems. In other words, the adaptation of the ideas to the procedure of our problem is not trivial at all, because of the presence of the nonlocal term ϕ_u. Hence, a more careful analysis of the interaction between the couple (u, ϕ) is required.

We introduce the variational setting and the compactness conditions in Section 2.1.2. In Section 2.1.3, we give the proofs of main results.

2.1.2   Variational setting and compactness condition

By [15], we know that the signs of ω are not relevant to the existence of solutions, so we assume that $\omega > 0$. In this section, we firstly give the variational setting of the problem $(KGM)_\lambda$ and then establish the compactness conditions.

Let $V(x) = V^+(x) - V^-(x)$, where $V^\pm = \max\{\pm V(x), 0\}$. Let

$$E = \left\{ u \in H^1(\mathbb{R}^3) : \int_{\mathbb{R}^3} |\nabla u|^2 + V^+(x)u^2 dx < \infty \right\}$$

be equipped with the inner product

$$(u, v) = \int_{\mathbb{R}^3} (\nabla u \nabla v + V^+(x)uv)dx \text{ and the norm } \|u\| = (u, u)^{1/2}.$$

For $\lambda > 0$, we also need the following inner product and norm

$$(u, v)_\lambda = \int_{\mathbb{R}^3} (\nabla u \nabla v + \lambda V^+(x)uv)dx, \quad \|u\|_\lambda = (u, u)_\lambda^{1/2}.$$

It is clear $\|u\| \leqslant \|u\|_\lambda$ for $\lambda \geqslant 1$. Set $E_\lambda = (E, \|\cdot\|_\lambda)$. It follows from the Poincaré inequality and (V_0), (V_1), we know that the embedding $E_\lambda \hookrightarrow H^1(\mathbb{R}^3)$ is continuous, and therefore, for $s \in [2, 6]$, there exists $d_s > 0$(independent of $\lambda \geqslant 1$) such that

$$|u|_s \leqslant d_s \|u\|_\lambda, \quad \forall u \in E_\lambda. \tag{2.5}$$

Let

$$F_\lambda = \{u \in E_\lambda : \mathrm{supp}\, u \subset V^{-1}([0, \infty))\},$$

and $F_\lambda^\perp$ denote the orthogonal complement of F_λ in E_λ. Clearly, $F_\lambda = E_\lambda$ if $V \geqslant 0$, otherwise $F_\lambda^\perp \neq \{0\}$. Define

$$A_\lambda := -\Delta + \lambda V,$$

then A_λ is formally self-adjoint in $L^2(\mathbb{R}^3)$ and the associated bilinear form

$$a_\lambda(u, v) = \int_{\mathbb{R}^3} (\nabla u \nabla v + \lambda V(x) uv) dx$$

is continuous in E_λ. As in [82], for fixed $\lambda > 0$, we consider the eigenvalue problem

$$-\Delta u + \lambda V^+(x) u = \mu \lambda V^-(x) u, \quad u \in F_\lambda^\perp. \tag{2.6}$$

By (V_0), (V_1), we know that the quadratic form $u \mapsto \int_{\mathbb{R}^3} \lambda V^-(x) u^2 dx$ is weakly continuous. Hence following Theorem 4.45 and Theorem 4.46 in [201], we can deduce the following proposition, which is the spectral theorem for compact self-adjoint operators jointly with the Courant-Fischer minimax characterization of eigenvalues.

Proposition 2.1　*Suppose that (V_0), (V_1) hold, then for any fixed $\lambda > 0$, the eigenvalue problem (2.6) has a sequence of positive eigenvalues $\{\mu_j(\lambda)\}$, which may be characterized by*

$$\mu_j(\lambda) = \inf_{\dim M \geqslant j, M \subset F_\lambda^\perp} \sup \left\{ \|u\|_\lambda^2 : u \in M, \int_{\mathbb{R}^3} \lambda V^-(x) u^2 dx = 1 \right\}, \quad j = 1, 2, 3, \cdots.$$

Furthermore, $\mu_1(\lambda) \leqslant \mu_2(\lambda) \leqslant \cdots \leqslant \mu_j(\lambda) \to +\infty$ as $j \to +\infty$, and the corresponding eigenfunctions $\{e_j(\lambda)\}$, which may be be chosen so that $(e_i(\lambda), e_j(\lambda))_\lambda = \delta_{ij}$, are a basis of $F_\lambda^\perp$.

Next, we give some properties for the eigenvalues $\{\mu_j(\lambda)\}$ defined above.

Proposition 2.2[82]　*Assume that (V_0), (V_1) hold and $V^- \not\equiv \{0\}$. Then, for each fixed $j \in \mathbb{N}$,*

(i) $\mu_j(\lambda) \to 0$ *as* $\lambda \to +\infty$;

(ii) $\mu_j(\lambda)$ *is a non-increasing continuous function of λ.*

Remark 2.3　By Proposition 2.2, there exists $\Lambda_0 > 0$ such that $\mu_1(\lambda) \leqslant 1$ for all $\lambda > \Lambda_0$.

Denote

$$E_\lambda^- := \mathrm{span}\{e_j(\lambda) : \mu_j(\lambda) \leqslant 1\} \quad \text{and} \quad E_\lambda^+ := \mathrm{span}\{e_j(\lambda) : \mu_j(\lambda) > 1\}.$$

Then $E_\lambda = E_\lambda^- \oplus E_\lambda^+ \oplus F_\lambda$ is an orthogonal decomposition. The quadratic form a_λ is negative semidefinite on E_λ^-, positive definite on $E_\lambda^+ \oplus F_\lambda$ and it is easy to see that $a_\lambda(u, v) = 0$ if u, v are in different subspaces of the above decomposition of E_λ.

From Remark 2.3, we have that $\dim E_\lambda^- \geqslant 1$ when $\lambda > \Lambda_0$. Moreover, since $\mu_j(\lambda) \to +\infty$ as $j \to +\infty$, $\dim E_\lambda^- < +\infty$ for every fixed $\lambda > 0$.

System $(KGM)_\lambda$ has a variational structure. In fact, we consider the functional $\mathcal{J}_\lambda : E_\lambda \times D^{1,2}(\mathbb{R}^3) \to \mathbb{R}$ defined by

$$\mathcal{J}_\lambda(u, \phi) = \frac{1}{2} \int_{\mathbb{R}^3} (|\nabla u|^2 + \lambda V(x)u^2)dx$$
$$- \frac{1}{2} \int_{\mathbb{R}^3} |\nabla \phi|^2 dx - \frac{1}{2} \int_{\mathbb{R}^3} K(x)(2\omega + \phi)\phi u^2 dx$$
$$- \int_{\mathbb{R}^3} F(x, u)dx - \int_{\mathbb{R}^3} h(x)u dx.$$

The solutions $(u, \phi) \in E_\lambda \times D^{1,2}(\mathbb{R}^3)$ of system $(KGM)_\lambda$ are the critical points of $\mathcal{J}_\lambda$. By using the reduction method described in [26], we are led to the study of a new functional $I_\lambda(u)$ ($I_\lambda(u)$ is defined in (2.7)). We need the following technical result.

Proposition 2.3 *Let $K(x)$ satisfy the condition (K). Then for any $u \in E_\lambda$, there exists a unique $\phi = \phi_u \in D^{1,2}(\mathbb{R}^3)$ which satisfies*

$$\Delta \phi = K(x)(\phi + \omega)u^2 \quad in \quad \mathbb{R}^3.$$

Moreover, the map $\Phi : u \in E_\lambda \mapsto \phi_u \in D^{1,2}(\mathbb{R}^3)$ is continuously differentiable, and
  (i) *$-\omega \leqslant \phi_u \leqslant 0$ on the set $\{x \in \mathbb{R}^3 | u(x) \neq 0\}$;*

  (ii) *$\|\phi_u\|_D \leqslant C_1|K|_3\|u\|_\lambda^2$ and $\int_{\mathbb{R}^3} K(x)\phi_u u^2 dx \leqslant C_2|K|_3^2\|u\|_\lambda^4$, if $K \in L^3(\mathbb{R}^3)$;*

  (iii) *$\|\phi_u\|_D \leqslant C_3|K|_\infty\|u\|_\lambda^2$ and $\int_{\mathbb{R}^3} K(x)\phi_u u^2 dx \leqslant C_4|K|_\infty^2\|u\|_\lambda^4$, if $K \in L^\infty(\mathbb{R}^3)$.*

Proof. If $K(x) \in L^3(\mathbb{R}^3)$, $u \in E_\lambda$ and we define the following bilinear form

$$L(w_1, w_2) \in D^{1,2}(\mathbb{R}^3) \times D^{1,2}(\mathbb{R}^3) \mapsto \int_{\mathbb{R}^3} [\nabla w_1 \nabla w_2 + K(x)u^2 w_1 w_2]dx \in \mathbb{R}.$$

It is easy to see that L is well defined. Moreover, since $K(x) \geqslant 0$, $L(w_1, w_1) \geqslant \|w_1\|_D^2$. Furthermore, since $K(x) \in L^3(\mathbb{R}^3)$, by the Hölder inequality, we obtain that

$$L(w_1, w_2) = \int_{\mathbb{R}^3} [\nabla w_1 \nabla w_2 + K(x)u^2 w_1 w_2]dx$$

$$\leqslant \|w_1\|_D \|w_2\|_D + |K|_3 |u|_6^2 |w_1|_6 |w_2|_6$$

$$\leqslant \|w_1\|_D \|w_2\|_D + d_6^2 \bar{S}^{-2} |K|_3 \|u\|_\lambda^2 \|w_1\|_D \|w_2\|_D$$

$$= (1 + d_6^2 \bar{S}^{-2} |K|_3 \|u\|_\lambda^2) \|w_1\|_D \|w_2\|_D.$$

Hence L defines an inner product, equivalent to the standard inner product in $D^{1,2}(\mathbb{R}^3)$. Moreover $E_\lambda \subset L^4(\mathbb{R}^3)$ and then

$$\left| \int_{\mathbb{R}^3} \omega K(x) u^2 w_1 dx \right| \leqslant \bar{S}^{-1} \omega |K|_3 |u|_4^2 \|w_1\|_D.$$

Therefore, the linear map

$$w_1 \in D^{1,2}(\mathbb{R}^3) \mapsto \int_{\mathbb{R}^3} -\omega K(x) u^2 w_1 dx \in \mathbb{R}$$

is continuous. Hence, by the Lax-Milgram theorem, there exists a unique $\phi_u \in D^{1,2}(\mathbb{R}^3)$ such that

$$\int_{\mathbb{R}^3} [\nabla \phi_u \nabla w_1 + K(x) u^2 \phi_u w_1] dx = \int_{\mathbb{R}^3} -\omega K(x) u^2 w_1 dx, \quad \forall w_1 \in D^{1,2}(\mathbb{R}^3),$$

ϕ_u is the unique solution of $\Delta \phi = K(x)(\phi + \omega) u^2$.

For the case $K \in L^\infty(\mathbb{R}^3)$ is similar to Lemma 3.1 in [178], we omit here.

(i) Arguing by contradiction, we assume that there exists an open subset $\Omega \subset \mathbb{R}^3$ satisfying

$$\phi_u < -\omega.$$

Then, by ϕ_u solving equation $\Delta \phi = K(x)(\phi + \omega) u^2$, we have

$$-\Delta(\phi_u + \omega) + K(x)(\phi_u + \omega) u^2 = -\Delta \phi_u + K(x) u^2 \phi_u + \omega K(x) u^2 = 0.$$

Set $\varphi = \phi_u + \omega$, we obtain that

$$-\Delta \varphi + K(x) \varphi u^2 = 0 \text{ in } \Omega, \quad \varphi = 0 \text{ on } \partial\Omega.$$

Then $\varphi = 0$ contradicting with $\phi_u < -\omega$.

An analogous argument shows that $\phi \leqslant 0$.

(ii) Since ϕ_u solving the equation $\Delta \phi = K(x)(\phi + \omega) u^2$, $K \in L^3(\mathbb{R}^3)$ and $K(x) \geqslant 0$, we have

$$\|\phi_u\|_D^2 \leqslant -\int_{\mathbb{R}^3} (K(x) \phi_u^2 u^2 + \omega K(x) u^2 \phi_u) dx$$

$$\leqslant -\int_{\mathbb{R}^3} \omega K(x) u^2 \phi_u dx$$

$$\leqslant \omega |K|_3 |u|_4^2 |\phi_u|_6 \leqslant \omega \bar{S}^{-1} d_4^2 |K|_3 \|u\|_\lambda^2 \|\phi_u\|_D.$$

Hence

$$\|\phi_u\|_D \leqslant C_1 |K|_3 \|u\|_\lambda^2, \quad \text{where } C_1 = \omega \bar{S}^{-1} d_4^2.$$

For the second inequality, we obtain that

$$\int_{\mathbb{R}^3} K(x)\phi_u u^2 dx \leqslant |K|_3 |\phi_u|_6 |u|_4^2 \leqslant \bar{S}^{-1} d_4^2 |K|_3 \|\phi_u\|_D \|u\|_\lambda^2$$

$$\leqslant \omega \bar{S}^{-2} d_4^4 |K|_3^2 \|u\|_\lambda^4 \leqslant C_2 |K|_3^2 \|u\|_\lambda^4,$$

where $C_2 = \omega \bar{S}^{-2} d_4^4$.

(iii) Again by ϕ_u solving the equation $\Delta \phi = K(x)(\phi + \omega)u^2, K \in L^\infty(\mathbb{R}^3)$ and $K(x) \geqslant 0$, we have

$$\|\psi_u\|_D^2 \leqslant - \int_{\mathbb{R}^3} (K(x)\phi_u^2 u^2 + \omega K(x)u^2 \phi_u) dx$$

$$\leqslant - \int_{\mathbb{R}^3} \omega K(x)u^2 \phi_u dx$$

$$\leqslant \omega |K|_\infty |u|_{12/5}^2 |\phi_u|_6 \leqslant \omega \bar{S}^{-1} d_{12/5}^2 |K|_\infty \|u\|_\lambda^2 \|\phi_u\|_D.$$

Hence

$$\|\phi_u\|_D \leqslant C_3 |K|_\infty \|u\|_\lambda^2, \quad \text{where } C_3 = \omega \bar{S}^{-1} d_{12/5}^2.$$

For the second inequality,

$$\int_{\mathbb{R}^3} K(x)\phi_u u^2 dx \leqslant |K|_\infty |\phi_u|_6 |u|_{12/5}^2 \leqslant \bar{S}^{-1} d_{12/5}^2 |K|_\infty \|\phi_u\|_D \|u\|_\lambda^2$$

$$\leqslant \omega \bar{S}^{-2} d_{12/5}^4 |K|_\infty^2 \|u\|_\lambda^4 \leqslant C_4 |K|_\infty^2 \|u\|_\lambda^4,$$

where $C_4 = \omega \bar{S}^{-2} d_{12/5}^4$. The proof is complete. $\qquad \square$

Remark 2.4   By the proof of Proposition 2.3, we can know that the condition (K) can be replaced by

(K') $K(x) \in L^{q_1}(\mathbb{R}^3) \cup L^\infty(\mathbb{R}^3)$ and $K(x) \geqslant 0$ is not identically zero for a.e. $x \in \mathbb{R}^3$, where $q_1 \geqslant 3$.

Multiplying $-\Delta \phi_u + K(x)\phi_u u^2 = -\omega K(x)u^2$ by ϕ_u and integration by parts, we obtain

$$\int_{\mathbb{R}^3} (|\nabla \phi_u|^2 + K(x)\phi_u^2 u^2) dx = - \int_{\mathbb{R}^3} \omega K(x)\phi_u u^2 dx.$$

By above equality and the definition of $\mathcal{J}$, we obtain a C^1 functional $I_\lambda : E_\lambda \to \mathbb{R}$ given by

$$I_\lambda(u) = \mathcal{J}_\lambda(u, \phi_u)$$

$$= \frac{1}{2} \int_{\mathbb{R}^3} (|\nabla u|^2 + \lambda V(x)u^2) dx - \frac{1}{2} \int_{\mathbb{R}^3} (|\nabla \phi_u|^2 + K(x)\phi_u^2 u^2) dx$$

$$- \int_{\mathbb{R}^3} \omega K(x)\phi_u u^2 dx - \int_{\mathbb{R}^3} F(x,u) dx - \int_{\mathbb{R}^3} h(x)u dx$$

$$= \frac{1}{2} \int_{\mathbb{R}^3} (|\nabla u|^2 + \lambda V(x)u^2) dx$$

$$- \frac{1}{2} \int_{\mathbb{R}^3} K(x)\omega \phi_u u^2 dx - \int_{\mathbb{R}^3} F(x,u) dx - \int_{\mathbb{R}^3} h(x)u dx, \tag{2.7}$$

and its Gateaux derivative is

$$\langle I_\lambda'(u), v \rangle = \int_{\mathbb{R}^3} (\nabla u \cdot \nabla v + \lambda V(x)uv) dx - \int_{\mathbb{R}^3} K(x)(2\omega + \phi_u)\phi_u uv dx$$

$$- \int_{\mathbb{R}^3} f(x,u)v dx - \int_{\mathbb{R}^3} h(x)v dx,$$

for all $v \in E_\lambda$. Here we use the fact that $\phi_u = (\Delta - K(x)u^2)^{-1}[\omega K(x)u^2]$.

Set

$$M(u) = \int_{\mathbb{R}^3} -\omega K(x)\phi_u u^2 dx.$$

Now we give some properties about the function M and its derivative M' possess splitting property, which is similar to Brezis-Lieb Lemma[35].

Proposition 2.4   Let $K \in L^\infty(\mathbb{R}^3) \cup L^3(\mathbb{R}^3)$. If $u_n \rightharpoonup u$ in $H^1(\mathbb{R}^3)$ and $u_n(x) \to u(x)$ a.e. $x \in \mathbb{R}^3$, then

(i) $\phi_{u_n} \rightharpoonup \phi_u$ in $D^{1,2}(\mathbb{R}^3)$ and $M(u) \leqslant \liminf\limits_{n \to \infty} M(u_n)$;

(ii) $M(u_n - u) = M(u_n) - M(u) + o(1)$;

(iii) $M'(u_n - u) = M'(u_n) - M'(u) + o(1)$ in $H^{-1}(\mathbb{R}^3)$.

Proof. (i) A straight forward adaption of Lemma 2.1 in [214]. The proof of (ii) and (iii) have been given in [212] for $N(u) = \int_{\mathbb{R}^3} K(x)\phi_u u^2 dx$, and it is easy to see that the conclusions remain valid for $M(u)$. The proof is complete.   □

Next, we investigate the compactness conditions for the function I_λ. Recall that a C^1 function J satisfies (PS) condition at level c if any sequence $\{u_n\} \subset E$ such that $J(u_n) \to c$ and $J'(u_n) \to 0$ has a convergent subsequence; and such sequence is called a $(PS)_c$ sequence.

We only consider the case $K \in L^\infty(\mathbb{R}^3)$, the other case $K \in L^3(\mathbb{R}^3)$ is similar.

Lemma 2.1   Suppose that (V_0), (V_1), (f_1)—(f_4), (K) and (h) are satisfied. Then every $(PS)_c$ sequence of I_λ is bounded in E_λ for each $c \in \mathbb{R}$.

Proof. Let $\{u_n\} \subset E_\lambda$ be a $(PS)_c$ sequence of I_λ. Suppose by contradiction that

$$I_\lambda(u_n) \to c, \quad I_\lambda'(u_n) \to 0, \quad \|u_n\|_\lambda \to \infty \tag{2.8}$$

as $n \to \infty$ after passing to a subsequence. Take $w_n := u_n/\|u_n\|_\lambda$. Then $\|w_n\|_\lambda = 1, w_n \rightharpoonup w$ in E_λ and $w_n(x) \to w(x)$ a.e. $x \in \mathbb{R}^3$.

We first consider the case $w = 0$. By (2.8), (f_3), Proposition 2.3 and the fact $w_n \to 0$ in $L^2(\{x \in \mathbb{R}^3 : V(x) < 0\})$, we obtain

$$
\begin{aligned}
o(1) &= \frac{1}{\|u_n\|_\lambda^2}\left(I_\lambda(u_n) - \frac{1}{4}\langle I_\lambda'(u_n), u_n\rangle\right) \\
&= \frac{1}{4}\|w_n\|_\lambda^2 - \frac{\lambda}{4}\int_{\mathbb{R}^3} V^-(x)w_n^2 dx + \frac{1}{4\|u_n\|_\lambda^2}\int_{\mathbb{R}^3} K(x)\phi_{u_n}^2 u_n^2 dx \\
&\quad + \frac{1}{\|u_n\|_\lambda^2}\int_{\mathbb{R}^3} \mathcal{F}(x, u_n)dx - \frac{3}{4\|u_n\|_\lambda^2}\int_{\mathbb{R}^3} h(x)u_n dx \\
&\geqslant \frac{1}{4} - \frac{\lambda}{4}|V^-|_\infty\int_{suppV^-} w_n^2 dx - \frac{3}{4}|h|_2 d_2\frac{1}{\|u_n\|_\lambda} \\
&= \frac{1}{4} + o(1),
\end{aligned}
$$

which is a contradiction.

If $w \neq 0$, then $\Omega_1 := \{x \in \mathbb{R}^3 : w(x) \neq 0\}$ has a positive Lebesgue measure. For $x \in \Omega_1$, one has $|u_n(x)| \to \infty$ as $n \to \infty$, and then, by (f_2),

$$\frac{F(x, u_n(x))}{u_n^4(x)}w_n^4(x) \to +\infty \quad \text{as } n \to \infty,$$

which, jointly with Fatou's lemma, shows that

$$\int_{\Omega_1} \frac{F(x, u_n)}{u_n^4}w_n^4 dx \to +\infty \quad \text{as } n \to \infty. \tag{2.9}$$

Combining this with (f_1), (2.7), the first limit of (2.8), (K), (h) and Proposition 2.3(ii), we obtain that

$$\frac{C_4}{2}|K|_\infty\omega \geqslant \limsup_{n\to\infty}\int_{\mathbb{R}^3} \frac{F(x, u_n)}{\|u_n\|_\lambda^4}dx \geqslant \limsup_{n\to\infty}\int_{\Omega_1} \frac{F(x, u_n)}{u_n^4}w_n^4 dx = +\infty.$$

This is impossible.

Hence $\{u_n\}$ is bounded in E_λ.

For the case $K \in L^3(\mathbb{R}^3)$, we can use the Cauchy-Schwarz inequality and the boundedness of ϕ_{u_n} to get the result. $\square$

Lemma 2.2 *Suppose that* (V_0), (V_1), (K), (h) *and* (2.3) *hold. If* $u_n \rightharpoonup u$ *in* E_λ, $u_n(x) \to u(x)$ *a.e. in* $\mathbb{R}^3$, *and we denote* $w_n := u_n - u$, *then*

$$I_\lambda(u_n) = I_\lambda(w_n) + I_\lambda(u) + o(1) \tag{2.10}$$

and

$$\langle I_\lambda'(u_n), \varphi \rangle = \langle I_\lambda'(w_n), \varphi \rangle + \langle I_\lambda'(u), \varphi \rangle + o(1), \quad uniformly \ for \ all \ \varphi \in E_\lambda \tag{2.11}$$

as $n \to \infty$. *In particular, if* $I_\lambda(u_n) \to c(\in \mathbb{R})$ *and* $I_\lambda'(u_n) \to 0$ *in* E_λ^* *(the dual space of* E_λ*), then* $I_\lambda'(u) = 0$ *and*

$$\begin{aligned}
I_\lambda(w_n) &\to c - I_\lambda(u), \\
\langle I_\lambda'(w_n), \varphi \rangle &\to 0, \ uniformly \ for \ all \ \varphi \in E_\lambda
\end{aligned} \tag{2.12}$$

after passing to a subsequence.

Proof. Since $u_n \rightharpoonup u$ in E_λ, we have $(u_n - u, u)_\lambda \to 0$ as $n \to \infty$, which implies that

$$\|u_n\|_\lambda^2 = (w_n + u, w_n + u)_\lambda = \|w_n\|_\lambda^2 + \|u\|_\lambda^2 + o(1). \tag{2.13}$$

By (V_0), the Hölder inequality and $w_n \rightharpoonup 0$, we have

$$\left| \int_{\mathbb{R}^3} V^-(x) w_n u dx \right| = \left| \int_{\text{supp}V^-} V^- w_n u dx \right| \leqslant |V^-|_\infty \left(\int_{\text{supp}V^-} w_n^2 dx \right)^{1/2} |u|_2 \to 0$$

as $n \to \infty$. Thus

$$\int_{\mathbb{R}^3} V^-(x) u_n^2 dx = \int_{\mathbb{R}^3} V^-(x) w_n^2 dx + \int_{\mathbb{R}^3} V^-(x) u^2 dx + o(1).$$

By Proposition 2.4 (ii), we have

$$M(u_n) = M(w_n) + M(u) + o(1).$$

Since $h \in L^2(\mathbb{R}^3)$,

$$\int_{\mathbb{R}^3} h(x) u_n dx = \int_{\mathbb{R}^3} h(x) w_n dx + \int_{\mathbb{R}^3} h(x) u dx,$$

therefore, to prove (2.10) and (2.11), it suffices to check that

$$\int_{\mathbb{R}^3} (F(x, u_n) - F(x, w_n) - F(x, u)) dx = o(1) \tag{2.14}$$

and

$$\sup_{\|\phi\|_\lambda=1} \int_{\mathbb{R}^3} (f(x,u_n) - f(x,w_n) - f(x,u))\phi dx = o(1). \qquad (2.15)$$

We prove (2.14) firstly. Inspired by [4], we observe that

$$F(x,u_n) - F(x,u_n - u) = -\int_0^1 \left(\frac{d}{dt}F(x,u_n - tu)\right) dt = \int_0^1 f(x,u_n - tu)u dt.$$

And hence, by (2.7), we obtain that

$$|F(x,u_n) - F(x,u_n - u)| \leqslant \varepsilon_1|u_n||u| + \varepsilon_1|u|^2 + C_{\varepsilon_1}|u_n|^{p-1}|u| + C_{\varepsilon_1}|u|^p,$$

where $\varepsilon_1, C_{\varepsilon_1} > 0$ and $p \in (4,6)$. Therefore, for each $\varepsilon > 0$, and the Young inequality, we get

$$|F(x,u_n) - F(x,w_n) - F(x,u)| \leqslant C[\varepsilon|u_n|^2 + C_\varepsilon|u|^2 + \varepsilon|u_n|^p + C_\varepsilon|u|^p].$$

Next, we consider the function f_n given by

$$f_n(x) := \max\left\{|F(x,u_n) - F(x,w_n) - F(x,u)| - C\varepsilon(|u_n|^2 + |u_n|^p), 0\right\}.$$

Then

$$0 \leqslant f_n(x) \leqslant CC_\varepsilon(|u|^2 + |u|^p) \in L^1(\mathbb{R}^3).$$

Moreover, by the Lebesgue Dominated Convergence theorem,

$$\int_{\mathbb{R}^3} f_n(x)dx \to 0 \quad \text{as } n \to \infty, \qquad (2.16)$$

since $u_n \to u$ a.e. in $\mathbb{R}^3$. By the definition of f_n, it follows that

$$|F(x,u_n) - F(x,w_n) - F(x,u)| \leqslant f_n(x) + C\varepsilon(|u_n|^2 + |u_n|^p).$$

Combining this with (2.16) and (2.4), it shows that

$$\int_{\mathbb{R}^3} |F(x,u_n) - F(x,w_n) - F(x,u)|\, dx \leqslant C\varepsilon$$

for n sufficiently large. It implies that

$$\int_{\mathbb{R}^3} [F(x,u_n) - F(x,w_n) - F(x,u)]dx = o(1).$$

The prove of (2.15) is similar to Lemma 4.7 in [223], we omit here.

Now, we check that $I_\lambda'(u) = 0$. In fact, for each $\psi \in C_0^\infty(\mathbb{R}^3)$, we have

$$(u_n - u, \psi)_\lambda \to 0 \quad \text{as } n \to \infty. \tag{2.17}$$

and

$$\left| \int_{\mathbb{R}^3} V^-(x)(u_n - u)\psi dx \right|$$

$$\leqslant |V^-|_\infty \left(\int_{\text{supp}\psi} (u_n - u)^2 dx \right)^{1/2} |\psi|_2 \to 0 \quad \text{as } n \to \infty, \tag{2.18}$$

since $u_n \to u$ in $L_{loc}^2(\mathbb{R}^3)$. By Proposition 2.4 (i), $u_n \rightharpoonup u$ in E_λ yields $\phi_{u_n} \rightharpoonup \phi_u$ in $D^{1,2}(\mathbb{R}^3)$. So

$$\phi_{u_n} \rightharpoonup \phi_u \text{ in } L^6(\mathbb{R}^3).$$

For every $\psi \in C_0^\infty(\mathbb{R}^3)$ and Proposition 2.4 (ii), we obtain

$$\int_{\mathbb{R}^3} 2\omega K(x)\phi_{u_n} u_n \psi dx = \int_{\mathbb{R}^3} 2\omega K(x)\phi_{w_n} w_n \psi dx + \int_{\mathbb{R}^3} 2\omega K(x)\phi_u u \psi dx + o(1).$$

Now we need to prove

$$\int_{\mathbb{R}^3} K(x)\phi_{u_n}^2 u_n \psi dx = \int_{\mathbb{R}^3} K(x)\phi_{w_n}^2 w_n \psi dx + \int_{\mathbb{R}^3} K(x)\phi_u^2 u \psi dx + o(1). \tag{2.19}$$

By $u_n \to u$ in $L_{loc}^s(\mathbb{R}^3), 1 \leqslant s < 6$; $\phi_{u_n} \to \phi_u$ in $L_{loc}^s(\mathbb{R}^3), 1 \leqslant s < 6$, the boundedness of (ϕ_{u_n}) and the Hölder inequality, we have

$$\int_{\mathbb{R}^3} K(x)(\phi_{u_n}^2 u_n - \phi_u^2 u)\psi dx$$

$$= \int_{\mathbb{R}^3} K(x)\phi_{u_n}^2(u_n - u)\psi dx + \int_{\mathbb{R}^3} K(x)(\phi_{u_n}^2 - \phi_u^2)u\psi dx$$

$$\leqslant C|K|_\infty \|\nabla\phi_{u_n}\|^2 \left(\int_{\Omega_\psi} |u_n - u|^{3/2} dx \right)^{2/3}$$

$$+ |K|_\infty \int_{\Omega_\psi} (\phi_{u_n}^2 - \phi_u^2)u\psi dx \to 0 \tag{2.20}$$

as $n \to \infty$, here Ω_ψ is the support set of ψ.

Furthermore, by the Lebesgue Dominated Convergence theorem and (2.3), we have

$$\int_{\mathbb{R}^3} [f(x, u_n) - f(x, u)]\psi dx = \int_{\Omega_\psi} [f(x, u_n) - f(x, u)]\psi dx = o(1).$$

Since $u_n \rightharpoonup u$ in $L^2(\mathbb{R}^3)$ and $h \in L^2(\mathbb{R}^3)$, we obtain

$$\int_{\mathbb{R}^3} h(u_n - u)dx = o(1).$$

This jointly with (2.17), (2.18), (2.20) and the Lebesgue Dominated Convergence theorem, shows that

$$\langle I_\lambda'(u), \psi \rangle = \lim_{n \to \infty} \langle I_\lambda'(u_n), \psi \rangle = 0, \quad \forall \psi \in C_0^\infty(\mathbb{R}^3).$$

Hence $I_\lambda'(u) = 0$. Combining with (2.10), (2.11) and Proposition 2.4 (iii), we obtain (2.12). The proof is complete.   □

Lemma 2.3   *Assume that* $V \geqslant 0$, (V_0), (V_1), (f_1)—(f_4), (K) *and* (h) *hold. Then, for any* $M > 0$, *there is* $\Lambda = \Lambda(M) > 0$ *such that* I_λ *satisfies* $(PS)_c$ *condition for all* $c < M$ *and* $\lambda > \Lambda$.

Proof. Let $\{u_n\} \subset E_\lambda$ be a $(PS)_c$ sequence with $c < M$. By Lemma 2.1, we know that $\{u_n\}$ is bounded in E_λ, and there exists $C > 0$ such that $\|u_n\|_\lambda \leqslant C$. Therefore, up to a subsequence, we can assume that

$$u_n \rightharpoonup u \text{ in } E_\lambda;$$

$$u_n \to u \text{ in } L_{loc}^s(\mathbb{R}^3)(1 \leqslant s < 2^*); \tag{2.21}$$

$$u_n(x) \to u(x) \text{ a.e. } x \in \mathbb{R}^3.$$

Now we can show that $u_n \to u$ in E_λ for $\lambda > 0$ large. Denote $w_n := u_n - u$, then $w_n \rightharpoonup 0$ in E_λ. According to Lemma 2.2 and the fact (2.2) holds uniformly for all $\varphi \in E_\lambda$, we have $I_\lambda'(u) = 0$, and

$$I_\lambda(w_n) \to c - I_\lambda(u), \quad I_\lambda'(w_n) \to 0 \quad \text{as } n \to \infty. \tag{2.22}$$

According to $V \geqslant 0$ and $(f3)$, we obtain

$$I_\lambda(u) = I_\lambda(u) - \frac{1}{4}\langle I_\lambda'(u), u \rangle$$

$$= \frac{1}{4}\|u\|_\lambda^2 + \frac{1}{4}\int_{\mathbb{R}^3} K(x)\phi_u^2 u^2 dx + \int_{\mathbb{R}^3} \mathcal{F}(x,u)dx - \frac{3}{4}\int_{\mathbb{R}^3} hudx$$

$$= \Phi_\lambda(u) - \frac{3}{4}\int_{\mathbb{R}^3} hudx,$$

here

$$\Phi_\lambda(u) = \frac{1}{4}\|u\|_\lambda^2 + \frac{1}{4}\int_{\mathbb{R}^3} K(x)\phi_u^2 u^2 dx + \int_{\mathbb{R}^3} \mathcal{F}(x,u)dx \geqslant 0.$$

Again by (2.22), (2.21) and Proposition 2.3 (i), we have

$$\frac{1}{4}\|w_n\|_\lambda^2 + \int_{\mathbb{R}^3} \mathcal{F}(x,w_n)dx = I_\lambda(w_n) - \frac{1}{4}\langle I_\lambda'(w_n), w_n \rangle + \frac{3}{4}\int_{\mathbb{R}^3} hw_ndx + o(1)$$

$$\leqslant c - I_\lambda(u) + o(1)$$

$$= c - \left[\Phi_\lambda(u) - \frac{3}{4}\int_{\mathbb{R}^3} hu dx\right] + \frac{3}{4}\int_{\mathbb{R}^3} hw_n dx + o(1)$$

$$= c - \Phi_\lambda(u) + \frac{3}{4}\int_{\mathbb{R}^3} hu dx + o(1)$$

$$\leqslant M + \tilde{M} + o(1). \tag{2.23}$$

Here we use the fact $c < M$ and

$$\frac{3}{4}|h|_2|u|_2 \leqslant \frac{3}{4}|h|_2 d_2\|u\|_\lambda \leqslant \frac{3}{4}|h|_2 d_2 \liminf_{n\to\infty}\|u_n\|_\lambda \leqslant |h|_2 d_2 C \leqslant \tilde{M},$$

where $\tilde{M}$ is a positive constant independent of λ. Hence

$$\int_{\mathbb{R}^3} \mathcal{F}(x, w_n) dx \leqslant M + \tilde{M} + o(1). \tag{2.24}$$

Because $V(x) < b$ on a set of finite measure and $w_n \rightharpoonup 0$, we obtain

$$|w_n|_2^2 \leqslant \frac{1}{\lambda b}\int_{V\geqslant b} \lambda V^+(x)w_n^2 dx + \int_{V<b} w_n^2 dx \leqslant \frac{1}{\lambda b}\|w_n\|_\lambda^2 + o(1). \tag{2.25}$$

For $2 < s < 2^*$, by the Hölder and Sobolev inequalities and (2.25), we have

$$|w_n|_s^s = \int_{\mathbb{R}^3} |w_n|^s dx \leqslant \left(\int_{\mathbb{R}^3} |w_n|^2 dx\right)^{\frac{6-s}{s}} \left(\int_{\mathbb{R}^3} |w_n|^6 dx\right)^{\frac{9s-18}{s}}$$

$$\leqslant \left[\frac{1}{\lambda b}\int_{\mathbb{R}^3} (|\nabla w_n|^2 + \lambda V^+ w_n^2)\, dx\right]^{\frac{6-s}{s}} \left(\bar{S}^{-6}\left[\int_{\mathbb{R}^3} |\nabla w_n|^2 dx\right]^3\right)^{\frac{9s-18}{s}} + o(1)$$

$$\leqslant \left(\frac{1}{\lambda b}\right)^{\frac{6-s}{4}} \bar{S}^{-\frac{3(s-2)}{2}}\|w_n\|_\lambda^s + o(1). \tag{2.26}$$

According to (f_1), for any $\varepsilon > 0$, there exists $\delta = \delta(\varepsilon) > 0$ such that $|f(x,t)| \leqslant \varepsilon|t|$ for all $x \in \mathbb{R}^3$ and $|t| \leqslant \delta$, and (f_4) is satisfied for $|t| \geqslant \delta$ (with the same τ but possibly larger than a_1). Hence we have that

$$\int_{|w_n|\leqslant\delta} f(x, w_n)w_n dx \leqslant \varepsilon \int_{|w_n|\leqslant\delta} w_n^2 dx \leqslant \frac{\varepsilon}{\lambda b}\|w_n\|_\lambda^2 + o(1) \tag{2.27}$$

and

$$\int_{|w_n|\geqslant\delta} f(x, w_n)w_n dx \leqslant \left(\int_{|w_n|\geqslant\delta} |\frac{f(x, w_n)}{w_n}|^\tau dx\right)^{1/\tau} |w_n|_s^2$$

$$\leqslant \left(\int_{|w_n| \geqslant \delta} a_1 \mathcal{F}(x, w_n) dx \right)^{1/\tau} |w_n|_s^2$$

$$\leqslant [a_1(M + \tilde{M})]^{1/\tau} \bar{S}^{-\frac{3(2s-4)}{2s}} \left(\frac{1}{\lambda b} \right)^\theta \|w_n\|_\lambda^2 + o(1) \qquad (2.28)$$

by (f_4), (2.24), (2.26) with $s = 2\tau/(\tau - 1)$ and the Hölder inequality, where $\theta = \dfrac{6-s}{2s} > 0$.

Since $u_n \rightharpoonup u$ in $L^2(\mathbb{R}^3)$ and $h \in L^2(\mathbb{R}^3)$, we obtain that

$$\int_{\mathbb{R}^3} h(u_n - u) dx \to 0 \quad \text{as } n \to \infty. \qquad (2.29)$$

Therefore, by (2.27)—(2.29) and Proposition 2.3(i), we have

$$o(1) = \langle I_\lambda'(w_n), w_n \rangle$$

$$\geqslant \|w_n\|_\lambda^2 - \int_{\mathbb{R}^3} K(x)(2\omega + \phi_{w_n})\phi_{w_n} w_n^2 dx - \int_{\mathbb{R}^3} f(x, w_n) w_n dx - \int_{\mathbb{R}^3} h w_n dx$$

$$\geqslant \left[1 - \frac{\varepsilon}{\lambda b} - [a_1(M + \tilde{M})]^{1/\tau} \bar{S}^{-\frac{3(2s-4)}{2s}} \left(\frac{1}{\lambda b} \right)^\theta \right] \|w_n\|_\lambda^2 + o(1). \qquad (2.30)$$

So, there exists $\Lambda = \Lambda(M) > 0$ such that $w_n \to 0$ in E_λ when $\lambda > \Lambda$. Since $w_n = u_n - u$, it follows that $u_n \to u$ in E_λ. This completes the proof. □

Lemma 2.4   Assume (V_0), (V_1), (f_1)—(f_4), (K) and (h) hold. Let $\{u_n\}$ be a $(PS)_c$ sequence of I_λ with level $c > 0$. Then for any $M > 0$, there is $\Lambda = \Lambda(M) > 0$ such that, up to a subsequence, $u_n \rightharpoonup u$ in E_λ with u being a nontrivial critical point of I_λ and satisfying $I_\lambda(u) \leqslant c$ for all $c < M$ and $\lambda > \Lambda$.

Proof. We modify the proof of Lemma 2.3. By Lemma 2.2, we obtain

$$I_\lambda'(u) = 0, \quad I_\lambda(w_n) \to c - I_\lambda(u), \quad I_\lambda'(u_n) \to 0 \quad \text{as } n \to \infty. \qquad (2.31)$$

However, since V is allowed to be sign-changing and the appearance of nonlinear term h, from

$$I_\lambda(u) = I_\lambda(u) - \frac{1}{4}\langle I_\lambda'(u), u \rangle$$

$$= \frac{1}{4}\|u\|_\lambda^2 - \frac{\lambda}{4} \int_{\mathbb{R}^3} V^-(x) u^2 dx$$

$$+ \frac{1}{4} \int_{\mathbb{R}^3} K(x)\phi_u^2 u^2 dx + \int_{\mathbb{R}^3} \mathcal{F}(x, u) dx - \frac{3}{4} \int_{\mathbb{R}^3} h u dx,$$

we cannot deduce that $I_\lambda(u) \geqslant 0$. We consider two possibilities:

(i) $I_\lambda(u) < 0$;

(ii) $I_\lambda(u) \geqslant 0$.

If $I_\lambda(u) < 0$, then $u \neq 0$ is nontrivial and the proof is done. If $I_\lambda(u) \geqslant 0$, following the argument in the proof of Lemma 2.3 step by step, we can get $u_n \to u$ in E_λ. Indeed, by (V_0) and $w_n \to 0$ in $L^2(\{x \in \mathbb{R}^3 : V(x) < b\})$, we obtain

$$\left| \int_{\mathbb{R}^3} V^-(x) w_n^2(x) dx \right| \leqslant |V^-|_\infty \int_{\text{supp} V^-} w_n^2 dx = o(1),$$

which jointly this with (2.31) and Proposition 2.3(i), we have

$$\int_{\mathbb{R}^3} \mathcal{F}(x, w_n) dx = I_\lambda(w_n) - \frac{1}{4} \langle I_\lambda'(w_n), w_n \rangle$$

$$- \frac{1}{4}\|w_n\|_\lambda^2 + \frac{1}{4} \int_{\mathbb{R}^3} \lambda V^-(x) w_n^2 dx - \frac{1}{4} \int_{\mathbb{R}^3} K(x) \phi_{w_n}^2 w_n^2 dx + \frac{3}{4} \int_{\mathbb{R}^3} h w_n dx$$

$$\leqslant c - I_\lambda(u) + o(1) \leqslant M + o(1).$$

It follows that (2.28)—(2.30) remain valid. Therefore $u_n \to u$ in E_λ and $I_\lambda(u) = c(> 0)$. The proof is complete. $\qquad\square$

2.1.3 Proofs of main results

If V is sign-changing, we first verify that the function I_λ have the linking geometry to apply the following linking theorem[154].

Proposition 2.5 Let $E = E_1 \oplus E_2$ be a Banach space with $\dim E_2 < \infty, \Phi \in C^1(E, \mathbb{R}^3)$. If there exist $R > \rho > 0, \alpha > 0$ and $e_0 \in E_1$ such that

$$\alpha := \inf \Phi(E_1 \cap S_\rho) > \sup \Phi(\partial Q),$$

where $S_\rho = \{u \in E : \|u\| = \rho\}, Q = \{u = v + te_0 : v \in E_2, t \geqslant 0, \|u\| \leqslant R\}$. Then Φ has a $(PS)_c$ sequence with $c \in [\alpha, \sup \Phi(Q)]$.

In our book, we use Proposition 2.5 with $E_1 = E_\lambda^+ \oplus F_\lambda$ and $E_2 = E_\lambda^-$. By Proposition 2.2, $\mu_j(\lambda) \to 0$ as $\lambda \to \infty$ for every fixed j. By Remark 2.3, there is $\Lambda_1 > 0$ such that $E_\lambda^- \neq \varnothing$ and E_λ^- is finite dimensional for $\lambda > \Lambda_1$. Now we can investigate the linking structure of the functional I_λ.

Lemma 2.5 Assume that (V_0), (V_1), (K), (h) and (2.3) with $p \in (4, 2^*)$ are satisfied. Then, for each $\lambda > \Lambda_1$(is the constant given in Remark 2.3), there exist $\alpha_\lambda, \rho_\lambda$ and $\eta_\lambda > 0$ such that

$$I_\lambda(u) \geqslant \alpha_\lambda \text{ for all } u \in E_\lambda^+ \oplus F_\lambda \text{ with } \|u\|_\lambda = \rho_\lambda \text{ and } |h|_2 < \eta_\lambda. \tag{2.32}$$

Furthermore, if $V \geqslant 0$, we can choose $\alpha, \rho, \eta > 0$ independent of λ.

Proof. For any $u \in E_\lambda^+ \oplus F_\lambda$, writing $u = u_1 + u_2$ with $u_1 \in E_\lambda^+$ and $u_2 \in F_\lambda$. Clearly, $(u_1, u_2)_\lambda = 0$, and

$$\int_{\mathbb{R}^3} (|\nabla u|^2 + \lambda V(x)u^2)dx = \int_{\mathbb{R}^3} (|\nabla u_1|^2 + \lambda V(x)u_1^2)dx + \|u_2\|_\lambda^2. \qquad (2.33)$$

By Proposition 2.1, we obtain that $\mu_j(\lambda) \to +\infty$ as $j \to +\infty$ for each fixed $\lambda > \Lambda_1$. So there is a positive integer n_λ such that $\mu_j(\lambda) \leqslant 1$ for $j \leqslant n_\lambda$ and $\mu_j(\lambda) > 1$ for $j > n_\lambda + 1$. For $u_1 \in E_\lambda^+$, we set $u_1 = \sum_{j=n_\lambda+1}^\infty \mu_j(\lambda)e_j(\lambda)$. Thus

$$\int_{\mathbb{R}^3} (|\nabla u_1|^2 + \lambda V(x)u_1^2)dx = \|u_1\|_\lambda^2 - \int_{\mathbb{R}^3} \lambda V^-(x)u_1^2 dx$$

$$\geqslant \left(1 - \frac{1}{\mu_{n_\lambda+1}(\lambda)}\right) \|u_1\|_\lambda^2. \qquad (2.34)$$

By using (2.5), (2.33), (2.34) and $-\omega \leqslant \phi_u \leqslant 0$ on the set $\{x \in \mathbb{R}^3 | u(x) \neq 0\}$, we have

$$I_\lambda(u) \geqslant \frac{1}{2}\left(1 - \frac{1}{\mu_{n_\lambda+1}(\lambda)}\right) \|u\|_\lambda^2 - \varepsilon|u|_2^2 - C_\varepsilon|u|_p^p - |h|_2|u|_2$$

$$\geqslant \frac{1}{2}\left(1 - \frac{1}{\mu_{n_\lambda+1}(\lambda)}\right) \|u\|_\lambda^2 - \varepsilon d_2^2\|u\|_\lambda^2 - C_\varepsilon d_p^p\|u\|_\lambda^p - d_2|h|_2\|u\|_\lambda$$

$$\geqslant \|u\|_\lambda \left\{\left[\frac{1}{2}\left(1 - \frac{1}{\mu_{n_\lambda+1}(\lambda)}\right) - \varepsilon d_2^2\right]\|u\|_\lambda - C_\varepsilon d_p^p\|u\|_\lambda^{p-1} - d_2|h|_2\right\}.$$

Let

$$g(t) = \left[\frac{1}{2}(1 - \frac{1}{\mu_{n_\lambda+1}(\lambda)}) - \varepsilon d_2^2\right]t - C_\varepsilon d_p^p t^{p-1}, \quad \text{for } t > 0, p \in (4,6),$$

there exists

$$\rho(\lambda) = \left[\frac{\frac{1}{2}\left(1 - \frac{1}{\mu_{n_\lambda+1}(\lambda)}\right) - \varepsilon d_2^2}{C_\varepsilon d_p^p(p-1)}\right]^{\frac{1}{p-2}}$$

such that $\max_{t \geqslant 0} g(t) = g(\rho(\lambda)) > 0$. It follows from above inequality,

$$I_\lambda(u)|_{\|u\|_\lambda=\rho(\lambda)} > 0, \quad \text{for all } |h|_2 < \eta_\lambda := \frac{g(\rho(\lambda))}{2d_2}.$$

Of course, $\rho(\lambda)$ can be chosen small enough, we can obtain the same result: there exists $\alpha_\lambda > 0$, such that $I_\lambda(u) \geqslant \alpha_\lambda$, here $\|u\|_\lambda = \rho_\lambda$.

If $V \geqslant 0$, since $E_\lambda = F_\lambda$, and

$$\int_{\mathbb{R}^3} (|\nabla u|^2 + \lambda V(x)u^2)dx = \|u\|_\lambda^2,$$

we can choose $\alpha, \rho, \eta > 0$ (independent of λ) such that (2.32) holds. $\square$

Lemma 2.6 *Suppose that* $(V_0), (V_1), (f_1), (f_2), (K)$ *and* (h) *are satisfied. Then, for any finite dimensional subspace* $\tilde{E}_\lambda \subset E_\lambda$, *there holds*

$$I_\lambda(u) \to -\infty \quad as \quad \|u\|_\lambda \to \infty, \ u \in \tilde{E}_\lambda.$$

Proof. Arguing indirectly, we can assume that there is a sequence $(u_n) \subset \tilde{E}_\lambda$ with $\|u_n\|_\lambda \to \infty$ such that

$$-\infty < \inf_n I_\lambda(u_n). \tag{2.35}$$

Take $v_n := u_n/\|u_n\|_\lambda$. Since $\dim \tilde{E}_\lambda < +\infty$, there exists $v \in \tilde{E}_\lambda \setminus \{0\}$ such that

$$v_n \to v \quad in \ \tilde{E}_\lambda, \qquad v_n(x) \to v(x) \text{ a.e. } x \in \mathbb{R}^3$$

after passing to a subsequence. If $v(x) \neq 0$, then $|u_n(x)| \to +\infty$ as $n \to \infty$, and hence by (f_2), we obtain that

$$\frac{F(x, u_n(x))}{u_n^4(x)} v_n^4(x) \to +\infty \quad as \ n \to \infty,$$

which jointly this with (f_1), (2.7), Proposition 2.3 (ii) and Fatou's lemma, we obtain

$$\begin{aligned}
\frac{I_\lambda(u_n)}{\|u_n\|_\lambda^4} &\leq \frac{1}{2\|u_n\|_\lambda^2} + \frac{C_4\omega}{2}|K|_\infty - \int_{\mathbb{R}^3} \frac{F(x, u_n)}{\|u_n\|_\lambda^4}dx - \int_{\mathbb{R}^3} h(x)\frac{u_n}{\|u_n\|_\lambda^4}dx \\
&\leq \frac{1}{2\|u_n\|_\lambda^2} + \frac{C_4\omega}{2}|K|_\infty - \left(\int_{v=0} + \int_{v\neq0}\right)\frac{F(x, u_n)}{u_n^4}v_n^4 dx + \frac{|h|_2 d_2}{\|u_n\|_\lambda^3} \\
&\leq \frac{1}{2\|u_n\|_\lambda^2} + \frac{C_4\omega}{2}|K|_\infty - \int_{v\neq0}\frac{F(x, u_n)}{u_n^4}v_n^4 dx + \frac{|h|_2 d_2}{\|u_n\|_\lambda^3} \\
&\to -\infty.
\end{aligned}$$

This contradicts (2.35). $\square$

Lemma 2.7 *Suppose that* $(V_0), (V_1), (h), (K)$ *and* $(f_1), (f_2)$ *are satisfied. If* $V(x) < 0$ *for some* x, *then , for each* $k \in \mathbb{N}$, *there exist* $\lambda_k > k, b_k > 0, w_k \in E_{\lambda_k}^+ \oplus F_{\lambda_k}, R_{\lambda_k} > \rho_{\lambda_k}(\rho_{\lambda_k}$ *is the constant given in Lemma 2.5) and* $\eta_k > 0$ *such that, for* $|h|_2 < \eta_k$, $|K|_\infty < b_k(or|K|_3 < b_k)$,

(i) $\sup I_{\lambda_k}(\partial Q_k) \leq 0$;

(ii) $\sup I_{\lambda_k}(Q_k)$ *is bounded above by a constant independent of* λ_k,

where $Q_k := \{u = v + tw_k : v \in E_{\lambda_k}^-, t \geq 0, \|u\|_{\lambda_k} \leq R_{\lambda_k}\}$.

Proof. We adapt an argument in Ding and Szulkin[82]. For each $k \in \mathbb{N}$, since $\mu_j(k) \to +\infty$ as $j \to \infty$, there exists $j_k \in \mathbb{N}$ such that $\mu_{j_k}(k) > 1$. By Proposition 2.2, there exists $\lambda_k > k$ such that

$$1 < \mu_{j_k}(\lambda_k) < 1 + \frac{1}{\lambda_k}.$$

Taking $w_k := e_{j_k}(\lambda_k)$ be an eigenfunction of $\mu_{j_k}(\lambda_k)$, then $w_k \in E_{\lambda_k}^+$ as $\mu_{j_k}(\lambda_k) > 1$. Because $\dim E_{\lambda_k}^- \oplus \mathbb{R}w_k < +\infty$, it follows directly from Lemma 2.6 that (i) holds with $R_{\lambda_k} > 0$ large enough.

According to (f_2), for each $\tilde{\eta} > |V^-|_\infty$, there is $r_{\tilde{\eta}} > 0$ such that

$$F(x,t) \geqslant \frac{1}{2}\tilde{\eta}t^2, \quad \text{if } |t| \geqslant r_{\tilde{\eta}}.$$

For $u = v + w \in E_{\lambda_k}^- \oplus \mathbb{R}w_k$, we have

$$\int_{\mathbb{R}^3} V^-(x)u^2 dx = \int_{\mathbb{R}^3} V^-(x)v^2 dx + \int_{\mathbb{R}^3} V^-(x)w^2 dx$$

by the orthogonality of $E_{\lambda_k}^-$ and $\mathbb{R}w_k$. Therefore, by Proposition 2.3 (ii), we obtain

$$I_{\lambda_k}(u) \leqslant \frac{1}{2}\int_{\mathbb{R}^3} \left(|\nabla w|^2 + \lambda_k V(x)w^2\right) dx - \frac{1}{2}\int_{\mathbb{R}^3} K(x)\omega\phi_u u^2 dx$$

$$- \int_{\text{supp}V^-} F(x,u)dx - \int_{\mathbb{R}^3} hu dx$$

$$\leqslant \frac{1}{2}[\mu_{j_k}(\lambda_k) - 1]\lambda_k \int_{\mathbb{R}^3} V^-(x)w^2 dx - \frac{1}{2}\int_{\text{supp}V^-} \tilde{\eta}u^2 dx$$

$$+ \frac{C_4\omega}{2}|K|_\infty \|u\|_{\lambda_k}^4 + d_2|h|_2\|u\|_{\lambda_k} - \int_{\text{supp}V^-,|u|\leqslant r_{\tilde{\eta}}} \left(F(x,u) - \frac{1}{2}\tilde{\eta}u^2\right) dx$$

$$\leqslant \frac{1}{2}\int_{\mathbb{R}^3} V^-(x)w^2 dx - \frac{\tilde{\eta}}{2|V^-|_\infty}\int_{\mathbb{R}^3} V^-(x)w^2 dx + C_{\tilde{\eta}}$$

$$+ \frac{C_4\omega}{2}|K|_\infty R_{\lambda_k}^4 + d_2|h|_2 R_{\lambda_k}$$

$$\leqslant C_{\tilde{\eta}} + 1,$$

for $u = v + w \in E_{\lambda_k}^- \oplus \mathbb{R}w_k$ with $\|u\|_{\lambda_k} \leqslant R_{\lambda_k}$, $|K|_\infty < b_k := (C_4\omega R_{\lambda_k}^4)^{-1/2}$, C_4 is defined in Proposition 2.3 (iii) and $|h|_2 < \eta_k := \dfrac{1}{2d_2 R_{\lambda_k}}$, where $C_{\tilde{\eta}}$ depends on $\tilde{\eta}$ but not λ_k.

If $K \in L^3(\mathbb{R}^3)$, by the Hölder inequality, we obtain that

$$\left|\int_{\mathbb{R}^3} K(x)\omega\phi_u u^2 dx\right|$$

$$\leqslant \omega |K|_3 |\phi_u|_6 |u|_4^2 \leqslant \omega |K|_3 \bar{S}^{-1} \|\phi_u\|_D d_4^2 \|u\|_\lambda^2$$

$$\leqslant C_1 |K|_3 \|u\|_\lambda^4 \leqslant C_1 |K|_3 R_{\lambda_k}^4.$$

for $|K|_3 < b_k := (C_1 R_{\lambda_k}^4)^{-1}$. $\qquad \square$

Lemma 2.8 *Suppose that $(V_0), (V_1), (h), (K)$ and $(f_1), (f_2)$ are satisfied. If $\Omega :=$ $\mathrm{int} V^{-1}(0)$ is nonempty, then, for each $\lambda > \Lambda_1($ is the constant given in Remark 2.3), there exist $w \in E_\lambda^+ \oplus F_\lambda, R_\lambda > 0, b_\lambda > 0$ and $\eta_\lambda > 0$ such that for $|h|_2 < \eta_\lambda, |K|_\infty < b_\lambda or (|K|_3 < b_\lambda),$*

(i) $\sup I_\lambda(\partial Q) \leqslant 0$;

(ii) $\sup I_\lambda(Q)$ is bounded above by a constant independent of λ,

where $Q := \{u = v + tw : v \in E_\lambda^-, t \geqslant 0, \|u\|_\lambda \leqslant R_\lambda\}$.

Proof. Choose $e_0 \in C_0^\infty(\Omega) \setminus \{0\}$, then $e_0 \in F_\lambda$. By Lemma 2.6, there is $R_\lambda > 0$ large such that $I_\lambda(u) \leqslant 0$ where $u \in E_\lambda^- \oplus \mathbb{R} e_0$ and $\|u\|_\lambda \geqslant R_\lambda$.

For $u = v + w \in E_\lambda^- \oplus \mathbb{R} e_0$, we have

$$I_\lambda(u) \leqslant \frac{1}{2} \int_{\mathbb{R}^3} |\nabla w|^2 dx - \frac{1}{2} \int_{\mathbb{R}^3} K(x) \omega \phi_u u^2 dx - \int_\Omega F(x, u) dx - \int_{\mathbb{R}^3} hu dx$$

$$\leqslant \frac{1}{2} \int_{\mathbb{R}^3} |\nabla w|^2 dx - \frac{\tilde{\eta}}{2} \int_\Omega u^2 dx - \int_{\Omega, |u| \leqslant r_{\tilde{\eta}}} \left(F(x, u) - \frac{\tilde{\eta}}{2} u^2 \right) dx$$

$$+ \frac{C_4 \omega}{2} |K|_\infty \|u\|_\lambda^4 + |h|_2 d_2 \|u\|_\lambda$$

$$\leqslant \frac{1}{2} \int_{\mathbb{R}^3} |\nabla w|^2 dx - \frac{\tilde{\eta}}{2} \int_\Omega u^2 dx + C_{\tilde{\eta}} + \frac{C_4 \omega}{2} |K|_\infty \|u\|_\lambda^4 + |h|_2 d_2 \|u\|_\lambda. \quad (2.36)$$

Observing $w \in C_0^\infty(\Omega)$, we have

$$\int_{\mathbb{R}^3} |\nabla w|^2 dx = \int_\Omega (-\Delta w) u dx \leqslant |\Delta w|_2 |u|_{2,\Omega}$$

$$\leqslant c_0 |\nabla w|_2 |u|_{2,\Omega} \leqslant \frac{c_0^2}{2\tilde{\eta}} |\nabla w|_2^2 + \frac{\tilde{\eta}}{2} |u|_{2,\Omega}^2, \quad (2.37)$$

where c_0 is a constant depending on e_0. Choosing $\tilde{\eta} > c_0^2$, we have

$$|\nabla w|_2^2 \leqslant \tilde{\eta} |u|_{2,\Omega}^2,$$

and it follows from (2.36) that

$$I_\lambda(u) \leqslant C_{\tilde{\eta}} + \frac{C_4 \omega}{2} |K|_\infty R_\lambda^4 + |h|_2 d_2 R_\lambda \leqslant C_{\tilde{\eta}} + 1,$$

for all $u \in E_\lambda^- \oplus \mathbb{R} e_0$ with $\|u\|_\lambda \leqslant R_\lambda, |h|_2 < \eta_\lambda := \dfrac{1}{2 d_2 R_\lambda}$ and $|K|_\infty < b_\lambda :=$ $(C_4 \omega R_\lambda^4)^{-1}$, where $C_{\tilde{\eta}}$ depends on $\tilde{\eta}$ but not λ.

If $K \in L^3(\mathbb{R}^3)$, by the Hölder inequality, we get that

$$\left| \int_{\mathbb{R}^3} K(x)\omega\phi_u u^2 dx \right|$$

$$\leqslant \omega|K|_3|\phi_u|_6|u|_4^2 \leqslant \omega|K|_3\bar{S}^{-1}\|\phi_u\|_D d_4^2\|u\|_\lambda^2$$

$$\leqslant C_1|K|_3\|u\|_\lambda^4 \leqslant C_1|K|_3 R_\lambda^4.$$

for $|K|_3 < b_\lambda := (C_1 R_\lambda^4)^{-1}$. □

Now we are in a position to prove our main results.

Proof of Theorem 2.1　The proof of Theorem 2.1 is divided in two steps.

Step 1　There exists a function $u_\lambda \in E_\lambda$ such that $I_\lambda'(u_\lambda) = 0$ and $I_\lambda(u_\lambda) < 0$. Since $h \in L^2(\mathbb{R}^3)$ and $h \geqslant 0 (\not\equiv 0)$, we can choose a function $\psi \in E_\lambda$ such that

$$\int_{\mathbb{R}^3} h(x)\psi(x)dx > 0.$$

Hence, by $-\omega \leqslant \phi_u \leqslant 0$ we obtain that

$$I_\lambda(t\psi) = \frac{t^2}{2}\|\psi\|_\lambda^2 - \frac{\lambda t^2}{2} \int_{\mathbb{R}^3} V^-(x)\psi^2 dx - \frac{1}{2} \int_{\mathbb{R}^3} K(x)\omega\phi_{t\psi}(t\psi)^2 dx$$

$$- \int_{\mathbb{R}^3} F(x,t\psi)dx - t \int_{\mathbb{R}^3} h(x)\psi dx$$

$$\leqslant \frac{t^2}{2}\|\psi\|_\lambda^2 + \frac{t^2}{2} \int_{\mathbb{R}^3} \omega^2\psi^2 dx + \frac{t^4}{4}C_1\|\psi\|_\lambda^4 - t \int_{\mathbb{R}^3} h(x)\psi dx$$

$$< 0, \quad \text{for } t > 0 \text{ small enough.}$$

Thus, there exists a u_λ small enough such that $I_\lambda(u_\lambda) < 0$. By Lemma 2.6, we have

$$c_{0,\lambda} = \inf\{I_\lambda(u) : u \in \bar{B}_{\rho_\lambda}\} < 0,$$

where $\rho_\lambda > 0$ is given by Lemma 2.5, $B_{\rho_\lambda} = \{u \in E_\lambda : \|u\|_\lambda < \rho_\lambda\}$. By the Ekeland's Variational Principle, there exists a minimizing sequence $\{u_{n,\lambda}\} \subset \bar{B}_{\rho_\lambda}$ such that

$$c_{0,\lambda} \leqslant I_\lambda(u_{n,\lambda}) < c_{0,\lambda} + \frac{1}{n_\lambda}$$

and

$$I_\lambda(w_\lambda) \geqslant I_\lambda(u_{n,\lambda}) - \frac{1}{n_\lambda}\|w_\lambda - u_{n,\lambda}\|_\lambda,$$

for all $w_\lambda \in \bar{B}_{\rho_\lambda}$. Therefore, $\{u_{n,\lambda}\}$ is a bounded Palais-Smale sequence of I_λ. Then, by a standard procedure, Lemma 2.3 and Lemma 2.2 imply that there is a function $u_\lambda \in E_\lambda$ such that $I_\lambda'(u_\lambda) = 0$ and $I_\lambda(u_\lambda) = c_{0,\lambda} < 0$.

If $V \geqslant 0$, we can get $\rho_\lambda, c_{0,\lambda}, u_{0,\lambda}$ are independent of λ.

Step 2   There exists a function $\tilde{u}_\lambda \in E_\lambda$ such that $I'_\lambda(\tilde{u}_\lambda) = 0$ and $I_\lambda(\tilde{u}_\lambda) > 0$.

It follows from Lemmas 2.5, 2.7 and Proposition 2.5 that, for each $k \in \mathbb{N}, \lambda = \lambda_k$ and $|h|_2 < \eta_k$, I_{λ_k} has a $(PS)_c$ sequence with $c \in [\alpha_{\lambda_k}, \sup I_{\lambda_k}(Q_k)]$. Setting $M := \sup I_{\lambda_k}(Q_k)$, then I_{λ_k} has a nontrivial critical point according to Lemmas 2.1, 2.4 and Proposition 2.5. Hence there exists a function $\tilde{u}_\lambda \in E_\lambda$ such that $I'_\lambda(\tilde{u}_\lambda) = 0$ and $I_\lambda(\tilde{u}_\lambda) = c \geqslant \alpha_{\lambda_k} > 0$. The proof is complete. □

Proof of Theorem 2.2   The first solution is similar to the first solution of Theorem 2.1. The second solution follows from Lemmas 2.1, 2.4, 2.5, 2.8 and Proposition 2.5. The proof is complete. □

Proof of Theorem 2.3   The proof of Theorem 2.3 is divided in two steps.

Step 1   There exists a function $u_0 \in E_\lambda$ such that $I'_\lambda(u_0) = 0$ and $I_\lambda(u_0) < 0$. In the proof of Theorem 2.1, we can choose $c_0 = c_{0,\lambda}, B_\rho = B_{\rho,\lambda}$, then by the Ekeland's Variational Principle, there exists a sequence $\{u_n\} \subset \bar{B}_\rho$ such that

$$c_0 \leqslant I_\lambda(u_n) < c_0 + \frac{1}{n}$$

and

$$I_\lambda(w) \geqslant I_\lambda(u_n) - \frac{1}{n}\|w - u_n\|_\lambda,$$

for all $w \in \bar{B}_\rho$. Then by a standard procedure, we can show that $\{u_n\}$ is a bounded Palais-Smale sequence of I_λ. Therefore Lemma 2.2 and Lemma 2.3 imply that there exists a function $u_0 \in E_\lambda$ such that $I'_\lambda(u_0) = 0$ and $I_\lambda(u_0) = c_0 < 0$.

Step 2   There exists a function $\tilde{u}_\lambda \in E_\lambda$ such that $I'_\lambda(\tilde{u}_\lambda) = 0$ and $I_\lambda(\tilde{u}_\lambda) > 0$.

Since we suppose $V \geqslant 0$, the functional I_λ has mountain pass geometry and the existence of nontrivial solutions can be obtained by Mountain Pass theorem, see [154,200,224]. Indeed, by Lemma 2.5, there exist constants $\alpha, \rho, \eta > 0$ (independent of λ) such that, for each $\lambda > \Lambda_0$,

$$I_\lambda(u) \geqslant \alpha, \quad \text{for } u \in E_\lambda \text{ with } \|u\|_\lambda = \rho \text{ and } |h|_2 < \eta.$$

Take $e \in C_0^\infty(\Omega) \setminus \{0\}$, by $(f_1), (f_2)$ and Fatou's lemma, we get

$$\frac{I_\lambda(te)}{t^4} \leqslant \frac{1}{2t^2} \int_\Omega |\nabla e|^2 dx - \frac{1}{2t^2} \int_\Omega K(x)\omega^2 e^2 dx - \int_{\{x \in \Omega : e(x) \neq 0\}} \frac{F(x, te)}{(te)^4} e^4 dx$$

$$- t^{-3} \int_\Omega he\, dx \to -\infty$$

as $t \to +\infty$, which yields that $I_\lambda(te) < 0$ for $t > 0$ large. Clearly, there is $C > 0$ (independent of λ) such that

$$c_\lambda := \inf_{\gamma \in \Gamma} \max_{t \in [0,1]} I_\lambda(\gamma(t)) \leqslant \sup_{t \geqslant 0} I_\lambda(te_0) \leqslant C,$$

where $\Gamma = \{\gamma \in C([0,1], E_\lambda) : \gamma(0) = 0, \|\gamma(1)\|_\lambda \geqslant \rho, I_\lambda(\gamma(1)) < 0\}$. By Mountain Pass theorem and Lemma 2.3, we obtain a nontrivial critical point $\tilde{u}_\lambda$ of I_λ with $I_\lambda(\tilde{u}_\lambda) \in [\alpha, C]$ for λ large. The proof is complete.   □

2.2   The primitive of the nonlinearity f is of 2-superlinear growth at infinity

2.2.1   Introduction and main results

In this section, we consider the following nonhomogeneous Klein-Gordon-Maxwell system:

$$(KGM) \begin{cases} -\Delta u + V(x)u - (2\omega + \phi)\phi u = f(x,u) + h(x), & x \in \mathbb{R}^3, \\ \Delta\phi = (\omega + \phi)u^2, & x \in \mathbb{R}^3, \end{cases}$$

where $\omega > 0$ is a constant. We are interested in the existence of two nontrivial solutions for system (KGM) under more general nonlinearity f, which doesn't satisfy the (local) (AR) condition or the (Je) condition of Jeanjean.

We consider the nonhomogeneous case, that is $h \not\equiv 0$. In [59], Chen and Song proved that (KGM) had two nontrivial solutions if $f(x,t)$ satisfies the local (AR) condition:

(CS) There exist $\mu > 2$ and $r_0 > 0$ such that $\mathcal{F}(x,t) := \dfrac{1}{\mu}f(x,t)t - F(x,t) \geqslant 0$

for every $x \in \mathbb{R}^3$ and $|t| \geqslant r_0$, where $F(x,t) = \displaystyle\int_0^t f(x,s)ds$.

Xu and Chen[207] studied the existence and multiplicity of solutions for system (KGM) for the pure power of nonlinearity with $f(x,u) = |u|^{q-2}u$. They also assumed that $V(x) \equiv 1$ and $h(x)$ is radially symmetric. For more results on the nonhomogeneous case see [59, 161] and the references therein.

Motivated by above works, we consider system (KGM) with more general assumptions on f and without any radially symmetric assumptions on f and h. More precisely, we assume

(V) $V \in C(\mathbb{R}^3, \mathbb{R})$ satisfies $V_0 = \inf\limits_{x \in \mathbb{R}^3} V(x) > 0$. Moreover, for every $M > 0$,

$\text{meas}\{x \in \mathbb{R}^3 : V(x) \leqslant M\} < +\infty$, where meas denotes the Lebesgue measures.

(f_1) $f \in C(\mathbb{R}^3 \times \mathbb{R}, \mathbb{R})$ and there exist $C_1 > 0$ and $p \in (2,6)$ such that

$$|f(x,t)| \leqslant C_1(|t| + |t|^{p-1}).$$

(f_2) $f(x,t) = o(t)$ uniformly in x as $|t| \to 0$.

(f_3) There exist $\theta > 2$ and $D_1, D_2 > 0$ such that $F(x,t) \geqslant D_1|t|^\theta - D_2$, for a.e. $x \in \mathbb{R}^3$ and every t sufficiently large.

(f_4) There exist C_2, r_0 are two positive constants and $\mu > 2$ such that

$$\mathcal{F}(x,t) := \frac{1}{\mu} f(x,t)t - F(x,t) \geqslant -C_2|t|^2, \quad |t| \geqslant r_0.$$

(H) $h \in L^2(\mathbb{R}^3), h(x) \geqslant 0, h(x) \not\equiv 0$.

Before giving our main results, we give some notations. Let $H^1(\mathbb{R}^3)$ be the usual Sobolev space endowed with the standard scalar and norm

$$(u,v)_H = \int_{\mathbb{R}^3} (\nabla u \nabla v + uv)dx, \quad \|u\|_H^2 = \int_{\mathbb{R}^3} (|\nabla u|^2 + |u|^2)dx.$$

$D^{1,2}(\mathbb{R}^3)$ is the completion of $C_0^\infty(\mathbb{R}^3)$ with respect to the norm

$$\|u\|_D^2 := \|u\|_{D^{1,2}(\mathbb{R}^3)}^2 = \int_{\mathbb{R}^3} |\nabla u|^2 dx.$$

The norm on $L^s = L^s(\mathbb{R}^3)$ with $1 < s < \infty$ is given by $|u|_s^s = \int_{\mathbb{R}^3} |u|^s dx$.

Under condition (V), we define a new Hilbert space

$$E := \left\{ u \in H^1(\mathbb{R}^3) : \int_{\mathbb{R}^3} (|\nabla u|^2 + V(x)u^2)dx < \infty \right\}$$

with the inner product

$$\langle u, v \rangle = \int_{\mathbb{R}^3} (\nabla u \cdot \nabla v + V(x)uv)\, dx,$$

and the norm $\|u\| = \langle u, u \rangle^{1/2}$. Obviously, the embedding $E \hookrightarrow L^s(\mathbb{R}^3)$ is continuous, for any $s \in [2, 2^*]$. Consequently, for each $s \in [2, 6]$, there exists a constant $d_s > 0$ such that

$$|u|_s \leqslant d_s\|u\|, \quad \forall u \in E. \tag{2.38}$$

Furthermore, it follows from the condition (V) that the embedding $E \hookrightarrow L^s(\mathbb{R}^3)$ is compact for any $s \in [2, 6)$(see [18]).

System (KGM) has a variational structure. In fact, we consider the function $\mathcal{J} : E \times D^{1,2}(\mathbb{R}^3) \to \mathbb{R}$ defined by

$$\mathcal{J}(u,\phi) = \frac{1}{2} \int_{\mathbb{R}^3} (|\nabla u|^2 + V(x)u^2)dx - \frac{1}{2} \int_{\mathbb{R}^3} |\nabla\phi|^2 dx - \frac{1}{2} \int_{\mathbb{R}^3} (2\omega + \phi)\phi u^2 dx$$

$$- \int_{\mathbb{R}^3} F(x,u)dx - \int_{\mathbb{R}^3} h(x)u dx.$$

The solutions $(u, \phi) \in E \times D^{1,2}(\mathbb{R}^3)$ of system (KGM) are the critical points of $\mathcal{J}$. As it is pointed in [59], the function $\mathcal{J}$ is strongly indefinite and is difficult to investigate. By using the reduction method described in [26], we are led to the study of a new function $I(u)$ ($I(u)$ is defined in (2.39)) which does not present such strongly indefinite nature.

Now we can state our main result.

Theorem 2.4 *Suppose (V), (f_1)—(f_4) and (H) hold. Then there exists a positive constant m_0 such that system (KGM) admits at least two different solutions $u_0, \tilde{u}_0$ in E satisfying $I(u_0) < 0$ and $I(\tilde{u}_0) > 0$ if $|h|_2 < m_0$.*

Remark 2.5 It is well known that, the (AR) condition is employed not only to prove that the Euler-Lagrange function associated has a mountain pass geometry, but also to guarantee that the Palais-Smale sequences, or Cerami sequences are bounded.

Compared with the local (AR) condition (CS), in our book $F(x,t)$ may have negative values.

Another widely used condition is the following condition introduced by Jeanjean[111].

(Je) There exists $\theta \geqslant 1$ such that $\theta \mathcal{F}_1(x, t) \geqslant \mathcal{F}_1(x, st)$ for all $s \in [0, 1]$ and $t \in \mathbb{R}$, where $\mathcal{F}_1(x, t) := \dfrac{1}{4}f(x, t)t - F(x, t)$.

We can observe that when $s = 0$, then $\mathcal{F}_1(x, t) \geqslant 0$, but for our condition (f_4), $F(x, t)$ may assume negative values.

In [4,58], the authors studied the Schrödinger-Poisson equation by assuming the following global condition to replace the (AR) condition:

(ASS) There exists $0 \leqslant \beta < \alpha$ such that $tf(t) - 4F(t) \geqslant -\beta t^2$, for all $t \in \mathbb{R}$, where α is a positive constant such that $\alpha \leqslant V(x)$.

Notice that we only need the local condition (f_4) in order to get nontrivial solutions.

In [118], Li and Tang used the following condition to get infinitely many solutions for homogenous system (KGM):

(LT) There exist two positive constants D_3 and r_0 such that

$$\frac{1}{4}f(x, t)t - F(x, t) \geqslant -D_3|t|^2, \quad \text{if } |t| \geqslant r_0.$$

Obviously, our condition (f_4) is weaker than (LT). Therefore, it is interesting to consider the nonhomogeneous system (KGM) under the conditions (f_3) and (f_4).

Remark 2.6 As it is pointed in [73], many technical difficulties arise to the presence of a nonlocal term ϕ, which is not homogeneous as it is in the Schrödinger-Poisson systems. Hence, a more careful analysis of the interaction between the couple (u, ϕ) is required.

In Section 2.2.2, we will introduce the variational setting for the problem and give some related preliminaries. We give the proof of our main result in Section 2.2.3.

2.2.2   Variational setting and compactness condition

By [15], we know that the signs of ω is not relevant for the existence of solutions, so we can assume that $\omega > 0$.

Evidently, the properties of ϕ_u plays an important role in the study of $\mathcal{J}$. So we need the following technical results.

Proposition 2.6   *For any $u \in H^1(\mathbb{R}^3)$, there exists a unique $\phi = \phi_u \in D^{1,2}(\mathbb{R}^3)$ which satisfies*

$$\Delta\phi = (\phi + \omega)u^2 \quad in \quad \mathbb{R}^3.$$

Moreover, the map $\Phi : u \in H^1(\mathbb{R}^3) \mapsto \phi_u \in D^{1,2}(\mathbb{R}^3)$ is continuously differentiable, and

(i) $-\omega \leqslant \phi_u \leqslant 0$ *on the set* $\{x \in \mathbb{R}^3 | u(x) \neq 0\}$;

(ii) $\|\phi_u\|_D^2 \leqslant C\|u\|^2$ *and* $\displaystyle\int_{\mathbb{R}^3} \phi_u u^2 dx \leqslant C|u|_{12/5}^4 \leqslant C\|u\|^4$.

The proof is similar to Proposition 2.1 in [104] by using the fact $E \hookrightarrow L^s(\mathbb{R}^3)$, for any $s \in [2, 6]$ is continuous.

Multiplying $-\Delta\phi_u + \phi_u u^2 = -\omega u^2$ by ϕ_u and integration by parts, we obtain

$$\int_{\mathbb{R}^3} (|\nabla\phi_u|^2 + \phi_u^2 u^2) dx = -\int_{\mathbb{R}^3} \omega\phi_u u^2 dx.$$

By above equality and the definition of $\mathcal{J}$, we obtain a C^1 functional $I : E \to \mathbb{R}$ given by

$$I(u) = \frac{1}{2}\int_{\mathbb{R}^3} (|\nabla u|^2 + V(x)u^2)dx$$
$$-\frac{1}{2}\int_{\mathbb{R}^3} \omega\phi_u u^2 dx - \int_{\mathbb{R}^3} F(x, u)dx - \int_{\mathbb{R}^3} h(x)u dx \qquad (2.39)$$

and its Gateaux derivative is

$$\langle I'(u), v \rangle = \int_{\mathbb{R}^3} (\nabla u \cdot \nabla v + V(x)uv)dx - \int_{\mathbb{R}^3} (2\omega + \phi_u)\phi_u uv dx$$
$$-\int_{\mathbb{R}^3} f(x, u)v dx - \int_{\mathbb{R}^3} h(x)v dx,$$

for all $v \in E$. Here we use the fact that $(\Delta - u^2)^{-1}[\omega u^2] = \phi_u$.

Now we will prove the function I has the mountain pass geometry.

Lemma 2.9   Let $h \in L^2(\mathbb{R}^3)$. Suppose (V), (f_1) and (f_2) hold. Then there exist some positive constants ρ, α, m_0 such that $I(u) \geqslant \alpha$ for all $u \in E$ satisfying $\|u\| = \rho$ and h satisfying $|h|_2 < m_0$.

Proof.   By (f_2), for any $\varepsilon > 0$, there exists $\delta > 0$ such that $|f(x,t)| \leqslant \varepsilon |t|$ for all $x \in \mathbb{R}^3$ and $|t| \leqslant \delta$. By (f_1), we obtain

$$|f(x,t)| \leqslant C_1(|t| + |t|^{p-1}) \leqslant C_1 \left(|t| \frac{t}{\delta}|^{p-2} + |t|^{p-1} \right)$$

$$= C_1 \left(\frac{1}{\delta^{p-2}} + 1 \right) |t|^{p-1}, \quad \text{for } |t| \geqslant \delta, \text{ a.e. } x \in \mathbb{R}^3.$$

Then for all $t \in \mathbb{R}$ and a.e. $x \in \mathbb{R}^3$, we have

$$|f(x,t)| \leqslant \varepsilon |t| + C_1 \left(\frac{1}{\delta^{p-2}} + 1 \right) |t|^{p-1} := \varepsilon |t| + C_\varepsilon |t|^{p-1}$$

and

$$|F(x,t)| \leqslant \frac{\varepsilon}{2}|t|^2 + \frac{C_\varepsilon}{p}|t|^p. \tag{2.40}$$

Therefore, due to (2.40), Proposition 2.6 and the Hölder inequality, we obtain

$$I(u) \geqslant \frac{1}{2}\|u\|^2 - \frac{\varepsilon}{2}\int_{\mathbb{R}^3} |u|^2 dx - \frac{C_\varepsilon}{p}\int_{\mathbb{R}^3} |u|^p dx - |h|_2 |u|_2$$

$$\geqslant \frac{1}{2}\|u\|^2 - \frac{\varepsilon}{2}d_2^2\|u\|^2 - \frac{C_\varepsilon}{p}d_p^p\|u\|^p - d_2|h|_2\|u\|$$

$$= \|u\| \left\{ \left(\frac{1}{2} - \frac{\varepsilon}{2}d_2^2 \right) \|u\| - \frac{C_\varepsilon}{p}d_p^p\|u\|^{p-1} - d_2|h|_2 \right\}.$$

Let $\varepsilon = \frac{1}{2d_2^2}$ and $g(t) = \frac{t}{4} - \frac{C_\varepsilon}{p}d_p^p t^{p-1}$ for $t \geqslant 0$. Because $2 < p < 6$, we can see that there exists a positive constant ρ such that

$$\tilde{m}_0 := g(\rho) = \max_{t \geqslant 0} g(t) > 0.$$

Taking $m_0 := \frac{1}{2d_2^2}\tilde{m}_0$, then it follows that there exists a positive constant α such that $I(u)|_{\|u\|=\rho} \geqslant \alpha$ for all h satisfying $|h|_2 < m_0$. The proof is complete. □

Lemma 2.10   Assume that (V), (f_1)—(f_4) are satisfied, then there exists a function $u_0 \in E$ with $\|u_0\| > \rho$ such that $I(u_0) < 0$, where ρ is given in Lemma 2.9.

Proof.   By (f_3), there exist $L_1 > 0$ large enough and $M_1 > 0$, such that

$$F(x,t) \geqslant M_1|t|^\theta, \quad \text{for } |t| \geqslant L_1. \tag{2.41}$$

By (2.40), we get that

$$|F(x,t)| \leqslant C_3(1+|t|^{p-2})|t|^2, \quad \text{where } C_3 = \max\left\{\frac{\varepsilon}{2}, \frac{C_\varepsilon}{p}\right\}, \qquad (2.42)$$

and then

$$|F(x,t)| \leqslant C_3(1+L_1^{p-2})|t|^2, \quad \text{when } |t| \leqslant L_1. \qquad (2.43)$$

By (2.41) and (2.43), we have

$$F(x,t) \geqslant M_1|t|^\theta - M_2|t|^2, \quad \text{for all } t \in \mathbb{R}, \qquad (2.44)$$

where $M_2 = M_1 L_1^{\theta-2} + C_3(1+L_1^{p-2})$.

Thus, by Proposition 2.6, taking $u \in E, u \neq 0$ and $t > 0$ we have

$$I(tu) = \frac{t^2}{2}\|u\|^2 - \frac{t^2}{2}\int_{\mathbb{R}^3}\omega\phi_{tu}u^2 dx - \int_{\mathbb{R}^3}F(x,tu)dx - t\int_{\mathbb{R}^3}h(x)udx$$

$$\leqslant \frac{t^2}{2}\|u\|^2 + \frac{t^2}{2}\int_{\mathbb{R}^3}\omega^2 u^2 dx - M_1 t^\theta \int_{\mathbb{R}^3}|u|^\theta dx + M_2 t^2 \int_{\mathbb{R}^3}u^2 dx - t\int_{\mathbb{R}^3}h(x)udx,$$

thus $I(tu) \to -\infty$ as $t \to +\infty$ and $\theta > 2$. The lemma is proved by taking $u_0 = t_0 u$ with $t_0 > 0$ large enough and $u \neq 0$. $\qquad \square$

Lemma 2.11 *Under assumptions* (V), (f_1)—(f_4) *and* (H), *any sequence* $\{u_n\} \subset E$ *satisfying*

$$I(u_n) \to c > 0, \quad \langle I'(u_n), u_n \rangle \to 0$$

is bounded in E. *Moreover,* $\{u_n\}$ *has a strongly convergent subsequence in* E.

Proof. To prove the boundedness of $\{u_n\}$, arguing by contradiction, suppose that, up to subsequences, we have $\|u_n\| \to +\infty$ as $n \to +\infty$. Let $v_n = \frac{u_n}{\|u_n\|}$, then $\{v_n\}$ is bounded. Going if necessary to a subsequence, for some $v \in E$, we obtain that

$$v_n \rightharpoonup v \text{ in } E,$$

$$v_n \to v \text{ in } L^s, \quad 2 \leqslant s < 6,$$

$$v_n(x) \to v(x) \quad \text{a.e. in } \mathbb{R}^3.$$

Let $\Lambda = \{x \in \mathbb{R}^3 : v(x) \neq 0\}$. Suppose that meas$(\Lambda) > 0$, then $|u_n(x)| \to +\infty$ as $n \to \infty$ for a.e. $x \in \Lambda$. By (2.38) and (2.44), we obtain

$$\int_{\mathbb{R}^3}\frac{F(x,u_n)}{\|u_n\|^\theta}dx \geqslant M_1\int_{\mathbb{R}^3}|v_n|^\theta dx - M_2\frac{|u_n|^2}{\|u_n\|^\theta}$$

$$\geqslant M_1 \int_{\mathbb{R}^3} |v_n|^\theta dx - \frac{M_2 d_2^2}{\|u_n\|^{\theta-2}}$$

$$\to M_1 \int_\Lambda |v|^\theta dx > 0 \quad \text{as } n \to \infty. \tag{2.45}$$

By Proposition 2.6, as from (2.42) and (2.44) it follows that $2 < \theta \leqslant p < 6$, so we can obtain that

$$\left| \int_{\mathbb{R}^3} \frac{\omega \phi_{u_n} u_n^2}{\|u_n\|^\theta} dx \right| \leqslant \frac{\omega^2 |u_n|_2^2}{\|u_n\|^\theta} \leqslant \frac{\omega^2 d_2^2}{\|u_n\|^{\theta-2}} \to 0 \quad \text{as } n \to \infty.$$

Since $h \in L^2(\mathbb{R}^3)$, we can obtain that

$$\left| \int_{\mathbb{R}^3} \frac{h(x) u_n}{\|u_n\|^\theta} dx \right| \leqslant \frac{|h|_2 |u_n|_2}{\|u_n\|^\theta} \leqslant \frac{|h|_2 d_2}{\|u_n\|^{\theta-1}} \to 0 \quad \text{as } n \to \infty.$$

By the definition of I, we have

$$0 = \lim_{n \to +\infty} \frac{I(u_n)}{\|u_n\|^\theta}$$

$$= \lim_{n \to +\infty} \left[\frac{1}{2\|u_n\|^{\theta-2}} - \int_{\mathbb{R}^3} \frac{\omega \phi_{u_n} u_n^2}{2\|u_n\|^\theta} dx - \int_{\mathbb{R}^3} \frac{F(x, u_n)}{\|u_n\|^\theta} dx - \int_{\mathbb{R}^3} \frac{h(x) u_n}{\|u_n\|^\theta} dx \right]$$

$$< 0,$$

which is a contradiction. Therefore, meas$(\Lambda) = 0$, which implies $v(x) = 0$ for almost everywhere $x \in \mathbb{R}^3$. By (f_1) and (2.42), we have for all $x \in \mathbb{R}^3$ and $|t| \leqslant r_0$,

$$|f(x, t)t - \mu F(x, t)| \leqslant |f(x, t)t| + \mu |F(x, t)|$$

$$\leqslant C_1(|t|^2 + |t|^p) + \mu C_3(1 + |t|^{p-2})t^2 \leqslant C_6(1 + |t|^{p-2})t^2$$

$$\leqslant C_6(1 + r_0^{p-2})t^2,$$

where $C_6 := 2\max\{C_1, \mu C_3\}$. Together with (f_4), we obtain

$$f(x, t)t - \mu F(x, t) \geqslant -C_7 t^2, \quad \text{for all } (x, t) \in \mathbb{R}^3 \times \mathbb{R}. \tag{2.46}$$

By $h \in L^2(\mathbb{R}^3)$, we can also obtain the following

$$\left| \int_{\mathbb{R}^3} \frac{h(x) u_n}{\|u_n\|^2} dx \right| \leqslant \frac{|h|_2 |u_n|_2}{\|u_n\|^2} \leqslant \frac{|h|_2 d_2}{\|u_n\|} \to 0 \quad \text{as } n \to \infty. \tag{2.47}$$

Case (i) $2 < \mu < 4$. By (2.46), (2.47), Proposition 2.6 and $2 < \mu < 4$, we have

$$\frac{\mu I(u_n) - \langle I'(u_n), u_n \rangle}{\|u_n\|^2}$$

$$= \left(\frac{\mu}{2} - 1\right) + \int_{\mathbb{R}^3} \frac{f(x, u_n)u_n - \mu F(x, u_n)}{\|u_n\|^2} dx + \left(2 - \frac{\mu}{2}\right) \int_{\mathbb{R}^3} \frac{\omega \phi_{u_n} u_n^2}{\|u_n\|^2} dx$$

$$+ \int_{\mathbb{R}^3} \frac{\phi_{u_n}^2 u_n^2}{\|u_n\|^2} dx + (1 - \mu) \int_{\mathbb{R}^3} \frac{h(x)u_n}{\|u_n\|^2} dx$$

$$\geqslant \left(\frac{\mu}{2} - 1\right) - C_7 |v_n|_2^2 + \left(2 - \frac{\mu}{2}\right) \int_{\mathbb{R}^3} \frac{\omega \phi_{u_n} u_n^2}{\|u_n\|^2} dx + (1 - \mu) \int_{\mathbb{R}^3} \frac{h(x)u_n}{\|u_n\|^2} dx$$

$$\geqslant \left(\frac{\mu}{2} - 1\right) - C_7 |v_n|_2^2 - \left(2 - \frac{\mu}{2}\right) \omega^2 |v_n|_2^2 + (1 - \mu) \int_{\mathbb{R}^3} \frac{h(x)u_n}{\|u_n\|^2} dx$$

$$\to \frac{\mu}{2} - 1 \quad \text{as } n \to \infty.$$

Then we get $0 \geqslant \dfrac{1}{2} - \dfrac{1}{\mu}$, which contradicts with $\mu > 2$.

Case (ii) $\mu \geqslant 4$. By (2.46), (2.47), Proposition 2.6 and $\mu \geqslant 4$, we have

$$\frac{\mu I(u_n) - \langle I'(u_n), u_n \rangle}{\|u_n\|^2}$$

$$\geqslant \left(\frac{\mu}{2} - 1\right) - C_7 |v_n|_2^2 + \left(2 - \frac{\mu}{2}\right) \int_{\mathbb{R}^3} \frac{\omega \phi_{u_n} u_n^2}{\|u_n\|^2} dx + (1 - \mu) \int_{\mathbb{R}^3} \frac{h(x)u_n}{\|u_n\|^2} dx$$

$$\geqslant \left(\frac{\mu}{2} - 1\right) - C_7 |v_n|_2^2 + (1 - \mu) \int_{\mathbb{R}^3} \frac{h(x)u_n}{\|u_n\|^2} dx$$

$$\to \frac{\mu}{2} - 1 \quad \text{as } n \to \infty.$$

Then we have $0 \geqslant \dfrac{1}{2} - \dfrac{1}{\mu}$, which contradicts with $\mu \geqslant 4$. Therefore $\{u_n\}$ is a bounded in E.

Now we shall prove $\{u_n\}$ contains a convergent subsequence. Without loss of generality, passing to a subsequence if necessary, there exists $u \in E$ such that $u_n \rightharpoonup u$ in E. By using the embedding $E \hookrightarrow L^s(\mathbb{R}^3)$ are compact for any $s \in [2, 6)$, $u_n \to u$ in $L^s(\mathbb{R}^3)$ for $2 \leqslant s < 6$ and $u_n(x) \to u(x)$ a.e. $x \in \mathbb{R}^3$. So by (2.40) and the Hölder inequality, we have

$$\int_{\mathbb{R}^3} (f(x, u_n) - f(x, u))(u_n - u) dx \to 0 \quad \text{as } n \to +\infty.$$

By an easy computing, we can get that

$$\langle I'(u_n) - I'(u), u_n - u \rangle \to 0 \quad \text{as } n \to \infty$$

and

$$\int_{\mathbb{R}^3} [(2\omega + \phi_{u_n})\phi_{u_n} u_n - (2\omega + \phi_u)\phi_u u](u_n - u) dx$$

$$= 2\omega \int_{\mathbb{R}^3} (\phi_{u_n} u_n - \phi_u u)(u_n - u) dx + \int_{\mathbb{R}^3} (\phi_{u_n}^2 u_n - \phi_u^2 u)(u_n - u) dx \to 0$$

as $n \to +\infty$. Indeed, by the Hölder inequality, the Sobolev inequality and Proposition 2.6, we can get

$$\left| \int_{\mathbb{R}^3} (\phi_{u_n} - \phi_u)(u_n - u) u_n dx \right| \leqslant |(\phi_{u_n} - \phi_u)(u_n - u)|_2 |u_n|_2$$

$$\leqslant |\phi_{u_n} - \phi_u|_6 |u_n - u|_3 |u_n|_2$$

$$\leqslant C \|\phi_{u_n} - \phi_u\|_D |u_n - u|_3 |u_n|_2,$$

where C is a positive constant. Since $u_n \to u$ in $L^s(\mathbb{R}^3)$ for $2 \leqslant s < 6$, we get

$$\left| \int_{\mathbb{R}^3} (\phi_{u_n} - \phi_u)(u_n - u) u_n dx \right| \to 0 \quad \text{as } n \to +\infty$$

and

$$\left| \int_{\mathbb{R}^3} \phi_u(u_n - u)(u_n - u) dx \right| \leqslant |\phi_u|_6 |u_n - u|_3 |u_n - u|_2 \to 0 \quad \text{as } n \to +\infty.$$

Thus we obtain

$$\int_{\mathbb{R}^3} (\phi_{u_n} u_n - \phi_u u)(u_n - u) dx$$

$$= \int_{\mathbb{R}^3} (\phi_{u_n} - \phi_u)(u_n - u) u_n dx + \int_{\mathbb{R}^3} \phi_u(u_n - u)(u_n - u) dx \to 0$$

as $n \to +\infty$.

In view of that the sequence $\{\phi_{u_n}^2 u_n\}$ is bounded in $L^{3/2}(\mathbb{R}^3)$, since

$$|\phi_{u_n}^2 u_n|_{3/2} \leqslant |\phi_{u_n}|_6^2 |u_n|_3,$$

so

$$\left| \int_{\mathbb{R}^3} (\phi_{u_n}^2 u_n - \phi_u^2 u)(u_n - u) dx \right| \leqslant |\phi_{u_n}^2 u_n - \phi_u^2 u|_{3/2} |u_n - u|_3$$

$$\leqslant (|\phi_{u_n}^2 u_n|_{3/2} + |\phi_u^2 u|_{3/2}) |u_n - u|_3 \to 0$$

as $n \to +\infty$. Thus, we get

$$\|u_n - u\|^2$$

$$= \langle I'(u_n) - I'(u), u_n - u \rangle - \int_{\mathbb{R}^3} [(2\omega + \phi_{u_n})\phi_{u_n} u_n - (2\omega + \phi_u)\phi_u u](u_n - u) dx$$

$$+ \int_{\mathbb{R}^3} (f(x, u_n) - f(x, u))(u_n - u) dx \to 0 \quad \text{as } n \to +\infty.$$

Therefore we get $\|u_n - u\| \to 0$ in E as $n \to \infty$. The proof is complete. $\quad\square$

2.2.3 Proofs of main results

Now, we are ready to prove our main result.

Proof of Theorem 2.4   Firstly, we prove that there exists a function $u_0 \in E$ such that $I'(u_0) = 0$ and $I(u_0) < 0$.

Since $h \in L^2(\mathbb{R}^3)$, $h \geqslant 0$ and $h \not\equiv 0$, we can choose a function $\varphi \in E$ such that

$$\int_{\mathbb{R}^3} h(x)\varphi(x)dx > 0.$$

Hence, by Proposition 2.6, $\theta > 2$ and (2.44), we obtain that

$$I(t\varphi) \leqslant \frac{t^2}{2}\|\varphi\|^2 + \frac{t^2}{2}\int_{\mathbb{R}^3} \omega^2\varphi^2 dx - M_1 t^\theta|\varphi|_\theta^\theta + M_2 t^2|\varphi|_2^2 - t\int_{\mathbb{R}^3} h(x)\varphi dx < 0,$$

for $t > 0$ small enough. Thus, we obtain

$$c_0 = \inf\{I(u) : u \in \bar{B}_\rho\} < 0,$$

where $\rho > 0$ is given by Lemma 2.9, $B_\rho = \{u \in E : \|u\| < \rho\}$. By the Ekeland's Variational Principle, there exists a sequence $\{u_n\} \subset \bar{B}_\rho$ such that

$$c_0 \leqslant I(u_n) < c_0 + \frac{1}{n}$$

and

$$I(v) \geqslant I(u_n) - \frac{1}{n}\|v - u_n\|,$$

for all $v \in \bar{B}_\rho$. Then by a standard procedure, we can prove that $\{u_n\}$ is a bounded (PS) sequence of I. Hence, by Lemma 2.11 we know that there exists a function $u_0 \in E$ such that $I'(u_0) = 0$ and $I(u_0) = c_0 < 0$.

Secondly, we prove that there exists a function $\tilde{u}_0 \in E$ such that $I'(\tilde{u}_0) = 0$ and $I(\tilde{u}_0) > 0$.

By Lemma 2.9, Lemma 2.10 and the Mountain Pass theorem, there is a sequence $\{u_n\} \subset E$ such that

$$I(u_n) \to \tilde{c}_0 > 0, \quad \text{and} \quad I'(u_n) \to 0.$$

In view of Lemma 2.11, we know that $\{u_n\}$ has a strongly convergent subsequence (still denoted by $\{u_n\}$) in E. So there exists a function $\tilde{u}_0 \in E$ such that $\{u_n\} \to \tilde{u}_0$ as $n \to \infty$ and $I'(\tilde{u}_0) = 0$ and $I(\tilde{u}_0) > 0$. The proof is complete. □

2.3   Proofs of results

In this part, we consider the following nonlinear Klein-Gordon-Maxwell system

$$(KGM1) \begin{cases} -\Delta u + V(x)u - (2\omega + \phi)\phi u = f(x,u), & x \in \mathbb{R}^3, \\ \Delta \phi = (\omega + \phi)u^2, & x \in \mathbb{R}^3, \end{cases}$$

where $\omega > 0$ is a constant. We are interested in the existence and multiplicity solutions of system $(KGM1)$ when the nonlinearity $f(x,u)$ is either asymptotically linear in u at infinity or the primitive of $f(x,u)$ is of 4-superlinear growth at infinity.

We first consider system $(KGM1)$ with the superlinear case, and hence make the following assumptions:

(V) $V \in C(\mathbb{R}^3, \mathbb{R})$ is bounded below and, for every $C > 0$, meas$\{x \in \mathbb{R}^3 : V(x) \leqslant C\} < +\infty$, where meas denotes the Lebesgue measures;

(f_1) $f \in C(\mathbb{R}^3 \times \mathbb{R}, \mathbb{R})$ and there exist $C > 0$ and $p \in (4,6)$ such that

$$|f(x,t)| \leqslant C(1 + |t|^{p-1});$$

(f_2) $f(x,t) = o(t)$ uniformly in x as $t \to 0$;

(f_3) $\dfrac{F(x,t)}{t^4} \to +\infty$ uniformly in x as $|t| \to +\infty$;

(f_4) There exists a positive constant b such that

$$\mathcal{F}(x,t) := \frac{1}{4}f(x,t)t - F(x,t) \geqslant -bt^2.$$

Remark 2.7   We emphasize that unlike all previous results about system $(KGM1)$, see e.g. [73, 104, 118], we have not assume that the potential V is positive. This means that we allow the potential V be sign changing.

Remark 2.8   It is well known that the condition (AR) is widely used in the studies of elliptic problem by variational methods. The condition (AR) is used not only to prove that the Euler-Lagrange function associated has a mountain pass geometry, but also to guarantee that the Palais-Smale sequences, or Cerami sequences are bounded. Obviously, we can observe that the condition (AR) implies the following condition:

(A_1) There exist $\theta > 4$ and $C_1, C_2 > 0$ such that $F(x,t) \geqslant C_1|t|^\theta - C_2$, for every t sufficiently large.

Moreover, the condition (A_1) implies our condition (f_3).

Another widely employed condition is the following condition, which is first introduced by Jeanjean[111].

(Je) There exist $\theta \geqslant 1$ such that $\theta \mathcal{F}(x,t) \geqslant \mathcal{F}(x,st)$ for all $s \in [0,1]$ and $t \in \mathbb{R}$, where $\mathcal{F}(x,t)$ is given in (f_4).

We can observe that when $s = 0$, then $\mathcal{F}(x,t) \geqslant 0$, but for our condition (f_4), $\mathcal{F}(x,t)$ may assume negative values. Therefore, it is interesting to consider 4-superlinear problems under the conditions (f_3) and (f_4).

The condition (f_4) is motivated by Alves, Soares and Souto[3]. Supposing in addition

$$\alpha = \inf_{x \in \mathbb{R}^3} V(x) > 0 \tag{2.48}$$

and $b \in [0, \alpha)$, they proved that all Cerami sequences are bounded. In 2015, Chen and Liu[58] also used conditions (f_3) and (f_4) to show the existence of infinitely many solutions for Schrödinger-Maxwell systems. In our case, however, many technical difficulties arise to the presence of a nonlocal term ϕ, which is not homogeneous as it is in the Schrödinger-Maxwell systems. Hence, a more careful analysis of the interaction between the couple (u, ϕ) is required.

By (V), we know that V is bounded from below, hence we may choose $V_0 > 0$ such that

$$\tilde{V}(x) := V(x) + V_0 > 1, \quad \forall x \in \mathbb{R}^3,$$

and define a new Hilbert space

$$E := \left\{ u \in H^1(\mathbb{R}^3) : \int_{\mathbb{R}^3} V(x)u^2 dx < \infty \right\}$$

with the inner product

$$\langle u, v \rangle = \int_{\mathbb{R}^3} \left(\nabla u \cdot \nabla v + \tilde{V}(x)uv \right) dx$$

and the norm $\|u\| = \langle u, u \rangle^{1/2}$. Obviously, the embedding $E \hookrightarrow L^s(\mathbb{R}^3)$ is continuous, for any $s \in [2, 2^*]$. The norm on $L^s = L^s(\mathbb{R}^3)$ with $1 < s < \infty$ is given by

$$|u|_s^s = \int_{\mathbb{R}^3} |u|^s dx.$$

Consequently, for each $s \in [2, 6]$, there exists a constant $d_s > 0$ such that

$$|u|_s \leqslant d_s \|u\|, \quad \forall u \in E. \tag{2.49}$$

Furthermore, we have that under the condition (V), the embedding $E \hookrightarrow L^s(\mathbb{R}^3)$ is compact for any $s \in [2, 6)$ (see [18]). By the compact embedding $E \hookrightarrow L^2(\mathbb{R}^3)$ and the standard elliptic theory[224], it is easy to see that the eigenvalue problem

$$-\Delta u + V(x)u = \lambda u, \quad u \in E \tag{2.50}$$

possesses a complete sequence of eigenvalues

$$-\infty < \lambda_1 \leqslant \lambda_2 \leqslant \lambda_3 \leqslant \cdots, \quad \lambda_j \to +\infty.$$

Each λ_j has finite multiplicity and $|\lambda_j|_2 = 1$. Denote e_j be the eigenfunction of λ_j. E^- is spanned by the eigenfunctions corresponding to negative eigenvalues. Note that the negative space E^- of the quadratic part of I is nontrivial if and only if some λ_j is negative.

Now we can state our first result.

Theorem 2.5 *Suppose (V), (f_1)—(f_4) are satisfied, and f is odd in t. If 0 is not an eigenvalue of (2.50), then $(KGM1)$ has a sequence of solutions $(u_n, \phi_n) \in E \times D^{1,2}(\mathbb{R}^3)$ such that the energy $\mathcal{J}(u_n, \phi_n) \to +\infty$.*

Remark 2.9 If u is a critical point of I, then $I(u) = \mathcal{J}(u, \phi_u)$ (see (2.51)). Therefore, in order to prove Theorem 1.1, we only need to find a sequence of critical points $\{u_n\}$ of I such that $I(u_n) \to +\infty$.

Remark 2.10 Theorem 2.5 improves the recent results in [104], the author assumed in addition (2.48), and (AR) or (Je). When V is positive, the quadratic part of the functional I (see (2.51)) is positively definite, and I has a mountain pass geometry. Therefore, the mountain pass lemma[154] can be applied. In our case, the quadratic part may possesses a nontrivial negative space E^-, so I no longer possesses the mountain pass geometry. Therefore the methods in [81,104] cannot be applied. To obtain our result, we adopt a technique developed in [58].

Next, we deal with the system $(KGM1)$ when the nonlinearity $f(x, t)$ is asymptotically linear at infinity in the second variable t. Set

$$\Omega = \inf_{u \in H^1(\mathbb{R}^3) \backslash \{0\}} \frac{\displaystyle\int_{\mathbb{R}^3} (|\nabla u|^2 + V(x)u^2) dx}{\displaystyle\int_{\mathbb{R}^3} u^2 dx},$$

i.e. Ω is the infimum of the spectrum of the Schrödinger operator $-\Delta + V$.

We make the following assumptions:

(H_1) $V(x) \in C(\mathbb{R}^3, \mathbb{R})$ satisfies $V(x) \geqslant D_0 > 0$ for all $x \in \mathbb{R}^3$;

(H_2) $\displaystyle\lim_{|x| \to +\infty} V(x) = V_\infty \in (0, +\infty)$;

(H_3) $f(x, t) \in C(\mathbb{R}^3 \times \mathbb{R}, \mathbb{R})$ and $\displaystyle\lim_{t \to 0} \frac{f(x, t)}{t} = 0$ uniformly in x;

(H_4) There exists $A \in (\Omega, V_\infty)$ such that $\displaystyle\lim_{t \to +\infty} \frac{f(x, t)}{t} = A$ uniformly in x and

$0 \leqslant \dfrac{f(x, t)}{t} \leqslant A$ for all $t \neq 0$.

Theorem 2.6 *Assume (H_1)—(H_4) hold, then there exists a constant $\omega^* > 0$ such that $(KGM1)$ has a positive solution for any $\omega \in (0, \omega^*)$.*

Remark 2.11 To our best knowledge, it seems that there are few results for system $(KGM1)$ in this case: the nonlinear term $f(x,t)$ is asymptotically linear at infinity with t. In order to get our results, we have to solve some difficulties. The first difficult is how to prove the variational function satisfies the assumptions of the Mountain Pass theorem. The second difficult is how to check the (PS) condition, i.e., how to verify the boundedness and compactness of a (PS) sequence. To overcome these difficulties, we use some techniques used in [152], [155] and [185]. However, it seems difficult to use this method to the case $f(x,t)$ is superlinear in t at infinity.

2.3.1   The proof of Theorem 2.5

By [15], we know that the signs of ω is not relevant for the existence of solutions, so we can assume that $\omega > 0$. Evidently, the properties of ϕ_u plays an important role in the study of $\mathcal{J}$. So we need the following technical results.

Proposition 2.7 *For any $u \in H^1(\mathbb{R}^3)$, there exists a unique $\phi = \phi_u \in D^{1,2}(\mathbb{R}^3)$ which satisfies*

$$\Delta\phi = (\phi + \omega)u^2 \quad in \quad \mathbb{R}^3.$$

Moreover, the map $\Phi : u \in H^1(\mathbb{R}^3) \mapsto \phi_u \in D^{1,2}(\mathbb{R}^3)$ is continuously differentiable, and

(i) $-\omega \leqslant \phi_u \leqslant 0$ *on the set* $\{x \in \mathbb{R}^3 | u(x) \neq 0\}$;

(ii) $\|\phi_u\|_D^2 \leqslant C\|u\|^2$ *and* $\displaystyle\int_{\mathbb{R}^3} \phi_u u^2 dx \leqslant C|u|_{12/5}^4 \leqslant C\|u\|^4$.

The proof is similar to Proposition 2.1 in [104] by using the fact $E \hookrightarrow L^s(\mathbb{R}^3)$, for any $s \in [2,6]$ is continuous.

By Proposition 2.7, we can consider the functional $I : H^1(\mathbb{R}^3) \mapsto \mathbb{R}$ defined by $I(u) = \mathcal{J}(u, \phi_u)$.

Multiplying $-\Delta\phi_u + \phi_u u^2 = -\omega u^2$ by ϕ_u and integration by parts, we obtain

$$\int_{\mathbb{R}^3} (|\nabla\phi_u|^2 + \phi_u^2 u^2) dx = -\int_{\mathbb{R}^3} \omega\phi_u u^2 dx.$$

By the above equality and the definition of $\mathcal{J}$, we obtain a C^1 function $I : H^1(\mathbb{R}^3) \to \mathbb{R}$ given by

$$I(u) = \frac{1}{2} \int_{\mathbb{R}^3} (|\nabla u|^2 + V(x)u^2) dx - \frac{1}{2} \int_{\mathbb{R}^3} \omega\phi_u u^2 dx - \int_{\mathbb{R}^3} F(x,u) dx, \qquad (2.51)$$

and its Gateaux derivative is

$$\langle I'(u), v \rangle = \int_{\mathbb{R}^3} (\nabla u \cdot \nabla v + V(x)uv) dx - \int_{\mathbb{R}^3} (2\omega + \phi_u)\phi_u uv dx - \int_{\mathbb{R}^3} f(x,u)v dx,$$

for all $v \in H^1(\mathbb{R}^3)$. Here we use the fact that $(\Delta - u^2)^{-1}[wu^2] = \phi_u$.

If $\lambda_1 > 0$, we can easy to prove that I has the mountain pass geometry, so we omit this case. Since 0 is not an eigenvalue of (2.50), we assume that there exists $l \geqslant 1$ such that $0 \in (\lambda_l, \lambda_{l+1})$. Set

$$E^- = \text{span}\{e_1, \cdots, e_l\}, \quad E^+ = (E^-)^{\perp}. \tag{2.52}$$

Then E^- and E^+ are the negative space and positive space of the quadratic form

$$N(u) = \frac{1}{2} \int_{\mathbb{R}^3} (|\nabla u|^2 + V(x)u^2)dx$$

respectively, and $\dim E^- < \infty$. Moreover, there is a positive constant B such that

$$\pm N(u) \geqslant B\|u\|^2, \quad u \in E^{\pm}. \tag{2.53}$$

In order to prove Theorem 2.5, we shall use the fountain theorem of Bartsch[18], see also Theorem 3.6 in [200]. For $k = 1, 2, \cdots$, set

$$Y_k = \text{span}\{e_1, \cdots, e_k\}, \quad Z_k = \overline{\text{span}\{e_{k+1}, \cdots\}}. \tag{2.54}$$

Proposition 2.8(Fountain Theorem)   *Assume that the even function $I \in C^1(E, \mathbb{R})$ satisfies the (PS) condition. If there is a positive constant K such that for any $k \geqslant K$ there exist $\rho_k > r_k > 0$ such that*
(i) $a_k = \max\limits_{u \in Y_k, \|u\| = \rho_k} I(u) \leqslant 0$;
(ii) $b_k = \inf\limits_{u \in Z_k, \|u\| = r_k} I(u) \to +\infty$ *as $k \to +\infty$,*
then I has a sequence of critical points $\{u_k\}$ such that $I(u_k) \to +\infty$.

In order to study the functional I, we write the function I in a form in which the quadratic part is $\|u\|^2$. Let $g(x, t) = f(x, t) + V_0 t$. Then, by an computation, we obtain that

$$G(x, t) := \int_0^t g(x, s)ds \leqslant \frac{t}{4}g(x, t) + \frac{\tilde{V}_0}{4}t^2, \quad \tilde{V}_0 := 4b + V_0 > 0. \tag{2.55}$$

By (f_3), we have

$$\lim_{|t| \to \infty} \frac{g(x, t)t}{t^4} = +\infty. \tag{2.56}$$

Furthermore, by (f_2) we obtain

$$\lim_{|t| \to 0} \frac{g(x, t)t}{t^4} = \lim_{|t| \to 0} \left(\frac{t^2}{t^4} \cdot \frac{f(x, t)t + V_0 t^2}{t^2}\right) = +\infty.$$

Hence there exists $M > 0$ such that

$$g(x,t)t \geqslant -Mt^4, \quad \forall t \in \mathbb{R}. \tag{2.57}$$

With the modified nonlinearity g, the function $I : E \to \mathbb{R}$ can be rewritten in the following

$$I(u) = \frac{1}{2}\|u\|^2 - \frac{\omega}{2}\int_{\mathbb{R}^3} \phi_u u^2 dx - \int_{\mathbb{R}^3} G(x,u)dx \tag{2.58}$$

with the derivative

$$\langle I'(u), v\rangle = \langle u, v\rangle - \int_{\mathbb{R}^3}(2\omega + \phi_u)\phi_u uvdx - \int_{\mathbb{R}^3} g(x,u)vdx.$$

Lemma 2.12 *Suppose* (V), (f_1)—(f_4) *are satisfied, then the function I satisfies the (PS) condition.*

Proof. It follows from $\frac{1}{4}tf(x,t) - F(x,t) \geqslant -bt^2$ that the condition (f_3) is equivalent to

$$\lim_{|t|\to+\infty} \frac{G(x,t)}{t^4} = +\infty.$$

Let $\{u_n\}$ be a (PS) sequence, i.e.,

$$\sup_n |I(u_n)| < \infty, \quad I'(u_n) \to 0.$$

We first prove that $\{u_n\}$ is bounded in E. Arguing by contradiction, suppose that $\{u_n\}$ is unbounded, passing to a subsequence, by (2.55), we obtian

$$4\sup_n I(u_n) + \|u_n\| \geqslant 4I(u_n) - \langle I'(u_n), u_n\rangle$$

$$= \|u_n\|^2 + \int_{\mathbb{R}^3} \phi_{u_n}^2 u_n^2 dx + \int_{\mathbb{R}^3}(g(x,u_n)u_n - 4G(x,u_n))dx$$

$$\geqslant \|u_n\|^2 - \tilde{V}_0 \int_{\mathbb{R}^3} u_n^2 dx. \tag{2.59}$$

Let $v_n = \dfrac{u_n}{\|u_n\|}$. Then, going if necessary to a subsequence, by the compact embedding $E \hookrightarrow L^2(\mathbb{R}^3)$ we may assume that

$$v_n \rightharpoonup v_0 \text{ in } E;$$

$$v_n \to v_0 \text{ in } L^2(\mathbb{R}^3);$$

$$v_n(x) \to v_0(x) \text{ a.e. in } \mathbb{R}^3.$$

Dividing both sides of (2.59) by $\|u_n\|^2$, we have

$$\tilde{V}_0 \int_{\mathbb{R}^3} v_0^2 dx \geqslant 1 \quad \text{as } n \to \infty.$$

Consequently, we have that $v_0 \neq 0$.

By (2.49) and (2.57), we have

$$\int_{v_0=0} \frac{g(x, u_n)u_n}{\|u_n\|^4} dx = \int_{v_0=0} \frac{g(x, u_n)u_n}{u_n^4} v_n^4 dx$$

$$\geqslant -M \int_{v_0=0} v_n^4 dx \geqslant -M \int_{\mathbb{R}^3} v_n^4 dx$$

$$= -M|v_n|_4^4 \geqslant -Md_4^4 > -\infty. \tag{2.60}$$

For $x \in \{x \in \mathbb{R}^3 | v_0 \neq 0\}$, we have $|u_n(x)| \to +\infty$ as $n \to \infty$. By (2.56) we have

$$\frac{g(x, u_n(x))u_n(x)}{\|u_n\|^4} = \frac{g(x, u_n(x))u_n(x)}{u_n^4(x)} v_n^4(x) \to +\infty. \tag{2.61}$$

Hence, by (2.60) and (2.61) and Fatou's lemma we obtain

$$\int_{\mathbb{R}^3} \frac{g(x, u_n)u_n}{\|u_n\|^4} dx \geqslant \int_{v_0 \neq 0} \frac{g(x, u_n)u_n}{u_n^4} v_n^4(x) dx - Md_4^4 \to +\infty. \tag{2.62}$$

Hence, we obtain that

$$\int_{\mathbb{R}^3} \frac{G(x, u_n)}{\|u_n\|^4} dx \to +\infty. \tag{2.63}$$

Since $\{u_n\}$ is a (PS) sequence, using Proposition 2.7 and (2.62), for n large enough, we obtain

$$c\omega + 1 \geqslant \frac{1}{\|u_n\|^4} \left(\frac{1}{2}\|u_n\|^2 - \frac{\omega}{2} \int_{\mathbb{R}^3} \phi_{u_n} u_n^2 dx - I(u_n) \right)$$

$$= \int_{\mathbb{R}^3} \frac{G(x, u_n)}{\|u_n\|^4} dx \to +\infty, \tag{2.64}$$

which is a contradict.

Now we have proved that $\{u_n\}$ is bounded in E. By a similar argument in [54], the compact embedding $E \hookrightarrow L^2(\mathbb{R}^3)$ and

$$E = \overline{\bigcup_{n \in \mathbb{N}} E_n},$$

we can show that $\{u_n\}$ has a subsequence converging to a critical point of I.   □

Lemma 2.13   *Let X be a finite dimensional subspace of E, then I is anti-coercive on X, i.e.*

$$I(u) \to -\infty, \quad as \ \|u\| \to \infty, \ u \in X.$$

Proof. If it is not true, we can choose a sequence $\{u_n\} \subset X$ and ξ is a real number such that

$$\|u_n\| \to \infty, \quad I(u_n) \geqslant \xi. \tag{2.65}$$

Let $v_n = \dfrac{u_n}{\|u_n\|}$. Since $\dim X < \infty$, going if necessary to a subsequence, we have

$$\|v_n - v_0\| \to 0, \quad v_n(x) \to v_0(x) \text{ a.e. in } \mathbb{R}^3$$

for every $v_0 \in X$, with $\|v_0\| = 1$. Since $v_0 \neq 0$, similar to (2.63) we obtain that

$$\int_{\mathbb{R}^3} \frac{G(x, u_n)}{\|u_n\|^4} dx \to +\infty.$$

And arguing similar to (2.64), it follows from $\sup_n |I(u_n)| < \infty$ that

$$I(u_n) = \|u_n\|^4 \left(\frac{1}{2\|u_n\|^2} - \frac{\omega}{2\|u_n\|^4} \int_{\mathbb{R}^3} \phi_{u_n} u_n^2 dx - \int_{\mathbb{R}^3} \frac{G(x, u_n)}{\|u_n\|^4} dx \right) \to -\infty,$$

which is contradict with $I(u_n) \geqslant \xi$. The proof is complete.   □

Now, we are ready to prove our main result.

Proof of Theorem 2.5   We will find a sequence of critical points $\{u_n\}$ of I such that $I(u_n) \to +\infty$.

Since $f(x, t)$ is odd in t, I is an even function. It follows from Lemma 2.12 that I satisfies (PS) condition. So it suffices to verify (i) and (ii) of Proposition 2.8.

(i) Since $\dim Y_k < \infty$, by Lemma 2.13, we get the conclusion of (i).

(ii) By $(f_1), (f_2)$, we have

$$|f(x, t)| \leqslant \epsilon|t| + C_\epsilon|t|^{p-1}, \quad |F(x, t)| \leqslant \frac{\epsilon}{2}t^2 + \frac{C_\epsilon}{p}|t|^p,$$

where $\epsilon > 0$ is very small. Then we have

$$|F(x, t)| \leqslant \frac{B}{2d_2^2}t^2 + \frac{CB}{p}|t|^p, \tag{2.66}$$

where B is defined in (2.53). We assume that $0 \in [\lambda_l, \lambda_{l+1})$. Then if $k > l$, we have that $Z_k \subset E^+$, where E^+ is defined in (2.52). Now we have

$$N(u) \geqslant B\|u\|^2, \quad u \in Z_k, \tag{2.67}$$

and, as proof of Lemma 3.8 in [200],

$$\beta_p(k) = \sup_{u \in Z_k, \|u\|=1} |u|_p \to 0 \quad \text{as } k \to \infty. \tag{2.68}$$

Let $r_k = (Cp\beta_p(k))^{1/(2-p)}$, where C is chosen as in (2.66). For $u \in Z_k \subset E^+$ with $\|u\| = r_k$, $\phi_u \leqslant 0$, by (2.67) we deduce that

$$I(u) = N(u) - \frac{1}{2}\omega \int_{\mathbb{R}^3} \phi_u u^2 dx - \int_{\mathbb{R}^3} F(x, u) dx$$

$$\geqslant B\|u\|^2 - \frac{D}{2d_2^2}|u|_2^2 - CB|u|_p^p$$

$$\geqslant B\left(\frac{1}{2}\|u\|^2 - C\beta_p^p\|u\|^p\right)$$

$$= B\left(\frac{1}{2} - \frac{1}{p}\right)(Cp\beta_p^p)^{2/(2-p)},$$

where $\beta_p^p := (\beta_p(k))^p$. Since $\beta_p(k) \to 0$ and $p > 2$, it follows that

$$b_k = \inf_{u \in Z_k, \|u\|=r_k} I(u) \to +\infty.$$

We get the conclusion of (ii). The proof is complete. $\qquad\qquad\qquad\square$

2.3.2   The proof of Theorem 2.6

Under the condition (H_1), we define a new Hilbert space

$$F := \left\{ u \in H^1(\mathbb{R}^3) : \int_{\mathbb{R}^3} (|\nabla u|^2 + V(x)u^2) dx < \infty \right\}$$

with the inner product

$$(u, v)_F = \int_{\mathbb{R}^3} (\nabla u \cdot \nabla v + V(x) uv) \, dx$$

and the norm $\|u\|_F = (u, u)_F^{1/2}$, which is equivalent to the usual Sobolev norm on $H^1(\mathbb{R}^3)$. Obviously, the embedding $F \hookrightarrow L^s(\mathbb{R}^3)$ is continuous, for any $s \in [2, 2^*]$. Consequently, for each $s \in [2, 6]$, there exists a constant $v_s > 0$ such that

$$|u|_s \leqslant v_s\|u\|_F, \quad \forall u \in F. \tag{2.69}$$

Furthermore, we know that under assumption (H_1), the embedding $F \hookrightarrow L^s(\mathbb{R}^3)$ is compact for any $s \in [2, 2^*)$(see [224]).

By Proposition 2.7, we can consider the functional I_ω on $(F, \| \cdot \|_F)$:

$$I_\omega(u) = \frac{1}{2} \int_{\mathbb{R}^3} (|\nabla u|^2 + V(x)u^2 - \omega\phi_u u^2)dx - \int_{\mathbb{R}^3} F(x, u)dx,$$

with its Gateaux derivative is

$$\langle I'_\omega(u), v \rangle = \int_{\mathbb{R}^3} [\nabla u \nabla v + V(x)uv - (2\omega + \phi_u)\phi_u uv - f(x, u)v]dx.$$

Lemma 2.14 *Suppose (H_1)—(H_4) hold. Then there exist some positive constants ρ_0, α_0 such that $I_\omega(u)|_{\|u\|_F=\rho_0} \geqslant \alpha_0$ for all $u \in F$. Moreover, there exists a function $u_0 \in F$ with $\|u_0\|_F > \rho_0$ and $\omega^* > 0$ such that $I_\omega(u_0) < 0$ for $0 < \omega < \omega^*$.*

Proof. By $(H_3), (H_4)$, for any $\varepsilon > 0$, there exists q with $1 < q < 5$ and $M_1 = M_1(\varepsilon, p) > 0$ such that

$$|F(x, t)| \leqslant \frac{\varepsilon}{2}t^2 + M_1 t^{q+1}, \quad for \ all \ t > 0. \tag{2.70}$$

By $\phi_u \leqslant 0$ and the Sobolev inequality, we get that

$$I_\omega(u) = \frac{1}{2} \int_{\mathbb{R}^3} (|\nabla u|^2 + V(x)u^2 - \omega\phi_u u^2)dx - \int_{\mathbb{R}^3} F(x, u)dx$$

$$\geqslant \frac{1}{2}\|u\|_F^2 - \frac{\varepsilon}{2}v_2^2\|u\|_F^2 - M_1 v_{q+1}^{q+1}\|u\|_F^{q+1}$$

$$= \left(\frac{1}{2} - \frac{\varepsilon}{2}v_2^2 \right) \|u\|_F^2 - M_1 v_{q+1}^{q+1}\|u\|_F^{q+1}.$$

Since $1 < q < 5$, let $\varepsilon = \dfrac{1}{2v_2^2}$ and $\|u\|_F = \rho_0 > 0$ small enough, then we can obtain

$$I_\omega(u)|_{\|u\|_F=\rho} \geqslant \alpha_0, \quad for \ all \ u \in F.$$

By (H_4), we have $A > \Omega$. From the definition of Ω, there exists a nonnegative function $u_1 \in H^1(\mathbb{R}^3)$ such that

$$\|u_1\|_F^2 = \int_{\mathbb{R}^3} (|\nabla u_1|^2 + V(x)u_1^2)dx < A \int_{\mathbb{R}^3} u_1^2 dx = A|u_1|_2^2.$$

Hence, by (H_4) and Fatou's lemma we obtain that

$$\lim_{t \to +\infty} \frac{I_0(tu_1)}{t^2} = \frac{1}{2}\|u_1\|_F^2 - \lim_{t \to +\infty} \int_{\mathbb{R}^3} \frac{F(x, tu_1)}{t^2 u_1^2} u_1^2 dx$$

$$\leqslant \frac{1}{2}\|u_1\|_F^2 - \frac{A}{2} \int_{\mathbb{R}^3} u_1^2 dx$$

$$= \frac{1}{2}(\|u_1\|_F^2 - A|u_1|_2^2) < 0.$$

If $I_0(tu_1) \to -\infty$ as $t \to +\infty$, then there is a $u_0 \in F$ with $\|u_0\|_F > \rho_0$ such that $I_0(u_0) < 0$. Since $I_\omega(u_0) \to I_0(u_0)$ as $\omega \to 0^+$. We have that there is a positive constant $\omega^* > 0$ such that $I_\omega(u_0) < 0$ for all $0 < \omega < \omega^*$. The proof is complete. $\square$

Lemma 2.15   *Suppose (H_1)—(H_4) hold. Then any sequence $\{u_n\} \subset F$ satisfying*

$$I_\omega(u_n) \to c > 0, \quad \langle I_\omega'(u_n), u_n \rangle \to 0$$

is bounded in F. Moreover, $\{u_n\}$ has a strongly convergent subsequence in F.

Proof.   (i) We first to prove that $\{u_n\}$ is bounded. For any fixed $L > 0$, let $\eta_L \in C^\infty(\mathbb{R}^3, \mathbb{R})$ be a cut-off function such that

$$\eta_L = \begin{cases} 0, & \text{for } |x| < L/2, \\ 1, & \text{for } |x| \geq L, \end{cases}$$

and $|\nabla \eta_L| \leq \dfrac{C}{L}$ for all $x \in \mathbb{R}^3$, and C is a positive constant. For any $u \in F$ and all $L \geq 1$, there exists a constant $C_0 > 0$, which is independent of L, such that

$$\|\eta_L u\|_F \leq C_0 \|u\|_F.$$

Since $I_\omega'(u_n) \to 0$ as $n \to +\infty$ in $H^{-1}(\mathbb{R}^3)$, for n large enough we have that

$$\langle I_\omega'(u_n), \eta_L u_n \rangle \leq \|I_\omega'(u_n)\|_{F^{-1}} \|\eta_L u_n\|_F \leq \|u_n\|_F \tag{2.71}$$

and

$$\int_{\mathbb{R}^3} (|\nabla u_n|^2 + V(x)u_n^2)\eta_L dx + \int_{\mathbb{R}^3} u_n \nabla u_n \nabla \eta_L dx - \int_{\mathbb{R}^3} (2\omega + \phi_{u_n})\phi_{u_n} \eta_L u_n^2 dx$$

$$\leq \int_{\mathbb{R}^3} f(x, u_n) u_n \eta_L dx + \|u_n\|_F, \tag{2.72}$$

where F^{-1} is the dual space of F.

By assumptions (H_2) and (H_4), there exist $\gamma > 0$ and $L_1 > 0$ such that $V(x) \geq A + \gamma$ for all $|x| \geq L_1$. Choosing $L > 2L_1$, since $|\nabla \eta_L(x)| \leq \dfrac{C}{L}$ for all $x \in \mathbb{R}^3$, $2\omega + \phi_{u_n} \geq 0$ and $f(x, u_n(x))u_n(x) \leq Au_n^2(x)$ for all $x \in \mathbb{R}^3$ by (H_4). Following from (2.72) we get that

$$\int_{\mathbb{R}^3} (|\nabla u_n|^2 + \gamma u_n^2)\eta_L dx \leq \frac{C}{L} \left(\int_{\mathbb{R}^3} u_n^2 dx + \int_{\mathbb{R}^3} \nabla u_n^2 dx \right) + \|u_n\|_F. \tag{2.73}$$

Similar to (2.71), we have that $\langle I'_\omega(u_n), u_n \rangle \leqslant \|u_n\|_F$, that is

$$\int_{\mathbb{R}^3} (|\nabla u_n|^2 + V(x)u_n^2 - 2\omega\phi_{u_n}u_n^2 - \phi_{u_n}^2 u_n^2 - f(x, u_n)u_n)dx \leqslant \|u_n\|_F. \qquad (2.74)$$

Motivated by [155](see also [207]), we give an inequality by using the second equality of system $(KGM1)$. Multiplying both sides of $\Delta\phi_{u_n} = (\omega + \phi_{u_n})u_n^2$ by $|u_n|$, integrating by parts and using the Young's inequality, we have

$$\sqrt{\frac{3}{4}} \int_{\mathbb{R}^3} (\omega + \phi_{u_n})|u_n|^3 dx \leqslant \frac{1}{4} \int_{\mathbb{R}^3} |\nabla u_n|^2 dx + \frac{3}{4} \int_{\mathbb{R}^3} |\nabla\phi_{u_n}|^2 dx. \qquad (2.75)$$

Then by Proposition 2.7, one has

$$\sqrt{3} \int_{\mathbb{R}^3} (\omega + \phi_{u_n})|u_n|^3 dx$$

$$\leqslant \frac{1}{2} \int_{\mathbb{R}^3} |\nabla u_n|^2 dx + \frac{3}{2} \int_{\mathbb{R}^3} |\nabla\phi_{u_n}|^2 dx$$

$$\leqslant \frac{1}{2} \int_{\mathbb{R}^3} |\nabla u_n|^2 dx - \frac{3}{2} \int_{\mathbb{R}^3} \omega\phi_{u_n}u_n^2 dx - \frac{3}{2} \int_{\mathbb{R}^3} \phi_{u_n}^2 u_n^2 dx$$

$$\leqslant \frac{1}{2} \int_{\mathbb{R}^3} |\nabla u_n|^2 dx - \frac{3}{2} \int_{\mathbb{R}^3} \omega\phi_{u_n}u_n^2 dx - \int_{\mathbb{R}^3} \phi_{u_n}^2 u_n^2 dx. \qquad (2.76)$$

By (2.74), (2.58), (2.76) and $V(x) > 0, \phi_{u_n} \leqslant 0$,

$$f(x, u_n(x))u_n(x) \leqslant Au_n^2(x), \quad \text{for all } x \in \mathbb{R}^3,$$

we have that

$$\frac{1}{2} \int_{\mathbb{R}^3} (|\nabla u_n|^2 + V(x)u_n^2)dx + \int_{\mathbb{R}^3} (\sqrt{3}(\omega + \phi_{u_n})|u_n|^3 - Au_n^2)dx$$

$$\leqslant \frac{1}{2} \int_{\mathbb{R}^3} (|\nabla u_n|^2 + V(x)u_n^2)dx + \frac{1}{2} \int_{\mathbb{R}^3} |\nabla u_n|^2 dx - \frac{3}{2} \int_{\mathbb{R}^3} \omega\phi_{u_n}u_n^2 dx$$

$$- \int_{\mathbb{R}^3} \phi_{u_n}^2 u_n^2 dx - \int_{\mathbb{R}^3} f(x, u_n)u_n dx$$

$$= \int_{\mathbb{R}^3} (|\nabla u_n|^2 + V(x)u_n^2 - 2\omega\phi_{u_n}u_n^2 - \phi_{u_n}^2 u_n^2 - f(x, u_n)u_n)dx$$

$$- \frac{1}{2} \int_{\mathbb{R}^3} V(x)u_n^2 dx + \frac{1}{2} \int_{\mathbb{R}^3} \omega\phi_{u_n}u_n^2 dx$$

$$\leqslant \|u_n\|_F,$$

that is

$$\frac{1}{2}\|u_n\|_F^2 + \int_{\mathbb{R}^3} h(u_n)dx \leqslant \|u_n\|_F, \tag{2.77}$$

where $h(u_n) = \sqrt{3}(\omega + \phi_{u_n})|u_n|^3 - Au_n^2$.

By (2.73), there is a positive constant $C_1 > 0$ (independent of L) such that

$$\int_{|x|\geqslant L} u_n^2 dx \leqslant \frac{C_1}{L}\|u_n\|_F^2 + C_1\|u_n\|_F.$$

Let $\delta = \inf_{t\in R} h(t)$. Then $\delta \in (-\infty, 0)$ and by above inequality we have

$$\int_{\mathbb{R}^3} h(u_n)dx \geqslant \int_{|x|\leqslant L} \delta dx + \int_{|x|\geqslant L}(-Au_n^2)dx$$

$$\geqslant \delta|B_L(0)| - \frac{AC_1}{L}\|u_n\|_F^2 - AC_1\|u_n\|_F, \tag{2.78}$$

where $|B_L(0)|$ denotes the volume of $B_L(0)$. It follows from (2.77) and (2.78) that

$$\frac{1}{2}\|u_n\|_F^2 \leqslant |\delta||B_L(0)| + \frac{AC_1}{L}\|u_n\|_F^2 + AC_1\|u_n\|_F + \|u_n\|_F.$$

Since C_1 is a constant independent of L, we can choose L large enough such that $\frac{AC_1}{L} < \frac{1}{2}$. Then we obtain that $\{u_n\}$ is bounded in F by above inequality.

(ii) Now we shall show that $\{u_n\}$ has a strongly convergent subsequence in F. From case (i), $\{u_n\}$ is bounded in F. Then (2.71) and (2.73) become

$$\langle I'_\omega(u_n), \eta_L u_n\rangle = o(1)$$

and

$$\int_{|x|\geqslant L}(|\nabla u_n|^2 + u_n^2)dx \leqslant \frac{C}{L}\|u_n\|_F^2 + o(1), \tag{2.79}$$

respectively. Therefore, for any $\varepsilon > 0$, there exists $L > 0$ such that for n large enough,

$$\int_{|x|\geqslant L}(|\nabla u_n|^2 + u_n^2)dx \leqslant \varepsilon. \tag{2.80}$$

Since $\{u_n\}$ is bounded in F, passing to a subsequence if necessary, there exists $u \in F$ such that $u_n \rightharpoonup u$ in F. In view of the embedding $F \hookrightarrow L^s(\mathbb{R}^3)$ are compact for any

$s \in [2,6)$, $u_n \to u$ in $L^s(\mathbb{R}^3)$ for $1 < s < 6$ and $u_n(x) \to u(x)$ a.e. $x \in \mathbb{R}^3$. Hence it follows from assumptions of Lemma 2.15 and the derivative of I_ω, we easily obtain

$$\|u_n - u\|_F^2 = \langle I'_\omega(u_n) - I'_\omega(u), u_n - u \rangle + \int_{\mathbb{R}^3} (f(x, u_n) - f(x, u))(u_n - u)dx$$

$$+ 2\omega \int_{\mathbb{R}^3} (\phi_{u_n} u_n - \phi_u u)(u_n - u)dx + \int_{\mathbb{R}^3} (\phi_{u_n}^2 u_n - \phi_u^2 u)(u_n - u)dx.$$

It is clear that

$$\langle I'_\omega(u_n) - I'_\omega(u), u_n - u \rangle \to 0 \quad \text{as } n \to \infty.$$

By Proposition 2.7, the Hölder inequality and the Sobolev inequality, we have

$$\left| \int_{\mathbb{R}^3} \phi_{u_n} u_n (u_n - u)dx \right| \leqslant |\phi_{u_n}|_6 |u_n|_{12/5} |u_n - u|_{12/5}$$

$$\leqslant C_1 \|\phi_{u_n}\|_D |u_n|_{12/5} |u_n - u|_{12/5}$$

$$\leqslant C_2 |u_n|_{12/5}^3 |u_n - u|_{12/5} \to 0.$$

Since $u_n \to u$ in $L^s(\mathbb{R}^3)$ for any $s \in [2, 2^*)$, we obtain

$$\int_{\mathbb{R}^3} (\phi_{u_n} - \phi_u) u_n (u_n - u)dx \to 0 \quad \text{as } n \to \infty$$

and

$$\int_{\mathbb{R}^3} \phi_u (u_n - u)^2 dx \leqslant |\phi_u|_6 |u_n - u|_3 |u_n - u|_2 \to 0 \quad \text{as } n \to \infty.$$

Thus, we get

$$\int_{\mathbb{R}^3} (\phi_{u_n} u_n - \phi_u u)(u_n - u)dx = \int_{\mathbb{R}^3} (\phi_{u_n} - \phi_u) u_n (u_n - u)dx + \int_{\mathbb{R}^3} \phi_u (u_n - u)^2 dx$$

$$\to 0 \quad \text{as } n \to \infty.$$

Now, we shall prove

$$\int_{\mathbb{R}^3} f(x, u_n)(u_n - u)dx = o(1) \quad \text{and} \quad \int_{\mathbb{R}^3} f(x, u)(u_n - u) = o(1). \quad (2.81)$$

We only to prove the first one and the second one is similar. Since $|f(x, u_n)| \leqslant A|u_n|$ and $\|u_n\|_F$ is bounded, by (2.80), the Hölder inequality and the Sobolev inequality, we have

$$\left| \int_{\mathbb{R}^3} f(x, u_n)(u_n - u)dx \right| \leqslant \left| \int_{|x| \leqslant L} f(x, u_n)(u_n - u)dx \right| + \left| \int_{|x| \geqslant L} f(x, u_n)(u_n - u)dx \right|$$

$$\leqslant C|u_n - u|_{L^2(B_L(0))} + C \left(\int_{|x| \geqslant L} u_n^2 dx \right)^{1/2}$$

$$\to 0 \quad \text{as } n \to \infty \text{ and } L \to +\infty.$$

So (2.81) hold. Therefore, $\|u_n - u\|_F \to 0$ as $n \to \infty$. The proof is complete. □

Now we can prove our main results Theorem 2.6.

Proof of Theorem 2.6   By Lemma 2.14 and Lemma 2.15, we can obtain that u is a solution of system $(KGM1)$. And by using bootstrap arguments and the maximum principle, we can conclude that u is positive. The proof is complete. □

2.4   Ground state solutions for critical Klein-Gordon-Maxwell equations

2.4.1   Introduction and main results

In this section we consider the following nonlinear Klein-Gordon-Maxwell system

$$(KGM2) \begin{cases} -\Delta u + V(x)u - (2\omega + \phi)\phi u = \lambda |u|^{q-2}u + |u|^{2^*-2}u, & x \in \mathbb{R}^3, \\ -\Delta \phi + \phi u^2 = -\omega u^2, & x \in \mathbb{R}^3, \end{cases}$$

where λ and ω are two positive constants, $2 < q < 6$ and $2^* = 6$ is the critical exponent in $\mathbb{R}^3$. We are interested in the existence of positive ground state solutions of $(KGM2)$.

In 2002, Benci and Fortunato[25] first studied the following system

$$\begin{cases} -\Delta u + [m^2 - (\omega + \phi)^2]\phi u = f(x, u), & x \in \mathbb{R}^3, \\ -\Delta \phi + \phi u^2 = -\omega u^2, & x \in \mathbb{R}^3 \end{cases} \tag{2.82}$$

with the pure power type nonlinearity, i.e. $f(x, u) = |u|^{q-2}u$, where ω and m are constants. By using a version of the mountain pass theorem, they proved that system (2.82) has infinitely many radially symmetric solutions under $|m| > |\omega|$ and $4 < q < 6$. It was complemented and improved by [75] and [15]. Motivated by the methods of Benci and Fortunato, Cassani[47], we considered system (2.82) for the critical case by adding a lower order perturbation

$$\begin{cases} -\Delta u + [m^2 - (\omega + \phi)^2]\phi u = \lambda |u|^{q-2}u + |u|^4 u, & x \in \mathbb{R}^3, \\ -\Delta \phi + \phi u^2 = -\omega u^2, & x \in \mathbb{R}^3, \end{cases} \tag{2.83}$$

where $\lambda > 0$. He showed that (2.83) has at least a radially symmetric solution under one of the following conditions:

(i) $4 < q < 6, |m| > |\omega|$ and $\lambda > 0$;

(ii) $q = 4, |m| > |\omega|$ and λ is sufficiently large.

Soon afterwards, it was improved and generalized by the results in [45,183]. Very recently, Carrião, Cunha and Miyagaki in [46] proved the existence of positive ground state solutions for the problem (2.83) with a periodic potential V, i.e. (KGM2). Under the conditions:

(H_1) $V(x)$ is a continuous function and $V(x + l) = V(x), x \in \mathbb{R}^3, l \in \mathbb{Z}^3$;

(H_2') There exists positive constant V_0 such that $V(x) \geqslant V_0$ for all $x \in \mathbb{R}^3$, where

$$\frac{V_0}{\omega^2} > \frac{2(4-q)}{q-2} \text{ if } 2 < q < 4.$$

They show that system (KGM2) has a positive ground state solution for each $\lambda > 0$ if $4 < q < 6$ and for λ is sufficiently large if $2 < q \leqslant 4$.

By [15], we know that the signs of ω is not relevant for the existence of solutions, so we can assume that $\omega > 0$.

In order to give our main result, we need a weaker assumption than (H_2'):

(H_2) There exists a positive constant V_0 such that $V(x) \geqslant V_0$ for all $x \in \mathbb{R}^3$, where $\dfrac{V_0}{\omega^2} > \dfrac{(4-q)^2}{4(q-2)}$ if $2 < q < 4$.

Now we can state our main result:

Theorem 2.7   *Assume that (H_1) and (H_2) are satisfied. System (KGM2) has a positive ground state solution that provides one of the following conditions is satisfied:*

(i) $4 < q < 6$ and $\lambda > 0$;

(ii) $2 < q \leqslant 4$ and $\lambda > 0$ sufficiently large.

Remark 2.12   Clearly, $\dfrac{(4-q)^2}{4(q-2)} < \dfrac{2(4-q)}{q-2}$ for all $2 < q < 4$. So our result give an improvement of the result in [46].

In Section 2.4.2, we introduce the variational setting for the problem and give some useful lemmas. In Section 2.4.3, we study the Nehari manifold $\mathcal{N}$. We give the proof of the main result in Section 2.4.4.

2.4.2   Variational setting and preliminaries

Let $H^1(\mathbb{R}^3)$ be the usual Sobolev space endowed with the standard scalar and norm

$$(u, v) = \int_{\mathbb{R}^3} (\nabla u \nabla v + uv)dx, \qquad \|u\|^2 = \int_{\mathbb{R}^3} (|\nabla u|^2 + |u|^2)dx.$$

$D^{1,2}(\mathbb{R}^3)$ is the completion of $C_0^\infty(\mathbb{R}^3)$ with respect to the norm

$$\|u\|_D^2 := \|u\|_{D^{1,2}(\mathbb{R}^3)}^2 = \int_{\mathbb{R}^3} |\nabla u|^2 dx.$$

Let

$$E := \left\{ u \in H^1(\mathbb{R}^3) : \int_{\mathbb{R}^3} (|\nabla u|^2 + V(x)u^2)dx < \infty \right\}.$$

Then E is a Hilbert space with the inner product

$$(u, v)_E = \int_{\mathbb{R}^3} (\nabla u \cdot \nabla v + V(x)uv)\, dx$$

and the norm $\|u\|_E = (u, u)_E^{1/2}$, which is equivalent to the usual Sobolev norm on $H^1(\mathbb{R}^3)$. Obviously, the embedding $E \hookrightarrow L^s(\mathbb{R}^3)$ is continuous, for any $s \in [2, 2^*]$. The norm on $L^s = L^s(\mathbb{R}^3)$ with $1 < s < \infty$ is given by $|u|_s^s = \int_{\mathbb{R}^3} |u|^s dx$. Consequently, for each $s \in [2, 6]$, there exists a constant $d_s > 0$ such that

$$|u|_s \leqslant d_s \|u\|_E, \quad \forall u \in E. \tag{2.84}$$

By a solution (u, ϕ), we mean $(u, \phi) \in E \times D^{1,2}(\mathbb{R}^3)$ satisfying $(KGM2)$ in the weak sense. Obviously, $(u, \phi) = (0, 0)$ is a trivial solution of $(KGM2)$. We define a functional $\Psi : E \times D^{1,2}(\mathbb{R}^3) \to \mathbb{R}$ by

$$\Psi(u, \phi) = \frac{1}{2} \int_{\mathbb{R}^3} \left(|\nabla u|^2 - |\nabla \phi|^2 + [V(x) - (2\omega + \phi)\phi]u^2\right) dx$$

$$- \frac{\lambda}{q} \int_{\mathbb{R}^3} |u|^q dx - \int_{\mathbb{R}^3} \frac{1}{6}|u|^6 dx.$$

By standard argument we can see that $\Psi \in C^1(E \times D^{1,2}(\mathbb{R}^3), \mathbb{R})$ and that weak solutions of $(KGM2)$ turn out to be critical points for the energy functional Ψ.

To obtain our main result, we have to overcome several difficulties. The first difficulty is that Ψ is strongly indefinite, i.e. it is unbounded both from below and from above on infinite-dimensional subspaces. To avoid this indefiniteness, we use the reduction method as in [45−47]. The second difficulty is the lack of compactness of the Sobolev embedding $H^1(\mathbb{R}^3)$ into $L^s(\mathbb{R}^3)$, $s \in (2, 6)$. Since we assume that the potential is nonradially symmetric, we cannot use the usual way to recover compactness, for example, restricting in the subspace $H^1_r(\mathbb{R}^3)$ of radially symmetric functions or using concentration compactness methods. To recover the compactness, we borrow some ideas used in [46] and obtain the result with periodicity condition on V.

The following two lemmas are obtained in [25, 74].

Lemma 2.16   *For any $u \in H^1(\mathbb{R}^3)$, there exists a unique $\phi = \phi_u \in D^{1,2}(\mathbb{R}^3)$ which satisfies*

$$\Delta \phi = (\phi + \omega)u^2 \quad in \quad \mathbb{R}^3. \tag{2.85}$$

Moreover, the map $\Phi : u \in H^1(\mathbb{R}^3) \mapsto \phi_u \in D^{1,2}(\mathbb{R}^3)$ *is continuously differentiable,* *and on the set* $\{x \in \mathbb{R}^3 | u(x) \neq 0\}$,

$$-\omega \leqslant \phi_u \leqslant 0.$$

Multiplying $-\Delta\phi_u + \phi_u u^2 = -\omega u^2$ by ϕ_u and integration by parts, we obtain

$$\int_{\mathbb{R}^3} (|\nabla\phi_u|^2 + \phi_u^2 u^2) dx = -\int_{\mathbb{R}^3} \omega\phi_u u^2 dx.$$

By the above equality and the definition of Ψ, we obtain a C^1 function $J : E \to \mathbb{R}$ given by

$$J(u) = \frac{1}{2}\left(\int_{\mathbb{R}^3} |\nabla u|^2 dx + \int_{\mathbb{R}^3} V(x)u^2 dx - \int_{\mathbb{R}^3} \omega\phi_u u^2 dx\right)$$
$$- \frac{\lambda}{q}\int_{\mathbb{R}^3} |u|^q dx - \frac{1}{6}\int_{\mathbb{R}^3} u^6 dx$$

and its Gateaux derivative is

$$\langle J'(u), v\rangle = \int_{\mathbb{R}^3} [\nabla u \cdot \nabla v + V(x)uv - (2\omega + \phi_u)\phi_u uv - \lambda|u|^{q-2}uv - u^5 v] dx,$$

for all $u, v \in E$. Here we use the fact that $(\Delta - u^2)^{-1}[\omega u^2] = \phi_u$.

Remark 2.13   Note that

$$\|\phi_u\|_D^2 \leqslant \omega\int_{\mathbb{R}^3} |\phi_u|u^2 dx \leqslant \omega|\phi_u|_6|u|_{12/5}^2,$$

and then

$$\|\phi_u\|_D \leqslant C\omega|u|_{12/5}^2.$$

Lemma 2.17   *The pair* $(u, \phi) \in E \times D^{1,2}(\mathbb{R}^3)$ *is a solution of* $(KGM2)$ *if and only if* u *is a critical point of*

$$J(u) = \Psi(u, \phi_u) = \int_{\mathbb{R}^3} \left[\frac{1}{2}(|\nabla u|^2 + V(x)u^2 - \omega\phi_u u^2) - \frac{\lambda}{q}|u|^q - \frac{u^6}{6}\right] dx$$

and $\phi = \phi_u$.

From Lemmas 2.16 and 2.17, in order to get a solution of $(KGM2)$, we only need to find a critical point of J in E.

Lemma 2.18[183]   *Let* $u \in H^1(\mathbb{R}^3)$, *and set* $\psi_u = \Phi'(u)[u]/2$. *Then the following hold:*

(i) ψ_u is a solution to the integral equation

$$\int_{\mathbb{R}^3} \omega \psi_u u^2 dx = \int_{\mathbb{R}^3} (\omega + \phi_u) \phi_u u^2 dx, \tag{2.86}$$

and satisfies

$$\Delta \psi_u = (\psi_u + \omega + \phi_u) u^2.$$

(ii) For almost everywhere on the set $\{x \in \mathbb{R}^3 : u(x) \neq 0\}$,

$$\max\{-\omega - \phi_u, \phi_u\} \leqslant \psi_u \leqslant 0.$$

2.4.3   The Nehari manifold $\mathcal{N}$

Set $Q(u) := \langle J'(u), u \rangle = 0$, that is,

$$Q(u) := \int_{\mathbb{R}^3} [(|\nabla u|^2 + V(x)u^2) - (2\omega + \phi_u)\phi_u u^2 - \lambda|u|^q - u^6] dx.$$

The manifold $\mathcal{N}$ is defined as

$$\mathcal{N} := \{u \in E \setminus \{0\} | Q(u) = 0\}.$$

It is well known that $\mathcal{N}$ is a Nehari manifold. Clearly, if u is a solution of system (KGM2) then $u \in \mathcal{N}$. Next we give some properties related to the manifold $\mathcal{N}$.

Lemma 2.19   There exists a positive constant C such that $\|u\|_E \geqslant C$ for all $u \in \mathcal{N}$.

Proof. By (2.84), the Hölder inequality and Lemma 2.16, for all $u \in \mathcal{N}$ we obtain that

$$0 = \langle J'(u), u \rangle = \|u\|_E^2 - 2\int_{\mathbb{R}^3} \omega\phi_u u^2 dx - \int_{\mathbb{R}^3} \phi_u^2 u^2 dx - \lambda|u|_q^q - |u|_6^6$$

$$\geqslant \|u\|_E^2 - \lambda d_q^q \|u\|_E^q - d_6^6 \|u\|_E^6.$$

Since $2 < q < 6$, there exists a positive constant C such that $\|u\|_E \geqslant C$ for all $u \in \mathcal{N}$. The proof is complete.   □

Lemma 2.20 $\mathcal{N}$ is a C^1 manifold.

Proof. For all $u \in E$, we have

$$Q(u) = 2J(u) - \int_{\mathbb{R}^3} \omega\phi_u u^2 dx - \int_{\mathbb{R}^3} \phi_u^2 u^2 dx + \frac{\lambda(2-q)}{q} \int_{\mathbb{R}^3} |u|^q dx - \frac{2}{3} \int_{\mathbb{R}^3} |u|^6 dx.$$

We shall prove that there exists a positive constant D_1 such that $\langle Q'(u), u \rangle \leqslant -D_1$ for all $u \in \mathcal{N}$.

If $u \in \mathcal{N}$, by Lemmas 2.17 and 2.18,

$$\langle Q'(u), u \rangle = (2-q) \int_{\mathbb{R}^3} |\nabla u|^2 dx + (2-q) \int_{\mathbb{R}^3} V(x) u^2 dx - 2(4-q) \int_{\mathbb{R}^3} \omega \phi_u u^2 dx$$

$$+ (q-6) \int_{\mathbb{R}^3} \phi_u^2 u^2 dx - 4 \int_{\mathbb{R}^3} \psi_u \phi_u u^2 dx + (q-6) \int_{\mathbb{R}^3} u^6 dx$$

$$\leqslant (2-q) \int_{\mathbb{R}^3} |\nabla u|^2 dx + (2-q) \int_{\mathbb{R}^3} V_0 u^2 dx - 2(4-q) \int_{\mathbb{R}^3} \omega \phi_u u^2 dx$$

$$+ (q-6) \int_{\mathbb{R}^3} (\omega \psi_u u^2 - \omega \phi_u u^2) dx - 4 \int_{\mathbb{R}^3} \psi_u \phi_u u^2 dx$$

$$= (2-q) \int_{\mathbb{R}^3} |\nabla u|^2 dx + (2-q) \int_{\mathbb{R}^3} V_0 u^2 dx + (q-2) \int_{\mathbb{R}^3} \omega \phi_u u^2 dx$$

$$- (6-q) \int_{\mathbb{R}^3} \omega \psi_u u^2 dx - 4 \int_{\mathbb{R}^3} \psi_u \phi_u u^2 dx$$

$$\leqslant (2-q) \int_{\mathbb{R}^3} |\nabla u|^2 dx + (2-q) \int_{\mathbb{R}^3} V_0 u^2 dx$$

$$- 2(4-q) \int_{\mathbb{R}^3} \omega \psi_u u^2 dx - 4 \int_{\mathbb{R}^3} \psi_u^2 u^2 dx,$$

that is,

$$\langle Q'(u), u \rangle \leqslant (2-q) \int_{\mathbb{R}^3} |\nabla u|^2 dx - \int_{\mathbb{R}^3} \Xi_u u^2 dx,$$

where

$$\Xi_u := 4\psi_u^2 - 2(q-4)\omega \psi_u + V_0(q-2).$$

Set

$$\gamma(t) := 4t^2 - 2(q-4)\omega t + V_0(q-2), \quad t \in [-\omega, 0].$$

Clearly,

$$\gamma(t) := 4 \left[t - \frac{\omega(q-4)}{4} \right]^2 - \frac{\omega^2(q-4)^2}{4} + V_0(q-2).$$

Now, we have to discuss the problem on two cases.

Case (i) $4 \leqslant q < 6$ and $V_0 > 0$.

Since $4 \leqslant q < 6$ and $\omega > 0$, we have $\dfrac{\omega(q-4)}{4} \geqslant 0$. We deduce that

$$\gamma(t) \geqslant \gamma(0) = V_0(q-2), \quad \forall t \in [-\omega, 0].$$

Case (ii) $2 < q < 4, V_0 > 0$ and $\dfrac{V_0}{\omega^2} > \dfrac{(4-q)^2}{4(q-2)}$.

Since $2 < q < 4$, we obtain $\dfrac{\omega(q-4)}{4} \in \left[-\dfrac{\omega}{2}, 0\right)$. Then we have

$$\gamma(t) \geqslant \gamma\left(\frac{\omega(q-4)}{4}\right) = V_0(q-2) - \frac{\omega^2(q-4)^2}{4}, \quad \forall t \in [-\omega, 0].$$

Therefore, under one of the following conditions,

(i) $4 \leqslant q < 6$ and $V_0 > 0$;

(ii) $2 < q < 4, V_0 > 0$ and $\dfrac{V_0}{\omega^2} > \dfrac{(4-q)^2}{4(q-2)}$,

we obtain

$$\langle Q'(u), u \rangle \leqslant (2-q) \int_{\mathbb{R}^3} |\nabla u|^2 dx - \int_{\mathbb{R}^3} \Xi_u u^2 dx$$

$$\leqslant -(q-2) \int_{\mathbb{R}^3} |\nabla u|^2 dx - M_1 \int_{\mathbb{R}^3} u^2 dx,$$

where

$$M_1 = \begin{cases} V_0(q-2), & 4 \leqslant q < 6, \\ V_0(q-2) - \dfrac{\omega^2(q-4)^2}{4} > 0, & 2 < q < 4. \end{cases}$$

By (H_2), we know that M_1 is a positive constant. The proof is complete. □

Lemma 2.21   *There exists a positive constant D_2 such that $J(u) \geqslant D_2$ for all $u \in \mathcal{N}$.*

Proof. For any $u \in \mathcal{N}$, we get the following

$$J(u) = \frac{q-2}{2q} \int_{\mathbb{R}^3} |\nabla u|^2 dx + \frac{q-2}{2q} \int_{\mathbb{R}^3} V(x) u^2 dx + \frac{4-q}{2q} \int_{\mathbb{R}^3} \omega \phi_u u^2 dx$$

$$+ \frac{1}{q} \int_{\mathbb{R}^3} \phi_u^2 u^2 dx + \frac{6-q}{6q} \int_{\mathbb{R}^3} u^6 dx$$

$$\geqslant \frac{q-2}{2q} \int_{\mathbb{R}^3} |\nabla u|^2 dx + \frac{1}{2q} \int_{\mathbb{R}^3} [2\phi_u^2 - (q-4)\omega\phi_u + (q-2)V_0] u^2 dx$$

$$= \frac{q-2}{2q} \int_{\mathbb{R}^3} |\nabla u|^2 dx + \frac{1}{2q} \int_{\mathbb{R}^3} \Pi_u u^2 dx,$$

where

$$\Pi_u := 2\phi_u^2 - (q-4)\omega\phi_u + (q-2)V_0.$$

Let

$$\eta(t) := 2t^2 - (q-4)\omega t + (q-2)V_0, \quad t \in [-\omega, 0].$$

It is easy to see that

$$\eta(t) = 2\left[t - \frac{\omega(q-4)}{4}\right]^2 - \frac{\omega^2(q-4)^2}{8} + V_0(q-2).$$

Similarly to the Lemma 2.20, we obtain

$$J(u) \geqslant \frac{q-2}{2q}\int_{\mathbb{R}^3}|\nabla u|^2 dx + \frac{1}{2q}\int_{\mathbb{R}^3}\Pi_u u^2 dx$$

$$\geqslant \frac{q-2}{2q}\int_{\mathbb{R}^3}|\nabla u|^2 dx + \frac{1}{2q}M_2\int_{\mathbb{R}^3}u^2 dx,$$

where

$$M_2 = \begin{cases} V_0(q-2), & 4 \leqslant q < 6, \\ V_0(q-2) - \dfrac{\omega^2(q-4)^2}{8} > 0, & 2 < q < 4. \end{cases}$$

By Lemma 2.19 and the equivalence of E and $H^1(\mathbb{R}^3)$, we complete the proof. □

2.4.4 Proofs of main results

Firstly, we show that the function J has the geometry of the mountain pass theorem.

Lemma 2.22   The functional J satisfies the following conditions:

(i) There exist two positive constants α and ρ such that $\inf\limits_{\|u\|_E=\rho} J(u) > \alpha$.

(ii) There exists $\tilde{u} \in E$ with $\|\tilde{u}\|_E > \rho$ such that $J(\tilde{u}) < 0$.

Proof. The proof of this lemma is similar to Lemma 4 of [45], but we exhibit it here for completeness.

By the Sobolev embedding, we have

$$J(u) \geqslant C_0\|u\|_E^2 - C_1\|u\|_E^q - C_2\|u\|_E^6,$$

where C_0, C_1 and C_2 are positive constants. Because $q > 2$, there exist two positive constant α, ρ such that $\inf\limits_{\|u\|_E=\rho} J(u) > \alpha$.

Let $u \in E$, by Lemma 2.16 and Lemma 2.17, for $t \geqslant 0$ we conclude that

$$J(tu) \leqslant C_3t^2\|u\|_E^2 + \frac{\omega^2 t^2}{2}|u|_2^2 - \frac{\lambda t^q}{q}|u|_q^q - \frac{t^6}{6}|u|_6^6 \to -\infty,$$

as $t \to +\infty$, since $q < 6$. Therefore, there exists $u \neq 0, \tilde{u} := tu$ with t sufficiently large such that $\|\tilde{u}\|_E > \rho$ such that $J(\tilde{u}) < 0$. The proof is complete. □

By Lemma 2.22 and the Ekeland Variational Principle, there exists a minimizing sequence $\{u_n\} \subset \mathcal{N}$, which can be considered as a $(PS)_c$, that is

$$J(u_n) \to c \quad \text{and} \quad J'(u_n) \to 0, \tag{2.87}$$

where c is characterized by

$$c := \inf_{\gamma \in \Gamma} \max_{0 \leqslant t \leqslant 1} J(\gamma(t)) \tag{2.88}$$

and

$$\Gamma = \{\gamma \in C([0,1], E) | J((\gamma(0)) = 0, J(\gamma(t)) < 0\}.$$

The authors in [46] used a technique by Brézis and Nirenberg[35] and some of its variants[97] to prove the following lemma.

Lemma 2.23[46]   *The number c given in (2.88) satisfies*

$$0 < c < \frac{1}{3}S^{3/2}, \tag{2.89}$$

where S is the best Sobolev constant

$$S := \inf \left\{ \frac{\int_{\mathbb{R}^3} |\nabla u|^2 dx}{\left(\int_{\mathbb{R}^3} u^6 dx\right)^{1/3}} : u \in D^{1,2}(\mathbb{R}^3) \setminus \{0\} \right\}.$$

Secondly, we give a lemma which is useful to prove our main result.

Lemma 2.24[15]   *If $u_n \rightharpoonup u_0$ in E, then, up to a subsequences, $\phi_{u_n} \rightharpoonup \phi_{u_0}$ in $D^{1,2}(\mathbb{R}^3)$. As a sequence $J'(u_n) \to J'(u_0)$ as $n \to \infty$.*

Now we are in a position to prove our main result.

Proof of Theorem 2.7   Let

$$\beta := \inf_{u \in \mathcal{N}} J(u).$$

We claim that there is a $u_0 \in \mathcal{N}$ with $J'(u_0) = 0$ and $J(u_0) = \beta$. Then we know that (u_0, ϕ_{u_0}) is a ground state solution of $(KGM1)$. In the following, we will prove the claim.

It follows from Lemma 2.21 that $\beta > 0$. Let $\{u_n\} \subset \mathcal{N}$ such that $J(u_n) \to \inf J|_{\mathcal{N}}$. We first show that $\{u_n\}$ is bounded in E. Indeed, for n large enough, we obtain

$$\inf J|_{\mathcal{N}} + 1 \geqslant J(u_n)$$

$$\geqslant \frac{q-2}{2q}\int_{\mathbb{R}^3}|\nabla u_n|^2 dx + \frac{1}{2q}M_2\int_{\mathbb{R}^3}u_n^2 dx,$$

where M_2 is defined in Lemma 2.21.

Then, going if necessary to a subsequence, we may assume that

$$u_n \rightharpoonup u_0 \text{ in } E,$$

$$u_n \to u_0 \text{ in } L^s_{loc}(\mathbb{R}^3), 2 \leqslant s < 6, \qquad (2.90)$$

$$u_n(x) \to u_0(x) \text{ a.e. } x \in \mathbb{R}^3.$$

By Lemma 2.24, $\phi_{u_n} \rightharpoonup \phi_{u_0}$ in $D^{1,2}(\mathbb{R}^3)$. Furthermore, we have

$$\phi_{u_n} \to \phi_{u_0} \text{ in } L^s_{loc}(\mathbb{R}^3), 2 \leqslant s < 6,$$

$$\phi_{u_n} \to \phi_{u_0} \text{ a.e. in } \mathbb{R}^3. \qquad (2.91)$$

Without loss of generality, we assume that $\{u_n\}$ is a Palais-Smale sequence for the functional $J|_{\mathcal{N}}$ such that

$$J(u_n) \to \beta \quad \text{and} \quad (J|_{\mathcal{N}})'(u_n) \to 0 \quad \text{as} \quad n \to \infty.$$

Then for suitable Lagrange multipliers λ_n, we can obtain that

$$o_n(1) = \langle (J|_{\mathcal{N}})'(u_n), u_n \rangle = \langle J'(u_n), u_n \rangle + \lambda_n \langle Q'(u_n), u_n \rangle$$

$$= \lambda_n \langle Q'(u_n), u_n \rangle. \qquad (2.92)$$

By Lemma 2.20, we can deduce that $\lambda_n = o_n(1)$. Combined with (2.92), we get that $J'(u_n) \to 0$ as $n \to \infty$. From Lemma 2.24, we obtain $J'(u_0) = 0$ and $u_0 \neq 0$. Then u_0 is a nontrivial solution of $(KGM2)$. Next we shall prove that $J(u_0) = \beta$.

Since $u_n \in \mathcal{N}$, we have

$$J(u_n) = \frac{q-2}{2q}\int_{\mathbb{R}^3}|\nabla u_n|^2 dx + \frac{q-2}{2q}\int_{\mathbb{R}^3}V(x)u_n^2 dx + \frac{4-q}{2q}\int_{\mathbb{R}^3}\omega\phi_{u_n}u_n^2 dx$$

$$+ \frac{1}{q}\int_{\mathbb{R}^3}\phi_{u_n}^2 u_n^2 dx + \frac{6-q}{6q}\int_{\mathbb{R}^3}u_n^6 dx$$

$$= \frac{q-2}{2q}\int_{\mathbb{R}^3}|\nabla u_n|^2 dx + \frac{1}{2q}\int_{\mathbb{R}^3}[2\phi_{u_n}^2 + (4-q)\omega\phi_{u_n} + (q-2)V(x)]u_n^2 dx$$

$$+ \frac{6-q}{6q}\int_{\mathbb{R}^3}u_n^6 dx.$$

Similar to the proof of Lemma 2.21, we have to divide the problem into two cases:
(i) $4 \leqslant q < 6$ and $V_0 > 0$,

(ii) $2 < q < 4$ and $\dfrac{V_0}{\omega^2} > \dfrac{(4-q)^2}{4(q-2)}$.

By (H_2), $V(x) \geqslant V_0 > 0$, it is easy to compute that

$$2\phi_{u_n}^2 + (4-q)\omega\phi_{u_n} + (q-2)V(x) \geqslant 2\phi_{u_n}^2 + (4-q)\omega\phi_{u_n} + (q-2)V_0 \geqslant 0.$$

Then, by (2.90), (2.91), the Fatou's lemma and the weak lower semicontinuity of the norm, we can obtain that $J(u_0) \leqslant \beta$. By the definition of β, we have $J(u_0) = \beta$.

Since $J(u_0) = \beta > 0$, by using bootstrap arguments, Lemma 3.8 in [46] and the maximum principle, we can get that the solution u_0 is positive. The proof is complete. $\square$

Chapter 3　Klein-Gordon Equation Coupled with Born-Infeld Theory

3.1　Introduction and main results

In this chapter, we consider the nonhomogeneous Klein-Gordon equation with Born-Infeld theory

$$(KGBI) \begin{cases} -\Delta u + V(x)u - (2\omega + \phi)\phi u = f(x,u) + h(x), & x \in \mathbb{R}^3, \\ \Delta \phi + \beta \Delta_4 \phi = 4\pi(\omega + \phi)u^2, & x \in \mathbb{R}^3, \end{cases}$$

where $\omega > 0$ is a constant. Under some assumptions on V, f and h, we obtain the existence of two solutions by the Mountain Pass theorem and the Ekeland's Variational Principle in critical point theory.

It is well known that Klein-Gordon equation can be used to develop the theory of electrically charged fields (see [87]), and Born-Infeld theory is proposed by Born[32−34] to overcome the infinite energy problem associated with a point-charge source in the original Maxwell theory. The presence of the nonlinear term f simulates the interaction between many particles or external nonlinear perturbations. For more details in the physical aspects, we refer the readers to [23, 44, 91, 146, 211].

In recent years, the Born-Infeld nonlinear electromagnetism has become more important since its relevance in the theory of superstring and membranes. By using variational methods, several existence results for problem $(KGBI)$ have been found with constant potential $V(x) = m^2 - \omega^2$. We recall some of them.

The case of $h \equiv 0$, that is the homogeneous case, has been widely studied in recent years. In 2002, [76] considered the following Klein-Gordon equation with Born-Infeld theory on $\mathbb{R}^3$

$$\begin{cases} -\Delta u + [m^2 - (\omega + \phi)^2]\phi u = f(x,u), & x \in \mathbb{R}^3, \\ \Delta \phi + \beta \Delta_4 \phi = 4\pi(\omega + \phi)u^2, & x \in \mathbb{R}^3, \end{cases} \tag{3.1}$$

for the pure power of nonlinearity, i.e., $f(x,u) = |u|^{p-2}u$, where ω and m are constants. By using the mountain pass theorem, they proved that (3.1) has infinitely many radially symmetric solutions under $|m| > |\omega|$ and $4 < p < 6$. Mugnai[146] covered the case $2 < p \leqslant 4$ assuming $\sqrt{\dfrac{p-2}{2}}|m| > \omega > 0$. Later, [175] obtained a nontrivial solution for the problem (3.1) with $f(x,u) = |u|^{p-2}u + |u|^{2^*-2}u$ under the conditions $4 \leqslant p < 6$ and $m > \omega$. [104] improved existence results from [175] and studied the existence of ground state solution for the problem (3.1) with $f(x,u) = |u|^{p-2}u + |u|^{2^*-2}u$.

Recently, for general potential $V(x)$, Chen and Song[60] obtained the existence of multiple nontrivial solutions for the problem (3.1) with the nonlinearity $f(x,u) = \lambda k(x)|u|^{q-2}u + g(x)|u|^{p-2}u$, that is, the Klein-Gordon equation with concave and convex nonlinearities coupled with Born-Infeld theory on $\mathbb{R}^3$. Other related results about homogeneous Klein-Gordon equation with Born-Infeld theory can be found in $[2, 176, 181, 199, 213, 218]$.

Next, we consider the nonhomogeneous case, that is $h \not\equiv 0$. In [56], Chen and Li proved that $(KGBI)$ had two nontrivial radially symmetric solutions if $f(x,t) = |u|^{p-2}u$ and $h(x)$ is radially symmetric.

Motivated by above works, in the present chapter we consider system $(KGBI)$ with more general assumptions on f and without any radially symmetric assumptions on f and h. More precisely, we assume

(V) $V \in C(\mathbb{R}^3, \mathbb{R})$ satisfies $V_0 = \inf\limits_{x \in \mathbb{R}^3} V(x) > 0$. Moreover, for every $M > 0$, meas$\{x \in \mathbb{R}^3 : V(x) \leqslant M\} < +\infty$, where meas denotes the Lebesgue measures in $\mathbb{R}^3$.

(f_1) $f \in C(\mathbb{R}^3 \times \mathbb{R}, \mathbb{R})$ and there exist $C_1 > 0$ and $p \in (2,6)$ such that

$$|f(x,t)| \leqslant C_1(|t| + |t|^{p-1}).$$

(f_2) $f(x,t) = o(t)$ uniformly in x as $|t| \to 0$, uniformly for $x \in \mathbb{R}^3$.

(f_3) There exist $\theta > 2$ and $D_1, D_2 > 0$ such that $F(x,t) \geqslant D_1|t|^\theta - D_2$, for a.e. $x \in \mathbb{R}^3$ and every t sufficiently large.

(f_4) There exist C_2, r_0 are two positive constants and $\mu > 2$ such that

$$\mathcal{F}(x,t) := \frac{1}{\mu}f(x,t)t - F(x,t) \geqslant -C_2|t|^2, \quad |t| \geqslant r_0.$$

(H) $h \in L^2(\mathbb{R}^3), h(x) \geqslant 0, h(x) \not\equiv 0$.

Before giving our main results, we give some notations. Let $H^1(\mathbb{R}^3)$ be the usual Sobolev space endowed with the standard scalar and norm

$$(u,v)_H = \int_{\mathbb{R}^3} (\nabla u \nabla v + uv)dx, \qquad \|u\|_H = \left(\int_{\mathbb{R}^3} (|\nabla u|^2 + |u|^2)dx\right)^{1/2}.$$

$D^{1,2}(\mathbb{R}^3)$ is the completion of $C_0^\infty(\mathbb{R}^3)$ with respect to the norm

$$\|u\|_{D^{1,2}(\mathbb{R}^3)} = \left(\int_{\mathbb{R}^3} |\nabla u|^2 dx\right)^{1/2}.$$

The norm on $L^s = L^s(\mathbb{R}^3)$ with $1 < s < \infty$ is given by $|u|_s^s = \int_{\mathbb{R}^3} |u|^s dx$. $D(\mathbb{R}^3)$ is the completion of $C_0^\infty(\mathbb{R}^3)$ with respect to the norm

$$\|u\|_D := |\nabla u|_2 + |\nabla u|_4.$$

$D(\mathbb{R}^3)$ is continuously embedded in $D^{1,2}(\mathbb{R}^3)$. By the Sobolev inequality, we know that $D^{1,2}(\mathbb{R}^3)$ is continuously embedded in $L^6 = L^6(\mathbb{R}^3)$ and $D(\mathbb{R}^3)$ is continuously embedded in $D(\mathbb{R}^3)$ is continuously embedded in $L^\infty = L^\infty(\mathbb{R}^3)$.

Under condition (V), we define a new Hilbert space

$$E := \left\{u \in H^1(\mathbb{R}^3) : \int_{\mathbb{R}^3} (|\nabla u|^2 + V(x)u^2)dx < \infty\right\}$$

with the inner product

$$\langle u, v \rangle = \int_{\mathbb{R}^3} (\nabla u \cdot \nabla v + V(x)uv)\, dx$$

and the norm $\|u\| = \langle u, u \rangle^{1/2}$. Obviously, the embedding $E \hookrightarrow L^s(\mathbb{R}^3)$ is continuous, for all $2 \leqslant s \leqslant 6$. Consequently, for each $2 \leqslant s \leqslant 6$, there exists a constant $d_s > 0$ such that

$$|u|_s \leqslant d_s\|u\|, \quad \forall u \in E. \tag{3.2}$$

Furthermore, it follows from the condition (V) that the embedding $E \hookrightarrow L^s(\mathbb{R}^3)$ is compact for any $s \in [2, 6)$ (see [18]).

System $(KGBI)$ has a variational structure. In fact, we consider the function $\mathcal{J} : E \times D(\mathbb{R}^3) \to \mathbb{R}$ defined by

$$\mathcal{J}(u, \phi) = \frac{1}{2}\int_{\mathbb{R}^3} (|\nabla u|^2 + V(x)u^2 - (2\omega + \phi)\phi u^2)dx - \frac{1}{8\pi}\int_{\mathbb{R}^3} |\nabla \phi|^2 dx$$

$$- \frac{\beta}{16\pi}\int_{\mathbb{R}^3} |\nabla \phi|^4 dx - \int_{\mathbb{R}^3} F(x, u)dx - \int_{\mathbb{R}^3} h(x)u dx.$$

The solutions $(u, \phi) \in E \times D(\mathbb{R}^3)$ of system $(KGBI)$ are the critical points of $\mathcal{J}$. As it is pointed in [60], the function $\mathcal{J}$ is strongly indefinite and is difficult to investigate. By the reduction method described in [25], we are led to the study of a new functional $I : E \to \mathbb{R}$ defined by $I(u) = J(u, \phi_u)$. By Proposition 3.1 (in the following), $I(u)$ is defined in the following which does not present such strongly indefinite nature.

We can obtain a C^1 functional $I : E \to \mathbb{R}$ given by

$$I(u) = \frac{1}{2} \int_{\mathbb{R}^3} [|\nabla u|^2 + V(x)u^2 - (2\omega + \phi_u)\phi_u u^2] dx$$

$$- \frac{1}{8\pi} \int_{\mathbb{R}^3} |\nabla \phi_u|^2 dx - \frac{\beta}{16\pi} \int_{\mathbb{R}^3} |\nabla \phi_u|^4 dx - \int_{\mathbb{R}^3} F(x, u) dx - \int_{\mathbb{R}^3} h(x)u dx$$

$$= \frac{1}{2} \int_{\mathbb{R}^3} (|\nabla u|^2 + V(x)u^2 + \phi_u^2 u^2) dx$$

$$+ \frac{1}{8\pi} \int_{\mathbb{R}^3} |\nabla \phi_u|^2 dx + \frac{3\beta}{16\pi} \int_{\mathbb{R}^3} |\nabla \phi_u|^4 dx - \int_{\mathbb{R}^3} F(x, u) dx - \int_{\mathbb{R}^3} h(x)u dx$$

$$= \frac{1}{2} \int_{\mathbb{R}^3} (|\nabla u|^2 + V(x)u^2 - \omega\phi_u u^2) dx$$

$$+ \frac{\beta}{16\pi} \int_{\mathbb{R}^3} |\nabla \phi_u|^4 dx - \int_{\mathbb{R}^3} F(x, u) dx - \int_{\mathbb{R}^3} h(x)u dx. \tag{3.3}$$

We consider the map $\Phi : E \to D, u \to \phi_u$. By standard arguments, $\Phi \in C^1(E, D)$. And the Gateaux derivative of I is

$$\langle I'(u), v \rangle = \int_{\mathbb{R}^3} (\nabla u \cdot \nabla v + V(x)uv - (2\omega + \phi_u)\phi_u uv dx$$

$$- \int_{\mathbb{R}^3} f(x, u)v dx - \int_{\mathbb{R}^3} h(x)v dx,$$

for all $u, v \in E$.

Now we can state our main result.

Theorem 3.1 *Suppose* (V), (f_1)—(f_4) *and* (H) *hold. Then there exists a positive constant* m_0 *such that system* $(KGBI)$ *admits at least two different solutions* $u_0, \tilde{u}_0$ *in* E *satisfying* $I(u_0) < 0$ *and* $I(\tilde{u}_0) > 0$ *if* $|h|_2 < m_0$.

Remark 3.1 In [55], Chen and Song proved that Klein-Gordon-Maxwell equation had two nontrivial solutions if $f(x, t)$ satisfies the local (AR) condition:

(LAR) There exist $\mu > 2$ and $r_0 > 0$ such that $\mathcal{F}(x, t) := \frac{1}{\mu}f(x, t)t - F(x, t) \geqslant 0$

for every $x \in \mathbb{R}^3$ and $|t| \geqslant r_0$, where $F(x, t) = \int_0^t f(x, s) ds$.

It is well-known that (AR) condition and (LAR) are employed not only to prove that the Euler-Lagrange function associated has a mountain pass geometry, but also to guarantee that the Palais-Smale sequences, or Cerami sequences are bounded.

Compared with (LAR), $\mathcal{F}(x,t)$ may have negative values.

Another widely used condition is the following condition introduced by Jeanjean[111].

(Je) There exists $\theta \geqslant 1$ such that $\theta\mathcal{F}_1(x,t) \geqslant \mathcal{F}_1(x,st)$ for all $s \in [0,1]$ and $t \in \mathbb{R}$, where $\mathcal{F}_1(x,t) := \dfrac{1}{4}f(x,t)t - F(x,t)$.

We can observe that when $s = 0$, then $\mathcal{F}_1(x,t) \geqslant 0$, but for our condition (f_4), $\mathcal{F}(x,t)$ may assume negative values.

In [3,58], the authors studied the Schrödinger-Poisson equation by assuming the following global condition to replace the (AR) condition:

(ASS) There exists $0 \leqslant \beta < \alpha$ such that $tf(t) - 4F(t) \geqslant -\beta t^2$, for all $t \in \mathbb{R}$, where α is a positive constant such that $\alpha \leqslant V(x)$.

Notice that we only need the local condition (f_4) in order to get nontrivial solutions.

In [118], Li and Tang used the following condition to get infinitely many solutions for homogenous system (KGM):

(LT) There exist two positive constants D_3 and r_0 such that $\dfrac{1}{4}f(x,t)t - F(x,t) \geqslant -D_3|t|^2$, if $|t| \geqslant r_0$.

Obviously, our condition (f_4) is weaker than (LT). Therefore, it is interesting to consider the nonhomogeneous system $(KGBI)$ under the conditions (f_3) and (f_4).

Remark 3.2   To the best of our knowledge, it seems that Theorem 3.1 is the first result about the existence of two solutions for the nonhomogeneous Klein-Gordon equation coupled with Born-Infeld theory on $\mathbb{R}^3$ with general nonlinearity f.

In Section 3.2, we will introduce the variational setting for the problem and give some related preliminaries. We give the proof of our main result in Section 3.3.

3.2   Variational setting and compactness condition

By [25], we know that the signs of ω is not relevant for the existence of solutions, so we can assume that $\omega > 0$.

Evidently, the properties of ϕ_u plays an important role in the study of $\mathcal{J}$. So we need the following technical results.

Proposition 3.1   *For any $u \in H^1(\mathbb{R}^3)$, there exists a unique $\phi = \phi_u \in D(\mathbb{R}^3)$ which satisfies*

$$\Delta\phi + \beta\Delta_4\phi = 4\pi(\phi + \omega)u^2 \quad in \quad \mathbb{R}^3.$$

Moreover, the map $\Phi : u \in H^1(\mathbb{R}^3) \mapsto \phi_u \in D(\mathbb{R}^3)$ is continuously differentiable, and

(i) $-\omega \leqslant \phi_u \leqslant 0$ *on the set $\{x \in \mathbb{R}^3 | u(x) \neq 0\}$;*

(ii) $\int_{\mathbb{R}^3} (|\nabla \phi_u|^2 + \beta |\nabla \phi_u|^4) dx \leqslant 4\pi\omega^2 |u|_2^2.$

Proposition 3.1 is proved in [60] for the first part and in [146] for the second part.

By Proposition 3.1 and $(KGBI)$, if $u \in E$ is a critical point of I, then $(u, \phi_u) \in E \times D(\mathbb{R}^3)$ is a critical point of $\mathcal{J}$, that is, $(u, \phi_u) \in E \times D(\mathbb{R}^3)$ is a solution of system $(KGBI)$.

Now we will prove the function I has the mountain pass geometry.

Lemma 3.1   Let $h \in L^2(\mathbb{R}^3)$. Suppose (V), (f_1) and (f_2) hold. Then there exist some positive constants ρ, α, m_0 such that $I(u) \geqslant \alpha$ for all $u \in E$ satisfying $\|u\| = \rho$ and h satisfying $|h|_2 < m_0$.

Proof. By (f_2), for any $\varepsilon > 0$, there exists $\delta > 0$ such that $|f(x,t)| \leqslant \varepsilon|t|$ for all $x \in \mathbb{R}^3$ and $|t| \leqslant \delta$. By (f_1), we obtain

$$|f(x,t)| \leqslant C_1(|t| + |t|^{p-1}) \leqslant C_1 \left(|t| \frac{t}{\delta}|^{p-2} + |t|^{p-1} \right)$$

$$= C_1 \left(\frac{1}{\delta^{p-2}} + 1 \right) |t|^{p-1}, \quad \text{for } |t| \geqslant \delta, \text{ a.e. } x \in \mathbb{R}^3.$$

Then for all $t \in \mathbb{R}$ and a.e. $x \in \mathbb{R}^3$ we have

$$|f(x,t)| \leqslant \varepsilon|t| + C_1 \left(\frac{1}{\delta^{p-2}} + 1 \right) |t|^{p-1} := \varepsilon|t| + C_\varepsilon|t|^{p-1}$$

and

$$|F(x,t)| \leqslant \frac{\varepsilon}{2}|t|^2 + \frac{C_\varepsilon}{p}|t|^p. \tag{3.4}$$

Therefore, due to (3.4), Proposition 3.1 and the Hölder inequality, we obtain

$$I(u) \geqslant \frac{1}{2}\|u\|^2 - \frac{\varepsilon}{2} \int_{\mathbb{R}^3} |u|^2 dx - \frac{C_\varepsilon}{p} \int_{\mathbb{R}^3} |u|^p dx - |h|_2|u|_2$$

$$\geqslant \frac{1}{2}\|u\|^2 - \frac{\varepsilon}{2}d_2^2\|u\|^2 - \frac{C_\varepsilon}{p}d_p^p\|u\|^p - d_2|h|_2\|u\|$$

$$= \|u\| \left\{ \left(\frac{1}{2} - \frac{\varepsilon}{2}d_2^2 \right) \|u\| - \frac{C_\varepsilon}{p}d_p^p\|u\|^{p-1} - d_2|h|_2 \right\}.$$

Let

$$\varepsilon = \frac{1}{2d_2^2} \quad \text{and} \quad g(t) = \frac{t}{4} - \frac{C_\varepsilon}{p}d_p^p t^{p-1}, \quad \text{for } t \geqslant 0.$$

Because $2 < p < 6$, we can see that there exists a positive constant ρ such that

$$\tilde{m}_0 := g(\rho) = \max_{t \geqslant 0} g(t) > 0.$$

Taking $m_0 := \dfrac{1}{2d_2^2}\tilde{m}_0$, then it follows that there exists a positive constant α such that $I(u)|_{\|u\|=\rho} \geqslant \alpha$ for all h satisfying $|h|_2 < m_0$. The proof is complete.   □

Lemma 3.2   *Assume that (V), (f_1)—(f_4) are satisfied, then there exists a function $u_0 \in E$ with $\|u_0\| > \rho$ such that $I(u_0) < 0$, where ρ is given in Lemma 3.1.*

Proof. By (f_3), there exist $L_1 > 0$ large enough and $M_1 > 0$, such that

$$F(x,t) \geqslant M_1|t|^\theta, \quad \text{for } |t| \geqslant L_1. \tag{3.5}$$

By (3.4), we get that

$$|F(x,t)| \leqslant C_3(1+|t|^{p-2})|t|^2, \quad \text{where } C_3 = \max\left\{\frac{\varepsilon}{2}, \frac{C_\varepsilon}{p}\right\}, \tag{3.6}$$

and then

$$|F(x,t)| \leqslant C_3(1+L_1^{p-2})|t|^2, \quad \text{when } |t| \leqslant L_1. \tag{3.7}$$

By (3.5) and (3.7), we have

$$F(x,t) \geqslant M_1|t|^\theta - M_2|t|^2, \quad \text{for all } t \in \mathbb{R}, \tag{3.8}$$

where $M_2 = M_1 L_1^{\theta-2} + C_3(1+L_1^{p-2})$.

Thus, by Proposition 3.1, taking $u \in E, u \neq 0$ and $\theta > 2$ we have

$$I(tu) = \frac{t^2}{2}\|u\|^2 - \frac{t^2}{2}\int_{\mathbb{R}^3}(2\omega\phi_{tu}u^2 + \phi_{tu}^2 u^2)dx - \frac{1}{8\pi}\int_{\mathbb{R}^3}|\nabla\phi_{tu}|^2 dx$$

$$- \frac{\beta}{16\pi}\int_{\mathbb{R}^3}|\nabla\phi_{tu}|^4 dx - \int_{\mathbb{R}^3}F(x,tu)dx - t\int_{\mathbb{R}^3}h(x)u dx$$

$$\leqslant \frac{t^2}{2}\|u\|^2 + \frac{t^2}{2}\int_{\mathbb{R}^3}\omega^2 u^2 dx - M_1 t^\theta\int_{\mathbb{R}^3}|u|^\theta dx + M_2 t^2\int_{\mathbb{R}^3}u^2 dx - t\int_{\mathbb{R}^3}h(x)u dx,$$

thus $I(tu) \to -\infty$ as $t \to +\infty$. The lemma is proved by taking $u_0 = t_0 u$ with $t_0 > 0$ large enough and $u \neq 0$.   □

Lemma 3.3   *Under assumptions (V), (f_1)—(f_4) and (H), any sequence $\{u_n\} \subset E$ satisfying*

$$I(u_n) \to c > 0, \quad \langle I'(u_n), u_n \rangle \to 0$$

is bounded in E. Moreover, $\{u_n\}$ has a strongly convergent subsequence in E.

Proof. To prove the boundedness of $\{u_n\}$, arguing by contradiction, suppose that, up to subsequences, we have $\|u_n\| \to +\infty$ as $n \to +\infty$. Let $v_n = \dfrac{u_n}{\|u_n\|}$, then

$\{v_n\}$ is bounded. Going if necessary to a subsequence, for some $v \in E$, we obtain that

$$v_n \rightharpoonup v \text{ in } E,$$

$$v_n \to v \text{ in } L^s(\mathbb{R}^3), \ 2 \leqslant s < 6,$$

$$v_n(x) \to v(x) \text{ a.e. in } \mathbb{R}^3.$$

Let $\Lambda = \{x \in \mathbb{R}^3 : v(x) \neq 0\}$. Suppose that $\text{meas}(\Lambda) > 0$, then $|u_n(x)| \to +\infty$ as $n \to \infty$ for a.e. $x \in \Lambda$. By (3.2) and (3.8), we obtain

$$\int_{\mathbb{R}^3} \frac{F(x, u_n)}{\|u_n\|^\theta} dx \geqslant M_1 \int_{\mathbb{R}^3} |v_n|^\theta dx - M_2 \frac{|u_n|^2}{\|u_n\|^\theta}$$

$$\geqslant M_1 \int_{\mathbb{R}^3} |v_n|^\theta dx - \frac{M_2 d_2^2}{\|u_n\|^{\theta-2}}$$

$$\to M_1 \int_\Lambda |v|^\theta dx > 0 \quad \text{as } n \to \infty. \tag{3.9}$$

By Proposition 3.1, from (3.2) and $\theta > 2$, so we can obtain that

$$\left| \int_{\mathbb{R}^3} \frac{\omega \phi_{u_n} u_n^2}{\|u_n\|^\theta} dx \right| \leqslant \frac{\omega^2 |u_n|_2^2}{\|u_n\|^\theta} \leqslant \frac{\omega^2 d_2^2}{\|u_n\|^{\theta-2}} \to 0 \quad \text{as } n \to \infty,$$

$$\left| \int_{\mathbb{R}^3} \frac{\beta |\nabla \phi_{u_n}|^4}{\|u_n\|^\theta} dx \right| \leqslant \frac{4\pi \omega^2 |u_n|_2^2}{\|u_n\|^\theta} \leqslant \frac{4\pi \omega^2 d_2^2}{\|u_n\|^{\theta-2}} \to 0 \quad \text{as } n \to \infty.$$

Since $h \in L^2(\mathbb{R}^3)$, we can obtain that

$$\left| \int_{\mathbb{R}^3} \frac{h(x) u_n}{\|u_n\|^\theta} dx \right| \leqslant \frac{|h|_2 |u_n|_2}{\|u_n\|^\theta} \leqslant \frac{|h|_2 d_2}{\|u_n\|^{\theta-1}} \to 0 \quad \text{as } n \to \infty.$$

By the definition of I , (3.8) and above inequalities, we have

$$0 = \lim_{n \to +\infty} \frac{I(u_n)}{\|u_n\|^\theta}$$

$$= \lim_{n \to +\infty} \left[\frac{1}{2\|u_n\|^{\theta-2}} - \int_{\mathbb{R}^3} \frac{\omega \phi_{u_n} u_n^2}{2\|u_n\|^\theta} dx + \frac{\beta}{16\pi} \int_{\mathbb{R}^3} \frac{|\nabla \phi_{u_n}|^4}{\|u_n\|^\theta} dx \right.$$

$$\left. - \int_{\mathbb{R}^3} \frac{F(x, u_n)}{\|u_n\|^\theta} dx - \int_{\mathbb{R}^3} \frac{h(x) u_n}{\|u_n\|^\theta} dx \right]$$

$$< 0,$$

which is a contradiction. Therefore, $\text{meas}(\Lambda) = 0$, which implies $v(x) = 0$ for almost everywhere $x \in \mathbb{R}^3$. By (f_1) and (3.6), we have for all $x \in \mathbb{R}^3$ and $|t| \leqslant r_0$,

$$|f(x, t)t - \mu F(x, t)| \leqslant |f(x, t)t| + \mu|F(x, t)|$$

$$\leqslant C_1(|t|^2 + |t|^p) + \mu C_3(1 + |t|^{p-2})t^2 \leqslant C_6(1 + |t|^{p-2})t^2$$

$$\leqslant C_6(1 + r_0^{p-2})t^2,$$

where $C_6 := 2\max\{C_1, \mu C_3\}$. Together with (f_4), we obtain

$$f(x, t)t - \mu F(x, t) \geqslant -C_7 t^2, \quad \text{for all } (x, t) \in \mathbb{R}^3 \times \mathbb{R}. \tag{3.10}$$

By $h \in L^2(\mathbb{R}^3)$, we can also obtain the following

$$\left| \int_{\mathbb{R}^3} \frac{h(x)u_n}{\|u_n\|^2} dx \right| \leqslant \frac{|h|_2 |u_n|_2}{\|u_n\|^2} \leqslant \frac{|h|_2 d_2}{\|u_n\|} \to 0 \quad \text{as } n \to \infty. \tag{3.11}$$

By (3.10), (3.11), Proposition 3.1, $v = 0$ and $\mu > 2$, we have

$$\frac{\mu I(u_n) - \langle I'(u_n), u_n \rangle}{\|u_n\|^2}$$

$$= \left(\frac{\mu}{2} - 1 \right) + \int_{\mathbb{R}^3} \frac{f(x, u_n)u_n - \mu F(x, u_n)}{\|u_n\|^2} dx + \left(\frac{\mu}{2} + 1 \right) \int_{\mathbb{R}^3} \frac{\phi_{u_n} u_n^2}{\|u_n\|^2} dx$$

$$+ 2\omega \int_{\mathbb{R}^3} \frac{\phi_{u_n} u_n^2}{\|u_n\|^2} dx + \frac{\mu}{8\pi} \int_{\mathbb{R}^3} \frac{|\nabla \phi_{u_n}|^2}{\|u_n\|^2} dx + \frac{3\beta\mu}{16\pi} \int_{\mathbb{R}^3} \frac{|\nabla \phi_{u_n}|^4}{\|u_n\|^2} dx$$

$$+ (1 - \mu) \int_{\mathbb{R}^3} \frac{h(x)u_n}{\|u_n\|^2} dx$$

$$\geqslant \left(\frac{\mu}{2} - 1 \right) - C_7 |v_n|_2^2 - 2\omega^2 |v_n|_2^2 + (1 - \mu) \int_{\mathbb{R}^3} \frac{h(x)u_n}{\|u_n\|^2} dx$$

$$\geqslant \left(\frac{\mu}{2} - 1 \right) - (C_7 + 2\omega^2)|v_n|_2^2 + (1 - \mu) \int_{\mathbb{R}^3} \frac{h(x)u_n}{\|u_n\|^2} dx$$

$$\to \frac{\mu}{2} - 1 \quad \text{as } n \to \infty.$$

Then we get $0 \geqslant \frac{1}{2} - \frac{1}{\mu}$, which contradicts with $\mu > 2$.

Therefore $\{u_n\}$ is a bounded in E.

Now we shall prove $\{u_n\}$ contains a convergent subsequence. Without loss of generality, passing to a subsequence if necessary, there exists $u \in E$ such that $u_n \rightharpoonup u$ in E. By using the embedding $E \hookrightarrow L^s(\mathbb{R}^3)$ are compact for any $s \in [2, 6)$, $u_n \to u$

in $L^s(\mathbb{R}^3)$ for $2 \leqslant s < 6$ and $u_n(x) \to u(x)$ a.e. $x \in \mathbb{R}^3$. By (3.3) and the Gateaux derivative of I, we can get that

$$\int_{\mathbb{R}^3} (|\nabla(u_n - u)|^2 + V(x)(u_n - u)^2) dx$$

$$= \langle I'(u_n) - I'(u), u_n - u \rangle + 2\omega \int_{\mathbb{R}^3} (\phi_{u_n} u_n - \phi_u u)(u_n - u) dx$$

$$+ \int_{\mathbb{R}^3} (f(x, u_n) - f(x, u))(u_n - u) dx + \int_{\mathbb{R}^3} (\phi_{u_n}^2 u_n - \phi_u^2 u)(u_n - u) dx.$$

By an easy computing, we can get that

$$\langle I'(u_n) - I'(u), u_n - u \rangle \to 0 \quad \text{as } n \to \infty$$

and

$$\int_{\mathbb{R}^3} [(2\omega + \phi_{u_n})\phi_{u_n} u_n - (2\omega + \phi_u)\phi_u u](u_n - u) dx$$

$$= 2\omega \int_{\mathbb{R}^3} (\phi_{u_n} u_n - \phi_u u)(u_n - u) dx + \int_{\mathbb{R}^3} (\phi_{u_n}^2 u_n - \phi_u^2 u)(u_n - u) dx$$

$$\to 0 \quad \text{as } n \to +\infty.$$

Indeed, by the Hölder inequality, the Sobolev inequality and Proposition 3.1, we can get

$$\left| \int_{\mathbb{R}^3} (\phi_{u_n} - \phi_u)(u_n - u) u_n dx \right| \leqslant |(\phi_{u_n} - \phi_u)(u_n - u)|_2 |u_n|_2$$

$$\leqslant |\phi_{u_n} - \phi_u|_6 |u_n - u|_3 |u_n|_2$$

$$\leqslant C \|\phi_{u_n} - \phi_u\|_D |u_n - u|_3 |u_n|_2,$$

where C is a positive constant. Since $u_n \to u$ in $L^s(\mathbb{R}^3)$ for $2 \leqslant s < 6$, we get

$$\left| \int_{\mathbb{R}^3} (\phi_{u_n} - \phi_u)(u_n - u) u_n dx \right| \to 0 \quad \text{as } n \to +\infty$$

and

$$\left| \int_{\mathbb{R}^3} \phi_u(u_n - u)(u_n - u) dx \right| \leqslant |\phi_u|_6 |u_n - u|_3 |u_n - u|_2 \to 0 \quad \text{as } n \to +\infty.$$

Thus we obtain

$$\int_{\mathbb{R}^3} (\phi_{u_n} u_n - \phi_u u)(u_n - u) dx$$

$$= \int_{\mathbb{R}^3} (\phi_{u_n} - \phi_u)(u_n - u)u_n dx + \int_{\mathbb{R}^3} \phi_u(u_n - u)(u_n - u)dx \to 0$$

as $n \to +\infty$. In view of that the sequence $\{\phi_{u_n}^2 u_n\}$ is bounded in $L^{3/2}(\mathbb{R}^3)$, since

$$|\phi_{u_n}^2 u_n|_{3/2} \leqslant |\phi_{u_n}|_6^2 |u_n|_3,$$

so

$$\left| \int_{\mathbb{R}^3} (\phi_{u_n}^2 u_n - \phi_u^2 u)(u_n - u)dx \right| \leqslant |\phi_{u_n}^2 u_n - \phi_u^2 u|_{3/2} |u_n - u|_3$$

$$\leqslant (|\phi_{u_n}^2 u_n|_{3/2} + |\phi_u^2 u|_{3/2})|u_n - u|_3$$

$$\to 0 \quad \text{as } n \to +\infty.$$

By $u_n \to u$ in $L^s(\mathbb{R}^3)$ for $2 \leqslant s < 6$, we have

$$\int_{\mathbb{R}^3} (f(x, u_n) - f(x, u))(u_n - u)dx \to 0 \quad \text{as } n \to +\infty.$$

Thus, we get

$$\|u_n - u\|^2$$

$$= \langle I'(u_n) - I'(u), u_n - u \rangle + 2\omega \int_{\mathbb{R}^3} (\phi_{u_n} u_n - \phi_u u)(u_n - u)dx$$

$$+ \int_{\mathbb{R}^3} (f(x, u_n) - f(x, u))(u_n - u)dx + \int_{\mathbb{R}^3} (\phi_{u_n}^2 u_n - \phi_u^2 u)(u_n - u)dx$$

$$\to 0 \quad \text{as } n \to +\infty.$$

Therefore we get $\|u_n - u\| \to 0$ in E as $n \to \infty$. The proof is complete. $\qquad\square$

3.3   Proofs of main results

Now, we are ready to prove our main result.

Proof of Theorem 3.1   Firstly, we prove that there exists a function $u_0 \in E$ such that $I'(u_0) = 0$ and $I(u_0) < 0$.

Since $h \in L^2(\mathbb{R}^3)$, $h \geqslant 0$ and $h \not\equiv 0$, we can choose a function $\varphi \in E$ such that

$$\int_{\mathbb{R}^3} h(x)\varphi(x)dx > 0.$$

Hence, by Proposition 3.1, $\theta > 2$ and (3.8), we obtain that

$$I(t\varphi) \leqslant \frac{t^2}{2}\|\varphi\|^2 + t^2 \int_{\mathbb{R}^3} \omega^2 \varphi^2 dx - M_1 t^\theta |\varphi|_\theta^\theta + M_2 t^2 |\varphi|_2^2 - t \int_{\mathbb{R}^3} h(x)\varphi dx < 0,$$

for $t > 0$ small enough. Thus, we obtain

$$c_0 = \inf\{I(u) : u \in \bar{B}_\rho\} < 0,$$

where $\rho > 0$ is given by Lemma 3.1, $B_\rho = \{u \in E : \|u\| < \rho\}$. By the Ekeland's Variational Principle [85], there exists a sequence $\{u_n\} \subset \bar{B}_\rho$ such that

$$c_0 \leqslant I(u_n) < c_0 + \frac{1}{n}$$

and

$$I(v) \geqslant I(u_n) - \frac{1}{n}\|v - u_n\|,$$

for all $v \in \bar{B}_\rho$. Then by a standard procedure, we can prove that $\{u_n\}$ is a bounded (PS) sequence of I. Hence, by Lemma 3.3 we know that there exists a function $u_0 \in E$ such that $I'(u_0) = 0$ and $I(u_0) = c_0 < 0$.

Secondly, we prove that there exists a function $\tilde{u}_0 \in E$ such that $I'(\tilde{u}_0) = 0$ and $I(\tilde{u}_0) > 0$.

By Lemma 3.1, Lemma 3.2 and the Mountain Pass theorem[200, 224], there is a sequence $\{u_n\} \subset E$ such that

$$I(u_n) \to \tilde{c}_0 > 0, \quad \text{and} \quad I'(u_n) \to 0.$$

In view of Lemma 3.3, we know that $\{u_n\}$ has a strongly convergent subsequence (still denoted by $\{u_n\}$) in E. So there exists a function $\tilde{u}_0 \in E$ such that $\{u_n\} \to \tilde{u}_0$ as $n \to \infty$ and $I'(\tilde{u}_0) = 0$ and $I(\tilde{u}_0) > 0$. The proof is complete.   □

Chapter 4   Localized Nodal Solutions for Kirchhoff Equations

4.1   Introduction and main results

In this Chapter, we study the following semiclassical states of nonlinear Kirchhoff equation

$$(SK_\varepsilon) \begin{cases} -\left(\varepsilon^2 a + \varepsilon b \int_{\mathbb{R}^3} |\nabla u|^2 dx\right) \Delta u + V(x)u = |u|^{p-2}u, \quad x \in \mathbb{R}^3, \\ u \in H^1(\mathbb{R}^3), \end{cases}$$

where $p \in (4, 2^*), 2^* = 6$, $\varepsilon > 0$ is a small parameter and $V : \mathbb{R}^3 \to \mathbb{R}$ is a continuous function satisfying the following conditions:

(V_1) $V \in C^1(\mathbb{R}^3, \mathbb{R})$ and there exist $n_0 > m_0 > 0$ such that $m_0 \leqslant V(x) \leqslant n_0$ for any $x \in \mathbb{R}^3$.

(V_2) There is a bounded domain $\Lambda \subset \mathbb{R}^3$ with smooth boundary $\partial \Lambda$ such that

$$\vec{n}(x) \cdot \nabla V(x) > 0, \quad \text{for any } x \in \partial \Lambda, \tag{4.1}$$

where $\vec{n}(x)$ denotes the outward normal to $\partial \Lambda$ at x and "$\cdot$" denotes the inner product in $\mathbb{R}^3$.

Note that if V has an isolated local minimum set, the condition (V_2) is satisfied. That is, V has a local trapping potential well. Under (V_2), the set of critical points of V is

$$A = \{x \in \Lambda | \nabla V(x) = 0\} \neq \varnothing, \tag{4.2}$$

and A is a compact subset of Λ. In the following, we will assume $0 \in A$.

Equation (SK_ε) or a more general versions of (SK_ε) with $\varepsilon = 1$

$$-\left(a + b \int_{\mathbb{R}^3} |\nabla u|^2 dx\right) \Delta u + V(x)u = f(x, u), \quad x \in \mathbb{R}^N \tag{4.3}$$

has been studied recently under some different conditions on $f(x, u)$ and $V(x)$, where $N = 1, 2, 3$ and a, b are two positive constants. It is well known that problem (4.3) is a nonlocal problem since the presence of the term $b \int_{\mathbb{R}^3} |\nabla u|^2 dx$. This fact indicates that (4.3) is not a pointwise identity. It causes some mathematical difficulties, and in the mean time, makes the study of such a problem particularly interesting. For a pure power $f(x,u) := |u|^{p-2}u$ $(3 < p \leqslant 6)$, Li and Ye[119] studied the existence of a positive ground state solution by using a monotonicity trick and a new version of global compactness lemma. The authors used the constrained minimization on a new manifold which is related to the Pohozaev's identity to get a positive ground state solution to (4.3).

We note that if $V(x) = 0$ and $\mathbb{R}^N$ is replaced by a bounded domain $\Omega \subset \mathbb{R}^N$ in (4.3), then we have the following Kirchhoff Dirichlet problem

$$\begin{cases} -\left(a + b \int_{\Omega} |\nabla u|^2 dx\right) \Delta u = f(x,u), & x \in \Omega, \\ u = 0, & x \in \partial\Omega, \end{cases}$$

which is arised to seek for standing wave solutions of the equation

$$\rho \frac{\partial^2 u}{\partial t^2} - \left(\frac{P_0}{h} + \frac{E}{2L} \int_0^L |\frac{\partial u}{\partial x}|^2 dx\right) \frac{\partial^2 u}{\partial x^2} = 0.$$

It is related to the stationary analogue of the Kirchhoff equation

$$u_{tt} - \left(a + b \int_{\mathbb{R}^3} |\nabla u|^2 dx\right) \Delta u = g(x,t), \tag{4.4}$$

which is proposed by Kirchhoff[114] as an extension of the classical D'Alembert's wave equation for free vibrations of elastic strings. Kirchhoff's model takes into account the changes in length of the string produced by transverse vibrations. In [63], the authors pointed out that Problem (4.4) models several physical and biological systems, where u describes a process which depends on the average of itself (for example, population density).

Motivated by the works above, we study the existence of localized sign-changing solutions to the semiclassical nonlinear Kirchhoff equation (SK_ε). Before giving our main results, we give some notations. Let $H^1(\mathbb{R}^3)$ be the usual Sobolev space endowed with the standard scalar and norm

$$(u,v) = \int_{\mathbb{R}^3} (\nabla u \nabla v + uv) dx, \qquad \|u\| = \left(\int_{\mathbb{R}^3} (|\nabla u|^2 + |u|^2) dx\right)^{1/2}.$$

$D^{1,2}(\mathbb{R}^3)$ is the completion of $C_0^\infty(\mathbb{R}^3)$ with respect to the norm

$$\|u\|_D := \|u\|_{D^{1,2}(\mathbb{R}^3)} = \left(\int_{\mathbb{R}^3} |\nabla u|^2 dx\right)^{1/2}.$$

The norm on $L^s = L^s(\mathbb{R}^3)$ with $1 < s < \infty$ is given by $|u|_s = \left(\int_{\mathbb{R}^3} |u|^s dx \right)^{1/s}$.

Assume the functional space is

$$H_\varepsilon = \left\{ u \in H^1(\mathbb{R}^3) : \|u\|_\varepsilon = \left(\int_{\mathbb{R}^3} (|\nabla u|^2 + V(\varepsilon x)u^2) dx \right)^{1/2} < \infty \right\}.$$

Since $0 < m_0 \leqslant V(x) \leqslant n_0$, we have

$$\min(1, m_0)\|u\|^2 \leqslant \int_{\mathbb{R}^3} (|\nabla u|^2 + V(\varepsilon x)u^2) dx \leqslant \max\{1, n_0\}\|u\|^2,$$

$$H_\varepsilon(\mathbb{R}^3) \hookrightarrow L^p(\mathbb{R}^3), \quad 2 \leqslant p \leqslant 6$$

and

$$|u|_p \leqslant C_p\|u\| \leqslant C_p'\|u\|_\varepsilon.$$

Moreover we make the following assumptions. For any set $\Omega \subset \mathbb{R}^3, \varepsilon > 0$ and $\delta > 0$, we set

$$\begin{aligned}
\Omega_\varepsilon &= \{x \in \mathbb{R}^3 : \varepsilon x \in \Omega\}, \\
\Omega^\delta &= \{x \in \mathbb{R}^3 : dist(x, \Omega) := \inf_{z \in \Omega} |x - z| < \delta\}.
\end{aligned} \tag{4.5}$$

A function $u \in H^1(\mathbb{R}^3)$ is called sign-changing if $u^+ \neq 0$ and $u^- \neq 0$, where $u^\pm = \max\{\pm u, 0\}$.

Now we state our main result.

Theorem 4.1 *Suppose that $4 < p < 6$, (V_1) and (V_2) hold. Then for any positive integer N, there exists $\varepsilon_N > 0$ such that if $0 < \varepsilon < \varepsilon_N$, (SK_ε) has at least N pairs of sign-changing solutions $\pm v_{j,\varepsilon}, j = 1, 2, \cdots, N$, satisfying that, for any $\delta > 0$, there exist $c = c(\delta, N) > 0$ and $C = C(\delta, N) > 0$ such that*

$$|v_{j,\varepsilon}(x)| \leqslant C \exp\left(-\frac{cdist(x, A^\delta)}{\varepsilon} \right), \quad 1 \leqslant j \leqslant N.$$

In recent years, the existence and multiplicity solutions for (SK_ε) have been studied by many researchers under different assumptions on the potential and nonlinearity. Figueiredo[88] constructed a family of positive solutions which concentrates around the local minima of V as $\varepsilon \to 0$, the nonlinearities is subcritical. Motivated by [88], He[105] extended the result of Figueiredo to the case where the nonlinearity is of critical growth. In [217] the authors consider the stability of ground states to a nonlinear focusing Schrödinger equation in presence of a Kirchhoff term. Zhang and Perera[221] considered sign changing solutions of Kirchhoff type problems via invariant sets of descent flow. Perera and Zhang[151] also considered nontrivial solutions of Kirchhoff type problems via the Yang index.

Especially, if $a = 1, b = 0$ and $\mathbb{R}^3$ replaced by $\mathbb{R}^N$, (SK_ε) is reduced to a singular perturbed Schrödinger equation i.e.

$$-\varepsilon^2 \Delta u + V(x)u = |u|^{p-2}u, \quad x \in \mathbb{R}^N, 2 < p < 2^*, N \geqslant 1. \qquad (4.6)$$

Floer and Weinstein[90] constructed a single peak solution which concentrates around any given non-degenerate critical point of the potential V. Oh[149] showed the existence of muli-peak solutions which concentrate around any finite subsets of the non-degenerate critical points of V. The methods in [90, 149] are mainly used a Lyapunov-Schmidt reduction.

The concentration behavior of the positive solutions also has been considered by variational methods. When $\varepsilon > 0$ small enough, by using the Mountain-Pass theorem, Rabinowitz[154] proved that (4.6) possesses a positive ground state solution under the following condition:

(V_3) $V_\infty = \liminf\limits_{|x| \to \infty} V(x) > V_0 = \inf\limits_{x \in \mathbb{R}^N} V(x) > 0$.

Other results on the concentration behavior for the family of positive ground solution can see [65]. By using the same arguments as in [65, 135, 154], He and Zou[103] considered the existence, concentration and multiplicity of solutions for (SK_ε) with general nonlinearity $f(u)$, and the potential $V(x)$ satisfy the following condition:

(V_4) $0 < V_0 := \inf V(x) < \liminf\limits_{|x| \to \infty} V(x) = V_\infty$, where $V_\infty \leqslant +\infty$ and $f(u) \in$

$C^1(\mathbb{R}^+, \mathbb{R}^+)$ is a subcritical function satisfying the Ambrosetti-Rabinowtiz condition, which is concentrate on the minima of $V(x)$ as $\varepsilon \to 0$.

Now we give the outline of the proof, we set $v(x) = u(\varepsilon x)$. Then (SK_ε) is changed to

$$-\left(a + b\int_{\mathbb{R}^3} |\nabla v|^2 dx\right) \Delta v + V(\varepsilon x)v = |v|^{p-2}v, x \in \mathbb{R}^3, \quad v \in H^1(\mathbb{R}^3), \qquad (4.7)$$

and the corresponding energy function is

$$I_\varepsilon(v) = \frac{1}{2}\int_{\mathbb{R}^3} (a|\nabla v|^2 + V(\varepsilon x)v^2)dx + \frac{b}{4}\left(\int_{\mathbb{R}^3} |\nabla v|^2 dx\right)^2 - \frac{1}{p}\int_{\mathbb{R}^3} v^p dx. \qquad (4.8)$$

It is well known that, by using Rabinowitz[154], we can prove that I_ε satisfies the $(PS)_c$ condition if c is smaller than the mountain pass value of the limiting function

$$I(v) = \frac{1}{2} \int_{\mathbb{R}^3} (a|\nabla v|^2 + V_0 v^2) dx + \frac{b}{4} \left(\int_{\mathbb{R}^3} |\nabla v|^2 dx \right)^2 - \frac{1}{p} \int_{\mathbb{R}^3} v^p dx,$$

where $V_0 = \liminf_{|x| \to \infty} V(x)$. However, we will construct the solutions in Theorem 4.1 have larger critical values. The variational problem does not satisfy the compact condition anymore. By the Byeon-Wang's penalization method[37], we difine $\Gamma_\varepsilon :$ $H_\varepsilon \to \mathbb{R}$ by

$$\Gamma_\varepsilon(v) = I_\varepsilon(v) + Q_\varepsilon(v),$$

where

$$Q_\varepsilon(v) = \left(\int_{\mathbb{R}^3} \chi_\varepsilon v^2 dx - 1 \right)_+^\beta$$

and

$$\chi_\varepsilon(x) = \begin{cases} 0, & \text{if } x \in \Lambda_\varepsilon, \\ \varepsilon^{-6} \xi(\text{dist}(x, \Lambda_\varepsilon)), & \text{if } x \notin \Lambda_\varepsilon. \end{cases}$$

The function Q_ε will act as a penalization to force the concentration phenomena to occur inside the set of A. The function Γ_ε has an advantage that it has a higher threshold for $(PS)_c$ condition to hold. Indeed, for any positive integer L, there exists $\varepsilon_L > 0$ such that Γ_ε satisfies the $(PS)_c$ condition for every $c < L$ if $0 < \varepsilon < \varepsilon_L$.

By using a new minimax theorem for sign-changing solutions (see [131]) and the genus (see [154]), we obtain that, for any positive integer N, there exists $\varepsilon_N > 0$ such that Γ_ε has at least N pairs of sign-changing critical points $v_{j,\varepsilon}$ $(1 \leqslant j \leqslant N)$ if $0 < \varepsilon < \varepsilon_N$.

To verify the critical point $v_{j,\varepsilon}$ of Γ_ε is a solution of the original problem (4.6), we need a finer asymptotic analysis and the local Pohozaev identity. Moreover, we show that the concentration points of these solutions lie in A as $\varepsilon \to 0$.

Remark 4.1 As it is pointed in [53, 156] considered the critical frequency case, that is, V satisfies

(V_5) $\liminf_{|x| \to \infty} V(x) > \inf_{x \in \mathbb{R}^N} V(x) = 0$;

(V_6) There exists a closed subset Z with a nonempty interior such that $V(x) = 0$ for $x \in Z$.

By using minimax theorem, they obtained that for any integer N, there exists $\varepsilon_N > 0$ such that for $0 < \varepsilon < \varepsilon_N$, (4.6) has at least N solutions. Under the assumption of critical frequency, one can use higher dimensional symmetric structures to

construct minimax values below the mountain pass value of the limiting function
I. However, in our case with positive potentials, the energies of the sequence of
localized nodal solutions tend to infinity.

Remark 4.2 We note that, to the best of our knowledge, there is no result on the
existence and concentration of sign-changing solutions for Kirchhoff type equation
under $(V_1), (V_2)$. In the present, we will adopt the ideas of Chen and Wang[53] to
study the existence of sign-changing solutions for (SK_ε). But the method of Chen
and Wang[53] can not be used directly because the nonlocal term and more careful
analysis is needed.

Throughout this Chapter, the letters C, C' will be used to denote various positive
constants which may vary from line to line and are not essential to the problem. E'
is a dual space for a Banach space E. The closure and the boundary of set G
are denoted by $\bar{G}$ and ∂G respectively. For $F \in C^1(E, \mathbb{R})$, we denote the Fréchet
derivative of F at u by $F'(u)$, and the Gateaux derivative of F by $\langle F'(u), v \rangle$ for all
$u, v \in E$. We denote "$\rightharpoonup$" weak convergence and "$\rightarrow$" strong convergence. Also if
we take a subsequence of a sequence $\{u_n\}$, we shall denote it again $\{u_n\}$.

Chapter 4 is organized as follows. In Section 4.2, we introduce the penalized
function Γ_ε, which show that Γ_ε satisfy $(PS)_c$ condition for $c < L$ and ε small
enough. In Section 4.3, when ε is small, we show the existence of multiple sign-
changing solutions of the problem through an abstract critical point theorem. In
Section 4.4, we give the proof of Theorem 4.1. We prove the solutions obtained in
Section 4.3 are in fact solutions of the original problem for ε small.

4.2 Variational setting and compactness condition

Set $\xi \in C^\infty(\mathbb{R})$ be a cut-off function such that $0 \leqslant \xi(t) \leqslant 1$ and $\xi'(t) \geqslant 0$ for any
$t \in \mathbb{R}$. $\xi(t) > 0$ if $t > 0$, $\xi(t) = 1$ if $t \geqslant 1$ and $\xi(t) = 0$ if $t \leqslant 0$. Define

$$\chi_\varepsilon(x) = \begin{cases} 0, & \text{if } x \in \Lambda_\varepsilon, \\ \varepsilon^{-6}\xi(\text{dist}(x, \Lambda_\varepsilon)), & \text{if } x \notin \Lambda_\varepsilon. \end{cases} \tag{4.9}$$

Obviously, for ε small, χ_ε is a C^1 function and

$$\begin{cases} \chi_\varepsilon(x) = 0, & \text{if } x \in \Lambda_\varepsilon, \\ \chi_\varepsilon(x) = \varepsilon^{-6}, & \text{if } x \notin (\Lambda_\varepsilon)^1. \end{cases}$$

For $u \in H^1(\mathbb{R}^3)$, we define the penalization function

$$Q_\varepsilon(v) = \left(\int_{\mathbb{R}^3} \chi_\varepsilon v^2 dx - 1 \right)_+^\beta, \tag{4.10}$$

which β satisfies $2 < 2\beta < p$ and $(t)_+ = \max\{t, 0\}$. For $v \in H^1(\mathbb{R}^3)$, define

$$\Gamma_\varepsilon(v) = I_\varepsilon(v) + Q_\varepsilon(v), \tag{4.11}$$

where I_ε is defined by (4.8). For any $u, v \in H(\mathbb{R}^3)$,

$$\langle \Gamma'_\varepsilon(v), u \rangle = \int_{\mathbb{R}^3} (a\nabla v\nabla u + V(\varepsilon x)vu)dx + b\int_{\mathbb{R}^3} |\nabla v|^2 dx \int_{\mathbb{R}^3} \nabla v\nabla u dx$$

$$+ 2\beta \left(\int_{\mathbb{R}^3} \chi_\varepsilon v^2 dx - 1 \right)_+^{\beta-1} \int_{\mathbb{R}^3} \chi_\varepsilon vu dx - \int_{\mathbb{R}^3} |v|^{p-2}vu dx. \tag{4.12}$$

The critical point v of Γ_ε is a solution of

$$- \left(a + b\int_{\mathbb{R}^3} |\nabla v|^2 dx \right) \Delta v + V(\varepsilon x)v$$

$$+ 2\beta \left(\int_{\mathbb{R}^3} \chi_\varepsilon v^2 dx - 1 \right)_+^{\beta-1} \chi_\varepsilon v = |v|^{p-2}v, \tag{4.13}$$

for any $v \in H^1(\mathbb{R}^3)$. If v is a critical point of Γ_ε with $Q_\varepsilon(v) = 0$, then v is a solution of (4.7).

Lemma 4.1 *For any $L > 0$, there exists $\varepsilon_L > 0$ such that, for any $\varepsilon \in (0, \varepsilon_L)$ and $c < L$, Γ_ε satisfies $(PS)_c$ condition.*

Proof. Let $\{u_n\} \subset H^1(\mathbb{R}^3)$ satisfy the following condition:

$$\Gamma_\varepsilon(u_n) \to c, \quad \Gamma'_\varepsilon(u_n) \to 0 \quad \text{in } (H^1(\mathbb{R}^3))'.$$

Now we can show that $\{u_n\}$ contains a convergent subsequence in $H^1(\mathbb{R}^3)$. By

$$o(\|u_n\|) + L \geqslant o(\|u_n\|) + c = \Gamma_\varepsilon(u_n) - \frac{1}{p}\langle \Gamma'_\varepsilon(u_n), u_n \rangle$$

$$= \frac{1}{2}\int_{\mathbb{R}^3} (a|\nabla u_n|^2 + V(\varepsilon x)u_n^2)dx + \frac{b}{4}\left(\int_{\mathbb{R}^3} |\nabla u_n|^2 dx \right)^2 - \frac{1}{p}\int_{\mathbb{R}^3} |u_n|^p dx$$

$$+ \left(\int_{\mathbb{R}^3} \chi_\varepsilon u_n^2 dx - 1 \right)_+^\beta - \frac{1}{p}\int_{\mathbb{R}^3} (a|\nabla u_n|^2 + V(\varepsilon)u_n^2)\,dx - \frac{b}{p}\left(\int_{\mathbb{R}^3} |\nabla u_n|^2 dx \right)^2$$

$$+ \frac{1}{p}\int_{\mathbb{R}^3} |u_n|^p dx - \frac{2\beta}{p}\left(\int_{\mathbb{R}^3} \chi_\varepsilon u_n^2 dx - 1 \right)_+^{\beta-1} \int_{\mathbb{R}^3} \chi_\varepsilon u_n^2 dx$$

$$= \left(\frac{1}{2} - \frac{1}{p} \right)\int_{\mathbb{R}^3} (a|\nabla u_n|^2 + V(\varepsilon x)u_n^2)dx + b\left(\frac{1}{4} - \frac{1}{p} \right)\left(\int_{\mathbb{R}^3} |\nabla u_n|^2 dx \right)^2$$

$$+ \left(\int_{\mathbb{R}^3} \chi_\varepsilon u_n^2 dx - 1 \right)_+^\beta - \frac{2\beta}{p} \left(\int_{\mathbb{R}^3} \chi_\varepsilon u_n^2 dx - 1 \right)_+^{\beta-1} \int_{\mathbb{R}^3} \chi_\varepsilon u_n^2 dx,$$

and $2 < 2\beta < p$, there exists $\eta_L > 0$ independent of ε such that $\|u_n\| \leqslant \eta_L$ and $Q_\varepsilon(u_n) \leqslant \eta_L$. Suppose that $u_n \rightharpoonup u$ in $H^1(\mathbb{R}^3)$ as $n \to \infty$ and

$$\lambda_n := 2\beta \left(\int_{\mathbb{R}^3} \chi_\varepsilon u_n^2 dx - 1 \right)_+^{\beta-1} \to \lambda, \quad n \to \infty.$$

Easily to prove that u solves

$$- \left(a + b \int_{\mathbb{R}^3} |\nabla u|^2 dx \right) \Delta u + V(\varepsilon x)u + \lambda \chi_\varepsilon u = |u|^{p-2}u. \tag{4.14}$$

Hence, for any $v \in H^1(\mathbb{R}^3)$,

$$a \int_{\mathbb{R}^3} \nabla(u_n - u) \nabla v dx + b \int_{\mathbb{R}^3} |\nabla u|^2 dx \int_{\mathbb{R}^3} \nabla(u_n - u) \nabla v dx$$

$$+ b \int_{\mathbb{R}^3} (|\nabla u_n|^2 - |\nabla u|^2) dx \int_{\mathbb{R}^3} \nabla u_n \nabla v dx + \int_{\mathbb{R}^3} V(\varepsilon x)(u_n - u) v dx$$

$$+ \lambda \int_{\mathbb{R}^3} \chi_\varepsilon(u_n - u) v dx + (\lambda_n - \lambda) \int_{\mathbb{R}^3} \chi_\varepsilon u_n v dx - \int_{\mathbb{R}^3} (|u_n|^{p-2}u_n - |u|^{p-2}u) v dx$$

$$= \langle \Gamma_\varepsilon'(u_n), v \rangle = o(\|v\|), \quad n \to \infty. \tag{4.15}$$

Since Λ is a bounded set, there exists $r_0 > 0$ satisfy $\Lambda \subset B(0, r_0)$. Let ϕ_ε be a C^∞ cut-off function such that $0 \leqslant \phi_\varepsilon \leqslant 1$ and $|\nabla \phi_\varepsilon| \leqslant 4$ in $\mathbb{R}^3$, $\phi_\varepsilon(x) = 1$ if $|x| \geqslant \varepsilon^{-1}r_0 + 2$ and $\phi_\varepsilon(x) = 0$ if $|x| \leqslant \varepsilon^{-1}r_0 + 1$. We choose $v = \phi_\varepsilon^2(u_n - u)$ in (4.14) we obtain that

$$\left(a + b \int_{\mathbb{R}^3} |\nabla u|^2 dx \right) \int_{\mathbb{R}^3} |\nabla(\phi_\varepsilon(u_n - u))|^2 dx + \int_{\mathbb{R}^3} V(\varepsilon x)\phi_\varepsilon^2(u_n - u)^2 dx$$

$$+ b \int_{\mathbb{R}^3} (|\nabla u_n|^2 - |\nabla u|^2) dx \int_{\mathbb{R}^3} \nabla u_n \left(2\phi_\varepsilon \nabla \phi_\varepsilon(u_n - u) + \phi_\varepsilon^2 \nabla(u_n - u) \right) dx$$

$$+ \lambda \int_{\mathbb{R}^3} \chi_\varepsilon \phi_\varepsilon^2(u_n - u)^2 dx + (\lambda_n - \lambda) \int_{\mathbb{R}^3} \chi_\varepsilon \phi_\varepsilon^2(u_n - u)^2 dx$$

$$- (p-1) \int_{\mathbb{R}^3} (\theta u_n + (1-\theta)u)^{p-2} \phi_\varepsilon^2(u_n - u)^2 dx$$

$$- \left(a + b \int_{\mathbb{R}^3} |\nabla u|^2 dx \right) \int_{\mathbb{R}^3} (u_n - u)^2 |\nabla \phi_\varepsilon|^2 dx = o(1) \quad \text{as } n \to \infty, \tag{4.16}$$

where $0 < \theta < 1$ comes from the mean value theorem. By $\lambda_n \to \lambda, n \to \infty, |\nabla \phi_\varepsilon|^2$ has a compact support, and $u_n \rightharpoonup u$ in $H^1(\mathbb{R}^3)$ as $n \to \infty$, we have that

$$(\lambda_n - \lambda) \int_{\mathbb{R}^3} \chi_\varepsilon \phi_\varepsilon^2 (u_n - u) u_n dx = o(1), \qquad \int_{\mathbb{R}^3} (u_n - u)^2 |\nabla \phi_\varepsilon|^2 = o(1),$$

as $n \to \infty$. Then by $V \geqslant m_0$ in $\mathbb{R}^3$ and (4.15) , we obtain that

$$\min \left\{ a + b \int_{\mathbb{R}^3} |\nabla u|^2 dx, m_0 \right\} \| \phi_\varepsilon (u_n - u) \|^2$$

$$\leqslant \left(a + b \int_{\mathbb{R}^3} |\nabla u|^2 dx \right) \int_{\mathbb{R}^3} |\nabla \phi_\varepsilon (u_n - u)|^2 dx + \int_{\mathbb{R}^3} V(\varepsilon x) \phi_\varepsilon^2 (u_n - u)^2 dx$$

$$+ b \int_{\mathbb{R}^3} (|\nabla u_n|^2 - |\nabla u|^2) dx \int_{\mathbb{R}^3} \nabla u_n \{ 2\phi_\varepsilon \nabla \phi_\varepsilon (u_n - u) + \phi_\varepsilon^2 \nabla (u_n - u) \} dx$$

$$\leqslant (p-1) \int_{\mathbb{R}^3} |\theta u_n + (1-\theta) u|^{p-2} \phi_\varepsilon^2 (u_n - u)^2 dx + o(1)$$

$$\leqslant (p-1) \left(\int_{\mathbb{R}^3} |\theta u_n + (1-\theta) u|^p dx \right)^{(p-2)/p} \left(\int_{\mathbb{R}^3} \phi_\varepsilon^p (u_n - u)^p dx \right)^{2/p} + o(1)$$

$$\leqslant C(p-1) \left\{ \left(\int_{|x| \geqslant \varepsilon^{-1} r_0 + 1} |u_n|^p dx \right)^{(p-2)/p} + \left(\int_{|x| \geqslant \varepsilon^{-1} r_0 + 1} |u|^p dx \right)^{(p-2)/p} \right\}$$

$$\times \| \phi_\varepsilon (u_n - u) \|^2 + o(1) \quad \text{as } n \to \infty, \tag{4.17}$$

where $C > 0$ is a constant independent of n and ε. By Fatou lemma, we get that

$$\int_{\mathbb{R}^3} (\nabla u_n \phi_\varepsilon^2 \nabla u_n - \nabla u_n \phi_\varepsilon^2 \nabla u) dx = \int_{\mathbb{R}^3} (|\nabla u_n|^2 \phi_\varepsilon^2 - |\nabla u_n||\nabla u| \phi_\varepsilon^2) dx \geqslant 0,$$

then

$$\int_{\mathbb{R}^3} 2 \nabla u_n \phi_\varepsilon \nabla \phi_\varepsilon (u_n - u) u_n dx = o(1).$$

By $Q_\varepsilon(u_n) \leqslant \eta_L$ and $(A_\varepsilon)^1 \subset B(0, \varepsilon^{-1} r_0 + 1)$, we have that

$$\int_{|x| \geqslant \varepsilon^{-1} r_0 + 1} u_n^2 dx \leqslant (1 + \hat{\eta}_L)^{1/\beta} \varepsilon^6.$$

It follows that

$$\int_{|x| \geqslant \varepsilon^{-1} r_0 + 1} u^2 dx \leqslant (1 + \hat{\eta}_L)^{1/\beta} \varepsilon^6.$$

Assume $p < q < 6$. By the inequality

$$|u|_p \leqslant |u|_2^t |u|_q^{1-t} \leqslant C'|u|_2^t \|u\|^{1-t},$$

where the positive C' is independent of n and ε, and $\dfrac{1}{p} = \dfrac{t}{2} + \dfrac{1-t}{q}$, by above two inequalities and $\|u_n\| \leqslant \hat{\eta}_L$, we infer that there is a constant $C_L > 0$ independent of ε and n such that

$$\int_{|x| \geqslant \varepsilon^{-1} r_0 + 1} u_n^p dx \leqslant C_L \varepsilon^{3pt}, \quad \int_{|x| \geqslant \varepsilon^{-1} r_0 + 1} u^p dx \leqslant C_L \varepsilon^{3pt}.$$

Let $\varepsilon_L > 0$ satisfying that, for $0 < \varepsilon < \varepsilon_L$,

$$C(p-1)(2C_L^{\frac{p-2}{p}} \varepsilon^{3(p-2)t}) < \frac{1}{2} \min\{a + b \int_{\mathbb{R}^3} |\nabla u|^2 dx, m_0\}.$$

Then by (4.15) we get that

$$\lim_{n \to \infty} \|\phi_\varepsilon(u_n - u)\| = 0. \tag{4.18}$$

Choosing $v = (1 - \phi_\varepsilon)^2(u_n - u)$ in (4.14), we get (4.15) still holds if we replace ϕ_ε with $1 - \phi_\varepsilon$. Indeed, $1 - \phi_\varepsilon$ has a compact support and $u_n \to u$ in $L^q_{loc}(\mathbb{R}^3)$ for any $2 \leqslant q < 2^*$,

$$\left(a + b \int_{\mathbb{R}^3} |\nabla u|^2 dx\right) \int_{\mathbb{R}^3} |\nabla((1 - \phi_\varepsilon)^2(u_n - u))|^2 dx - \left(a + b \int_{\mathbb{R}^3} |\nabla u|^2 dx\right)$$

$$\times \int_{\mathbb{R}^3} |\nabla(1 - \phi_\varepsilon)|^2(u_n - u)^2 dx + b \int_{\mathbb{R}^3} (|\nabla u_n|^2 - |\nabla u|^2) dx$$

$$+ \int_{\mathbb{R}^3} \{\nabla u_n \nabla(1 - \phi_\varepsilon)^2(u_n - u) + \nabla u_n(1 - \phi_\varepsilon)^2 \nabla(u_n - u)\} dx$$

$$+ \int_{\mathbb{R}^3} V(\varepsilon x)(1 - \phi_\varepsilon)^2(u_n - u)^2 dx + \lambda \int_{\mathbb{R}^3} \chi_\varepsilon(1 - \phi_\varepsilon)^2(u_n - u)^2 dx$$

$$+ (\lambda_n - \lambda) \int_{\mathbb{R}^3} \chi_\varepsilon(1 - \phi_\varepsilon)^2(u_n - u)^2 dx$$

$$- (p-1) \int_{\mathbb{R}^3} (\theta u_n + (1 - \theta)u)^{p-2}(1 - \phi_\varepsilon)^2(u_n - u)^2 dx = o(1) \quad \text{as } n \to \infty.$$

This implies that

$$\lim_{n \to \infty} \|(1 - \phi_\varepsilon)(u_n - u)\| = 0 \tag{4.19}$$

and

$$\lim_{n\to\infty} \|u_n - u\| = \lim_{n\to\infty} \|(1 - \phi_\varepsilon)(u_n - u) + \phi_\varepsilon(u_n - u)\|$$

$$\leqslant \lim_{n\to\infty} \|(1 - \phi_\varepsilon)(u_n - u)\| + \lim_{n\to\infty} \|\phi_\varepsilon(u_n - u)\| = 0.$$

The proof is complete.   □

4.3 Existence of multiple sign-changing critical points of Γ_ε

We will use an abstract critical point theorem in [131] to obtain multiple sign-changing critical points for Γ_ε. Now we give some definitions and notations first.

Let X be a Banach space. For $P \subset X$, define $-P = \{-u : u \in P\}$. The genus (see [154]) of a closed symmetric subset $B(i.e. - B = B)$ of X is denoted by $\gamma(B)$. For $J \in C^1(X, \mathbb{R})$ and $c \in \mathbb{R}$, denote

$$J^c = \{u \in X : J(u) \leqslant c\}$$

and

$$K_c = \{u \in X : J(u) = c, J'(u) = 0\}.$$

Definition 4.1[131]   *Let $J \in C^1(X, \mathbb{R})$ be an even function. Let $P \subset X$ be a nonempty open set and $W = P \cup (-P)$. P is called an admissible invariant set with respect to J at level c, if the following deformation property holds, there is $\tau_0 > 0$ and a symmetric open neighborhood $\mathbb{M}$ of $K_c \setminus W$ with $\gamma(\mathbb{M}) < \infty$, such that for $\tau \in (0, \tau_0)$, there exists $\eta \in C(X, X)$ satisfying*
  (i) $\eta(\partial P) \subset P, \eta(\partial(-P)) \subset -P, \eta(P) \subset P, \eta(-P) \subset -P$;
  (ii) $\eta(-u) = -\eta(u)$, *for every $u \in X$;*
  (iii) $\eta|_{J^{c-2\tau}} = id$;
  (iv) $\eta(J^{c+\tau} \setminus (\mathbb{M} \cup W)) \subset J^{c-\tau}$.

Proposition 4.1   *Assume $J \in C^1(X, \mathbb{R})$ is an even function, $P \subset X$ is a nonempty open set, $M = P \cap (-P), W = P \cup (-P)$ and $\Sigma = \partial P \cap \partial(-P)$. Let P be an admissible invariant set with respect to J for $c \in [c^*, L]$ for some $L > c^*$, where $c^* = \inf_{u \in \Sigma} J(u)$ and for any $n \in \mathbb{N}$, there is a continuous map $\phi_n : B_n := \{x \in \mathbb{R}^n : |x| \leqslant 1\} \to X$ satisfying*
  (i) $\phi_n(0) \in M, \phi_n(-t) = -\phi_n(t)$, *for any $t \in B_n$;*
  (ii) $\phi_n(\partial B_n) \cap M = \varnothing$;
  (iii) $\max\{J(0), \sup_{u \in \phi_n(\partial B_n)} J(u)\} < c^*$.

For $j \in \mathbb{N}$, define

$$c_j = \inf_{B \in \Lambda_j} \sup_{u \in B \setminus W} J(u),$$

where

$$\Lambda_j = \{B : B = \phi(B_n \setminus Y) \text{ for some } \phi \in G_n, n \geqslant j,$$

$$\text{and open } Y \subset B_n \text{ such that } -Y = Y \text{ and } \gamma(\bar{Y}) \leqslant n - j\}$$

and

$$G_n = \{\phi : \phi \in C(B_n, X), \phi(-t) = -\phi(t) \text{ for any } t \in B_n, \phi|_{\partial B_n} = \phi_n|_{\partial B_n}\}.$$

Then for $j \geqslant 2$, if $L > c_j$,

$$K_{c_j} \setminus W \neq \varnothing. \tag{4.20}$$

Furthermore, if $j \geqslant 2$ and $L > c := c_j = \cdots = c_{j+m} \geqslant c_*$, we have that

$$\gamma(K_c \setminus W) \geqslant m + 1. \tag{4.21}$$

The proposition is proved in Theorem 2.5 of [131]. If we choose $k = 1$ and $G = -id$ in [131], we can obtain (4.19). The result (4.20) is proved in [53] by a variant of the argument in the proof of Theorem 2.5 in [131]. So we omit here.

Let $P_\pm := \{u \in H^1(\mathbb{R}^3) : u \geqslant (\leqslant)0\}$. For $\sigma > 0$, let

$$P_+^\sigma := \{u \in H^1(\mathbb{R}^3) : \text{dist}_{H^1}(u, P_+) < \sigma\}$$

and

$$P_-^\sigma := \{u \in H^1(\mathbb{R}^3) : \text{dist}_{H^1}(u, P_-) < \sigma\},$$

where $\text{dist}_{H^1}(u, B) := \inf_{v \in B} \|u - v\|$ for $u \in H^1(\mathbb{R}^3)$ and $B \subset H^1(\mathbb{R}^3)$. It is easy to see that $P_-^\sigma = -P_+^\sigma$.

In order to apply Proposition 4.1 to obtain multiple sign-changing critical points of Γ_ε, we let

$$X = H^1(\mathbb{R}^3), \quad P = P_+^\sigma, \quad W = P_-^\sigma \cup P_+^\sigma, \quad \text{and } J = \Gamma_\varepsilon \tag{4.22}$$

in Definition 4.1 and Proposition 4.1. It is easy to know that W is a symmetric and open subset of $H^1(\mathbb{R}^3)$ and sign-changing functions are contained in $H^1(\mathbb{R}^3) \setminus W$. Furthermore, since 0 is a strict local minimum point of Γ_ε, the constant c^* in Proposition 4.1 satisfies

$$c^* = \inf_{\partial(P_-^\sigma) \cap \partial(P_+^\sigma)} \Gamma_\varepsilon > 0,$$

when $\sigma > 0$ is small enough.

Without loss of generality, we assume that

$$0 \in A. \tag{4.23}$$

For $z \in \mathbb{R}^3$ and $r > 0$, we define

$$B(z, r) = \{x \in \mathbb{R}^3 : |x - z| < r\}.$$

From (4.21), we can obtain that

$$B(0, 1) \subset \Lambda_\varepsilon, \tag{4.24}$$

if $\varepsilon > 0$ small enough.

Now we define a function

$$J_0(u) = \frac{1}{2} \int_{B(0,1)} (a|\nabla u|^2 + n_0 u^2) dx - \frac{1}{p} \int_{B(0,1)} |u|^p dx + \frac{b}{4} \left(\int_{B(0,1)} |\nabla u|^2 dx \right)^2,$$

$u \in H_0^1(B(0, 1))$.

Assume $E_n := \mathrm{span}\{e_1, \cdots, e_n\}$, where $\{e_n\} \subset H_0^1(B(0, 1))$ is an orthonormal basis. From $p > 2$, we can infer that there is an increasing sequence of positive numbers $\{R_n\}$ satisfying

$$J_0(u) < 0, \quad \text{for all } u \in E_n \text{ and } \|u\| \geqslant R_n.$$

We also define $\phi_n \in C(B_n, H_0^1(B(0, 1)))$ as

$$\phi_n(t) = R_n \sum_{i=1}^{n} t_i e_i, \quad t = (t_1, \cdots, t_n) \in B_n. \tag{4.25}$$

One can easily to prove that under (4.22), ϕ_n satisfied (i)—(iii) in Proposition 4.1. For $j \in \mathbb{N}$, we define four sets

$$\Lambda_j = \{B : B = \phi(B_n \setminus Y) \text{ for some } \phi \in G_n, n \geqslant j,$$
$$\text{and open } Y \subset B_n \text{ such that } -Y = Y \text{ and } \gamma(\bar{Y}) \leqslant n - j\},$$

$$\tilde{\Lambda}_j = \{B : B = \phi(B_n \setminus Y) \text{ for some } \phi \in \tilde{G}_n, n \geqslant j,$$
$$\text{and open } Y \subset B_n \text{ such that } -Y = Y \text{ and } \gamma(\bar{Y}) \leqslant n - j\},$$

$$G_n = \{\phi : \phi \in C(B_n, H^1(\mathbb{R}^3)), \phi(-t) = -\phi(t) \text{ for any } t \in B_n, \phi|_{\partial B_n} = \phi_n|_{\partial B_n}\},$$

$$\tilde{G}_n = \{\phi : \phi \in C(B_n, H_0^1(B(0, 1))), \phi(-t) = -\phi(t) \text{ for any } t \in B_n, \phi|_{\partial B_n} = \phi_n|_{\partial B_n}\}.$$

Then we can give the the the minimax values

$$c_j^\varepsilon = \inf_{B \in \Lambda_j} \sup_{u \in B \setminus W} \Gamma_\varepsilon(u), \quad \tilde{c}_j = \inf_{B \in \tilde{\Lambda}_j} \sup_{u \in B \setminus W} J_0(u).$$

We obtain

$$0 < c_2^\varepsilon \leqslant c_3^\varepsilon \leqslant \cdots, \quad \tilde{c}_2 \leqslant \tilde{c}_3 \leqslant \cdots. \tag{4.26}$$

Because $\chi_\varepsilon = 0$ in Λ_ε, from $V \leqslant n_0$ and (4.23), for all $u \in H_0^1(B(0,1))$, we can obtain that $\Gamma_\varepsilon(u) \leqslant J_0(u)$. And then by $\tilde{\Lambda}_j \subset \Lambda_j$, for any $j \geqslant 2$ and sufficiently small $\varepsilon > 0$, we have

$$0 < c_j^\varepsilon \leqslant \tilde{c}_j. \tag{4.27}$$

Proposition 4.2   *Assume that $\sigma_0 > 0$ and $L > 0$. Then for any $\sigma \in (0, \sigma_0)$ and $\varepsilon \in (0, \varepsilon_L)$, P_+^σ is an admissible invariant set with respect to Γ_ε for $c < L$, where ε_L is from Lemma 4.1.*

We give the proof in the last of this chapter.

Proposition 4.3   *For any $N \in \mathbb{N}$, there exists $\varepsilon_N' > 0$ such that, for any $\varepsilon \in (0, \varepsilon_N')$, Γ_ε has at least N pairs of sign-changing critical points*

$$\{\pm v_{j,\varepsilon} : 1 \leqslant j \leqslant N\}$$

satisfying that

$$\Gamma_\varepsilon(v_{j,\varepsilon}) = c_{j+1}^\varepsilon \leqslant \tilde{c}_{N+1}, \quad 1 \leqslant j \leqslant N.$$

Proof. By Proposition 4.1, Proposition 4.2 and under (4.21), (4.25) and (4.26), we can get the results. The proof is complete.   □

4.4   The proof of Theorem 4.1

In this part, we first verify that the sign-changing critical points $\{v_{j,\varepsilon}\}$ obtained in Proposition 4.3 are solutions of (4.7), then we can prove the main theorem.

Lemma 4.2   *For any $N \in \mathbb{N}$ and $0 < \varepsilon < \varepsilon_N'$, there exist $\rho = \rho(a, m_0, p) > 0$ and $\eta_N > 0$ such that*

$$\rho \leqslant \|v_{j,\varepsilon}\| \leqslant \eta_N \quad \text{and} \quad Q_\varepsilon(v_{j,\varepsilon}) \leqslant \eta_N, \quad 1 \leqslant j \leqslant N,$$

where η_N is independent of ε.

Proof. Since

$$\tilde{c}_{N+1} \geqslant c_{j+1}^\varepsilon$$

$$= \Gamma_\varepsilon(v_{j,\varepsilon}) - \frac{1}{p}\langle \Gamma'_\varepsilon(v_{j,\varepsilon}), v_{j,\varepsilon}\rangle$$

$$= I_\varepsilon(v_{j,\varepsilon}) + Q_\varepsilon(v_{j,\varepsilon}) - \frac{1}{p}\langle \Gamma'_\varepsilon(v_{j,\varepsilon}), v_{j,\varepsilon}\rangle$$

$$= \left(\frac{1}{2} - \frac{1}{p}\right)\int_{\mathbb{R}^3}(a|\nabla v_{j,\varepsilon}|^2 + V(\varepsilon x)v_{j,\varepsilon}^2)dx + b\left(\frac{1}{4} - \frac{1}{p}\right)\left(\int_{\mathbb{R}^3}|\nabla v_{j,\varepsilon}|^2dx\right)^2$$

$$+ \left(\int_{\mathbb{R}^3}\chi_\varepsilon v_{j,\varepsilon}^2 dx - 1\right)_+^\beta - \frac{2\beta}{p}\left(\int_{\mathbb{R}^3}\chi_\varepsilon v_{j,\varepsilon}^2 dx - 1\right)_+^{\beta-1}\int_{\mathbb{R}^3}\chi_\varepsilon v_{j,\varepsilon}^2 dx$$

and $2 < 2\beta < p$, we can have that there exists $\eta_N > 0$ independent of ε such that

$$\|v_{j,\varepsilon}\| \leqslant \eta_N \quad \text{and} \quad Q_\varepsilon(v_{j,\varepsilon}) \leqslant \eta_N.$$

From $\langle \Gamma'_\varepsilon(v_{j,\varepsilon}), v_{j,\varepsilon}\rangle = 0$, we obtain that

$$\min\{a, m_0\}\|v_{j,\varepsilon}\|^2$$

$$\leqslant \int_{\mathbb{R}^3}(a|\nabla v_{j,\varepsilon}|^2 + V(\varepsilon x)v_{j,\varepsilon}^2)dx + b\left(\int_{\mathbb{R}^3}|\nabla v_{j,\varepsilon}|^2dx\right)^2$$

$$+ 2\beta\left(\int_{\mathbb{R}^3}\chi_\varepsilon v_{j,\varepsilon}^2 dx - 1\right)_+^{\beta-1}\int_{\mathbb{R}^3}\chi_\varepsilon v_{j,\varepsilon}^2 dx$$

$$= \int_{\mathbb{R}^3}|v_{j,\varepsilon}|^p dx \leqslant C\|v_{j,\varepsilon}\|^p,$$

where $C = C(p)$ comes from the constant in Sobolev inequality. Since $v_{j,\varepsilon}$ are sign-changing functions, $v_{j,\varepsilon} \neq 0$ and $p > 2$, it follows that there exists $\rho = \rho(a, m_0, p) > 0$ such that $\|v_{j,\varepsilon}\| \geqslant \rho$ for $1 \leqslant j \leqslant N$. The proof is complete.　□

Lemma 4.3　*For any $\delta > 0$, $\lim_{\varepsilon\to 0}\|v_{j,\varepsilon}\|_{L^\infty(\mathbb{R}^3\setminus(\Lambda_\varepsilon)^\delta)} = 0, 1 \leqslant j \leqslant N$.*

Proof. From $Q_\varepsilon(v_{j,\varepsilon}) \leqslant \eta_N$ and the definition of cut-off function χ_ε, we have that, for any $\delta > 0$, there exists a positive constant $C = C(\delta, N)$ such that

$$\int_{\mathbb{R}^3\setminus(\Lambda_\varepsilon)^\delta}v_{j,\varepsilon}^2 dx \leqslant C\varepsilon^6, \quad 1 \leqslant j \leqslant N. \tag{4.28}$$

Since $v_{j,\varepsilon}$ solves (4.13), $\|v_{j,\varepsilon}\| \leqslant \eta_N$, by using the bootstrap argument and (4.27), we have that

$$\|v_{j,\varepsilon}\|_{L^\infty(\mathbb{R}^3\setminus(\Lambda_\varepsilon)^\delta)} \leqslant C\varepsilon^3, \quad 1 \leqslant j \leqslant N.$$

The proof is complete.　□

Lemma 4.4　*Assume $\varsigma > 0$, $\{y_\varepsilon\} \subset \mathbb{R}^3$ and $\{v_\varepsilon\} \subset H^1(\mathbb{R}^3) \cap L^\infty(\mathbb{R}^3)$ satisfy*

$$\sup_{\varepsilon>0}\|v_\varepsilon\| < +\infty, \tag{4.29}$$

$$\int_{B(y_\varepsilon,1)} v_\varepsilon^2 dx \geqslant \varsigma, \tag{4.30}$$

$$\sup\{\langle \Gamma'_\varepsilon(v_\varepsilon), u \rangle : u \in H_0^1(\Lambda_\varepsilon), \|u\|_{H_0^1(\Lambda_\varepsilon)} \leqslant 1\} \to 0 \quad as \ \varepsilon \to 0, \tag{4.31}$$

and for any $\delta > 0$,

$$\lim_{\varepsilon \to 0} \|v_\varepsilon\|_{L^\infty(\mathbb{R}^3 \setminus (\Lambda_\varepsilon)^\delta)} = 0. \tag{4.32}$$

Then $y_\varepsilon \in \Lambda_\varepsilon$ and $\lim_{\varepsilon \to 0} \mathrm{dist}(y_\varepsilon, \partial \Lambda_\varepsilon) = +\infty$.

Proof. It follows from (4.29) and (4.31) that $y_\varepsilon \in (\Lambda_\varepsilon)^1$. Assume

$$w_\varepsilon = v_\varepsilon(\cdot + y_\varepsilon).$$

By (4.29), we obtain that

$$\int_{B(0,1)} w_\varepsilon^2 dx \geqslant \varsigma. \tag{4.33}$$

If not, we suppose

$$\lim_{\varepsilon \to 0} \mathrm{dist}(y_\varepsilon, \partial \Lambda_\varepsilon) = l < +\infty. \tag{4.34}$$

By changing variables, without loss of generality, we may assume that

$$y_\varepsilon = 0, \tag{4.35}$$

and there is $z_\varepsilon = (a_\varepsilon, 0, \cdots, 0) \in \partial \Lambda_\varepsilon$ such that

$$|\alpha_\varepsilon| = \mathrm{dist}(y_\varepsilon, \partial \Lambda_\varepsilon) \to l \quad as \ \varepsilon \to 0. \tag{4.36}$$

Up to a subsequence, we assume $\lim_{\varepsilon \to 0} \alpha_\varepsilon = \alpha$.

By $y_\varepsilon \in (\Lambda_\varepsilon)^1$ and (4.33)—(4.35), we can infer that $-1 \leqslant \alpha < +\infty$. Due to $\|w_\varepsilon\| = \|v_\varepsilon\|$ and (4.28), we can set that $w_\varepsilon \rightharpoonup w$ in $H^1(\mathbb{R}^3)$ as $\varepsilon \to 0$. From (4.32), we can obtain $w \neq 0$. And from (4.31) and (4.35), if $x_1 \geqslant \alpha$, we get the following

$$w(x) = 0, \tag{4.37}$$

where $x = (x_1, x_2, x_3)$. By $\chi_\varepsilon = 0$ in Λ_ε and (4.34), we obtain

$$a \int_{\mathbb{R}^3} \nabla w_\varepsilon \nabla u dx + \int_{\mathbb{R}^3} V(\varepsilon x) w_\varepsilon u dx + b \int_{\mathbb{R}^3} |\nabla w_\varepsilon|^2 dx \int_{\mathbb{R}^3} \nabla w_\varepsilon \nabla u dx$$

$$= \int_{\mathbb{R}^3} |w_\varepsilon|^{p-2} w_\varepsilon u dx + \langle \Gamma'_\varepsilon(w_\varepsilon), u \rangle, \quad \forall u \in H_0^1(\Lambda_\varepsilon). \tag{4.38}$$

By (4.30), (4.36) and (4.37), we infer that w is a weak solution of

$$-\left(a + b \int_{\mathbb{R}^3} |\nabla w_\varepsilon|^2 dx\right) \Delta w + V(0)w = |w|^{p-2}w \text{ in } \{x \in \mathbb{R}^3 : x_1 < \alpha\}, \ w|_{x_1=\alpha} = 0.$$

By the result of Theorem I.1 in [86], the only solution of this equation in $H^1(\mathbb{R}^3)$ is $w = 0$. This contradicts with $w \neq 0$. The proof is complete. □

Lemma 4.5   Let $v_{j,\varepsilon} \rightharpoonup \tilde{v}_0$ in $H^1(\mathbb{R}^3)$ as $\varepsilon \to 0$. If $\liminf\limits_{\varepsilon \to 0} \|v_{j,\varepsilon} - \tilde{v}_0\|_{L^p(\mathbb{R}^3)} > 0$, then there exists $m_j \in \mathbb{N}, m_j$ nonzero functions $\tilde{v}_i$ in $H^1(\mathbb{R}^3), 1 \leqslant i \leqslant m_j$ and m_j sequences $\{y^i_{j,\varepsilon}\} \subset \Lambda_\varepsilon, 1 \leqslant i \leqslant m_j$ satisfy

(i) $\lim\limits_{\varepsilon \to 0} |y^i_{j,\varepsilon}| = +\infty$, $\lim\limits_{\varepsilon \to 0} \text{dist}(y^i_{j,\varepsilon}, \partial \Lambda_\varepsilon) = +\infty, 1 \leqslant i \leqslant m_j$, and

$$\lim_{\varepsilon \to 0} |y^i_{j,\varepsilon} - y^{i'}_{j,\varepsilon}| = +\infty, \quad \text{if } i \neq i'.$$

(ii) $\tilde{v}_0$ is a solution of

$$-(a + bA_j)\Delta v + V(0)v = |v|^{p-2}v, \quad v \in H^1(\mathbb{R}^3), \tag{4.39}$$

where $A_j := \lim\limits_{\varepsilon \to 0} \int_{\mathbb{R}^3} |\nabla v_{j,\varepsilon}|^2 dx$ and $\int_{\mathbb{R}^3} |\nabla \tilde{v}_0|^2 dx \leqslant A_j$.

For every $1 \leqslant i \leqslant m_j$, $\tilde{v}_i$ is a nontrivial solution of

$$-(a + bA_j)\Delta v + V(y^i_j)v = |v|^{p-2}v, \quad v \in H^1(\mathbb{R}^3), \tag{4.40}$$

where $y^i_j = \lim\limits_{\varepsilon \to 0} \varepsilon y^i_{j,\varepsilon} \in \bar{\Lambda}$.

(iii) For any $2 < q < 6$,

$$\lim_{\varepsilon \to 0} \left\| v_{j,\varepsilon} - \tilde{v}_0 - \sum_{i=1}^{m_j} \tilde{v}_i(\cdot - y^i_{j,\varepsilon}) \right\|_{L^q(\mathbb{R}^3)} = 0. \tag{4.41}$$

Proof. Since $\|v_{j,\varepsilon}\|$ and $Q(v_{j,\varepsilon})$ are bounded and $v_{j,\varepsilon}$ solves (4.13), we can prove that $\tilde{v}_0$ is a solution of (4.38). Indeed, since $v_{j,\varepsilon} \rightharpoonup \tilde{v}_0$ in $H^1(\mathbb{R}^3)$ as $\varepsilon \to 0$, we assume that for some constant $A_j \in \mathbb{R}$,

$$\lim_{\varepsilon \to 0} \int_{\mathbb{R}^3} |\nabla v_{j,\varepsilon}|^2 dx = A_j.$$

For any $\phi \in C_0^\infty(\mathbb{R}^3)$, we have that $\langle \Gamma'_\varepsilon(v_{j,\varepsilon}), \phi \rangle \to 0$, i.e.

$$\left(a + b \int_{\mathbb{R}^3} |\nabla v_{j,\varepsilon}|^2 dx\right) \int_{\mathbb{R}^3} \nabla v_{j,\varepsilon} \nabla \phi dx + \int_{\mathbb{R}^3} V(\varepsilon x) v_{j,\varepsilon} \phi dx - \int_{\mathbb{R}^3} |v_{j,\varepsilon}|^{p-2} v_{j,\varepsilon} \phi dx$$

$$+ 2\beta \left(\int_{\mathbb{R}^3} \chi_\varepsilon v_{j,\varepsilon}^2 dx - 1 \right)_+^{\beta-1} \int_{\mathbb{R}^3} \chi_\varepsilon v_{j,\varepsilon} \phi dx = o(1),$$

which implies that as $\varepsilon \to 0$,

$$(a + bA_j) \int_{\mathbb{R}^3} \nabla \tilde{v}_0 \nabla \phi dx + V(0) \int_{\mathbb{R}^3} \tilde{v}_0 \phi dx - \int_{\mathbb{R}^3} |v_0|^{p-2} v_0 \phi dx = 0.$$

Since $C_0^\infty(\mathbb{R}^3)$ is dense in $H^1(\mathbb{R}^3)$, we have that $\tilde{v}_0$ solves

$$-(a + bA_j)\Delta v + V(0)v = |v|^{p-2}v, \quad v \in H^1(\mathbb{R}^3).$$

Let $v_{j,\varepsilon}^1 = v_{j,\varepsilon} - \tilde{v}_0$ and $\{y_{j,\varepsilon}^1\} \subset \mathbb{R}^3$, we have

$$\int_{B(y_{j,\varepsilon}^1, 1)} (v_{j,\varepsilon}^1)^2 dx = \sup_{y \in \mathbb{R}^3} \int_{B(y,1)} (v_{j,\varepsilon}^1)^2 dx := \varsigma_\varepsilon^1.$$

Since $v_{j,\varepsilon}^1 \to 0$ as $\varepsilon \to 0$, we have $|y_{j,\varepsilon}^1| \to \infty$ as $\varepsilon \to 0$ if $\liminf_{\varepsilon \to 0} \varsigma_\varepsilon > 0$.

Since $v_{j,\varepsilon}$ solves (4.13) and $\tilde{v}_0$ solves (4.38), we have

$$- a\Delta v_{j,\varepsilon}^1 - b \int_{\mathbb{R}^3} |\nabla v_{j,\varepsilon}|^2 dx \Delta v_{j,\varepsilon}^1 - b \left(\int_{\mathbb{R}^3} |\nabla v_{j,\varepsilon}|^2 dx - A_j \right) \Delta \tilde{v}_0$$
$$+ V(\varepsilon x) v_{j,\varepsilon}^1 + (V(\varepsilon x) - V(0))\tilde{v}_0 + \xi_\varepsilon \chi_\varepsilon v_\varepsilon^1 + \xi_\varepsilon \chi_\varepsilon \tilde{v}_0$$
$$= |v_{j,\varepsilon}|^{p-2} v_{j,\varepsilon} - |\tilde{v}_0|^{p-2}\tilde{v}_0, \tag{4.42}$$

where

$$\xi_\varepsilon = 2\beta \left(\int_{\mathbb{R}^3} \chi_\varepsilon v_{j,\varepsilon}^2 dx - 1 \right)_+^{\beta-1}. \tag{4.43}$$

By (4.12) and (4.41), for $u \in H^1(\Lambda_\varepsilon)$,

$$\langle \Gamma_\varepsilon'(v_{j,\varepsilon}^1), u \rangle$$
$$= \int_{\mathbb{R}^3} (|v_{j,\varepsilon}|^{p-2} v_{j,\varepsilon} - |\tilde{v}_0|^{p-2}\tilde{v}_0 - |v_{j,\varepsilon}^1|^{p-2} v_{j,\varepsilon}^1) u dx$$
$$- \int_{\mathbb{R}^3} (V(\varepsilon x) - V(0))\tilde{v}_0 u dx + b \left(\int_{\mathbb{R}^3} (|\nabla v_{j,\varepsilon}^1|^2 - |\nabla v_{j,\varepsilon}|^2) \right) \int_{\mathbb{R}^3} \nabla v_{j,\varepsilon}^1 \nabla u dx$$
$$- b \left(\int_{\mathbb{R}^3} |\nabla v_{j,\varepsilon}|^2 - A_j \right) \int_{\mathbb{R}^3} \nabla \tilde{v}_0 \nabla u dx. \tag{4.44}$$

By Lemma 8.1 of [200] and

$$\sup \left\{ \int_{\mathbb{R}^3} (V(\varepsilon x) - V(0))\tilde{v}_0 u dx : u \in H^1(\mathbb{R}^3), \|u\| \leqslant 1 \right\} \to 0 \quad \text{as } \varepsilon \to 0. \tag{4.45}$$

By (4.43), we obtain that

$$\sup\left\{\langle\Gamma_\varepsilon'(v_{j,\varepsilon}^1), u\rangle : u \in H_0^1(\Lambda_\varepsilon), \|u\|_{H_0^1(\Lambda_\varepsilon)} \leqslant 1\right\} \to 0 \quad \text{as } \varepsilon \to 0. \tag{4.46}$$

Since $\tilde{v}_0 \in H_0^1(\mathbb{R}^3)$ and $\tilde{v}_0$ solves (4.38), we have that $\lim\limits_{|x|\to\infty} \tilde{v}_0(x) = 0$. By Lemma 4.3, we have that, for any $\delta > 0$,

$$\lim_{\varepsilon\to 0} \|v_{j,\varepsilon}^1\|_{L^\infty(\mathbb{R}^3\backslash(\Lambda_\varepsilon)^\delta)} = 0. \tag{4.47}$$

By the Lions lemma[200] and $\liminf\limits_{\varepsilon\to 0} \|v_{j,\varepsilon} - \tilde{v}_0\|_{L^p(\mathbb{R}^3)} > 0$,

$$\liminf_{\varepsilon\to 0} \varsigma_\varepsilon^1 > 0.$$

Then by Lemma 4.4, (4.45) and (4.46), we get that

$$y_{j,\varepsilon}^1 \in \Lambda_\varepsilon, \quad \lim_{\varepsilon\to 0} \text{dist}(y_{j,\varepsilon}^1, \partial\Lambda_\varepsilon) = +\infty. \tag{4.48}$$

Let $w_{j,\varepsilon}^1 = v_{j,\varepsilon}^1(\cdot + y_{j,\varepsilon}^1)$. Then

$$\liminf_{\varepsilon\to 0} \int_{B(0,1)} (w_{j,\varepsilon}^1)^2 dx = \liminf_{\varepsilon\to 0} \varsigma_\varepsilon^1 > 0. \tag{4.49}$$

Let $w_{j,\varepsilon}^1 \rightharpoonup \tilde{v}_1$ as $\varepsilon \to 0$. By (4.12) and (4.45), we deduce that for any $u \in H_0^1(y_{j,\varepsilon}^1 + \Lambda_\varepsilon)$, as $\varepsilon \to 0$,

$$\left(a + b\int_{\mathbb{R}^3} |\nabla w_{j,\varepsilon}^1|^2 dx\right)\int_{\mathbb{R}^3} \nabla w_{j,\varepsilon}^1 \nabla u dx + \int_{\mathbb{R}^3} V(\varepsilon(x + y_{j,\varepsilon}^1))w_{j,\varepsilon}^1 u dx$$

$$- \int_{\mathbb{R}^3} |w_{j,\varepsilon}^1|^{p-2} w_{j,\varepsilon}^1 u dx \to 0, \tag{4.50}$$

where $y_{j,\varepsilon}^1 + \Lambda_\varepsilon = \{x + y_{j,\varepsilon}^1 : x \in \Lambda_\varepsilon\}$.

By (4.47) and (4.49), we know that $\tilde{v}_1$ is a solution of (4.39) with $i = 1$. From Lemma 4.2, we get that there exists a positive constant ρ depending only on a, m_0 and p such that

$$\|\tilde{v}_1\| \geqslant \rho. \tag{4.51}$$

Let $v_{j,\varepsilon}^2 = v_{j,\varepsilon}^1 - \tilde{v}_1(\cdot - y_{j,\varepsilon}^1)$. Since $\tilde{v}_1 \in H^1(\mathbb{R}^3)$ is a solution of (4.39), we can deduce that $\lim\limits_{|x|\to\infty} \tilde{v}_1(x) = 0$. Then by (4.46) and (4.47), we obtain that, for any $\delta > 0$,

$$\lim_{\varepsilon\to 0} \|v_{j,\varepsilon}^2\|_{L^\infty(\mathbb{R}^3\backslash(\Lambda_\varepsilon)^\delta)} = 0. \tag{4.52}$$

Since $v_{j,\varepsilon}, \tilde{v}_0$ and $\tilde{v}_1$ solve (4.13),(4.38) and (4.39) with $i = 1$ respectively, we have that

$$
-a\Delta v_{j,\varepsilon}^2 - b\int_{\mathbb{R}^3}|\nabla v_{j,\varepsilon}|^2 dx \Delta v_{j,\varepsilon}^2 - b\left(\int_{\mathbb{R}^3}|\nabla v_{j,\varepsilon}|^2 - A_j\right)\Delta\tilde{v}_0
$$
$$
-b\left(\int_{\mathbb{R}^3}|\nabla v_{j,\varepsilon}|^2 - A_j\right)\Delta\tilde{v}_1 + \xi_\varepsilon\chi_\varepsilon v_{j,\varepsilon}^2 + \xi_\varepsilon\chi_\varepsilon\tilde{v}_0 + \xi_\varepsilon\chi_\varepsilon\tilde{v}_1
$$
$$
+V(\varepsilon x)v_{j,\varepsilon}^2 + (V(\varepsilon x) - V(0))\tilde{v}_0 + (V(\varepsilon x) - V(y_j^i))\tilde{v}_1(\cdot - y_{j,\varepsilon}^1)
$$
$$
= |v_{j,\varepsilon}|^{p-2}v_{j,\varepsilon} - |\tilde{v}_0|^{p-2}\tilde{v}_0 - |\tilde{v}_1|^{p-2}\tilde{v}_1(\cdot - y_{j,\varepsilon}^1). \tag{4.53}
$$

By (4.12), (4.52) and Lemma 8.1 of [200], for any $u \in H_0^1(\Lambda_\varepsilon)$ with $\|u\|_{H_0^1(\Lambda_\varepsilon)} \leqslant 1$,

$$
\langle\Gamma_\varepsilon'(v_{j,\varepsilon}^2), u\rangle
$$
$$
= \int_{\mathbb{R}^3}\left(|v_{j,\varepsilon}|^{p-2}v_{j,\varepsilon} - |\tilde{v}_0|^{p-2}\tilde{v}_0 - |\tilde{v}^1(\cdot - y_{j,\varepsilon}^1)|^{p-2}\tilde{v}^1(\cdot - y_{j,\varepsilon}^1) - |v_{j,\varepsilon}^2|^{p-2}v_{j,\varepsilon}^2\right)u\,dx
$$
$$
-\int_{\mathbb{R}^3}(V(\varepsilon x) - V(0))\,\tilde{v}_0 u\,dx - \int_{\mathbb{R}^3}(V(\varepsilon x) - V(y_j^1))\tilde{v}_1(\cdot - y_{j,\varepsilon}^1)u\,dx
$$
$$
+b\left(\int_{\mathbb{R}^3}(|\nabla v_{j,\varepsilon}^2|^2 - |\nabla v_{j,\varepsilon}|^2)\right)\int_{\mathbb{R}^3}\nabla v_{j,\varepsilon}^2\nabla u\,dx - b\left(\int_{\mathbb{R}^3}|\nabla v_{j,\varepsilon}|^2 - A_j\right)\int_{\mathbb{R}^3}\nabla\tilde{v}_0\nabla u\,dx
$$
$$
-b\left(\int_{\mathbb{R}^3}|\nabla v_{j,\varepsilon}|^2 - A_j\right)\int_{\mathbb{R}^3}\nabla\tilde{v}_1(\cdot - y_{j,\varepsilon}^1)\nabla u\,dx + o(1) \quad\text{as } \varepsilon \to 0. \tag{4.54}
$$

Since $\lim_{\varepsilon\to 0}\varepsilon y_{j,\varepsilon}^1 = y_j^1$, we obtain that

$$
\sup\left\{\int_{\mathbb{R}^3}(V(\varepsilon(x + y_{j,\varepsilon}^1)) - V(y_j^1))\tilde{v}_1 u\,dx : u \in H^1(\mathbb{R}^3), \|u\| \leqslant 1\right\} \to 0 \quad\text{as } \varepsilon \to 0.
$$

It follows that

$$
\sup\left\{\int_{\mathbb{R}^3}(V(\varepsilon x)) - V(y_j^1))\tilde{v}_1(\cdot - y_{j,\varepsilon}^1)u\,dx : u \in H^1(\mathbb{R}^3), \|u\| \leqslant 1\right\} \to 0 \quad\text{as } \varepsilon \to 0. \tag{4.55}
$$

By (4.44), (4.53),(4.54) and $\int_{\mathbb{R}^3}|\nabla v_{j,\varepsilon}|^2 dx \to A_j$, we have

$$
\sup\left\{\langle\Gamma_\varepsilon'(v_{j,\varepsilon}^2), u\rangle : u \in H_0^1(\Lambda_\varepsilon), \|u\|_{H_0^1(\Lambda_\varepsilon)} \leqslant 1\right\} \to 0 \quad\text{as } \varepsilon \to 0. \tag{4.56}
$$

Let $\{y_{j,\varepsilon}^2\} \subset \mathbb{R}^3$ be such that

$$
\int_{B(y_{j,\varepsilon}^2,1)}(v_{j,\varepsilon}^2)^2 dx = \sup_{y\in\mathbb{R}^3}\int_{B(y,1)}(v_{j,\varepsilon}^2)^2 dx := \varsigma_\varepsilon^2.
$$

By (4.51),(4.55) and Lemma 4.4, we have that $y_{j,\varepsilon}^2 \in \Lambda_\varepsilon, \mathrm{dist}(y_{j,\varepsilon}^2, \partial\Lambda_\varepsilon) \to +\infty$ as $\varepsilon \to 0$, $\lim\limits_{\varepsilon\to0} |y_{j,\varepsilon}^2| = +\infty$, $\lim\limits_{\varepsilon\to0} |y_{j,\varepsilon}^2 - y_{j,\varepsilon}^1| = +\infty$ if $\liminf\limits_{\varepsilon\to0} \varsigma_\varepsilon^2 > 0$.

Iterating the above argument we can know that the iteration procedure has to stop in finite number of steps, since $\|v_{j,\varepsilon}\| \leqslant \eta_N, \|\tilde{v}_i\| \geqslant \rho$ for all $1 \leqslant i \leqslant m_j$, and

$$\|v_{j,\varepsilon}^i\|^2 = \|v_{j,\varepsilon}^{i-1}\|^2 - \|\tilde{v}_{i-1}\|^2 + o(1)$$

$$= \|v_{j,\varepsilon}\|^2 - \sum_{n=1}^{i-1} \|\tilde{v}_n\|^2 + o(1), \quad \varepsilon \to 0. \tag{4.57}$$

Hence, we obtain $m_j \in \mathbb{N}$ such that $v_{j,\varepsilon}^{m_j+1} = v_{j,\varepsilon}^{m_j} - \tilde{v}_{m_j}(\cdot - y_{j,\varepsilon}^{m_j})$ satisfies

$$\sup_{y\in\mathbb{R}^3} \int_{B(y,1)} (v_{j,\varepsilon}^{m_j+1})^2 dx = 0 \quad \text{as } \varepsilon \to 0. \tag{4.58}$$

It follows from the Lions lemma and (4.57), we get, for any $2 < q < 2^* = 6$,

$$\int_{\mathbb{R}^3} |v_{j,\varepsilon}^{m_j+1}|^q dx = 0 \quad \text{as } \varepsilon \to 0.$$

Hence, we obtain m_j nonzero functions $\tilde{v}_i$ in $H^1(\mathbb{R}^3), 1 \leqslant i \leqslant m_j$ and m_j sequences $\{y_{j,\varepsilon}^i\} \subset \Lambda_\varepsilon, 1 \leqslant i \leqslant m_j$ such that the results (i),(ii) and (iii) hold.

The proof is complete.   □

Next, for any $\varepsilon > 0$ and any $1 \leqslant j \leqslant N$, assume

$$y_{j,\varepsilon}^0 = 0.$$

Let $\varepsilon_n > 0$ be such that

$$\lim_{n\to\infty} \varepsilon_n = 0.$$

Up to a subsequence, we assume that $\lim\limits_{n\to\infty} \varepsilon_n y_{j,\varepsilon_n}^i$ exists for every i. We may write the set of these limiting points by

$$\{x_1^*, \cdots, x_{s_j}^*\} = \{\lim_{n\to\infty} \varepsilon_n y_{j,\varepsilon_n}^i : 0 \leqslant i \leqslant m_j\} \subset \bar{\Lambda}, \tag{4.59}$$

for some $1 \leqslant s_j \leqslant m_j$. Set

$$\theta_* = \begin{cases} \dfrac{1}{100}\min\{|x_s^* - x_{s'}^*| : 1 \leqslant s < s' \leqslant s_j\}, & \text{if } s_j \geqslant 2, \\ +\infty, & \text{if } s_j = 1. \end{cases}$$

Lemma 4.6   *If* $0 < \delta < \theta_*$, *then there exist two positive constants* C *and* c *independent of* n *such that, for every* $0 \leqslant i \leqslant m_j$, *when* n *is large enough,*

$$|\nabla v_{j,\varepsilon_n}(x)| + |v_{j,\varepsilon_n}(x)| \leqslant C\exp(-c\varepsilon_n^{-1}), \quad for\ x \in \partial B(y_{j,\varepsilon_n}^i, \delta\varepsilon_n^{-1}). \tag{4.60}$$

Proof. Define

$$A_n^i = B\left(y_{j,\varepsilon_n}^i, \frac{3}{2}\delta\varepsilon_n^{-1}\right) \setminus B\left(y_{j,\varepsilon_n}^i, \frac{1}{2}\delta\varepsilon_n^{-1}\right).$$

By $0 < \delta < \theta_*$, we can deduce that, for every $0 \leqslant i, i' \leqslant m_j$,

$$\mathrm{dist}(y_{j,\varepsilon_n}^{i'}, A_n^i) \to \infty \quad \text{as } n \to \infty. \tag{4.61}$$

From Lemma 4.5, (4.60) and

$$\lim_{R \to \infty} \int_{\mathbb{R}^3 \setminus B(y_{j,\varepsilon_n}^i, R)} |\bar{v}_i(\cdot - y_{j,\varepsilon_n}^i)|^p dx = 0, \quad 0 \leqslant i \leqslant m_j, \tag{4.62}$$

we obtain that

$$\lim_{R \to \infty} \int_{A_n^i} |v_{j,\varepsilon_n}|^p dx = 0, \quad \text{for every } 0 \leqslant i \leqslant m_j. \tag{4.63}$$

Then there exists $n_1 \in \mathbb{N}$ such that for $n \geqslant n_1$,

$$\|v_{j,\varepsilon_n}\|_{L^\infty(A_n^i)}^{p-2} < a/2. \tag{4.64}$$

For $m \in \mathbb{N}$, let

$$R_m = B\left(y_{j,\varepsilon_n}^i, \frac{3}{2}\delta\varepsilon_n^{-1} - m\right) \setminus B\left(y_{j,\varepsilon_n}^i, \frac{1}{2}\delta\varepsilon_n^{-1} + m\right).$$

Let ζ_m be a cut-off function satisfying that $0 \leqslant \xi_m(t) \leqslant 1$ for all $t \in \mathbb{R}$,

$$\zeta_m(t) = \begin{cases} 0, & \text{if } t \leqslant \frac{1}{2}\delta\varepsilon_n^{-1} + m - 1 \text{ or } t \geqslant \frac{3}{2}\delta\varepsilon_n^{-1} - m + 1, \\ 1, & \text{if } \frac{1}{2}\delta\varepsilon_n^{-1} + m \leqslant t \leqslant \frac{3}{2}\delta\varepsilon_n^{-1} - m, \end{cases}$$

and $|\zeta_m'(t)| \leqslant 4$ for all t. For $x \in \mathbb{R}^3$, let $\psi_m(x) = \zeta_m(|x - y_{j,\varepsilon_n}^i|)$. Multiplying both sides of (4.13) by $\psi_m^2 v_{j,\varepsilon_n}$ and integrating on $\mathbb{R}^3$, by (4.63) we have that

$$\left(a + b\int_{\mathbb{R}^3} |\nabla v_{j,\varepsilon_n}|^2 dx\right)\int_{R_{m-1}} |\nabla v_{j,\varepsilon_n}|^2 \psi_m^2 dx + \int_{R_{m-1}} V(\varepsilon x) v_{j,\varepsilon_n}^2 \psi_m^2 dx$$

$$\xi_n \int_{R_{m-1}} \chi_{\varepsilon_n} v_{j,\varepsilon_n}^2 \psi_m^2 dx - \int_{R_{m-1}} |v_{j,\varepsilon_n}|^p \psi_m^2 dx$$

$$\geqslant \min\left\{a + b\frac{A_j}{2}, \frac{m_0}{2}\right\}\int_{R_m}(|\nabla v_{j,\varepsilon_n}|^2 + v_{j,\varepsilon_n}^2)dx \tag{4.65}$$

and

$$\left(a + b\int_{\mathbb{R}^3}|\nabla v_{j,\varepsilon_n}|^2dx\right)\int_{R_{m-1}}|\nabla v_{j,\varepsilon_n}|^2\psi_m^2dx + \int_{R_{m-1}}V(\varepsilon x)v_{j,\varepsilon_n}^2\psi_m^2dx$$

$$\xi_n\int_{R_{m-1}}\chi_{\varepsilon_n}v_{j,\varepsilon_n}^2\psi_m^2dx - \int_{R_{m-1}}|v_{j,\varepsilon_n}|^p\psi_m^2dx$$

$$\leqslant 8(a + bA_j)\int_{R_{m-1}\backslash R_m}(|\nabla v_{j,\varepsilon_n}|^2 + v_{j,\varepsilon_n}^2)dx, \tag{4.66}$$

where

$$\xi_n := 2\beta\left(\int_{\mathbb{R}^3}\chi_{\varepsilon_n}v_{j,\varepsilon_n}^2dx - 1\right)_+^{\beta-1},$$

here we have used the fact,

$$\lim_{n\to\infty}\int_{\mathbb{R}^3}|\nabla v_{j,\varepsilon_n}|^2dx = A_j,$$

then there exists $n_2 \in \mathbb{N}$, such that

$$\int_{\mathbb{R}^3}|\nabla v_{j,\varepsilon_n}|^2dx > \frac{A_j}{2}, \quad \text{when } n > n_2.$$

By above inequalities, let $C = \dfrac{8(a + bA_j)}{\min\{a + bA_j/2, m_0/2\}}$, we have that

$$\int_{R_m}(|\nabla v_{j,\varepsilon_n}|^2 + v_{j,\varepsilon_n}^2)dx \leqslant C\int_{R_m\backslash R_{m-1}}(|\nabla v_{j,\varepsilon_n}|^2 + v_{j,\varepsilon_n}^2)dx. \tag{4.67}$$

Let

$$a_m = \int_{R_m}(|\nabla v_{j,\varepsilon_n}|^2 + v_{j,\varepsilon_n}^2)dx,$$

we obtain that $a_m \leqslant C(a_{m-1} - a_m)$ which gives $a_m \leqslant \theta a_{m-1}$ with $\theta = C/(1 + C) < 1$. Therefore $a_m \leqslant a_0\theta^m$. By Lemma 4.2, we obtain $a_0 \leqslant \eta_N^2$. Hence, for sufficiently large n, $a_m \leqslant \eta_N^2 e^{m\ln\theta}$. Denote $[x]$ be the integer part of x. Choosing $m = [\delta\varepsilon^{-1}/2] - 1$ and noting that $[\delta\varepsilon^{-1}/2] - 1 \leqslant \delta\varepsilon^{-1}/4$ when n is large enough, we get that

$$\int_{D_n^i}(|\nabla v_{j,\varepsilon_n}|^2 + v_{j,\varepsilon_n}^2)dx \leqslant a_m \leqslant \eta_N^2\exp(([\delta\varepsilon^{-1}/2] - 1)\ln\theta)$$

$$\leqslant \eta_N^2\exp\left(\frac{1}{4}\delta\varepsilon_n^{-1}\ln\theta\right), \tag{4.68}$$

where

$$D_n^i = \overline{B(y_{j,\varepsilon_n}^i, \delta\varepsilon_n^{-1} + 1)} \setminus B(y_{j,\varepsilon_n}^i, \delta\varepsilon_n^{-1} - 1).$$

By the standard regularity of elliptic equation, we can get the result of this lemma. The proof is complete.   □

Lemma 4.7   For any $0 \leqslant i \leqslant m_j$, $\lim_{\varepsilon \to 0} \text{dist}(\varepsilon y_{j,\varepsilon}^i, A) = 0$.

Proof. If not, we assume that there exist $1 \leqslant i_0 \leqslant m_j$ and $\varepsilon_n > 0$ such that $\lim_{n \to \infty} \varepsilon_n = 0$ and

$$\lim_{n \to \infty} \text{dist}(\varepsilon_n y_{j,\varepsilon_n}^{i_0}, A) > 0.$$

Without loss of generality, we assume that for every i, $\lim_{\varepsilon \to \infty} \varepsilon_n y_{j,\varepsilon_n}^i$ exists.

By the condition of (V_2), we deduce that there exists $\delta' > 0$ such that, for every $y \in \Lambda^{\delta'}$,

$$\inf_{x \in B(y,\delta') \setminus \Lambda} \nabla V(y) \cdot \nabla \text{dist}(x, \partial\Lambda) > 0. \tag{4.69}$$

Since $y_j^{i_0} = \lim_{n \to \infty} \varepsilon_n y_{j,\varepsilon_n}^{i_0} \notin A$, we infer that there exists $\delta'' > 0$ such that, for sufficiently large n,

$$\inf_{x \in B(y_{j,\varepsilon_n}^{i_0}, \delta'' \varepsilon_n^{-1})} \nabla V(\varepsilon_n x) \cdot \nabla V(\varepsilon_n y_{j,\varepsilon_n}^{i_0}) \geqslant \frac{1}{2} |\nabla V(y_j^{i_0})|^2 > 0. \tag{4.70}$$

Set

$$0 < \delta_0 < \min\{\delta', \delta'', \vartheta_*\}.$$

Shortly, we denote $w_n = v_{j,\varepsilon_n}$, $\tilde{B} = B(y_{j,\varepsilon_n}^{i_0}, \delta_0\varepsilon_n^{-1})$. Because $0 < \delta_0 < \vartheta_*$ and Lemma 4.5, there exist constants $c, C > 0$ independent of n such that

$$|\nabla w_n(x)| + |w_n(x)| \leqslant C \exp(-c\varepsilon_n^{-1}), \quad x \in \partial\tilde{B}, \tag{4.71}$$

for sufficiently large n.

From Lemma 4.2, we infer that there exists $C > 0$ independent of n such that

$$0 \leqslant \xi_n \leqslant C, \quad \text{for all } n. \tag{4.72}$$

Denote $\vec{t}_n = \nabla V(\varepsilon_n y_{j,\varepsilon_n}^{i_0})$. Since w_n solves (4.13) and the coefficients of (4.13) are all C^1 functions, we infer that w_n is a C^2 function. Multiplying both sides of (4.13) by $\vec{t}_n \cdot \nabla w_n$ and integrating in $\tilde{B}$, we get the following local Pohozaev type identity

$$\frac{1}{2} \int_{\tilde{B}} \left(\varepsilon_n \vec{t}_n \cdot (\nabla V)(\varepsilon_n x) + \xi_n \nabla \chi_{\varepsilon_n} \vec{t}_n \right) w_n^2 \, dx$$

$$
= \left(a + b\int_{\mathbb{R}^3}|\nabla w_n|^2 dx\right)\int_{\partial \tilde{B}}\frac{1}{2}|\nabla w_n|^2\vec{t}_n \cdot \nu
$$

$$
- \left(a + b\int_{\mathbb{R}^3}|\nabla w_n|^2 dx\right)\int_{\partial \tilde{B}}(\nabla w_n \cdot \nu)(\nabla w_n \cdot \vec{t}_n)ds
$$

$$
- \frac{1}{p}\int_{\partial \tilde{B}}|w_n|^p(\vec{t}_n \cdot \nu)ds, \tag{4.73}
$$

where ν denotes the unit outward normal to the boundary of $\tilde{B}$.

From (4.69) and $w(\cdot + y_{j,\varepsilon_n^{-1}}^{i_0}) \rightharpoonup \tilde{v}_{i_0} \neq 0$ in $H^1(\mathbb{R}^3)$, we obtain that

$$
\varepsilon_n\int_{\tilde{B}}(\vec{t}_n \cdot (\nabla V)(\varepsilon_n x))w_n^2 dx \geqslant \frac{\varepsilon_n}{2}|\nabla V(y_j^{i_0})|^2\int_{B(0,\delta_0\varepsilon_n^{-1})}w_n^2(\cdot + y_{j,\varepsilon_n}^{i_0})dx \geqslant C\varepsilon_n, \tag{4.74}
$$

where

$$
C = \frac{1}{4}|\nabla V(y_j^{i_0})|^2\int_{\mathbb{R}^3}\tilde{v}_{i_0}^2 > 0.
$$

By (4.68), we obtain that, for any $x \in \tilde{B} \setminus \Lambda_{\varepsilon_n}$,

$$
\vec{t}_n \cdot \nabla \chi_{\varepsilon_n}(x) \geqslant 0. \tag{4.75}
$$

Furthermore, by (4.70) and (4.71), there exist two positive constants C, c independent of n such that, for sufficiently large n,

$$
\left(a + b\int_{\mathbb{R}^3}|\nabla w_n|^2 dx\right)\int_{\partial \tilde{B}}\frac{1}{2}|\nabla w_n|^2\vec{t}_n \cdot \nu
$$

$$
- \left(a + b\int_{\mathbb{R}^3}|\nabla w_n|^2 dx\right)\int_{\partial \tilde{B}}(\nabla w_n \cdot \nu)(\nabla w_n \cdot \vec{t}_n)ds
$$

$$
- \frac{1}{p}\int_{\partial \tilde{B}}|w_n|^p(\vec{t}_n \cdot \nu)ds
$$

$$
\leqslant C\exp(-c\varepsilon_n^{-1}). \tag{4.76}
$$

This contradicts (4.72). The proof is complete. □

Lemma 4.8 *For any $\delta > 0$, there exist two positive constant $C = C(\delta, N)$ and $c = c(\delta, N)0$ independent of ε such that for every $1 \leqslant j \leqslant N$,*

$$
|v_{j,\varepsilon}(x)| \leqslant C\exp(-c\mathrm{dist}(x,(A_\varepsilon)^\delta)), \quad x \in \mathbb{R}^3.
$$

Proof. By (4.50), (4.61) and Lemma 4.7, we infer that there is $R_0 > 0$ independent of ε such that, for sufficiently small $\varepsilon > 0$,

$$
|v_{j,\varepsilon}(x)|^{p-2} < m_0/2, \quad \text{if } \mathrm{dist}(x,(\overline{A_\varepsilon})^\delta) \geqslant R_0. \tag{4.77}
$$

To prove the result, it is only need to show

$$|v_{j,\varepsilon}(x)| \leqslant C \exp(-c\mathrm{dist}(x,(A_\varepsilon)^\delta)), \quad \text{if}\quad \mathrm{dist}(x,(\overline{A_\varepsilon})^\delta) \geqslant R_0. \tag{4.78}$$

For $m \in \mathbb{N}$, let

$$B_m = \{x \in \mathbb{R}^3 : \mathrm{dist}(x,\overline{(A_\varepsilon)^\delta} \geqslant R_0 - m + 1\}.$$

Let ρ_m be a cut-off function satisfying $0 \leqslant \rho_m(t) \leqslant 1$, $|\rho_m'(t)| \leqslant 4$ for all $t \in \mathbb{R}$ and

$$\rho_m(t) = \begin{cases} 0, & \text{if } t \leqslant R_0 + m - 1, \\ 1, & \text{if } t \leqslant R_0 + m. \end{cases}$$

For $x \in \mathbb{R}^3$, set $\phi_m(x) = \rho_m(\mathrm{dist}(x,\overline{A_\varepsilon^\delta}))$. Multiplying both sides of (4.13) by $\phi_m^2 v_{j,\varepsilon}$ and integrating on $\mathbb{R}^3$, we have that

$$\left(a + b\int_{\mathbb{R}^3}|\nabla v_{j,\varepsilon}|^2 dx\right)\int_{B_m}|\nabla v_{j,\varepsilon}|^2\phi_m^2 dx + \int_{B_m}V(\varepsilon x)v_{j,\varepsilon}^2\phi_m^2 dx$$

$$\xi_\varepsilon \int_{B_m}\chi_\varepsilon v_{j,\varepsilon}^2\phi_m^2 dx - \int_{B_m}|v_{j,\varepsilon}|^p\phi_m^2 dx$$

$$\leqslant 8(a + bA_j)\int_{B_m\setminus B_{m+1}}(|\nabla v_{j,\varepsilon}|^2 + v_{j,\varepsilon}^2)dx, \tag{4.79}$$

and by (4.76), we obtain that

$$\left(a + b\int_{\mathbb{R}^3}|\nabla v_{j,\varepsilon}|^2 dx\right)\int_{B_{m+1}}|\nabla v_{j,\varepsilon}|^2\phi_m^2 dx + \int_{B_{m+1}}V(\varepsilon x)v_{j,\varepsilon}^2\phi_m^2 dx$$

$$\xi_\varepsilon \int_{B_{m+1}}\chi_\varepsilon v_{j,\varepsilon}^2\phi_m^2 dx - \int_{B_{m+1}}|v_{j,\varepsilon}|^p\psi_m^2 dx$$

$$\geqslant \min\left\{a + b\frac{A_j}{2}, \frac{m_0}{2}\right\}\int_{B_{m+1}}(|\nabla v_{j,\varepsilon}|^2 + v_{j,\varepsilon}^2)dx, \tag{4.80}$$

where ξ_ε is defined by (4.45).

By above two inequalities, we have that

$$\left(a + b\int_{\mathbb{R}^3}|\nabla v_{j,\varepsilon}|^2 dx\right)\int_{B_m}|\nabla v_{j,\varepsilon}|^2\phi_m^2 dx \leqslant C\int_{B_m\setminus B_{m+1}}(|\nabla v_{j,\varepsilon}|^2 + v_{j,\varepsilon}^2)dx, \tag{4.81}$$

where $C = 8/\min\{a + bA_j/2, m_0/2\}$. Then similar to the proof of Lemma 4.5, we can get (4.77). The proof is complete. □

Lemma 4.9   *There exists $\varepsilon_N > 0$ such that if $0 < \varepsilon < \varepsilon_N$, then for every $1 \leqslant j \leqslant N$, $v_{j,\varepsilon}$ is a solution of (4.13).*

Proof. Since A is a compact subset of Λ, $\text{dist}(A, \partial\Lambda) > 0$. By choosing $0 < \delta < \text{dist}(A, \partial\Lambda)$, from Lemma 4.8, we obtain that, for every $1 \leqslant j \leqslant N$,

$$\lim_{\varepsilon \to 0} \int_{\mathbb{R}^3} \chi_\varepsilon v_{j,\varepsilon}^2 dx = 0. \tag{4.82}$$

It follows from that $Q_\varepsilon(v_{j,\varepsilon}) = 0$ if $\varepsilon > 0$ is small enough. Hence there exists $\varepsilon_N > 0$ such that if $0 < \varepsilon < \varepsilon_N$, then for every $1 \leqslant j \leqslant N, v_{j,\varepsilon}$ is a solution of (4.13). The proof is complete.   □

Proof of Theorem 4.1   By Proposition 4.3, Lemma 4.8 and Lemma 4.9, we can get the results of Theorem 4.1. The proof is complete.   □

4.5   Proof of Proposition 4.2

In this section, we give the proof of Proposition 4.2. Let G is an operator on $H^1(\mathbb{R}^3)$. For $u \in H^1(\mathbb{R}^3)$, we define $w = G(u)$ is

$$-\left(a + b \int_{\mathbb{R}^3} |\nabla u|^2 dx\right) \Delta w + V(\varepsilon x)w + 2\beta \left(\int_{\mathbb{R}^3} \chi_\varepsilon u^2 dx - 1\right)_+^{\beta-1} \chi_\varepsilon w = |u|^{p-2}u, \tag{4.83}$$

where $w \in H^1(\mathbb{R}^3)$.

We know that G is odd on $H^1(\mathbb{R}^3)$.

Lemma 4.10 G is well defined and continuous on $H^1(\mathbb{R}^3)$.

Proof. Since

$$\xi(u) := 2\beta \left(\int_{\mathbb{R}^3} \chi_\varepsilon u^2 dx - 1\right)_+^{\beta-1} \tag{4.84}$$

is non-negative, G is well defined and continuous on $H^1(\mathbb{R}^3)$. If $u_n \to u$ in $H^1(\mathbb{R}^3)$, we can obtain that

$$\min\left\{a + b \int_{\mathbb{R}^3} |\nabla u|^2 dx, a_0\right\} \|A(u_n) - A(u)\|^2$$

$$\leqslant \int_{\mathbb{R}^3} \left||u_n|^{p-2}u_n - |u|^{p-2}u\right| |A(u_n) - A(u)| dx$$

$$+ |\xi(u_n) - \xi(u)| \int_{\mathbb{R}^3} \chi_\varepsilon |A(u_n) - A(u)||A(u)| dx.$$

Since $|\xi(u_n) - \xi(u)| \to 0$ is obvious, by Sobolev embedding, we can get the conclusion. The proof is complete.   □

Lemma 4.11   *For any $u \in H^1(\mathbb{R}^3)$,*

$$\langle \Gamma'_\varepsilon(u), u - A(u)\rangle = \left(a + b\int_{\mathbb{R}^3} |\nabla u|^2 dx\right) \int_{\mathbb{R}^3} |\nabla(u - A(u))|^2 dx \tag{4.85}$$

$$+ \int_{\mathbb{R}^3} V(\varepsilon x)(u - A(u))^2 dx + \xi(u) \int_{\mathbb{R}^3} \chi_\varepsilon (u - A(u))^2 dx.$$

And for any $u \in H^1(\mathbb{R}^3)$, there exists a positive constant C such that

$$\|\Gamma'_\varepsilon(u)\| \leqslant \|u - A(u)\| \left(\max\left\{a + b\int_{\mathbb{R}^3} |\nabla u|^2 dx, 1\right\} + C\|u\|^{2\beta-2}\right). \tag{4.86}$$

Proof. By a direct computation, we can get (4.84). In the following, we only need to show (4.85). For any $\psi \in H^1(\mathbb{R}^3)$,

$$\langle \Gamma'_\varepsilon(u), \psi\rangle = \left(a + b\int_{\mathbb{R}^3} |\nabla u|^2 dx\right) \int_{\mathbb{R}^3} \nabla u \nabla \psi dx + \int_{\mathbb{R}^3} V(\varepsilon x) u\psi dx$$

$$+ \xi(u) \int_{\mathbb{R}^3} \chi_\varepsilon u\psi dx - \int_{\mathbb{R}^3} |u|^{p-2} u\psi dx. \tag{4.87}$$

(4.82) times ψ, then integrate on both sides, we can get

$$\left(a + b\int_{\mathbb{R}^3} |\nabla u|^2 dx\right) \int_{\mathbb{R}^3} \nabla w \nabla \psi dx + \int_{\mathbb{R}^3} V(\varepsilon x) w\psi dx + \xi(u) \int_{\mathbb{R}^3} \chi_\varepsilon w\psi dx$$

$$= \int_{\mathbb{R}^3} |u|^{p-2} u\psi dx. \tag{4.88}$$

By (4.86) and (4.87), we have

$$\langle \Gamma'_\varepsilon(u), \psi\rangle = \left(a + b\int_{\mathbb{R}^3} |\nabla u|^2 dx\right) \int_{\mathbb{R}^3} \nabla(u - w) \nabla \psi dx + \int_{\mathbb{R}^3} V(\varepsilon x)(u - w)\psi dx$$

$$+ \xi(u) \int_{\mathbb{R}^3} \chi_\varepsilon (u - w)\psi dx.$$

Then

$$|\langle \Gamma'_\varepsilon(u), \psi\rangle|$$

$$\leqslant \max\left\{a + b\int_{\mathbb{R}^3} |\nabla u|^2 dx, 1\right\} \|u - A(u)\|\|\psi\| + C\|u\|^{2\beta-2}\|u - A(u)\|\|\psi\|,$$

that is, for any $u \in H^1(\mathbb{R}^3)$, we obtain that

$$\|\Gamma'_\varepsilon(u)\| \leqslant \|u - A(u)\| \left(\max\left\{a + b\int_{\mathbb{R}^3} |\nabla u|^2 dx, 1\right\} + C\|u\|^{2\beta-2}\right).$$

The proof is complete.　　　　　　　　　　　　　　　　　　　　□

Lemma 4.12   *There exists $\sigma_0 > 0$ such that for $\sigma \in (0, \sigma_0)$,*

$$G(\partial(P_-^\sigma)) \subset P_-^\sigma, \quad G(\partial(P_+^\sigma)) \subset P_+^\sigma.$$

Proof. We only proof $G(\partial(P_-^\sigma)) \subset P_-^\sigma$. For $u \in H^1(\mathbb{R}^3)$, let

$$w = G(u), \quad C_1 := \left(\min\left\{ a + b \int_{\mathbb{R}^3} |\nabla u|^2 dx, m_0 \right\} \right)^{-1}.$$

We obtain

$$\mathrm{dist}_{H^1}(w, P_-) \|w^+\|$$

$$\leqslant C_1 \|w^+\|^2 \leqslant \left\{ \left(a + b \int_{\mathbb{R}^3} |\nabla u|^2 dx \right) \int_{\mathbb{R}^3} |\nabla w|^2 dx + \int_{\mathbb{R}^3} V(\varepsilon x) w^2 dx \right\}$$

$$= C_1 \left\{ \left(a + b \int_{\mathbb{R}^3} |\nabla u|^2 dx \right) \int_{\mathbb{R}^3} w w^+ dx + \int_{\mathbb{R}^3} V(\varepsilon x) w w^+ dx \right\}$$

$$= C_1 \int_{\mathbb{R}^3} |u|^{p-2} u w^+ dx - C_1 \xi(u) \int_{\mathbb{R}^3} \chi_\varepsilon w w^+ \psi dx$$

$$\leqslant C_1 \int_{\mathbb{R}^3} |u|^{p-2} u w^+ dx \leqslant C_1 \int_{\mathbb{R}^3} |u|^{p-2} u^+ w^+ dx$$

$$\leqslant C_1 \|u^+\|_p^{p-1} \|w^+\|_p$$

$$= C_1 (\mathrm{dist}_{L^p}(u, P_-))^{p-1} \|w^+\|_p$$

$$\leqslant C_1 C (\mathrm{dist}_{H^1}(u, P_-))^{p-1} \|w^+\|.$$

Then we can infer that $\mathrm{dist}_{H^1}(w, P_-) \leqslant C\sigma^{p-1}$. For $\sigma > 0$ small enough, we can get the conclusion. The proof is complete. $\square$

We need to have a locally Lipschitz perturbation of G, here G may be only continuous. We $E_0 = H^1(\mathbb{R}^3) \setminus K$, where K is the set of fixed points of G, that is, the set of critical points of Γ_ε.

Lemma 4.13   *There exists a locally Lipschitz continuous operator $B : E_0 \to H^1(\mathbb{R}^3)$ such that*

(i) $B(\partial(P_+^\sigma)) \subset P_+^\sigma$ *and* $B(\partial(P_-^\sigma)) \subset P_-^\sigma$, *for $\sigma \in (0, \sigma_0)$;*

(ii) $\dfrac{1}{2} \|u - B(u)\| \leqslant \|u - G(u)\| \leqslant 2\|u - B(u)\|$, *for $u \in E_0$;*

(iii) $\langle \Gamma_\varepsilon'(u), u - B(u) \rangle \geqslant \dfrac{1}{2} \|u - G(u)\|^2$, *for $u \in E_0$;*

(iv) B *is odd.*

Since the proof is similar to the proofs of Lemma 4.1 in [19] and Lemma 7 in [20], we omit the proof.

Γ_ε satisfies $(PS)_c$ condition for $c < L$ if $0 < \varepsilon < \varepsilon_L$, by using the map B and similar argument of Lemma 3.5 of [131], we can obtain the following lemma.

Lemma 4.14   *Assume that $0 < \varepsilon < \varepsilon_L$, $c < L$ and N is a symmetric closed neighborhood of K_c. Then there exist a positive constant ι_0 such that for $0 < \iota < \iota' < \iota_0$, there exists a continuous map $\zeta : [0,1] \times H^1(\mathbb{R}^3) \to H^1(\mathbb{R}^3)$ satisfying*

(i) $\zeta(0, u) = u$ *for all* $u \in H^1(\mathbb{R}^3)$;

(ii) $\zeta(t, u) = u$ *for* $t \in [0,1], \Gamma_\varepsilon(u) \notin [c - \iota', c + \iota']$;

(iii) $\zeta(t, -u) = -\zeta(t, u)$ *for all* $t \in [0,1]$ *and* $u \in H^1(\mathbb{R}^3)$;

(iv) $\zeta(1, (\Gamma_\varepsilon)^{c+\iota}) \subset (\Gamma_\varepsilon)^{c-\iota}$;

(v) $\zeta(t, \partial(P_+^\sigma)) \subset P_+^\sigma, \zeta(t, \partial(P_-^\sigma)) \subset P_-^\sigma, \zeta(t, P_+^\sigma) \subset P_+^\sigma, \zeta(t, P_-^\sigma) \subset P_-^\sigma, t \in [0,1]$.

Proof of Proposition 4.2   Set D is a closed symmetric neighborhood of $K_c \setminus W$. Notice that $N = D \cup \overline{P_+^\sigma} \cup \overline{P_-^\sigma}$ is a closed symmetric neighborhood of K_c. By Lemma 4.14, we can choose $\eta = \zeta(1, \cdot)$ in Definition 4.1. The proof is complete.   □

Chapter 5 Infinitely Many Sign-Changing Solutions

5.1 Sign-changing solutions for an elliptic equation involving critical Sobolev and Hardy-Sobolev exponent

5.1.1 Introduction and main results

Let $\mu \geqslant 0, N \geqslant 7, 0 < t < 2, 2^* = \dfrac{2N}{N-2}$ is the critical Sobolev exponent and $2^*(t) = \dfrac{2(N-t)}{N-2}$ is the critical Hardy-Sobolev exponent, Ω is a bounded domain in $\mathbb{R}^N, 0 \in \partial\Omega$, all the principal curvatures of $\partial\Omega$ at 0 are negative. We study the following Dirichlet's problem

$$\begin{cases} -\Delta u = \mu|u|^{2^*-2}u + \dfrac{|u|^{2^*(t)-2}u}{|x|^t} + a(x)u, & \text{in } \Omega, \\ u = 0, & \text{on } \partial\Omega, \end{cases} \tag{5.1}$$

where $a(x)$ is a positive function. It is well known that solutions of (5.1) are critical points of the corresponding functional $J : H_0^1(\Omega) \to \mathbb{R}$ given by

$$J(u) = \frac{1}{2}\int_\Omega \left(|\nabla u|^2 - a(x)u^2\right) dx - \frac{\mu}{2^*}\int_\Omega |u|^{2^*} dx - \frac{1}{2^*(t)}\int_\Omega \frac{|u|^{2^*(t)}}{|x|^t} dx. \tag{5.2}$$

By using the following Hardy-Sobolev inequality (Lemma 5.1), we know that J is well defined and C^1 function on $H_0^1(\Omega)$ for any open subset of $\mathbb{R}^N$.

Since problem (5.1) involves the critical Sobolev exponent and the critical Hardy-Sobolev exponent, we can use the pioneering idea of Brézis and Nirenberg[36], or the concentration compactness principle of Lions[128], or the global compactness of Struwe[164] to show (5.2) has a critical point, then we get a positive solution to (5.1).

When $t = \mu = 0$ and $a(x) = \lambda$, (5.1) is related to the well known Brézis-Nirenberg problem[36]:

$$\begin{cases} -\Delta u = \lambda u + |u|^{2^*-2}u, & \text{in } \Omega, \\ u = 0, & \text{on } \partial\Omega, \end{cases} \tag{5.3}$$

where $2^* = \dfrac{2N}{N-2}$ is the critical Sobolev exponent. Since the pioneering work of [36], there are some important results on this problem, see e.g. [12, 43, 50, 51, 61, 71, 80, 173, 222]. Here we would like to point out [79], in the paper Devillanova and Solimini proved that, when $N \geqslant 7$, (5.3) has infinitely many solutions for each $\lambda > 0$. Let us now briefly recall the main results concerning the sign-changing solutions of (5.3) obtained before. If $N \geqslant 4$ and Ω is a ball, then for any $\lambda > 0$, (5.3) has infinitely many nodal solutions which are built using particular symmetries of the domain Ω (see [91]). In [162], Solimini proved that if Ω is a ball and $N \geqslant 7$, for each $\lambda > 0$, (5.3) has infinitely many sign-changing radial solutions. When Ω is a ball and $4 \leqslant N \leqslant 6$, there is a $\lambda^* > 0$ such that (5.3) has no radial solutions which change sign if $\lambda \in (0, \lambda^*)$ (see [13]). In [91, 162], the symmetry of the ball plays an essential role, hence their methods are invalid for general domains.

When $\Omega = \mathbb{R}^N$, $a(x)$ is singular at the origin, by using Mountain Pass theorem of Ambrosetti and Rabinowtiz[9], the existence of positive solution to more general equations was studied by Fillippucci[89]. For the existence of infinitely many solutions or infinitely many sign-changing solutions for the related equations see [30, 121, 166, 205, 220] and the references therein. Very recently, M. Bhakta[29] proved the existence of infinitely many sign-changing solutions for (5.3).

Theorem 5.1 *Suppose that $N \geqslant 7, \mu \geqslant 0$ and $0 \in \partial\Omega$, all the principal curvatures of $\partial\Omega$ at 0 are negative and $a \in C^1(\bar{\Omega}), a(x) > 0, 0 < t < 2, 2^*(t) = \dfrac{2(N-t)}{N-2}$, then* (5.3) *has infinitely many sign-changing solutions.*

M. Bhakta also considered the following non-existence theorem.

Theorem 5.2[29] *Suppose $N \geqslant 3, a \in C^1(\bar{\Omega})$ and $\left(ax + \dfrac{1}{2}x \cdot \nabla a \right) \leqslant 0$ for every $x \in \Omega$. Then* (5.3) *does not have nontrivial solution in a domain which is star shaped domain with respect to the origin.*

Remark 5.1 Let λ_1 be the first eigenvalue of

$$\begin{cases} -\Delta u = \lambda a(x)u, & \text{in } \Omega, \\ u = 0, & \text{on } \partial\Omega. \end{cases} \tag{5.4}$$

Since $a \in C^1(\bar{\Omega})$ and strictly positive, then (5.4) has infinitely many eigenvalues $\{\lambda_1, \lambda_2, \cdots\}$ such that $0 < \lambda_1(\Omega) < \lambda_2(\Omega) \leqslant \lambda_3(\Omega) \leqslant \cdots \leqslant \lambda_l(\Omega) \leqslant \cdots$. It is characterized by the following variational principle:

$$\lambda_1(\Omega) = \inf_{u \in H_0^1(\Omega), u \neq 0} \frac{\displaystyle\int_\Omega |\nabla u|^2 dx}{\displaystyle\int_\Omega a(x)u^2 dx}. \tag{5.5}$$

Let e_m be the orthonormal eigenfunction corresponding to λ_m and $e_m > 0$. Denote
$$H_m := \text{span}\{e_1, e_2, \cdots, e_m\}.$$
Then $H_m \subset H_{m+1}$ and $H_0^1(\Omega) = \overline{\cup_{m=1}^{\infty} H_m}$. It is easy to know that if $\lambda_1 \leqslant 1$, equation (5.1) has infinitely many sign-changing solutons. Indeed, by multiplying the first eigenfunction e_1 and integrating both sides, then we can check that if $\lambda_1 \leqslant 1$, any nontrivial solution of (5.3) has to change sign. Therefore, by the result of [209], to prove Theorem 5.1 it suffices to consider the case of $\lambda_1 > 1$.

Remark 5.2   In [40],the following problem was considered:

$$\begin{cases} -\Delta u = |u|^{2^*-2}u + \mu \dfrac{u}{|x|^2} + a(x)u, & \text{in } \Omega, \\ u = 0, & \text{on } \partial\Omega. \end{cases} \tag{5.6}$$

They obtained a pair of sign changing solutions to (5.6). In [61, 220], the authors get the infinitely many sign changing solutions for (5.6) when $a(x) = \lambda$. They only considered the case $0 \in \Omega$. In another case, $0 \in \partial\Omega$, the mean curvature of $\partial\Omega$ at 0 plays an important role in the existence of mountain pass solutions, see [19, 40, 62, 99, 101, 106, 118]. As it is pointed in [29, 209], there are some differences between the case $t = 2$ and $t \in (0, 2)$. When $t = 2$, solutions of (5.6) have a singularity at 0, Chen[61] and Zhang[220] impose the condition $\mu \in \left[0, \dfrac{(N-2)^2}{4} - 4 \right)$. If $t \in (0, 2)$, no such condition is needed. So the estimates for the case $t \in (0, 2)$ and the case $t = 2$ are very different. Therefore we have generalize the result in [220] to include the case $0 \in \partial\Omega$.

Remark 5.3   In order to prove the results, M. Bhakta[29] first used an abstract theorem which is introduced by Schechter and Zou[158]. Then by combining this with the uniform bounded theorem due to [209], the author obtained infinitely many sign-changing solutions. The method introduced in [29, 61, 93, 158, 209] sometimes are limited. Because by general minimax procedure to get the Morse indices of sign-changing critical points sometimes are not clear. Another limited condition is that the corresponding functional is also needed to be C^2.

Before giving our main results, we give some notations first. We will always denote $0 < t < 2$. Let $E = H_0^1(\Omega)$ be endowed with the standard scalar and norm

$$(u, v) = \int_\Omega \nabla u \nabla v dx, \qquad \|u\| = \left(\int_\Omega |\nabla u|^2 dx \right)^{1/2}.$$

The norm on $L^s = L^s(\Omega)$ with $1 \leqslant s < \infty$ is given by $|u|_s = \left(\int_\Omega |u|^s dx \right)^{1/s}$,

$L_t^q(\Omega)(1 \leqslant q < \infty, 0 \leqslant t < 2)$ with the norm $|u|_{q,t,\Omega} = \left(\int_\Omega \frac{|u|^q}{|x|^t} dx \right)^{1/q}$, where dx denote the Lebesgue measure in $\mathbb{R}^N$. Denote $B_r = \{u \in E : \|u\| \leqslant r\}$ and $B_r^c := E \setminus B_r$.

We will use the usual Ljusternik-Schnirelman type minimax method and invariant set method to prove Theorem 5.1. Our method is much simpler than the proof of [29]. In fact, our approach also works for the Brézis-Nirenberg problem involving subcritical perturbation term $f(x, u)$ which is not C^1. However, the techniques developed by M. Bhakta[29] or Schechter and Zou[158] can not be applied directly. Let us outline the proof of Theorem 5.1 and explain the difficulties we will encounter.

In general, by using the combination of invariant sets method and minimax method to obtain infinitely many nodal critical points, we need the energy functional satisfie the Palais-Smale condition in all energy level. This fact prevents us from using the variational methods directly to prove the existence of infinitely many sign-changing solutions for (5.1). Because $J(u)$ does not satisfy the Palais-Smale condition for large energy level due to the critical Sobolev exponent $2^*(t)$.

In order to overcome the difficulty, we will adopt the idea in [79,166] and [29,209]. We first study the following perturbed problem:

$$\begin{cases} -\Delta u = \mu |u|^{2^*-2-\varepsilon} u + \dfrac{|u|^{2^*(t)-2-\varepsilon} u}{|x|^t} + a(x)u, & \text{in } \Omega, \\ u = 0, & \text{on } \partial\Omega, \end{cases} \tag{5.7}$$

where $\varepsilon > 0$ is a small constant. The corresponding energy functional is

$$J_\varepsilon(u) = \frac{1}{2} \int_\Omega \left(|\nabla u|^2 - a(x)u^2 \right) dx - \frac{\mu}{2^* - \varepsilon} \int_\Omega |u|^{2^*-\varepsilon} dx$$

$$- \frac{1}{2^*(t) - \varepsilon} \int_\Omega \frac{|u|^{2^*(t)-\varepsilon}}{|x|^t} dx. \tag{5.8}$$

By the following lemmas, we will know $J_\varepsilon(u)$ is a C^1 function on $H_0^1(\Omega)$ and satisfies the Palais-Smale condition. It follows from [9,154], $J_\varepsilon(u)$ has infinitely many critical points. More precisely, there are positive numbers $c_{\varepsilon,l}$, $l = 2, 3, \cdots$, with $c_{\varepsilon,l} \to +\infty$ as $l \to \infty$. Moreover, a critical point $u_{\varepsilon,l}$ for $J_\varepsilon(u)$ satisfying

$$J_\varepsilon(u_{\varepsilon,l}) = c_{\varepsilon,l}.$$

Next, we will show that for any fixed $l \geqslant 2$, $\|u_{\varepsilon,l}\|$ are uniformly bounded with respect to ε, then we can apply the following compactness result Proposition 5.1 (see Theorem 1.1 in [209]) which essentially follows from the uniform bounded theorem due to Devillanova and Solimini[79] to show that $u_{\varepsilon,l}$ converges strongly to u_l in E

as $\varepsilon \to 0$. Therefore it is easy to prove that u_l is a solution of (5.1) with $J(u_l) = c_l := \lim_{\varepsilon \to 0} c_{\varepsilon,l}$.

Proposition 5.1[209]   *Suppose that $a(0) \geqslant 0$ and $0 \in \partial\Omega$, all the principle curvatures of $\partial\Omega$ at 0 are negative. If $N \geqslant 7$, then for any sequence u_n, which is a solution of (5.1) with $\varepsilon = \varepsilon_n \to 0$, satisfying $\|u_n\| \leqslant C$ for some constant independent of n, u_n has a sequence, which converges strongly in $H_0^1(\Omega)$ as $n \to \infty$.*

In the end, we will distinguish two cases to prove that $J(u)$ has infinitely many sign-changing critical points.

Case (i)   There are $2 \leqslant l_1 < \cdots < l_i < \cdots$, satisfying $c_{l_1} < \cdots < c_{l_i} < \cdots$.

Case (ii)   There is a positive integer L such that $c_l = c$ for all $l \geqslant L$.

The central task in this procedure is to deal with Case (ii). In fact, we can prove that the usual Krasnoselskii genus of $K_c \setminus W$ (W is denoted in Section 5.1.2) is at least two, where $K_c := \{u \in E : J(u) = c, J'(u) = 0\}$. Then our result is obtained.

In Section 5.1.2, we introduce some notations and Hardy-Sobole inequality. In Section 5.1.3, we give an auxiliary operator A_ε and construct the invariant sets. We give the proof of Theorem 5.1 in Section 5.1.4.

5.1.2 Preliminaries

Now we give some integrals inequalities, for details we refer to [38].

Lemma 5.1(Hardy-Sobolev inequality)   *Let $N \geqslant 3, 0 \leqslant t < 2$, then there exists a positive constant $C = C(N, t)$ such that*

$$\left(\int_{\mathbb{R}^N} \frac{|u|^{2^*(t)}}{|x|^t} dx \right)^{2/2^*(t)} \leqslant C \int_{\mathbb{R}^N} |\nabla u|^2 dx, \tag{5.9}$$

for all $u \in C_0^\infty(\mathbb{R}^N)$.

Lemma 5.2[93]   *If Ω is a bounded subset of $\mathbb{R}^N, 0 \leqslant t < 2, N \geqslant 3$, then*

$$L_t^p(\Omega) \subset L_t^q(\Omega)$$

with the inclusion being continuous, whenever $1 \leqslant q \leqslant p < \infty$.

Remark 5.4   If $f \in L_t^p(\Omega)$ for $1 \leqslant p < \infty$, then $f \in L^p(\Omega)$ with

$$|f|_p \leqslant C|f|_{p,t,\Omega}.$$

For each ε and $u \in E$, we define

$$\|u\|_* = \mu|u|_{2^*-\varepsilon} + \left(\int_\Omega \frac{|u|^{2^*(t)-\varepsilon}}{|x|^t} dx \right)^{1/(2^*(t)-\varepsilon)}.$$

Lemma 5.3[93]   *Let $1 \leqslant q < 2^*(t), 0 \leqslant t < 2$ and $N \geqslant 3$, then the embedding $H_0^1(\Omega) \hookrightarrow L_t^q(\Omega)$ is compact.*

By Lemma 5.2, Lemma 5.3 and Hardy-Sobolev inequality, we know that the singular term $\int_\Omega \dfrac{|u|^{2^*(t)-\varepsilon}}{|x|^t}$ is finite and $\|u\|_* \leqslant C\|u\|$ where C is independent of ε. Therefore J_ε is a C^1 function on $H_0^1(\Omega)$. By Lemma 5.3, J_ε satisfies the Palais-Smale condition. In order to prove Theorem 5.1, it is enough to obtain sign-changing critical points for the functional J_ε.

Fix $\xi \in (2, 2^*(t))$. In the following, we will always assume that $\varepsilon \in (0, 2^*(t) - \xi)$. In order to construct the minimax values for the perturbed functional J_ε, the following two technique lemmas are needed.

Lemma 5.4 *Assume* $m \geqslant 1$. *Then there exists* $R = R(H_m) > 0$, *such that for all* $\varepsilon \in (0, 2^*(t) - \xi)$,

$$\sup_{B_R^c \cap H_m} J_\varepsilon(u) < 0,$$

where $B_R^c := E \setminus B_R$.

Proof. Since H_m is finite dimensional, by Lemma 5.2 we know that $\|\cdot\|_*$ is defined a norm on $H_0^1(\Omega)$, there is a constant $C > 0$ such that

$$\|u\|^{2^*-\varepsilon} \leqslant C\|u\|_*^{2^*-\varepsilon}, \quad \text{for all } u \in H_m.$$

Therefore,

$$J_\varepsilon(u) \leqslant \frac{1}{2}\|u\|^2 - \frac{\mu}{2^*-\varepsilon}\int_\Omega |u|^{2^*-\varepsilon}dx - \frac{1}{2^*(t)-\varepsilon}\int_\Omega \frac{|u|^{2^*(t)-\varepsilon}}{|x|^t}dx$$

$$\leqslant \frac{1}{2}\|u\|^2 - C\|u\|^{2^*-\varepsilon}.$$

Since $2^* - \varepsilon > 2^*(t) - \varepsilon > \xi > 2$ and $\lambda_1 > 1$, we have that

$$\lim_{\|u\|\to\infty, u\in H_m} J_\varepsilon(u) = -\infty.$$

The proof is complete. $\square$

Lemma 5.5 *For any* $\varepsilon \in (0, 2^*(t) - \xi)$, $\lambda_1 > 1$, *there exist* $\rho = \rho(\varepsilon)$, $\alpha = \alpha(\varepsilon) > 0$ *such that*

$$\inf_{\partial B_\rho} J_\varepsilon(u) \geqslant \alpha.$$

Proof.

$$J_\varepsilon(u) = \frac{1}{2}\int_\Omega (|\nabla u|^2 - a(x)u^2)\,dx - \frac{\mu}{2^*-\varepsilon}\int_\Omega |u|^{2^*-\varepsilon}dx - \frac{1}{2^*(t)-\varepsilon}\int_\Omega \frac{|u|^{2^*(t)-\varepsilon}}{|x|^t}dx$$

$$\geqslant \frac{1}{2}(\lambda_1 - 1)\int_\Omega a(x)u^2 dx - C_1|u|_{2^*-\varepsilon}^{2^*-\varepsilon} - C_2|u|_{2^*(t)-\varepsilon}^{2^*(t)-\varepsilon}.$$

Since $2^* - \varepsilon > 2^*(t) - \varepsilon > \xi > 2$ and $\lambda_1 > 1$, there exist $\rho = \rho(\varepsilon), \alpha = \alpha(\varepsilon) > 0$ such that

$$\inf_{\partial B_\rho} J_\varepsilon(u) \geqslant \alpha.$$

The proof is complete. $\hspace{11cm} \square$

Lemma 5.5 implies that 0 is a strict local minimum critical point. Then we can construct invariant sets containing all the positive and negative solutions of (5.1) for the gradient flow of J_ε. Therefore, nodal solutions can be found outside of these sets.

5.1.3   Auxiliary operator and invariant subsets of descending flow

For any $\varepsilon \in (0, 2^*(t) - \xi)$, let $A_\varepsilon : E \to E$ be given by

$$A_\varepsilon(u) := (-\Delta)^{-1}(G_\varepsilon(u) + L(u)) = (-\Delta)^{-1}\left(\mu|u|^{2^* - 2 - \varepsilon}u + \frac{|u|^{2^*(t) - 2 - \varepsilon}u}{|x|^t} + a(x)u\right),$$

where

$$G_\varepsilon(u) = \mu|u|^{2^* - 2 - \varepsilon}u + \frac{|u|^{2^*(t) - 2 - \varepsilon}u}{|x|^t}, \quad L(u) = a(x)u, \quad \text{for } u \in E.$$

Then

$$\langle L(u), v \rangle = \int_\Omega a(x)uv dx, \langle G_\varepsilon(u, v) \rangle_{H_0^1(\Omega)}$$

$$= \mu \int_\Omega |u|^{2^* - 2 - \varepsilon}uv dx + \int_\Omega \frac{|u|^{2^*(t) - 2 - \varepsilon}uv}{|x|^t} dx,$$

the gradient of J_ε has the form

$$\nabla J_\varepsilon(u) = u - A_\varepsilon(u).$$

Note that the set of fixed points of A_ε is the same as the set of critical points of J_ε, which is $K := \{u \in E : \nabla J_\varepsilon(u) = 0\}$. It is easy to check that ∇J_ε is locally Lipschitz continuous.

We consider the negative gradient flow ϕ_ε of J_ε defined by

$$\begin{cases} \dfrac{d}{dt}\phi_\varepsilon(t, u) = -\nabla J_\varepsilon(\phi_\varepsilon(t, u)), & \text{for } t \geqslant 0, \\[2mm] \phi_\varepsilon(0, u) = u. \end{cases}$$

Here and in the sequel, for $u \in E$, denote $u^\pm(x) := \max\{\pm u(x), 0\}$, the convex cones

$$+P = \{u \in E : u \geqslant 0\}, \quad -P = \{u \in E : -u \geqslant 0\}.$$

For $\theta > 0$, define
$$(\pm P)_\theta := \{u \in E : \operatorname{dist}(u, \pm P) < \theta\}.$$

We will show that there exists a $\theta_0 > 0$ such that $(\pm P)_\theta$ is an invariant set under the descending flow for all $0 < \theta \leqslant \theta_0$ (c.f. Lemma 5.6 below). Note that $E \setminus W$ contains only sign-changing functions, where
$$W := \overline{(+P)_\theta} \cup \overline{(-P)_\theta}.$$

Thus it follows from a version of the symmetric Mountain Pass theorem which provides the minimax critical values on $E \setminus W$ that (5.6) has infinitely many sign-changing solutions.

For any $N \subset E$ and $\delta > 0$, N_δ denotes the open δ-neighborhood of N, i.e.
$$N_\delta := \{u \in E : \operatorname{dist}(u, N) < \delta\},$$

whose closure and boundary are denoted by $\overline{N_\delta}$ and ∂N_δ. The following result shows that a neighborhood of $\pm P$ is an invariant set. We can use similar way as Lemma 2 in [71] and Lemma 3.1 in [19] to get the following lemma.

Lemma 5.6   *There exists a $\theta_0 > 0$ such that for any $\theta \in (0, \theta_0]$, there holds*
$$A_\varepsilon(\partial(\pm P)_\theta) \subset (\pm P)_\theta$$

and
$$\phi_\varepsilon(t, u) \in (\pm P)_\theta, \quad \text{for all } t > 0 \text{ and } u \in \overline{(\pm P)_\theta}.$$

Moreover, every nontrivial solutions $u \in (+P)_\theta$ and $u \in (-P)_\theta$ of (5.5) are positive and negative, respectively.

To prove our main result, we need to construct nodal solution by using the combination of invariant sets method and minimax method, we need a deformation lemma in the presence of invariant sets.

Definition 5.1   *A subset $W \subset E$ is an invariant set with respect to ϕ_ε if, for any $u \in W$, $\phi_\varepsilon(t, u) \in W$ for all $t \geqslant 0$.*

From Lemma 5.6, we may choose an $\theta > 0$ sufficiently small such that $\overline{(\pm P)_\theta}$ are invariant set. Set $W := \overline{(+P)_\theta} \cup \overline{(-P)_\theta}$. Note that $\phi_\varepsilon(t, \partial W) \subset \operatorname{int}(W)$ and $Q := E \setminus W$ only contains sign-changing functions.

Since J_ε satisfies the Palais-Smale condition, we have the following deformation lemma which follows from Lemma 5.1 in [130] (also see Lemma 2.4 in [122]). Define
$$K^1_{\varepsilon,c} := K_{\varepsilon,c} \cap W, \quad K^2_{\varepsilon,c} := K_{\varepsilon,c} \cap Q,$$

where
$$K_{\varepsilon,c} := \{u \in E : J_\varepsilon(u) = c, J'_\varepsilon(u) = 0\}.$$

Let $\rho > 0$ be such that $(K_{\varepsilon,c}^1)_\rho \subset W$, where $(K_{\varepsilon,c}^1)_\rho := \{u \in E : \text{dist}(u, K_{\varepsilon,c}^1) < \rho\}$.

We can use the similar method of the proof of Lemma 5.1 in [130] and Lemma 2.4 in [122] to prove the following lemma.

Lemma 5.7 *Assume that J_ε satisfies Palais-Smale condition, then there exists an $\delta_0 > 0$ such that for any $0 < \delta < \delta_0$, there exists $\eta \in C([0,1] \times E, E)$ satisfying:*

(i) $\eta(t, u) = u$ *for* $t = 0$ *or* $u \notin J_\varepsilon^{-1}([c - \delta_0, c + \delta_0]) \setminus (K_{\varepsilon,c}^2)_\rho$.

(ii) $\eta(1, J_\varepsilon^{c+\delta} \cup W \setminus (K_{\varepsilon,c}^2)_{3\rho}) \subset J_\varepsilon^{c-\delta} \cup W$ *and* $\eta(1, J_\varepsilon^{c+\delta} \cup W) \subset J_\varepsilon^{c-\delta} \cup W$ *if* $K_{\varepsilon,c}^2 = \varnothing$. *Here* $J_\varepsilon^d = \{u \in E : J_\varepsilon(u) \leqslant d\}$ *for any* $d \in \mathbb{R}$.

(iii) $\eta(t, \cdot)$ *is odd and a homeomorphism of E for* $t \in [0, 1]$.

(iv) $J_\varepsilon(\eta(\cdot, u))$ *is non-increasing.*

(v) $\eta(t, W) \subset W$ *for any* $t \in [0, 1]$.

5.1.4 The proof of Theorem 5.1

In the following, we assume that $\lambda_1 > 1$. For any $\varepsilon \in (0, 2^*(t) - \xi)$ small, we define the minimax value $c_{\varepsilon,l}$ for the perturbed functional $J_\varepsilon(u)$ with $l = 2, 3, \cdots$. We now define a family of sets for the minimax procedure here. We essentially follow [19], also see [130] and [154]. Define

$$G_m := \{h \in C(B_R \cap H_m, E) : h \text{ is odd and } h = id \text{ on } \partial B_R \cap H_m\},$$

where $R > 0$ is given by Lemma 5.4. Note that $G_m \neq \varnothing$, since $id \in G_m$. Set

$$\Gamma_l := \{h(B_R \cap H_m \setminus Y) : h \in G_m, m \geqslant l, Y = -Y \text{ is open and } \gamma(Y) \leqslant m - l\},$$

for $k \geqslant 2$. From [154], Γ_l possess the following properties:

(1°) $\Gamma_l \neq \varnothing$ and $\Gamma_{l+1} \subset \Gamma_l$ for all $l \geqslant 2$.

(2°) If $\phi \in C(E, E)$ is odd and $\phi = id$ on $\partial B_R \cap H_m$, then $\phi(A) \in \Gamma_l$ if $A \in \Gamma_l$ for all $l \geqslant 2$.

(3°) If $A \in \Gamma_l$, $Z = -Z$ is open and $\gamma(Z) \leqslant s < l$ and $l - s \geqslant 2$, then $A \setminus Z \in \Gamma_{l-s}$.

Now, for $l \geqslant 2$, we can define the minimax value $c_{\varepsilon,l}$ given by

$$c_{\varepsilon,l} := \inf_{A \in \Gamma_l} \sup_{u \in A \cap Q} J_\varepsilon(u).$$

Lemma 5.8 *For any $A \in \Gamma_l$ and $l \geqslant 2$, $A \cap Q \neq \varnothing$, then $c_{\varepsilon,l}$ are well defined, and $c_{\varepsilon,l} \geqslant \alpha > 0$ where α is given by Lemma 5.5.*

Proof. Consider the attracting domain of 0 in E:

$$D := \{u \in E : \phi_\varepsilon(t, u) \to 0, \text{ as } t \to \infty\}.$$

Note that D is open since 0 is a local minimum of J_ε and by the continuous dependence of ODE on initial data. Moreover, ∂D is an invariant set and $\overline{(+P)_\delta} \cap \overline{(-P)_\delta} \subset D$. In particular there holds

$$J_\varepsilon(u) > 0,$$

for every $u \in \overline{(+P)_\delta} \cap \overline{(-P)_\delta} \setminus \{0\}$ (see Lemma 3.4 in [19]). Now we claim that for any $A \in \Gamma_l$ with $l \geqslant 2$, it holds

$$A \cap Q \cap \partial D \neq \varnothing. \tag{5.10}$$

If this is true, then we have $A \cap Q \neq \varnothing$ and $c_{\varepsilon,2} \geqslant \alpha > 0$, because $\partial B_\rho \subset D$ and $\sup\limits_{A \cap Q} J_\varepsilon(u) \geqslant \inf\limits_{\partial D} J_\varepsilon(u) \geqslant \inf\limits_{\partial B_\rho} J_\varepsilon(u) \geqslant \alpha > 0$ by Lemma 5.5.

To prove (5.10), let

$$A = h(B_R \cap H_m \setminus Y)$$

with $\gamma(Y) \leqslant m - l$ and $l \geqslant 2$.

Define

$$O := \{u \in B_R \cap H_m : h(u) \in D\}.$$

Then O is a bounded open symmetric set with $0 \in O$ and $O \subset B_R \cap H_m$. Thus, it follows from the Borsuk-Ulam theorem that $\gamma(\partial O) = m$ and by the continuity of h, $h(\partial O) \subset \partial D$. As a consequence,

$$h(\partial O \setminus Y) \subset A \cap \partial D,$$

and therefore

$$\gamma(A \cap \partial D) \geqslant \gamma(h(\partial O \setminus Y)) \geqslant \gamma(\partial O \setminus Y) \geqslant \gamma(\partial O) - \gamma(Y) \geqslant l,$$

by the "monotone, sub-additive and supervariant" property of the genus (Proposition 5.4 in [165]). Since $(+P)_\delta \cap (-P)_\delta \cap \partial D = \varnothing$,

$$\gamma(W \cap \partial D) \leqslant 1.$$

Thus for $l \geqslant 2$, we conclude that

$$\gamma(A \cap Q \cap \partial D) \geqslant \gamma(A \cap \partial D) - \gamma(W \cap \partial D) \geqslant l - 1 \geqslant 1,$$

which proves (5.10).

Thus $c_{\varepsilon,l}$ are well defined for all $l \geqslant 2$ and $0 < \alpha \leqslant c_{\varepsilon,2} \leqslant c_{\varepsilon,3} \leqslant \cdots \leqslant c_{\varepsilon,l} \leqslant \cdots$. The proof is complete.   □

Lemma 5.9

$$K_{\varepsilon,c_{\varepsilon,l}} \cap Q \neq \varnothing. \tag{5.11}$$

Proof. If not, we assume that

$$K_{\varepsilon,c_{\varepsilon,l}} \cap Q = \varnothing.$$

By Lemma 5.7, for the functional J_ε, there exist $\delta > 0$ and a map $\eta \in C([0,1] \times E, E)$ such that $\eta(1, \cdot)$ is odd, $\eta(1, u) = u$ for $u \in J_\varepsilon^{c_{\varepsilon,l} - 2\delta}$ and

$$\eta(1, J_\varepsilon^{c_{\varepsilon,l}+\delta} \cup W) \subset J_\varepsilon^{c_{\varepsilon,l}-\delta} \cup W. \tag{5.12}$$

By the definition of $c_{\varepsilon,l}$, there exists $A \in \Gamma_l$ such that

$$\sup_{A \cap Q} J_\varepsilon(u) \leqslant c_{\varepsilon,l} + \delta.$$

Let $B = \eta(1, A)$. It follows from (5.14) that

$$\sup_{B \cap Q} J_\varepsilon(u) \leqslant c_{\varepsilon,l} - \delta.$$

On the other hand, it is easy to show that $B \in \Gamma_l$ by Lemma 5.4 and the property of $(2°)$ of Γ_l above. As a result, $c_{\varepsilon,l} \leqslant c_{\varepsilon,l} - \delta$. This contradicts with $\delta > 0$. The proof is complete. $\qquad \square$

Lemma 5.9 implies that there exists a sign-changing critical point $u_{\varepsilon,l}$ such that

$$J_\varepsilon(u_{\varepsilon,l}) = c_{\varepsilon,l}.$$

As a consequence of Lemma 5.8, we have that $c_{\varepsilon,l}$ are well defined for all $l \geqslant 2$ and $0 < \alpha \leqslant c_{\varepsilon,2} \leqslant c_{\varepsilon,3} \leqslant \cdots \leqslant c_{\varepsilon,l} \leqslant \cdots$. Now we can show the following lemma.

Lemma 5.10 $c_{\varepsilon,l} \to \infty$ as $l \to \infty$.

Proof.   Here we deduce by a negation. Suppose $c_{\varepsilon,l} \to \bar{c}_\varepsilon < \infty$ as $l \to \infty$. Since J_ε satisfies Palais-Smale condition, it follows that $K_{\varepsilon,\bar{c}_\varepsilon} \neq \varnothing$ and is compact. Moreover, we have

$$K_{\varepsilon,\bar{c}_\varepsilon}^2 := K_{\varepsilon,\bar{c}_\varepsilon} \cap Q \neq \varnothing.$$

Indeed, assume $\{u_{\varepsilon,l_i}\}_{i \in \mathbb{N}}$ is a sequence of sign-changing solutions to (5.6) with $J_\varepsilon(u_{\varepsilon,l_i}) = c_{\varepsilon,l_i}$, we have

$$\int_\Omega |\nabla u_{\varepsilon,l_i}^\pm|^2 - a(x)|u_{\varepsilon,l_i}^\pm|^2 dx = \mu \int_\Omega |u_{\varepsilon,l_i}^\pm|^{2^*-\varepsilon} dx + \int_\Omega \frac{|u_{\varepsilon,l_i}^\pm|^{2^*(t)-\varepsilon}}{|x|^t} dx.$$

By using (5.5), we obtain

$$\left(1 - \frac{1}{\lambda_1}\right) \|u_{\varepsilon,l_i}^\pm\|^2 \leqslant \mu \int_\Omega |u_{\varepsilon,l_i}^\pm|^{2^*-\varepsilon} dx + \int_\Omega \frac{|u_{\varepsilon,l_i}^\pm|^{2^*(t)-\varepsilon}}{|x|^t} dx.$$

It follows that, by Sobolev embedding theorem, $\|u_{\varepsilon,l_i}^\pm\| \geqslant c_0 > 0$, where c_0 is a constant independent of i. This implies that the limit $\bar{u}_\varepsilon \in K_{\varepsilon,\bar{c}_\varepsilon}$ of the subsequence of $\{u_{\varepsilon,l_i}\}_{i \in \mathbb{N}}$ is still sign-changing.

Assume $\gamma(K_{\varepsilon,\bar{c}_\varepsilon}^2) = \tau$. Since $0 \notin K_{\varepsilon,\bar{c}_\varepsilon}^2$ and $K_{\varepsilon,\bar{c}_\varepsilon}^2$ is compact, by the "continuous" property of the genus (Proposition 5.4 in [165]), there exists an open neighborhood

N in E with $K_{\varepsilon,\bar{c}_\varepsilon}^2 \subset N$ such that $\gamma(N) = \tau$. Now using Lemma 5.7 for the functional J_ε, there exist $\delta > 0$ and a map $\eta \in C([0,1] \times E, E)$ such that $\eta(1, \cdot)$ is odd, $\eta(1, u) = u$ for $u \in J_\varepsilon^{\bar{c}_\varepsilon - 2\delta}$ and

$$\eta(1, J_\varepsilon^{\bar{c}_\varepsilon + \delta} \cup W \setminus N) \subset J_\varepsilon^{\bar{c}_\varepsilon - \delta} \cup W. \tag{5.13}$$

Since $c_{\varepsilon,l} \to \bar{c}_\varepsilon$ as $l \to \infty$, we can choose l sufficiently large, such that $c_{\varepsilon,l} \geq \bar{c}_\varepsilon - \frac{1}{2}\delta$. Clearly, $c_{\varepsilon,l+\tau} \geq c_{\varepsilon,l} \geq \bar{c}_\varepsilon - \frac{1}{2}\delta$. By the definition of $c_{\varepsilon,l+\tau}$, we can find a set $A \in \Gamma_{l+\tau}$, that is $A = h(B_R \cap H_m \setminus Y)$, where $h \in G_m$, $m \geq l+\tau$, $\gamma(Y) \leq m-(l+\tau)$, such that

$$J_\varepsilon(u) \leq c_{\varepsilon,l+\tau} + \frac{1}{4}\delta < \bar{c}_\varepsilon + \delta, \quad \text{for any } u \in A \cap Q,$$

which implies $A \subset J_\varepsilon^{\bar{c}_\varepsilon + \delta} \cup W$.

It follows from (5.13) that

$$\eta(1, A \setminus N) \subset J_\varepsilon^{\bar{c}_\varepsilon - \delta} \cup W. \tag{5.14}$$

Let $Y_1 = Y \cup h^{-1}(N)$. Then Y_1 is symmetric and open, and

$$\gamma(Y_1) \leq \gamma(Y) + \gamma(h^{-1}(N)) \leq m - (l+\tau) + \tau = m - l.$$

Then it is easy to check $\tilde{A} := \eta(1, h(B_R \cap H_m \setminus Y_1)) \in \Gamma_l$ by (2°) and (3°) above.

As a result, by (5.14),

$$c_{\varepsilon,l} \leq \sup_{\tilde{A} \cap Q} J_\varepsilon(u) \leq \sup_{\eta(1, A \setminus N) \cap Q} J_\varepsilon(u) \leq \bar{c}_\varepsilon - \delta.$$

This is a contradiction to $c_{\varepsilon,l} \geq \bar{c}_\varepsilon - \frac{1}{2}\delta$. The proof is complete. $\square$

Lemma 5.11   For any fixed $l \geq 2$, $\|u_{\varepsilon,l}\|$ is uniformly bounded with respect to ε, and then $u_{\varepsilon,l}$ converges strongly to u_l in E as $\varepsilon \to 0$.

Proof.   In deed, by using the same Γ_l above, we can also define the minimax value for the following auxiliary function

$$J_*(u) = \frac{1}{2}\int_\Omega (|\nabla u|^2 - a(x)|u|^2)dx - \frac{1}{2^*}\int_\Omega |u|^\xi dx - \frac{1}{2^*(t)}\int_\Omega \frac{|u|^\xi}{|x|^t}dx,$$

$$\alpha_l := \inf_{A \in \Gamma_l} \sup_{u \in A} J_*(u), \quad l = 2, 3, \cdots.$$

Here, we choose $R > 0$ sufficiently large if necessary, such that Lemma 5.4 also holds for J_*. Then by a $\mathbb{Z}_2$ version of the Mountain Pass theorem (Theorem 9.2 in [154]), for each $l \geq 2$, $\alpha_l > 0$ is well defined and $\alpha_l \to \infty$ as $l \to \infty$. Because

$$J_\varepsilon(u) \leq \frac{1}{2}\int_\Omega (|\nabla u|^2 - a(x)|u|^2)dx - \frac{1}{2^*}\int_\Omega (|u|^\xi - 1)dx - \frac{1}{2^*(t)}\int_\Omega \frac{|u|^\xi - 1}{|x|^t}dx$$

$$= J_*(u) + \frac{\mu|\Omega|}{2^*} + d_0,$$

where $d_0 = \dfrac{1}{2^*(t)} \displaystyle\int_\Omega \frac{1}{|x|^t} dx$.

Therefore, for any fixed $l \geqslant 2$, $c_{\varepsilon,l}$ is uniformly bounded for $\varepsilon \in (0, 2^*(t) - \xi)$, that is, there is $C = C(\alpha_l, \Omega) > 0$ independent on ε, such that $c_{\varepsilon,l} \leqslant C$ uniformly for ε. Because $u_{\varepsilon,l}$ is a nodal solution of (5.6) and $J_\varepsilon(u_{\varepsilon,l}) = c_{\varepsilon,l}$. By the definition of λ_1, we can obtain the following

$$C \geqslant c_{\varepsilon,l} = J_\varepsilon(u_{\varepsilon,l}) = J_\varepsilon(u_{\varepsilon,l}) - \frac{1}{2^*(t) - \varepsilon} \langle J_\varepsilon'(u_{\varepsilon,l}), u_{\varepsilon,l} \rangle$$

$$= \left(\frac{1}{2} - \frac{1}{2^*(t) - \varepsilon}\right) \int_\Omega (|\nabla u_{\varepsilon,l}|^2 - a(x)u_{\varepsilon,l}^2) \, dx$$

$$+ \mu \left(\frac{1}{2^*(t) - \varepsilon} - \frac{1}{2^* - \varepsilon}\right) \int_\Omega |u_{\varepsilon,l}|^{2^* - \varepsilon} dx$$

$$\geqslant \left(\frac{1}{2} - \frac{1}{2^*(t) - \varepsilon}\right) \int_\Omega (|\nabla u_{\varepsilon,l}|^2 - a(x)u_{\varepsilon,l}^2) \, dx$$

$$\geqslant \left(\frac{1}{2} - \frac{1}{\xi}\right) \left(1 - \frac{1}{\lambda_1}\right) \|u_{\varepsilon,l}\|^2 > 0,$$

where $\lambda_1 > 1, \varepsilon \in (0, 2^*(t) - \xi)$ and $2 < \xi < 2^*(t)$. Therefore $\|u_{\varepsilon,l}\|$ is uniformly with respect to ε. So we can apply Proposition 5.1 and obtain a subsequence $\{u_{\varepsilon_l,l}\}_{l \in \mathbb{N}}$, such that $u_{\varepsilon_l,l} \to u_l$ strongly in E for some u_l and also $c_{\varepsilon_l,l} \to c_l$. Thus u_l is a solution of (5.5) and $J_\varepsilon(u_l) = c_l$. Moreover, since $u_{\varepsilon_l,l}$ is sign-changing, similar to Lemma 5.10, by Sobolev embedding theorem, we can prove that u_l is still sign-changing. The proof is complete. □

Proof of Theorem 5.1 Now we are in a position to prove Theorem 5.1. Noting that c_l is non-decreasing with respect to l, we have the following two cases:

Case (i) There are $2 \leqslant l_1 < \cdots < l_i < \cdots$, satisfying $c_{l_1} < \cdots < c_{l_i} < \cdots$. Obviously, in this case, equation (5.1) has infinitely many sign solutions such that $J(u_i) = c_{l_i}$.

Case (ii) There is a positive integer L such that $c_l = c$ for all $l \geqslant L$.

From now on we assume that there exists a $\delta > 0$, such that $J(u)$ has no sign-changing critical point u with

$$J(u) \in [c - \delta, c) \cup (c, c + \delta].$$

Otherwise we are done. In this case, we claim that $\gamma(K_c^2) \geqslant 2$, where $K_c := \{u \in E : J(u) = c, J'(u) = 0\}$ and $K_c^2 = K_c \cap Q$. Then as a consequence, $J(u)$ has infinitely many sign-changing critical points.

Now we adopt a technique in the proof of Theorem 1.1 in [41]. Suppose, on the contrary, that $\gamma(K_c^2) = 1$ (note that $K_c^2 \neq \varnothing$). Moreover, we assume K_c^2 contains only finitely many critical points, otherwise we are done. Then it follows that K_c^2 is compact. Obviously, $0 \notin K_c^2$. Then there exists a open neighborhood N in E with $K_c^2 \subset N$ such that $\gamma(N) = \gamma(K_c^2)$.

Define

$$V_\varepsilon := (J_\varepsilon^{c+\delta} \setminus J_\varepsilon^{c-\delta}) \setminus N.$$

We now claim that if $\varepsilon > 0$ small, J_ε has no sign-changing critical point $u \in V_\varepsilon$. Indeed, arguing indirectly, suppose that there exist $\varepsilon \to 0$ and $u_\varepsilon \in V_\varepsilon$ satisfying $J_\varepsilon'(u_\varepsilon) = 0$, with $u_\varepsilon^\pm \neq 0$, and $u_\varepsilon \notin N$.

Then, by Proposition 5.1, up to a subsequence, u_n converges strongly to u in E. Therefore $J'(u) = 0$,

$$J(u) \in [c - \delta, c + \delta]$$

and $u \notin K_c^2$.

This is a contradiction to our assumption and the fact that u is still sign-changing. The following proof is similar to that of Lemma 5.1. By using Lemma 5.7, for the functional J_ε, there exist $\delta > 0$ and a map $\eta \in C([0,1] \times E, E)$ such that $\eta(1, \cdot)$ is odd, $\eta(1, u) = u$ for $u \in J_\varepsilon^{c-2\delta}$ and

$$\eta(1, J_\varepsilon^{c+\delta} \cup W \setminus N) \subset J_\varepsilon^{c-\delta} \cup W. \tag{5.15}$$

Now fix $l > L$. Since $c_{\varepsilon,l}, c_{\varepsilon,l+1} \to c$ as $\varepsilon \to 0$, we can find an $\varepsilon > 0$ small, such that $c_{\varepsilon,l}, c_{\varepsilon,l+1} \in \left(c - \frac{1}{2}\delta, c + \frac{1}{2}\delta\right)$. By the definition of $c_{\varepsilon,l+1}$, we can find a set $A \in \Gamma_{l+1}$, that is

$$A = h(B_R \cap H_m \setminus Y),$$

where $h \in G_m$, $m \geqslant l + 1$, $\gamma(Y) \leqslant m - (l+1)$, such that

$$J_\varepsilon(u) \leqslant c_{\varepsilon,l+1} + \frac{1}{4}\delta < c + \delta,$$

for any $u \in A \cap Q$, which implies $A \subset J_\varepsilon^{c+\delta} \cup W$. Then by (5.15), we have

$$\eta(1, A \setminus N) \subset J_\varepsilon^{c-\delta} \cup W. \tag{5.16}$$

Let $\widetilde{Y} = Y \cup h^{-1}(N)$. Then $\widetilde{Y}$ is symmetric and open, and

$$\gamma(\widetilde{Y}) \leqslant \gamma(Y) + \gamma(h^{-1}(N)) \leqslant m - (l+1) + 1 = m - l.$$

Then it is easy to check $\widehat{A} := \eta(1, h(B_R \cap H_m \setminus \widetilde{Y})) \in \Gamma_l$ by (2°) and (3°) above. As a result, by (5.16)

$$c_{\varepsilon,l} \leqslant \sup_{\widehat{A} \cap Q} J_\varepsilon(u) \leqslant \sup_{\eta(1,A\setminus N) \cap Q} J_\varepsilon(u) \leqslant c - \delta.$$

This contradicts to $c_{\varepsilon,l} > c - \dfrac{1}{2}\delta$. Then the proof for the *Case* (ii) is finished. The proof is complete.   □

5.2 Infinitely many sign-changing solutions for an elliptic equation involving double critical Hardy-Sobolev-Maz'ya terms

5.2.1 Introduction and main results

Let $N \geqslant 3, \mu \geqslant 0, 0 \leqslant t < s < 2$, $2^*(t) = \dfrac{2(N-t)}{N-2}$ and $2^*(s) = \dfrac{2(N-s)}{N-2}$ are the critical Hardy-Sobolev-Maz'ya exponents, Ω is an open bounded domain in $\mathbb{R}^N$. We study the following equation

$$\begin{cases} -\Delta u = \mu \dfrac{|u|^{2^*(t)-2}u}{|y|^t} + \dfrac{|u|^{2^*(s)-2}u}{|y|^s} + a(x)u, & \text{in } \Omega, \\ u = 0, & \text{on } \partial\Omega, \end{cases} \tag{5.17}$$

where $a(x)$ is a positive function, $x = (y, z) \in \mathbb{R}^k \times \mathbb{R}^{N-k}, 2 \leqslant k < N$. It is well known that solutions of (5.17) are critical points of the corresponding functional $J : H_0^1(\Omega) \to \mathbb{R}$ given by

$$J(u) = \frac{1}{2} \int_\Omega (|\nabla u|^2 - a(x)u^2)\, dx - \frac{\mu}{2^*(t)} \int_\Omega \frac{|u|^{2^*(t)}}{|y|^t}\, dx$$

$$- \frac{1}{2^*(s)} \int_\Omega \frac{|u|^{2^*(s)}}{|y|^s}\, dx. \tag{5.18}$$

By using the following Hardy-Sobolev-Maz'ya inequality (Lemma 5.12), we know that J is well defined and C^1 functional on $H_0^1(\Omega)$ for any open subset of $\mathbb{R}^N$.

Since (5.17) involves the double critical Hardy-Sobolev-Maz'ya exponents, we can use the pioneering idea of Brézis and Nirenberg[35], or the concentration compactness principle of Lions[128], or the global compactness of Struwe[165] to show (5.18) has a critical point, then get a positive solution to (5.17).

When $s = \mu = 0$, $a(x) = \lambda$ and $k = N$, (5.17) is related to the well known Brézis-Nirenberg problem[35]:

$$\begin{cases} -\Delta u = \lambda u + |u|^{2^*-2}u, & \text{in } \Omega, \\ u = 0, & \text{on } \partial\Omega, \end{cases} \tag{5.19}$$

where $2^* = \dfrac{2N}{N-2}$ is the critical Sobolev exponent. Since the pioneering work of [35], there are some important results on this problem, see e.g. [40,61,71,80,173]. Here we would like to point out [79], in the paper Devillanova and Solimini proved that, when $N \geqslant 7$, (5.19) has infinitely many solutions for each $\lambda > 0$. Let us now briefly recall the main results concerning the sign-changing solutions of (5.19) obtained before. If $N \geqslant 4$ and Ω is a ball, then for any $\lambda > 0$, (5.19) has infinitely many nodal solutions which are built by using particular symmetries of the domain Ω (see [91]). In [162], Solimini proved that if Ω is a ball and $N \geqslant 7$, for each $\lambda > 0$, (1.3) has infinitely many sign-changing radial solutions. When Ω is a ball and $4 \leqslant N \leqslant 6$, there is a $\lambda^* > 0$ such that (5.19) has no radial solutions which change sign if $\lambda \in (0, \lambda^*)$ (see [13]). In [91, 162], the symmetry of the ball plays an essential role, hence their methods are invalid for general domains.

When $t = 2, a(x) = \lambda, k - N$, (5.17) is becoming Hardy-Sobolev-Maz'ya equation:

$$
\begin{cases}
-\Delta u - \dfrac{\mu u}{|y|^2} = \lambda u + \dfrac{|u|^{2^*(s)-2}u}{|y|^s}, & \text{in } \Omega, \\
u = 0, & \text{on } \partial\Omega.
\end{cases}
$$

By using the idea of [79], the authors of [185] obtained infinitely many solutions for Hardy-Sobolev-Maz'ya equation. Ganguly[93] and Wang[189] by using different methods to get infintely many sign-changing solutions. For the existence of infinitely many solutions or infinitely many sign-changing solutions for the related equations, see [99, 166, 205, 220] and the references therein. Very recently, Wang and Yang[184] proved the existence of infinitely many sign-changing solutions for (5.17).

Theorem 5.3   *Suppose that $a((0, z^*)) > 0$ and Ω is a bounded domain. If $(0, z^*) \in \partial\Omega$, $(x - (0, z^*)) \cdot \nu \leqslant 0$ in a neighborhood of $(0, z^*)$, where ν is the outward normal of $\partial\Omega$. If $N > 6 + t$ when $\mu > 0$, and if $N > 6 + s$, when $\mu = 0$, then (5.17) has infinitely many sign-changing solutions.*

Wang and Yang also considered the following non-existence theorem.

Theorem 5.4[184]   *Suppose that $N \geqslant 3, a(x) \in C^1(\bar{\Omega})$ and $\left(a(x) + \dfrac{1}{2}x \cdot \nabla a\right) \leqslant 0$ for every $x \in \Omega$. Then (5.17) does not have nontrivial solution in a domain which is star shaped domain with respect to the origin.*

Remark 5.5   Let λ_1 be the first eigenvalue of

$$
\begin{cases}
-\Delta u = \lambda a(x)u & \text{in } \Omega, \\
u = 0, & \text{on } \partial\Omega.
\end{cases}
\tag{5.20}
$$

Since $a(x) \in C^1(\bar{\Omega})$ and is strictly positive, (5.20) has infinitely many eigenvalues $\{\lambda_1, \lambda_2, \cdots\}$ such that $0 < \lambda_1(\Omega) < \lambda_2(\Omega) \leqslant \lambda_3(\Omega) \leqslant \cdots \leqslant \lambda_m(\Omega) \leqslant \cdots$. It is characterized by the following variational principle:

$$\lambda_1(\Omega) = \inf_{u \in H_0^1(\Omega), u \neq 0} \frac{\int_\Omega |\nabla u|^2}{\int_\Omega a(x)u^2}. \tag{5.21}$$

Let e_m be the orthonormal eigenfunction corresponding to λ_m and $e_m > 0$. Denote

$$H_m := \text{span}\{e_1, e_2, \cdots, e_m\}.$$

Then $H_m \subset H_{m+1}$ and $H_0^1(\Omega) = \overline{\cup_{m=1}^\infty H_m}$. It is easy to know that if $\lambda_1 \leqslant 1$, equation (5.17) has infinitely many sign-changing solutions. Indeed, by multiplying the first eigenfunction e_1 and integrating both sides, then we can check that if $\lambda_1 \leqslant 1$, any nontrivial solution of (5.17) has to change sign. Therefore, by the result of [186], to prove Theorem 5.3 it suffices to consider the case of $\lambda_1 > 1$.

Remark 5.6 When $s = 0, t = 2$ and $k = N$, Cao and Peng[40] considered the following system:

$$\begin{cases} -\Delta u = |u|^{2^*-2}u + \mu \dfrac{u}{|x|^2} + \lambda u, & \text{in } \Omega, \\ u = 0, & \text{on } \partial\Omega. \end{cases} \tag{5.22}$$

They obtained a pair of sign-changing solutions to (5.22). In [61, 220], the authors get infinitely many sign-changing solutions for (1.6). They only considered the case $0 \in \Omega$. In another case, $0 \in \partial\Omega$, the mean curvature of $\partial\Omega$ at 0 plays an important role in the existence of mountain pass solutions, see [19, 40, 99]. As it is pointed in [29, 209], there are some differences between the case $t = 2$ and $t \in (0, 2)$. When $t = 2$, solutions of (5.22) have a singularity at 0, and the authors of [61, 220] impose the condition $\mu \in [0, \dfrac{(N-2)^2}{4} - 4)$. If $t \in (0, 2)$, no such condition is needed. So the estimates for the case $t \in (0, 2)$ and the case $t = 2$ are very different. Therefore we have generalize the results in [220] to the case $0 \in \partial\Omega$.

Remark 5.7 In order to prove the results, Wang and Yang[184] first used an abstract theorem which is introduced by Schechter and Zou[158]. Then by combining with the uniform bounded theorem due to [186], the authors of [184] obtained infinitely many sign-changing solutions. The method introduced in [29, 61, 93, 158, 209] sometimes are limited. Because by general minimax procedure to get the Morse indices of sign-changing critical points sometimes are not clear.

Another limited condition is that the corresponding functional is also needed to be C^2.

Before giving our main results, we give some notations first. We will always denote $0 < t < 2$. Let $E = H_0^1(\Omega)$ be endowed with the standard scalar and norm

$$(u, v) = \int_\Omega \nabla u \nabla v dx, \qquad \|u\| = \left(\int_\Omega |\nabla u|^2 dx \right)^{1/2}.$$

The norm on $L^s = L^s(\Omega)$ with $1 \leqslant s < \infty$ is given by

$$|u|_s = \left(\int_\Omega |u|^s dx \right)^{1/s} \quad L_t^q(\Omega), \quad 1 \leqslant q < \infty, 0 \leqslant t < 2$$

with the norm $|u|_{q,t,\Omega} = \left(\int_\Omega \frac{|u|^q}{|x|^t} dx \right)^{1/q}$, where dx denote the Lebesgue measure in $\mathbb{R}^N$. Denote $B_r = \{u \in E : \|u\| \leqslant r\}$ and $B_r^c := E \setminus B_r$.

We will use the usual Ljusternik-Schnirelman type minimax method and invariant set method to prove Theorem 5.3. Our method is much simpler than the proof of [184]. In fact, our approach also works for the Brézis-Nirenberg problem involving subcritical perturbation term $f(x, u)$ which is not C^1. However, the techniques developed by Wang and Yang[184] or Schechter and Zou[158] can not be applied directly. Let us outline the proof of Theorem 5.3 and explain the difficulties we will encounter.

In general, by using the combination of invariant sets method and minimax method to obtain infinitely many nodal critical points, we need the energy functional satisfies the Palais-Smale condition in all energy level. This fact prevents us from using the variational methods directly to prove the existence of infinitely many sign-changing solutions for (5.17). Because $J(u)$ does not satisfy the Palais-Smale condition for large energy level due to the double critical Sobolev-Hardy-Maz'ya exponents $2^*(t)$ and $2^*(s)$.

In order to overcome the difficulty, we will adopt the idea in [79,166] and [29,209]. We first study the following perturbed problem:

$$\begin{cases} -\Delta u = \mu |u|^{2^*-2} u + \dfrac{|u|^{2^*(t)-2} u}{|x|^t} + a(x) u, & \text{in } \Omega, \\ u = 0, & \text{on } \partial\Omega. \end{cases} \tag{5.23}$$

where $\varepsilon > 0$ is a small constant. The corresponding energy functional is

$$J_\varepsilon(u) = \frac{1}{2} \int_\Omega \left(|\nabla u|^2 - a(x) u^2 \right) - \frac{\mu}{2^*(t) - \varepsilon} \int_\Omega \frac{|u|^{2^*(t)-\varepsilon}}{|y|^t}$$

$$-\frac{1}{2^*(s) - \varepsilon} \int_\Omega \frac{|u|^{2^*(s) - \varepsilon}}{|y|^s}. \tag{5.24}$$

By the following lemmas, we will know $J_\varepsilon(u)$ is a C^1 function on $H_0^1(\Omega)$ and satisfies the Palais-Smale condition. It follows from [9,154], $J_\varepsilon(u)$ has infinitely many critical points. More precisely, there are positive numbers $c_{\varepsilon,l}$, $l = 2, 3, \cdots$, with $c_{\varepsilon,l} \to +\infty$ as $l \to \infty$. Moreover, a critical point $u_{\varepsilon,l}$ for $J_\varepsilon(u)$ satisfying

$$J_\varepsilon(u_{\varepsilon,l}) = c_{\varepsilon,l}.$$

Next, we will show that for any fixed $l \geqslant 2$, $\|u_{\varepsilon,l}\|$ are uniformly bounded with respect to ε, then we can apply the following compactness result Proposition 5.2 (see Theorem 1.3 in [186]) which essentially follows from the uniform bounded theorem due to Devillanova and Solimini[79] to show that $u_{\varepsilon,l}$ converges strongly to u_l in E as $\varepsilon \to 0$. Therefore it is easy to prove that u_l is a solution of (5.17) with $J(u_l) = c_l := \lim_{\varepsilon \to 0} c_{\varepsilon,l}$.

Proposition 5.2[186] *Suppose that $a((0, z^*)) > 0$ and Ω satisfies the conditions in Theorem 5.3. If $N \geqslant 6 + t$ when $\mu > 0$, and $N > 6 + s$ when $\mu = 0$, then for any sequence u_n, which is a solution of (5.23) with $\varepsilon = \varepsilon_n \to 0$, satisfying $\|u_n\| \leqslant C$ for some constant independent of n, u_n has a sequence, which converges strongly in $H_0^1(\Omega)$ as $n \to \infty$.*

In the end, we will distinguish two cases to prove that $J(u)$ has infinitely many sign-changing critical points.

Case (i)   There are $2 \leqslant l_1 < \cdots < l_i < \cdots$, satisfying $c_{l_1} < \cdots < c_{l_i} < \cdots$.

Case (ii)   There is a positive integer L such that $c_l = c$ for all $l \geqslant L$.

The central task in this procedure is to deal with Case (ii). In fact, we can prove that the usual Krasnoselskii genus of $K_c \setminus W$ (W is denoted in Section 5.2.2) is at least two, where $K_c := \{u \in E : J(u) = c, J'(u) = 0\}$. Then our result is obtained.

In Section 5.2.2, we introduce some notations and Hardy-Sobole-Maz'ya inequality. In Section 5.2.3, we give an auxiliary operator A_ε and construct the invariant sets. We give the proof of Theorem 5.3 in Section 5.2.4.

5.2.2 Preliminaries

Now we give some integrals inequalities, for details we refer to [179].

Lemma 5.12(Hardy-Sobolev-Maz'ya inequality)   *Let $N \geqslant 3, 0 \leqslant t < 2$, then there exist a positive constant $S = S(\Omega, s)$ such that*

$$\left(\int_\Omega \frac{|u|^{2*(s)}}{|y|^s} dx \right)^{\frac{2}{2*(s)}} \leqslant S^{-1} \int_\Omega |\nabla u|^2 dx, \tag{5.25}$$

for all $u \in H_0^1(\Omega)$.

Lemma 5.13[93]　*If Ω is a bounded subset of $\mathbb{R}^N, 0 \leqslant t < 2, N \geqslant 3$, then*

$$L_t^p(\Omega) \subset L_t^q(\Omega)$$

with the inclusion being continuous, whenever $1 \leqslant q \leqslant p < \infty$.

Remark 5.8　If $f \in L_t^p(\Omega)$ for $1 \leqslant p < \infty$, then $f \in L^p(\Omega)$ with

$$|f|_p \leqslant C|f|_{p,t,\Omega}.$$

For each ε and $u \in E$, we define

$$\|u\|_* = \mu \left(\int_\Omega \frac{|u|^{2^*(t)-\varepsilon}}{|y|^t} dx \right)^{1/(2^*(t)-\varepsilon)} + \left(\int_\Omega \frac{|u|^{2^*(s)-\varepsilon}}{|y|^s} dx \right)^{1/(2^*(s)-\varepsilon)}.$$

Lemma 5.14[93]　Let $1 \leqslant q < 2^*(t), 0 \leqslant t < 2$ and $N \geqslant 3$, then the embedding $H_0^1(\Omega) \hookrightarrow L_t^q(\Omega)$ is compact.

By Lemma 5.13, Lemma 5.14 and Hardy-Sobolev-Maz'ya inequality, we know that the singular term $\int_\Omega \frac{|u|^{2^*(t)-\varepsilon}}{|y|^t}$ and $\int_\Omega \frac{|u|^{2^*(s)-\varepsilon}}{|y|^s}$ are finite and $\|u\|_* \leqslant C\|u\|$ where C is independent of ε. Therefore J_ε is a C^1 function on $H_0^1(\Omega)$. By Lemma 5.14, J_ε satisfies the Palais-Smale condition. In order to prove Theorem 5.3, it is enough to obtain sign-changing critical points for the functional J_ε.

Fix $\xi \in (2, 2^*(s))$. In the following, we will always assume that $\varepsilon \in (0, 2^*(s) - \xi)$. In order to construct the minimax values for the perturbed functional J_ε, the following two technique lemmas are needed.

Lemma 5.15　Assume $m \geqslant 1$. Then there exists a $R = R(H_m) > 0$, such that for all $\varepsilon \in (0, 2^*(s) - \xi)$,

$$\sup_{B_R^c \cap H_m} J_\varepsilon(u) < 0,$$

where $B_R^c := E \setminus B_R$.

Proof.　Since H_m is finite dimensional, by Lemma 5.13 we know that $\|\cdot\|_*$ is defined a norm on $H_0^1(\Omega)$, there is a constant $C > 0$ such that

$$\|u\|^{2^*-\varepsilon} \leqslant C\|u\|_*^{2^*-\varepsilon}, \quad \text{for all } u \in H_m.$$

Therefore

$$J_\varepsilon(u) \leqslant \frac{1}{2}\|u\|^2 - \frac{\mu}{2^*(t)-\varepsilon} \int_\Omega \frac{|u|^{2^*(t)-\varepsilon}}{|y|^t} - \frac{1}{2^*(s)-\varepsilon} \int_\Omega \frac{|u|^{2^*(s)-\varepsilon}}{|y|^s}$$

$$\leqslant \frac{1}{2}\|u\|^2 - C\|u\|^{2^*(s)-\varepsilon}.$$

Since $2^*(s) - \varepsilon > 2$ and $\lambda_1 > 1$, we have that

$$\lim_{\|u\| \to \infty, u \in H_m} J_\varepsilon(u) = -\infty.$$

The proof is complete.　　　　　　　　　　　　　　　　　　　　　　　　□

Lemma 5.16　*For any* $\varepsilon \in (0, 2^*(s) - \xi), \lambda_1 > 1$, *there exists* $\rho = \rho(\varepsilon), \alpha = \alpha(\varepsilon) > 0$ *such that*

$$\inf_{\partial B_\rho} J_\varepsilon(u) \geqslant \alpha.$$

Proof.

$$J_\varepsilon(u) = \frac{1}{2} \int_\Omega \left(|\nabla u|^2 - a(x)u^2 \right) - \frac{\mu}{2^*(t) - \varepsilon} \int_\Omega \frac{|u|^{2^*(t) - \varepsilon}}{|y|^t} - \frac{1}{2^*(s) - \varepsilon} \int_\Omega \frac{|u|^{2^*(s) - \varepsilon}}{|y|^s}$$

$$\geqslant \frac{1}{2} (\lambda_1 - 1) \int_\Omega a(x)u^2 - C_1 |u|_{2^*(t) - \varepsilon}^{2^*(t) - \varepsilon} - C_2 |u|_{2^*(s) - \varepsilon}^{2^*(s) - \varepsilon}.$$

Since $2^* - \varepsilon > 2^*(t) - \varepsilon > 2^*(s) - \varepsilon > \xi > 2$ and $\lambda_1 > 1$, there exist $\rho = \rho(\varepsilon), \alpha = \alpha(\varepsilon) > 0$ such that

$$\inf_{\partial B_\rho} J_\varepsilon(u) \geqslant \alpha.$$

The proof is complete.　　　　　　　　　　　　　　　　　　　　　　　　□

Lemma 5.16 implies that 0 is a strict local minimum critical point. Then we can construct invariant sets containing all the positive and negative solutions of (5.17) for the gradient flow of J_ε. Therefore, nodal solutions can be found outside of these sets.

5.2.3　Auxiliary operator and invariant subsets of descending flow

For any $\varepsilon \in (0, 2^*(s) - \xi)$, let $A_\varepsilon : E \to E$ be given by

$$A_\varepsilon(u) := (-\Delta)^{-1} \left(\mu \frac{|u|^{2^*(t) - 2 - \varepsilon} u}{|y|^t} + \frac{|u|^{2^*(s) - 2 - \varepsilon} u}{|y|^s} + a(x)u \right),$$

for $u \in E$. Then the gradient of J_ε has the form

$$\nabla J_\varepsilon(u) = u - A_\varepsilon(u).$$

Note that the set of fixed points of A_ε is the same as the set of critical points of J_ε, which is $K := \{u \in E : \nabla J_\varepsilon(u) = 0\}$. It is easy to check that ∇J_ε is locally Lipschitz continuous.

We consider the negative gradient flow ϕ_ε of J_ε defined by

$$\begin{cases} \dfrac{d}{dt} \phi_\varepsilon(t, u) = -\nabla J_\varepsilon(\phi_\varepsilon(t, u)), & \text{for } t \geqslant 0, \\ \phi_\varepsilon(0, u) = u, \end{cases}$$

Here and in the sequel, for $u \in E$, denote $u^{\pm}(x) := \max\{\pm u(x), 0\}$, the convex cones

$$+P = \{u \in E : u \geqslant 0\}, \quad -P = \{u \in E : -u \geqslant 0\}.$$

For $\theta > 0$, we define

$$(\pm P)_{\theta} := \{u \in E : \operatorname{dist}(u, \pm P) < \theta\}.$$

In the following, we will show that there exists a $\theta_0 > 0$ such that $(\pm P)_{\theta}$ is an invariant set under the descending flow for all $0 < \theta \leqslant \theta_0$. Note that $E \setminus W$ contains only sign-changing functions, where

$$W := \overline{(+P)_{\theta}} \cup \overline{(-P)_{\theta}}.$$

Since $E \setminus W$ contains only sign-changing functions. By a version of the symmetric Mountain Pass theorem which provides the minimax critical values on $E \setminus W$, we can prove that (5.22) has infinitely many sign-changing solutions.

For any $N \subset E$ and $\delta > 0$, N_{δ} denotes the open δ-neighborhood of N, i.e.

$$N_{\delta} := \{u \in E : \operatorname{dist}(u, N) < \delta\},$$

whose closure and boundary are denoted by $\overline{N_{\delta}}$ and ∂N_{δ}. By the following result we can know that a neighborhood of $\pm P$ is an invariant set. We can use similar way as Lemma 2 in [71] and Lemma 3.1 in [19] to get the following lemma.

Lemma 5.17   *There exists a $\theta_0 > 0$ such that for any $\theta \in (0, \theta_0]$, there holds*

$$A_{\varepsilon}(\partial(\pm P)_{\theta}) \subset (\pm P)_{\theta}$$

and

$$\phi_{\varepsilon}(t, u) \in (\pm P)_{\theta}, \quad \text{for all } t > 0 \text{ and } u \in \overline{(\pm P)_{\theta}}.$$

Moreover, every nontrivial solutions $u \in (+P)_{\theta}$ and $u \in (-P)_{\theta}$ of (5.21) are positive and negative, respectively.

By using the combination of invariant sets method and minimax method, we can construct a nodal solution first, then to prove our main result. We need a deformation lemma in the presence of invariant sets.

Definition 5.2   *A subset $W \subset E$ is an invariant set with respect to ϕ_{ε} if, for any $u \in W$, $\phi_{\varepsilon}(t, u) \in W$ for all $t \geqslant 0$.*

From Lemma 5.17, we may choose an $\theta > 0$ sufficiently small such that $\overline{(\pm P)_{\theta}}$ are invariant set. Set $W := \overline{(+P)_{\theta}} \cup \overline{(-P)_{\theta}}$. Note that $\phi_{\varepsilon}(t, \partial W) \subset \operatorname{int}(W)$ and $Q := E \setminus W$ only contains sign-changing functions.

Since J_{ε} satisfies the Palais-Smale condition, we have the following deformation lemma which follows from Lemma 5.1 in [130] (also see Lemma 2.4 in [122]).

Define

$$K^1_{\varepsilon,c} := K_{\varepsilon,c} \cap W, \quad K^2_{\varepsilon,c} := K_{\varepsilon,c} \cap Q,$$

where

$$K_{\varepsilon,c} := \{u \in E : J_{\varepsilon}(u) = c, J'_{\varepsilon}(u) = 0\}.$$

Let $\rho > 0$ be such that $(K^1_{\varepsilon,c})_\rho \subset W$, where

$$(K^1_{\varepsilon,c})_\rho := \{u \in E : \text{dist}(u, K^1_{\varepsilon,c}) < \rho\}.$$

We can use the similar method to the proof of Lemma 5.1 in [130] and Lemma 2.4 in [122] to prove the following lemma.

Lemma 5.18 *Assume that J_{ε} satisfies Palais-Smale condition, then there exists an $\delta_0 > 0$ such that for any $0 < \delta < \delta_0$, there exists a $\eta \in C([0,1] \times E, E)$ satisfying:*

(i) $\eta(t, u) = u$ for $t = 0$ or $u \notin J^{-1}_{\varepsilon}([c - \delta_0, c + \delta_0]) \setminus (K^2_{\varepsilon,c})_\rho$.

(ii) $\eta(1, J^{c+\delta}_{\varepsilon} \cup W \setminus (K^2_{\varepsilon,c})_{3\rho}) \subset J^{c-\delta}_{\varepsilon} \cup W$ and $\eta(1, J^{c+\delta}_{\varepsilon} \cup W) \subset J^{c-\delta}_{\varepsilon} \cup W$ if $K^2_{\varepsilon,c} = \varnothing$. *Here $J^d_{\varepsilon} = \{u \in E : J_{\varepsilon}(u) \leqslant d\}$ for any $d \in \mathbb{R}$.*

(iii) $\eta(t, \cdot)$ *is odd and a homeomorphism of E for $t \in [0,1]$.*

(iv) $J_{\varepsilon}(\eta(\cdot, u))$ *is non-increasing.*

(v) $\eta(t, W) \subset W$ *for any $t \in [0,1]$.*

5.2.4   The proof of Theorem 5.3

In the following, we assume that $\lambda_1 > 1$. For any $\varepsilon \in (0, 2^*(s) - \xi)$ small, we define the minimax value $c_{\varepsilon,l}$ for the perturbed functional $J_{\varepsilon}(u)$ with $l = 2, 3, \cdots$. We now define a family of sets for the minimax procedure here. We essentially follow [19], also see [130] and [154]. Define

$$G_m := \{h \in C(B_R \cap H_m, E) : h \text{ is odd and } h = id \text{ on } \partial B_R \cap H_m\},$$

where $R > 0$ is given by Lemma 5.15. Note that $G_m \neq \varnothing$, since $id \in G_m$. Set

$$\Gamma_l := \{h(B_R \cap H_m \setminus Y) : h \in G_m, m \geqslant l, Y = -Y \text{ is open and } \gamma(Y) \leqslant m - l\}$$

for $k \geqslant 2$. From [154], Γ_l possess the following properties:

(1°) $\Gamma_l \neq \varnothing$ and $\Gamma_{l+1} \subset \Gamma_l$ for all $l \geqslant 2$.

(2°) If $\phi \in C(E, E)$ is odd and $\phi = id$ on $\partial B_R \cap H_m$, then $\phi(A) \in \Gamma_l$ if $A \in \Gamma_l$ for all $l \geqslant 2$.

(3°) If $A \in \Gamma_l$, $Z = -Z$ is open and $\gamma(Z) \leqslant s < l$ and $l - s \geqslant 2$, then $A \setminus Z \in \Gamma_{l-s}$.

Now, for $l \geqslant 2$, we can define the minimax value $c_{\varepsilon,l}$ given by

$$c_{\varepsilon,l} := \inf_{A \in \Gamma_l} \sup_{u \in A \cap Q} J_{\varepsilon}(u).$$

Lemma 5.19   *For any $A \in \Gamma_l$ and $l \geqslant 2$, $A \cap Q \neq \varnothing$, then $c_{\varepsilon,l}$ are well defined, and $c_{\varepsilon,l} \geqslant \alpha > 0$ where α is given by Lemma 5.16.*

Proof. Consider the attracting domain of 0 in E:

$$D := \{u \in E : \phi_\varepsilon(t, u) \to 0, \text{ as } t \to \infty\}.$$

Note that D is open since 0 is a local minimum of J_ε and by the continuous dependence of ODE on initial data. Moreover, ∂D is an invariant set and $\overline{(+P)_\delta} \cap \overline{(-P)_\delta} \subset D$. In particular there holds

$$J_\varepsilon(u) > 0,$$

for every $u \in \overline{(+P)_\delta} \cap \overline{(-P)_\delta} \setminus \{0\}$ (see Lemma 3.4 in [19]). Now we claim that for any $A \in \Gamma_l$ with $l \geqslant 2$, it holds

$$A \cap Q \cap \partial D \neq \varnothing. \tag{5.26}$$

If this is true, then we have $A \cap Q \neq \varnothing$ and $c_{\varepsilon,2} \geqslant \alpha > 0$, because $\partial B_\rho \subset D$ and $\sup\limits_{A \cap Q} J_\varepsilon(u) \geqslant \inf\limits_{\partial D} J_\varepsilon(u) \geqslant \inf\limits_{\partial B_\rho} J_\varepsilon(u) \geqslant \alpha > 0$ by Lemma 5.16.

To prove (5.26), let

$$A = h(B_R \cap H_m \setminus Y)$$

with $\gamma(Y) \leqslant m - l$ and $l \geqslant 2$. Define

$$O := \{u \in B_R \cap H_m : h(u) \in D\}.$$

Then O is a bounded open symmetric set with $0 \in O$ and $\bar{O} \subset B_R \cap H_m$. Thus, it follows from the Borsuk-Ulam theorem that $\gamma(\partial O) = m$ and by the continuity of h, $h(\partial O) \subset \partial D$. As a consequence,

$$h(\partial O \setminus Y) \subset A \cap \partial D,$$

and therefore

$$\gamma(A \cap \partial D) \geqslant \gamma(h(\partial O \setminus Y)) \geqslant \gamma(\partial O \setminus Y) \geqslant \gamma(\partial O) - \gamma(Y) \geqslant l,$$

by the "monotone, sub-additive and supervariant" property of the genus (Proposition 5.4 in [165]). Since $(+P)_\delta \cap (-P)_\delta \cap \partial D = \varnothing$,

$$\gamma(W \cap \partial D) \leqslant 1.$$

Thus for $l \geqslant 2$, we conclude that

$$\gamma(A \cap Q \cap \partial D) \geqslant \gamma(A \cap \partial D) - \gamma(W \cap \partial D) \geqslant l - 1 \geqslant 1,$$

which proves (5.26).

Thus $c_{\varepsilon,l}$ are well defined for all $l \geqslant 2$ and $0 < \alpha \leqslant c_{\varepsilon,2} \leqslant c_{\varepsilon,3} \leqslant \cdots \leqslant c_{\varepsilon,l} \leqslant \cdots$. The proof is complete.   □

Lemma 5.20

$$K_{\varepsilon,c_{\varepsilon,l}} \cap Q \neq \varnothing. \tag{5.27}$$

Proof. If not, we assume that

$$K_{\varepsilon,c_{\varepsilon,l}} \cap Q = \varnothing.$$

By Lemma 5.14, for the functional J_ε, there exist $\delta > 0$ and a map $\eta \in C([0,1] \times E, E)$ such that $\eta(1,\cdot)$ is odd, $\eta(1,u) = u$ for $u \in J_\varepsilon^{c_{\varepsilon,l}-2\delta}$ and

$$\eta(1, J_\varepsilon^{c_{\varepsilon,l}+\delta} \cup W) \subset J_\varepsilon^{c_{\varepsilon,l}-\delta} \cup W. \tag{5.28}$$

By the definition of $c_{\varepsilon,l}$, there exists $A \in \Gamma_l$ such that $\sup\limits_{A \cap Q} J_\varepsilon(u) \leqslant c_{\varepsilon,l} + \delta$. Let $B = \eta(1, A)$. It follows from (5.28) that

$$\sup\limits_{B \cap Q} J_\varepsilon(u) \leqslant c_{\varepsilon,l} - \delta.$$

On the other hand, it is easy to show that $B \in \Gamma_l$ by Lemma 5.15 and the property of $(2°)$ of Γ_l above. As a result, $c_{\varepsilon,l} \leqslant c_{\varepsilon,l} - \delta$. This contradicts with $\delta > 0$. The proof is complete.   □

Lemma 5.20 implies that there exists a sign-changing critical point $u_{\varepsilon,l}$ such that

$$J_\varepsilon(u_{\varepsilon,l}) = c_{\varepsilon,l}.$$

As a consequence of Lemma 5.19, we have that $c_{\varepsilon,l}$ are well defined for all $l \geqslant 2$ and $0 < \alpha \leqslant c_{\varepsilon,2} \leqslant c_{\varepsilon,3} \leqslant \cdots \leqslant c_{\varepsilon,l} \leqslant \cdots$. Now we can show the following lemma.

Lemma 5.21 $c_{\varepsilon,l} \to \infty$ as $l \to \infty$.

Proof. Here we deduce by a negation. Suppose $c_{\varepsilon,l} \to \bar{c}_\varepsilon < \infty$ as $l \to \infty$. Since J_ε satisfies Palais-Smale condition, it follows that $K_{\varepsilon,\bar{c}_\varepsilon} \neq \varnothing$ and is compact. Moreover, we have

$$K_{\varepsilon,\bar{c}_\varepsilon}^2 := K_{\varepsilon,\bar{c}_\varepsilon} \cap Q \neq \varnothing.$$

Indeed, assume $\{u_{\varepsilon,l_i}\}_{i \in \mathbb{N}}$ is a sequence of sign-changing solutions to (5.22) with $J_\varepsilon(u_{\varepsilon,l_i}) = c_{\varepsilon,l_i}$, we have

$$\int_\Omega |\nabla u_{\varepsilon,l_i}^\pm|^2 - a(x)|u_{\varepsilon,l_i}^\pm|^2 = \mu \int_\Omega \frac{|u_{\varepsilon,l_i}^\pm|^{2^*(t)-\varepsilon}}{|y|^t} + \int_\Omega \frac{|u_{\varepsilon,l_i}^\pm|^{2^*(s)-\varepsilon}}{|y|^s}.$$

By using the variational principle of (5.21), we obtain

$$\left(1 - \frac{1}{\lambda_1}\right) \|u_{\varepsilon,l_i}^{\pm}\|^2 \leq \mu \int_\Omega \frac{|u_{\varepsilon,l_i}^{\pm}|^{2^*(t)-\varepsilon}}{|y|^t} + \int_\Omega \frac{|u_{\varepsilon,l_i}^{\pm}|^{2^*(s)-\varepsilon}}{|y|^s}.$$

It follows that, by Sobolev embedding theorem, $\|u_{\varepsilon,l_i}^{\pm}\| \geq c_0 > 0$, where c_0 is a constant independent of i. This implies that the limit $\bar{u}_\varepsilon \in K_{\varepsilon,\bar{c}_\varepsilon}$ of the subsequence of $\{u_{\varepsilon,l_i}\}_{i\in\mathbb{N}}$ is still sign-changing.

Assume $\gamma(K_{\varepsilon,\bar{c}_\varepsilon}^2) = \tau$. Since $0 \notin K_{\varepsilon,\bar{c}_\varepsilon}^2$ and $K_{\varepsilon,\bar{c}_\varepsilon}^2$ is compact, by the "continuous" property of the genus (Proposition 5.4 in [165]), there exists an open neighborhood N in E with $K_{\varepsilon,\bar{c}_\varepsilon}^2 \subset N$ such that $\gamma(N) = \tau$. Now using Lemma 5.19 for the function J_ε, there exist $\delta > 0$ and a map $\eta \in C([0,1] \times E, E)$ such that $\eta(1,\cdot)$ is odd, $\eta(1,u) = u$ for $u \in J_\varepsilon^{\bar{c}_\varepsilon - 2\delta}$ and

$$\eta(1, J_\varepsilon^{\bar{c}_\varepsilon+\delta} \cup W \setminus N) \subset J_\varepsilon^{\bar{c}_\varepsilon-\delta} \cup W. \tag{5.29}$$

Since $c_{\varepsilon,l} \to \bar{c}_\varepsilon$ as $l \to \infty$, we can choose l sufficiently large, such that $c_{\varepsilon,l} \geq \bar{c}_\varepsilon - \frac{1}{2}\delta$. Clearly, $c_{\varepsilon,l+\tau} \geq c_{\varepsilon,l} \geq \bar{c}_\varepsilon - \frac{1}{2}\delta$. By the definition of $c_{\varepsilon,l+\tau}$, we can find a set $A \in \Gamma_{l+\tau}$, that is $A = h(B_R \cap H_m \setminus Y)$, where $h \in G_m$, $m \geq l+\tau$, $\gamma(Y) \leq m-(l+\tau)$, such that

$$J_\varepsilon(u) \leq c_{\varepsilon,l+\tau} + \frac{1}{4}\delta < \bar{c}_\varepsilon + \delta, \quad \text{for any } u \in A \cap Q,$$

which implies $A \subset J_\varepsilon^{\bar{c}_\varepsilon+\delta} \cup W$. It follows from (5.29) that

$$\eta(1, A \setminus N) \subset J_\varepsilon^{\bar{c}_\varepsilon-\delta} \cup W. \tag{5.30}$$

Let $Y_1 = Y \cup h^{-1}(N)$. Then Y_1 is symmetric and open, and

$$\gamma(Y_1) \leq \gamma(Y) + \gamma(h^{-1}(N)) \leq m - (l+\tau) + \tau = m - l.$$

Then it is easy to check $\tilde{A} := \eta(1, h(B_R \cap H_m \setminus Y_1)) \in \Gamma_l$ by (2°) and (3°) above. As a result, by (5.19)

$$c_{\varepsilon,l} \leq \sup_{\tilde{A}\cap Q} J_\varepsilon(u) \leq \sup_{\eta(1,A\setminus N)\cap Q} J_\varepsilon(u) \leq \bar{c}_\varepsilon - \delta.$$

This is a contradiction to $c_{\varepsilon,l} \geq \bar{c}_\varepsilon - \frac{1}{2}\delta$. The proof is complete. $\square$

Lemma 5.22 *For any fixed $l \geq 2$, $\|u_{\varepsilon,l}\|$ is uniformly bounded with respect to ε, and then $u_{\varepsilon,l}$ converges strongly to u_l in E as $\varepsilon \to 0$.*

Proof. In deed, by using the same Γ_l above, we can also define the minimax value for the following auxiliary function

$$J_*(u) = \frac{1}{2} \int_\Omega (|\nabla u|^2 - a(x)|u|^2) - \frac{\mu}{2^*} \int_\Omega \frac{|u|^\xi}{|y|^t} - \frac{1}{2^*} \int_\Omega \frac{|u|^\xi}{|y|^s},$$

$$\alpha_l := \inf_{A \in \Gamma_l} \sup_{u \in A} J_*(u), \quad l = 2, 3, \cdots.$$

Here, we choose $R > 0$ sufficiently large if necessary, such that Lemma 5.15 also holds for J_*. Then by a $\mathbb{Z}_2$ version of the Mountain Pass theorem (Theorem 9.2 in [154]), for each $l \geqslant 2, \alpha_l > 0$ is well defined and $\alpha_l \to \infty$ as $l \to \infty$. Because

$$J_\varepsilon(u) \leqslant \frac{1}{2} \int_\Omega (|\nabla u|^2 - a(x)|u|^2) - \frac{\mu}{2^*} \int_\Omega \left(\frac{|u|^\xi - 1}{|y|^t} \right) - \frac{1}{2^*} \int_\Omega \frac{|u|^\xi - 1}{|y|^s}$$

$$= J_*(u) + d_0,$$

where

$$d_0 = \frac{\mu}{2^*} \int_\Omega \frac{1}{|y|^t} + \frac{1}{2^*} \int_\Omega \frac{1}{|y|^s}.$$

Therefore, for any fixed $l \geqslant 2$, $c_{\varepsilon,l}$ is uniformly bounded for $\varepsilon \in (0, 2^*(s) - \xi)$, that is, there is $C = C(\alpha_l, \Omega) > 0$ independent on ε, such that $c_{\varepsilon,l} \leqslant C$ uniformly for ε. Because $u_{\varepsilon,l}$ is a nodal solution of (5.22) and $J_\varepsilon(u_{\varepsilon,l}) = c_{\varepsilon,l}$. By the definition of λ_1, we can obtain the following

$$C \geqslant c_{\varepsilon,l} = J_\varepsilon(u_{\varepsilon,l}) = J_\varepsilon(u_{\varepsilon,l}) - \frac{1}{2^*(s) - \varepsilon} \langle J_\varepsilon'(u_{\varepsilon,l}), u_{\varepsilon,l} \rangle$$

$$= \left(\frac{1}{2} - \frac{1}{2^*(s) - \varepsilon} \right) \int_\Omega (|\nabla u_{\varepsilon,l}|^2 - a(x)u_{\varepsilon,l}^2)$$

$$+ \mu \left(\frac{1}{2^*(s) - \varepsilon} - \frac{1}{2^*(t) - \varepsilon} \right) \int_\Omega \frac{|u_{\varepsilon,l}|^{2^* - \varepsilon}}{|y|^t}$$

$$\geqslant \left(\frac{1}{2} - \frac{1}{2^*(s) - \varepsilon} \right) \int_\Omega (|\nabla u_{\varepsilon,l}|^2 - a(x)u_{\varepsilon,l}^2)$$

$$\geqslant \left(\frac{1}{2} - \frac{1}{\xi} \right) \left(1 - \frac{1}{\lambda_1} \right) \|u_{\varepsilon,l}\|^2 > 0,$$

where $\lambda_1 > 1, \varepsilon \in (0, 2^*(s) - \xi)$ and $2 < \xi < 2^*(s)$. Therefore $\|u_{\varepsilon,l}\|$ is uniformly with respect to ε. So we can apply Proposition 5.2 and obtain a subsequence $\{u_{\varepsilon_l,l}\}_{l \in \mathbb{N}}$, such that $u_{\varepsilon_l,l} \to u_l$ strongly in E for some u_l and also $c_{\varepsilon_l,l} \to c_l$. Thus u_l is a solution of (1.5) and $J_\varepsilon(u_l) = c_l$. Moreover, since $u_{\varepsilon_l,l}$ is sign-changing, similar to Lemma

4.3, by Sobolev embedding theorem, we can prove that u_l is still sign-changing. The proof is complete.   □

Proof of Theorem 5.3   Now we are in a position to prove Theorem 5.3. Noting that c_l is non-decreasing with respect to l, we have the following two cases:

Case (i)   There are $2 \leqslant l_1 < \cdots < l_i < \cdots$, satisfying $c_{l_1} < \cdots < c_{l_i} < \cdots$. Obviously, in this case, equation (5.17) has infinitely many sign solutions such that $J(u_i) = c_{l_i}$.

Case (ii)   There is a positive integer L such that $c_l = c$ for all $l \geqslant L$.

From now on we assume that there exists a $\delta > 0$, such that $J(u)$ has no sign-changing critical point u with

$$J(u) \in [c - \delta, c) \cup (c, c + \delta].$$

Otherwise we are done. In this case, we claim that $\gamma(K_c^2) \geqslant 2$, where $K_c := \{u \in E : J(u) = c, J'(u) = 0\}$ and $K_c^2 = K_c \cap Q$. Then as a consequence, $J(u)$ has infinitely many sign-changing critical points.

Now we adopt a technique in the proof of Theorem 1.1 in [41]. Suppose, on the contrary, that $\gamma(K_c^2) = 1$ (note that $K_c^2 \neq \varnothing$). Moreover, we assume K_c^2 contains only finitely many critical points, otherwise we are done. Then it follows that K_c^2 is compact. Obviously, $0 \notin K_c^2$. Then there exists a open neighborhood N in E with $K_c^2 \subset N$ such that $\gamma(N) = \gamma(K_c^2)$.

Define

$$V_\varepsilon := (J_\varepsilon^{c+\delta} \setminus J_\varepsilon^{c-\delta}) \setminus N.$$

We now claim that if $\varepsilon > 0$ small, J_ε has no sign-changing critical point $u \in V_\varepsilon$. Indeed, arguing indirectly, suppose that there exist $\varepsilon \to 0$ and $u_\varepsilon \in V_\varepsilon$ satisfying $J_\varepsilon'(u_\varepsilon) = 0$, with $u_\varepsilon^{\pm} \neq 0$, and $u_\varepsilon \notin N$.

Then, by Proposition 5.2, up to a subsequence, u_n converges strongly to u in E. Therefore $J'(u) = 0$,

$$J(u) \in [c - \delta, c + \delta]$$

and $u \notin K_c^2$.

This is a contradiction to our assumption and the fact that u is still sign-changing. The following proof is similar to that of Lemma 5.20. By using Lemma 5.18, for the function J_ε, there exist $\delta > 0$ and a map $\eta \in C([0, 1] \times E, E)$ such that $\eta(1, \cdot)$ is odd, $\eta(1, u) = u$ for $u \in J_\varepsilon^{c-2\delta}$ and

$$\eta(1, J_\varepsilon^{c+\delta} \cup W \setminus N) \subset J_\varepsilon^{c-\delta} \cup W. \tag{5.31}$$

Now fix $l > L$. Since $c_{\varepsilon,l}$, $c_{\varepsilon,l+1} \to c$ as $\varepsilon \to 0$, we can find an $\varepsilon > 0$ small, such that $c_{\varepsilon,l}, c_{\varepsilon,l+1} \in (c - \frac{1}{2}\delta, c + \frac{1}{2}\delta)$. By the definition of $c_{\varepsilon,l+1}$, we can find a set

$A \in \Gamma_{l+1}$, that is
$$A = h(B_R \cap H_m \setminus Y),$$
where $h \in G_m$, $m \geqslant l + 1$, $\gamma(Y) \leqslant m - (l + 1)$, such that
$$J_\varepsilon(u) \leqslant c_{\varepsilon, l+1} + \frac{1}{4}\delta < c + \delta,$$
for any $u \in A \cap Q$, which implies $A \subset J_\varepsilon^{c+\delta} \cup W$. Then by (5.31), we have
$$\eta(1, A \setminus N) \subset J_\varepsilon^{c-\delta} \cup W. \tag{5.32}$$

Let $\widetilde{Y} = Y \cup h^{-1}(N)$. Then $\widetilde{Y}$ is symmetric and open, and
$$\gamma(\widetilde{Y}) \leqslant \gamma(Y) + \gamma(h^{-1}(N)) \leqslant m - (l + 1) + 1 = m - l.$$

Then it is easy to checl $\widehat{A} := \eta(1, h(B_R \cap H_m \setminus \widetilde{Y})) \in \Gamma_l$ by $(2°)$ and $(3°)$ above. As a result, by (5.32)
$$c_{\varepsilon, l} \leqslant \sup_{\widehat{A} \cap Q} J_\varepsilon(u) \leqslant \sup_{\eta(1, A \setminus N) \cap Q} J_\varepsilon(u) \leqslant c - \delta.$$

This contradicts to $c_{\varepsilon, l} > c - \frac{1}{2}\delta$. Then the proof for the Case II is finished. The proof is complete.   □

5.3   Sign-changing solutions for Hardy-Sobolev-Maz'ya equation involving critical growth

5.3.1   Introduction and main results

Let $N \geqslant 3, \bar{\mu} = \dfrac{(k-2)^2}{4}, 2^*(t) = \dfrac{2(N-t)}{N-2}, 0 \leqslant t < 2$ and Ω be an open bounded domain in $\mathbb{R}^N$ which contains some points $x^0 = (0, z^0)$. We study the following Hardy-Sobolev-Maz'ya equation
$$\begin{cases} -\Delta u - \dfrac{\mu u}{|y|^2} = \lambda u + \dfrac{|u|^{2^*(t)-2}u}{|y|^t}, & \text{in } \Omega, \\ u = 0, & \text{on } \partial\Omega, \end{cases} \tag{5.33}$$
where $x = (y, z) \in \mathbb{R}^k \times \mathbb{R}^{N-k}, 2 \leqslant k < N, 0 \leqslant \mu < \bar{\mu}, \lambda > 0$ and the Hardy-Sobolev term $\dfrac{|u|^{2^*(t)-2}u}{|y|^t}$ is critical. It is well known that solutions of equation (5.33) are critical points of the corresponding functional $J : H_0^1(\Omega) \to \mathbb{R}$ given by
$$J(u) = \frac{1}{2}\int_\Omega \left(|\nabla u|^2 - \mu\frac{u^2}{|y|^2} - \lambda u^2\right) dx - \frac{1}{2^*(t)}\int_\Omega \frac{|u|^{2^*(t)}}{|y|^t} dx. \tag{5.34}$$

Equation (5.33) has been used to model some astrophysical phenomenon like stellar dynamics in [16, 22]. When $\mu = 0$, equation (5.33) was proposed as for describing the dynamics of galaxies. Various equations similar to (5.33) have been proposed to model several phenomena of interest in astrophysics. Such as Eddingtons and Matukumas equations have attracted much interest in recent years, see [16, 115−117]. Especially in [22], various astrophysical models were introduced, including some generalizations of Matukumas equation.

When Ω is a bounded domain of $\mathbb{R}^N$, (5.33) does not have a solution in general since the critical nature of the equation. By using Pohozaev identity, Bhakata and Sandeep[30] proved (5.33) does not have a nontrivial solution for the case $\lambda = 0$ and $2 \leqslant k < N$, if Ω is star shaped with respect to the point $(0, z_0)$. They also studied the equation in some special bounded domain. Jannelli[110] considered the existence of positive solution under suitable condition on μ and λ when $k = N$ and $t = 0$. Cao and Han[39] proved the existence of a nontrivial solution for (5.33) with $\lambda > 0$ if $\mu \in \left[0, \dfrac{(N-2)^2}{16} - \dfrac{(N+2)^2}{N^2}\right)$.

When $\Omega = \mathbb{R}^N$, Musina[147], Tertikas and Tintarev[177] considered the existence of positive solutions for (5.33). In [48, 137, 138], the authors considered the nondegeneracy of positive solutions for (5.33). Furthermore, Gazzini, Musina[96] and Mancini et al.[138] studied the qualitative properties, such as decay properties, cylindrical symmetry and uniqueness of positive solutions for (5.33). It is well known that problem (5.33) with $\Omega = \mathbb{R}^N$ is related to the Brézis-Nirenberg problem in the Hyperbolic space (see [30, 48, 137, 138]).

When $\mu = 0$ and $t = 0$, (5.33) is related to the well known Brézis-Nirenberg problem[35]:

$$\begin{cases} -\Delta u = \lambda u + |u|^{2^*-2}u, & \text{in } \Omega, \\ u = 0, & \text{on } \partial\Omega, \end{cases} \tag{5.35}$$

where $2^* = \dfrac{2N}{N-2}$ is the critical Sobolev exponent. One of the most important result is the existence of infinitely many solutions when $N \geqslant 7$ (see [30]), see e.g. [12, 43, 50, 51, 61, 71, 80, 173]. Here we would like to point out [79], in the paper Devillanova and Solimini proved that, when $N \geqslant 7$, (1.3) has infinitely many solutions for each $\lambda > 0$. Let us now briefly recall the main results concerning the sign-changing solutions of (1.3) obtained before. If $N \geqslant 4$ and Ω is a ball, then for any $\lambda > 0$, (5.35) has infinitely many nodal solutions which are built using particular symmetries of the domain Ω (see [91]). In [162], Solimini proved that if Ω is a ball and $N \geqslant 7$, for each $\lambda > 0$, (5.35) has infinitely many sign-changing radial solutions. When Ω is a ball and $4 \leqslant N \leqslant 6$, there is a $\lambda^* > 0$ such that (1.3) has no radial solutions which change sign if $\lambda \in (0, \lambda^*)$ (see [13]). In [91, 162], the symmetry of the ball plays an essential role, hence their methods are invalid for general domains. For the existence of infinitely many sign-changing solutions for the related equations see [121, 166, 205, 220] and the references therein. Very recently, Ganguly[93] proved the existence of infinitely many sign-changing solutions for (5.33).

Theorem 5.5   *Suppose that $N \geqslant 6 + t, \lambda > 0$ and $\mu \in \left[0, \dfrac{(k-2)^2}{4} - 4 \right)$, then* (5.33) *has infinitely many sign-changing solutions.*

He also consider the following existence theorem:

Theorem 5.6   *If $N \geqslant 7, k = N, t = 0, \lambda > 0$ and $\mu \in \left[0, \dfrac{(N-2)^2}{4} - 4 \right)$, then* (5.33) *has infinitely many sign-changing solutions.*

Remark 5.9   Let $\lambda_1(\mu)$ be the first eigenvalue of $\left(-\Delta - \dfrac{\mu}{|y|^2}, H_0^1(\Omega) \right)$, then it is characterized by the following variational principle:

$$\lambda_1(\mu) = \min_{u \in H_0^1(\Omega)} \frac{\displaystyle\int_\Omega |\nabla u|^2 dx - \int_\Omega \mu \frac{u^2}{|y|^2} dx}{\displaystyle\int_\Omega u^2 dx}. \tag{5.36}$$

It is easy to know that if $\lambda \geqslant \lambda_1(\mu)$, any nontrivial solution of (5.33) is sign-changing. Indeed, we can multiply the first eigenfunction of the operator $\left(-\Delta - \dfrac{\mu}{|y|^2} \right)$ in $H_0^1(\Omega)$ with zero-boundary value problem and integrating both sides. Therefore, by the result of [180], to prove Theorem 5.5 it suffices to consider the case of $\lambda \in (0, \lambda_1(\mu))$.

In order to prove the results, Ganguly[93] first used an abstract theorem which is introduced by Schechter and Zou[158]. Then by combining this with the uniform bounded theorem due to [180], the author obtained infinitely many sign-changing solutions. The method introduced in [93, 158] sometimes are limited. Because by general minimax procedure to get the Morse indices of sign-changing critical points sometimes are not clear. Another limited condition is that the corresponding functional is also needed to be C^2.

Before giving our main results, we give some notations first. We will always denote points in $\mathbb{R}^k \times \mathbb{R}^{N-k}$ as pairs $x = (y, z)$, assuming $2 \leqslant k < N$ and $0 \leqslant t < 2$. Let $E = H_0^1(\Omega)$ be endowed with the standard scalar and norm

$$(u, v) = \int_\Omega \nabla u \nabla v dx, \qquad \|u\| = \left(\int_\Omega |\nabla u|^2 dx \right)^{1/2}.$$

The norm on $L^s = L^s(\Omega)$ with $1 \leqslant s < \infty$ is given by

$$|u|_s = \left(\int_\Omega |u|^s dx \right)^{1/s} \quad L_t^q(\Omega), \quad 1 \leqslant q < \infty, 0 \leqslant t < 2$$

with the norm

$$|u|_{q,t,\Omega} = \left(\int_\Omega \frac{|u|^q}{|y|^t} dx \right)^{1/q},$$

where dx denote the Lebesgue measure in $\mathbb{R}^N$. Denote $B_r = \{u \in E : \|u\| \leqslant r\}$ and $B_r^c := E \setminus B_r$.

We will use the usual Ljusternik-Schnirelman type minimax method and invariant set method to prove Theorem 5.5. Our method is much simpler than the proof of [93]. In fact, our approach also works for the Brézis-Nirenberg problem involving subcritical perturbation term $f(x, u)$ which is not C^1. However, the techniques developed by Ganguly[93] or Schechter and Zou[158] can not be applied directly. Let us outline the proof of Theorem 5.5 and explain the difficulties we will encounter.

In general, by using the combination of invariant sets method and minimax method to obtain infinitely many nodal critical points, we need the energy function satisfies the Palais-Smale condition in all energy level. This fact prevents us from using the variational methods directly to prove the existence of infinitely many sign-changing solutions for (5.33). Because $J(u)$ does not satisfy the Palais-Smale condition for large energy level due to the critical Sobolev exponent $2^*(t)$. Another difficulty is that, every nontrivial solution of (5.33) is singular at $\{y = 0\}$ if $\mu \neq 0$ (see [30]).

In order to overcome the first difficulty, we will adopt the idea in [79,39]. We first study the following perturbed problem:

$$\begin{cases} -\Delta u - \dfrac{\mu u}{|y|^2} = \lambda u + \dfrac{|u|^{2^*(t)-2-\varepsilon}u}{|y|^t}, & \text{in } \Omega, \\ u = 0, & \text{on } \partial\Omega, \end{cases} \tag{5.37}$$

where $\varepsilon > 0$ small. The corresponding energy function is

$$J_\varepsilon(u) = \frac{1}{2} \int_\Omega \left(|\nabla u|^2 - \mu\frac{u^2}{|y|^2} - \lambda u^2 \right) dx - \frac{1}{2^*(t)-\varepsilon} \int_\Omega \frac{|u|^{2^*(t)-\varepsilon}}{|y|^t} dx. \tag{5.38}$$

By the following lemmas, we will know $J_\varepsilon(u)$ is a C^1 function on $H_0^1(\Omega)$ and satisfies the Palais-Smale condition. It follows from [9,154], $J_\varepsilon(u)$ has infinitely many critical points. More precisely, there are positive numbers $c_{\varepsilon,l}$, $l = 2, 3, \cdots$, with $c_{\varepsilon,l} \to +\infty$ as $l \to \infty$. Moreover, a critical point $u_{\varepsilon,l}$ for $J_\varepsilon(u)$ satisfying

$$J_\varepsilon(u_{\varepsilon,l}) = c_{\varepsilon,l}.$$

Next, we will show that for any fixed $l \geq 2$, $\|u_{\varepsilon,l}\|$ are uniformly bounded with respect to ε, then we can apply the following compactness result Proposition 1.3 (see Theorem 1.3 in [180]) which essentially follows from the uniform bounded theorem due to Devillanova and Solimini[79] to show that $u_{\varepsilon,l}$ converges strongly to u_l in E as $\varepsilon \to 0$. Therefore it is easy to prove that u_l is a solution of (5.33) with $J(u_l) = c_l := \lim_{\varepsilon \to 0} c_{\varepsilon,l}$.

Proposition 5.3[180]   *Suppose $N \geq 6 + t$, $\lambda > 0$ and $\mu \in [0, \bar{\mu} - 4)$. Then for any sequence u_n, which is a solution of (5.33) with $\varepsilon = \varepsilon_n \to 0$, satisfying $\|u_n\| \leq C$ for some constant independent of n, u_n has a sequence, which converges strongly in $H_0^1(\Omega)$ as $n \to \infty$.*

In the end, we will distinguish two cases to prove that $J(u)$ has infinitely many sign-changing critical points.

Case (i)   There are $2 \leq l_1 < \cdots < l_i < \cdots$, satisfying $c_{l_1} < \cdots < c_{l_i} < \cdots$.

Case (ii)   There is a positive integer L such that $c_l = c$ for all $l \geq L$.

The central task in this procedure is to deal with Case (ii). In fact, we can prove that the usual Krasnoselskii genus of $K_c \setminus W$ (W is denoted in Section 2) is at least two, where $K_c := \{u \in E : J(u) = c, J'(u) = 0\}$. Then our result is obtained.

Throughout this section, the closure and the boundary of set G are denoted by $\bar{G}$ and ∂G respectively. We denote "$\rightharpoonup$" weak convergence and by "$\to$" strong convergence. Also if we take a subsequence of a sequence $\{u_n\}$, we shall denote it again $\{u_n\}$.

In Section 5.3.2, we introduce some notations and Hardy-Sobolev-Maz'yz (HSM) inequality. In Section 5.3.3, we give an auxiliary operator A_ε and construct the invariant sets. We give the proof of Theorem 5.5 in Section 5.3.4.

5.3.2 Preliminaries

Now we give some integrals inequalities, for details we refer to [179].

Lemma 5.23(Hardy inequality)   *For $k > 2$, we have*

$$\frac{(k-2)^2}{4} \int_{\mathbb{R}^N} \frac{|u|^2}{|y|^2} dx \leq \int_{\mathbb{R}^N} |\nabla u|^2 dx, \tag{5.39}$$

for all $u \in D^{1,2}(\mathbb{R}^N) \cap L^2(\mathbb{R}^N; |y|^{-2} dx)$.

The constant $\dfrac{(k-2)^2}{4}$ in above inequality is the best constant and is not attained.

By Lemma 5.23, for $\mu < \dfrac{(k-2)^2}{4}$, the operator

$$L[\cdot] \equiv -\Delta - \frac{\mu}{|y|^2}$$

is positive and has discrete Spectrum in $H_0^1(\Omega)$.

Hardy-Sobolev-Maz'ya inequality was proved by Maz'ya in [179].

Lemma 5.24(Hardy-Sobolev-Maz'ya inequality) *Let $p > 2$ and $p \leqslant \dfrac{2N}{N-2}$ if $N \geqslant 3$. Assume $t = N - \dfrac{N-2}{2}p$. Then there exits a $C = C(N, p)$ such that*

$$\left(\int_{\mathbb{R}^k \times \mathbb{R}^{N-k}} \frac{|u|^p}{|y|^t} dydz \right)^{2/p} \leqslant C \int_{\mathbb{R}^k \times \mathbb{R}^{N-k}} \left[|\nabla u|^2 - \frac{(k-2)^2}{4} \frac{u^2}{|y|^2} \right] dydz,$$

for all $u \in C_c^\infty(\mathbb{R}^k \times \mathbb{R}^{N-k})$.

As a consequence of Hardy-Sobolev-Maz'ya inequality, if $\mu < \dfrac{(k-2)^2}{4}$, we have

$$\|u\|_\mu = \left[\int_{\mathbb{R}^N} \left(|\nabla u|^2 - \mu \frac{u^2}{|y|^2} dx \right) \right]^{1/2}, \quad u \in C_c^\infty(\Omega) \tag{5.40}$$

which is a norm, equivalent to the $H_0^1(\Omega)$ norm.

Then we will derive the weighted L^p embedding.

Lemma 5.25[93] *If Ω is a bounded subset of $\mathbb{R}^N = \mathbb{R}^k \times \mathbb{R}^{N-k}, t < 2$, then*

$$L_t^p(\Omega) \subset L_t^q(\Omega)$$

with the inclusion being continuous, whenever $1 \leqslant q \leqslant p < \infty$.

Remark 5.10 If $f \in L_t^p(\Omega)$ for $1 \leqslant p < \infty$, then $f \in L^p(\Omega)$ with

$$\|f\|_p \leqslant C|f|_{p,t,\Omega}.$$

For any $\varepsilon > 0$ small, we define

$$\|u\|_* = \left[\int_\Omega \frac{|u|^{2^*(t)-\varepsilon}}{|y|^t} dx \right]^{1/(2^*(t)-\varepsilon)}, \quad u \in H_0^1(\Omega).$$

Then by Hardy-Sobolev-Maz'ya inequality and Lemma 5.26, we can obtain that $\|u\|_* \leqslant C\|u\|_\mu$ for all $u \in H_0^1(\Omega)$ for some constant $C > 0$.

Lemma 5.26[93] *Let $1 \leqslant q < 2^*(t), 0 \leqslant t < 2$, then the embedding $H_0^1(\Omega) \hookrightarrow L_t^q(\Omega)$ is compact.*

By Lemma 5.24 and Hardy-Sobolev-Maz'ya inequality, we know that the singular term $\int_\Omega \dfrac{|u|^{2^*(t)-\varepsilon}}{|y|^t}$ is finite. Therefore J_ε is a C^1 function on $H_0^1(\Omega)$. By Lemma 5.26, J_ε satisfies the Palais-Smale condition. In order to prove Theorem 5.5, it is enough to obtain sign-changing critical points for the functional J_ε.

Let $0 < \lambda_1 < \lambda_2 \leqslant \lambda_3 \leqslant \cdots \leqslant \lambda_m \leqslant \cdots$ be the eigenvalues of $\left(-\Delta - \dfrac{\mu}{|y|^2}, H_0^1(\Omega)\right)$ and e_m be the eigenfunction corresponding to λ_m. Denote

$$H_m := \operatorname{span}\{e_1, e_2, \cdots, e_m\}.$$

Fix $\xi \in (2, 2^*(t))$. In the following, we will always assume that $\varepsilon \in (0, 2^*(t) - \xi)$. In order to construct the minimax values for the perturbed functional J_ε, the following two technique lemmas are needed.

Lemma 5.27 *Assume $m \geqslant 1$. Then there exists $R = R(H_m) > 0$ such that for all $\varepsilon \in (0, 2^*(t) - \xi)$,*

$$\sup_{B_R^c \cap H_m} J_\varepsilon(u) < 0,$$

where $B_R^c := E \setminus B_R$.

Proof. By Lemma 5.25 we know that $\| \cdot \|_*$ is defined a norm on $H_0^1(\Omega)$, since H_m is finite dimensional, there is a constant $C > 0$ such that $\|u\|_\mu \leqslant C\|u\|_*$ for all $u \in H_m$. Therefore

$$J_\varepsilon(u) \leqslant \frac{1}{2} \int_\Omega \left(|\nabla u|^2 - \mu \frac{u^2}{|y|^2}\right) dx - \frac{1}{2^*(t) - \varepsilon} \int_\Omega \frac{|u|^{2^*(t) - \varepsilon}}{|y|^t} dx$$

$$\leqslant \frac{1}{2}\|u\|_\mu^2 - C\|u\|_\mu^{2^*(t) - \varepsilon}.$$

Since $2^*(t) - \varepsilon > \xi > 2$, we have $\displaystyle \lim_{\|u\| \to \infty, u \in H_m} J_\varepsilon(u) = -\infty$. The proof is complete.

$\square$

Lemma 5.28 *For any $\varepsilon \in (0, 2^*(t) - \xi)$, there exist $\rho = \rho(\varepsilon), \alpha = \alpha(\varepsilon) > 0$ such that*

$$\inf_{\partial B_\rho} J_\varepsilon(u) \geqslant \alpha.$$

Proof.

$$J_\varepsilon(u) = \frac{1}{2} \int_\Omega \left(|\nabla u|^2 - \mu \frac{u^2}{|y|^2} - \lambda u^2\right) dx - \frac{1}{2^*(t) - \varepsilon} \int_\Omega \frac{|u|^{2^*(t) - \varepsilon}}{|y|^t} dx$$

$$= \frac{1}{2}\|u\|_\mu^2 - \frac{\lambda}{2} \int_\Omega u^2 dx - \frac{1}{2^*(t) - \varepsilon}\|u\|_*^{2^*(t) - \varepsilon}$$

$$\geqslant \frac{1}{2}\left(1 - \frac{\lambda}{\lambda_1}\right) \|u\|_\mu^2 - C\|u\|_\mu^{2^*(t) - \varepsilon}.$$

Since $2^*(t) - \varepsilon > \xi > 2$, there exist $\rho = \rho(\varepsilon), \alpha = \alpha(\varepsilon) > 0$ such that

$$\inf_{\partial B_\rho} J_\varepsilon(u) \geqslant \alpha.$$

The proof is complete. $\square$

Lemma 5.28 implies that 0 is a strict local minimum critical point. Then we can construct invariant sets containing all the positive and negative solutions of (5.33) for the gradient flow of J_ε. Therefore, nodal solutions can be found outside of these sets.

5.3.3 Auxiliary operator and invariant subsets of descending flow

For any $\varepsilon \in (0, 2^*(t) - \xi)$, let $A_\varepsilon : E \to E$ be given by

$$A_\varepsilon(u) := (-\Delta)^{-1}\left(\frac{\mu u}{|y|^2} + \lambda u + |u|^{2^*(t)-2-\varepsilon}u \right),$$

for $u \in E$. Then the gradient of J_ε has the form

$$\nabla J_\varepsilon(u) = u - A_\varepsilon(u).$$

Note that the set of fixed points of A_ε is the same as the set of critical points of J_ε, which is $K_\varepsilon := \{u \in E : \nabla J_\varepsilon(u) = 0\}$. It is easy to check that ∇J_ε is locally Lipschitz continuous.

We consider the negative gradient flow ϕ_ε of J_ε defined by

$$\begin{cases} \dfrac{d}{dt}\phi_\varepsilon(t, u) = -\nabla J_\varepsilon(\phi_\varepsilon(t, u)), & \text{for } t \geqslant 0, \\ \phi_\varepsilon(0, u) = u. \end{cases}$$

Here and in the sequel, for $u \in E$, denote $u^\pm(x) := \max\{\pm u(x), 0\}$, the convex cones

$$+P = \{u \in E : u \geqslant 0\}, \quad -P = \{u \in E : -u \geqslant 0\}.$$

For $\theta > 0$, define

$$(\pm P)_\theta := \{u \in E : \text{dist}(u, \pm P) < \theta\}.$$

We will show that there exists a $\theta_0 > 0$ such that $(\pm P)_\theta$ is an invariant set under the descending flow for all $0 < \theta \leqslant \theta_0$ (c.f. Lemma 5.29 below). Note that $E \setminus W$ contains only sign-changing functions, where

$$W := \overline{(+P)_\theta} \cup \overline{(-P)_\theta}.$$

Thus it follows from a version of the symmetric Mountain Pass theorem which provides the minimax critical values on $E \setminus W$ that (5.37) has infinitely many sign-changing solutions.

For any $N \subset E$ and $\delta > 0$, N_δ denotes the open δ-neighborhood of N, i.e.

$$N_\delta := \{u \in E : \text{dist}(u, N) < \delta\},$$

whose closure and boundary are denoted by $\overline{N_\delta}$ and ∂N_δ. The following result shows that a neighborhood of $\pm P$ is an invariant set. This result was proved in Lemma 2 in [71], also in Lemma 3.1 in [21].

Lemma 5.29   *There exists a $\theta_0 > 0$ such that for any $\theta \in (0, \theta_0]$, there holds*

$$A_\varepsilon(\partial(\pm P)_\theta) \subset (\pm P)_\theta,$$

and

$$\phi_\varepsilon(t, u) \in (\pm P)_\theta, \quad \text{for all } t > 0 \text{ and } u \in \overline{(\pm P)_\theta}.$$

Moreover, every nontrivial solutions $u \in (+P)_\theta$ and $u \in (-P)_\theta$ of (5.37) are positive and negative, respectively.

To prove our main result, we need to construct nodal solution by using the combination of invariant sets method and minimax method, we need a deformation lemma in the presence of invariant sets.

Definition 5.3   A subset $W \subset E$ is an invariant set with respect to ϕ_ε if, for any $u \in W$, $\phi_\varepsilon(t, u) \in W$ for all $t \geqslant 0$.

From Lemma 5.29, we may choose an $\theta > 0$ sufficiently small such that $\overline{(\pm P)_\theta}$ are invariant set. Set $W := \overline{(+P)_\theta} \cup \overline{(-P)_\theta}$. Note that $\phi_\varepsilon(t, \partial W) \subset \text{int}(W)$ and $Q := E \setminus W$ only contains sign-changing functions.

Since J_ε satisfies the Palais-Smale condition, we have the following deformation lemma which follows from Lemma 5.1 in [130] (also see Lemma 2.4 in [122]).

Define

$$K^1_{\varepsilon,c} := K_{\varepsilon,c} \cap W, \quad K^2_{\varepsilon,c} := K_{\varepsilon,c} \cap Q,$$

where

$$K_{\varepsilon,c} := \{u \in E : J_\varepsilon(u) = c, J'_\varepsilon(u) = 0\}.$$

Let $\rho > 0$ be such that $(K^1_{\varepsilon,c})_\rho \subset W$, where

$$(K^1_{\varepsilon,c})_\rho := \{u \in E : \text{dist}(u, K^1_{\varepsilon,c}) < \rho\}.$$

Lemma 5.30   *Assume that J_ε satisfies Palais-Smale condition, then there exists an $\delta_0 > 0$ such that for any $0 < \delta < \delta_0$, there exists $\eta \in C([0,1] \times E, E)$ satisfying:*

(i) $\eta(t, u) = u$ for $t = 0$ or $u \notin J_\varepsilon^{-1}([c - \delta_0, c + \delta_0]) \setminus (K^2_{\varepsilon,c})_\rho$.

(ii) $\eta(1, J_\varepsilon^{c+\delta} \cup W \setminus (K^2_{\varepsilon,c})_{3\rho}) \subset J_\varepsilon^{c-\delta} \cup W$ and $\eta(1, J_\varepsilon^{c+\delta} \cup W) \subset J_\varepsilon^{c-\delta} \cup W$ if $K^2_{\varepsilon,c} = \varnothing$. Here $J_\varepsilon^d = \{u \in E : J_\varepsilon(u) \leqslant d\}$ for any $d \in \mathbb{R}$.

(iii) $\eta(t, \cdot)$ is odd and a homeomorphism of E for $t \in [0, 1]$.

(iv) $J_\varepsilon(\eta(\cdot, u))$ is non-increasing.

(v) $\eta(t, W) \subset W$ for any $t \in [0, 1]$.

5.3.4   The proof of Theorem 5.5

In the following, $\lambda \in (0, \lambda_1)$ is fixed. For any $\varepsilon \in (0, 2^*(t) - \xi)$ small, we define the minimax value $c_{\varepsilon,l}$ for the perturbed functional $J_\varepsilon(u)$ with $l = 2, 3, \cdots$. We now define a family of sets for the minimax procedure here. We essentially follow [21], also see [130, 154]. Define

$$G_m := \{h \in C(B_R \cap H_m, E) : h \text{ is odd and } h = id \text{ on } \partial B_R \cap H_m\},$$

where $R > 0$ is given by Lemma 5.27. Note that $G_m \neq \varnothing$, since $id \in G_m$. Set

$$\Gamma_l := \{h(B_R \cap H_m \setminus Y) : h \in G_m, m \geqslant l, Y = -Y \text{ is open and } \gamma(Y) \leqslant m - l\},$$

for $k \geqslant 2$. From [154], Γ_l possess the following properties:

(1) $\Gamma_l \neq \varnothing$ and $\Gamma_{l+1} \subset \Gamma_l$ for all $l \geqslant 2$.

(2) If $\phi \subset C(E, E)$ is odd and $\phi - id$ on $\partial B_R \cap H_m$, then $\psi(A) \in \Gamma_l$ if $A \in \Gamma_l$ for all $l \geqslant 2$.

(3) If $A \in \Gamma_l$, $Z = -Z$ is open and $\gamma(Z) \leqslant s < l$ and $l - s \geqslant 2$, then $A \setminus Z \in \Gamma_{l-s}$.

Now, for $l \geqslant 2$, we can define the minimax value $c_{\varepsilon,l}$ given by

$$c_{\varepsilon,l} := \inf_{A \in \Gamma_l} \sup_{u \in A \cap Q} J_\varepsilon(u).$$

Lemma 5.31   *For any $A \in \Gamma_l$ and $l \geqslant 2$, $A \cap Q \neq \varnothing$, then $c_{\varepsilon,l}$ are well defined, and $c_{\varepsilon,l} \geqslant \alpha > 0$ where α is given by Lemma 5.28.*

Proof. Consider the attracting domain of 0 in E:

$$D := \{u \in E : \phi_\varepsilon(t, u) \to 0, \text{ as } t \to \infty\}.$$

Note that D is open since 0 is a local minimum of J_ε and by the continuous dependence of ODE on initial data. Moreover, ∂D is an invariant set and $\overline{(+P)_\delta} \cap \overline{(-P)_\delta} \subset D$. In particular there holds

$$J_\varepsilon(u) > 0,$$

for every $u \in \overline{(+P)_\delta} \cap \overline{(-P)_\delta} \setminus \{0\}$ (see Lemma 3.4 in [21]). Now we claim that for any $A \in \Gamma_l$ with $l \geqslant 2$, it holds

$$A \cap Q \cap \partial D \neq \varnothing. \tag{5.41}$$

If this is true, then we have $A \cap Q \neq \varnothing$ and $c_{\varepsilon,2} \geqslant \alpha > 0$, because $\partial B_\rho \subset D$ and

$$\sup_{A \cap Q} J_\varepsilon(u) \geqslant \inf_{\partial D} J_\varepsilon(u) \geqslant \inf_{\partial B_\rho} J_\varepsilon(u) \geqslant \alpha > 0$$

by Lemma 5.28.

To prove (5.41), let

$$A = h(B_R \cap H_m \setminus Y)$$

with $\gamma(Y) \leqslant m - l$ and $l \geqslant 2$. Define

$$O := \{u \in B_R \cap H_m : h(u) \in D\}.$$

Then O is a bounded open symmetric set with $0 \in O$ and $\bar{O} \subset B_R \cap H_m$. Thus, it follows from the Borsuk-Ulam theorem that $\gamma(\partial O) = m$ and by the continuity of h, $h(\partial O) \subset \partial D$. As a consequence,

$$h(\partial O \setminus Y) \subset A \cap \partial D,$$

and therefore

$$\gamma(A \cap \partial D) \geqslant \gamma(h(\partial O \setminus Y)) \geqslant \gamma(\partial O \setminus Y) \geqslant \gamma(\partial O) - \gamma(Y) \geqslant l,$$

by the "monotone, sub-additive and supervariant" property of the genus (Proposition 5.4 in [164]). Since $(+P)_\delta \cap (-P)_\delta \cap \partial D = \varnothing$,

$$\gamma(W \cap \partial D) \leqslant 1.$$

Thus for $l \geqslant 2$, we conclude that

$$\gamma(A \cap Q \cap \partial D) \geqslant \gamma(A \cap \partial D) - \gamma(W \cap \partial D) \geqslant l - 1 \geqslant 1,$$

which proves (5.41).

Thus $c_{\varepsilon,l}$ are well defined for all $l \geqslant 2$ and $0 < \alpha \leqslant c_{\varepsilon,2} \leqslant c_{\varepsilon,3} \leqslant \cdots \leqslant c_{\varepsilon,l} \leqslant \cdots$. The proof is complete. $\qquad\square$

Lemma 5.32

$$K_{\varepsilon,c_{\varepsilon,l}} \cap Q \neq \varnothing. \tag{5.42}$$

Proof. If not, we assume that

$$K_{\varepsilon,c_{\varepsilon,l}} \cap Q = \varnothing.$$

By Lemma 5.30, for the function J_ε, there exist $\delta > 0$ and a map $\eta \in C([0,1] \times E, E)$ such that $\eta(1, \cdot)$ is odd, $\eta(1, u) = u$ for $u \in J_\varepsilon^{c_{\varepsilon,l}-2\delta}$ and

$$\eta(1, J_\varepsilon^{c_{\varepsilon,l}+\delta} \cup W) \subset J_\varepsilon^{c_{\varepsilon,l}-\delta} \cup W. \tag{5.43}$$

By the definition of $c_{\varepsilon,l}$, there exists a $A \in \Gamma_l$ such that

$$\sup_{A \cap Q} J_\varepsilon(u) \leqslant c_{\varepsilon,l} + \delta.$$

Let $B = \eta(1, A)$. It follows from (5.43) that

$$\sup_{B \cap Q} J_\varepsilon(u) \leqslant c_{\varepsilon,l} - \delta.$$

On the other hand, it is easy to show that $B \in \Gamma_l$ by Lemma 5.27 and the property of (2) of Γ_l above. As a result, $c_{\varepsilon,l} \leqslant c_{\varepsilon,l} - \delta$. This contradicts with $\delta > 0$. The proof is complete. $\square$

Lemma 5.32 implies that there exists a sign-changing critical point $u_{\varepsilon,l}$ such that

$$J_\varepsilon(u_{\varepsilon,l}) = c_{\varepsilon,l}.$$

As a consequence of Lemma 5.32, we have that $c_{\varepsilon,l}$ are well defined for all $l \geqslant 2$ and $0 < \alpha \leqslant c_{\varepsilon,2} \leqslant c_{\varepsilon,3} \leqslant \cdots \leqslant c_{\varepsilon,l} \leqslant \cdots$. Now we can show the following lemma.

Lemma 5.33 $c_{\varepsilon,l} \to \infty$ as $l \to \infty$.

Proof. Here we deduce by a negation. Suppose $c_{\varepsilon,l} \to \bar{c}_\varepsilon < \infty$ as $l \to \infty$. Since J_ε satisfies Palais-Smale condition, it follows that $K_{\varepsilon,\bar{c}_\varepsilon} \neq \varnothing$ and is compact. Moreover, we have

$$K^2_{\varepsilon,\bar{c}_\varepsilon} := K_{\varepsilon,\bar{c}_\varepsilon} \cap Q \neq \varnothing.$$

Indeed, assume $\{u_{\varepsilon,l_i}\}_{i \in \mathbb{N}}$ is a sequence of sign-changing solutions to (5.37) with $J_\varepsilon(u_{\varepsilon,l_i}) = c_{\varepsilon,l_i}$, we have

$$\|u^\pm_{\varepsilon,l_i}\|^2 = \mu\|u^\pm_{\varepsilon,l_i}\|^2_2 + \|u^\pm_{\varepsilon,l_i}\|^{2^*(t)-\varepsilon}_*.$$

It follows that, by Sobolev embedding theorem, $\|u^\pm_{\varepsilon,l_i}\| \geqslant c_0 > 0$, where c_0 is a constant independent of i. This implies that the limit $\bar{u}_\varepsilon \in K_{\varepsilon,\bar{c}_\varepsilon}$ of the subsequence of $\{u_{\varepsilon,l_i}\}_{i \in \mathbb{N}}$ is still sign-changing.

Assume $\gamma(K^2_{\varepsilon,\bar{c}_\varepsilon}) = \tau$. Since $0 \notin K^2_{\varepsilon,\bar{c}_\varepsilon}$ and $K^2_{\varepsilon,\bar{c}_\varepsilon}$ is compact, by the "continuous" property of the genus (Proposition 5.4 in [164]), there exists an open neighborhood N in E with $K^2_{\varepsilon,\bar{c}_\varepsilon} \subset N$ such that $\gamma(N) = \tau$. Now using Lemma 5.31 for the functional J_ε, there exist $\delta > 0$ and a map $\eta \in C([0,1] \times E, E)$ such that $\eta(1, \cdot)$ is odd, $\eta(1, u) = u$ for $u \in J^{\bar{c}_\varepsilon-2\delta}_\varepsilon$ and

$$\eta(1, J^{\bar{c}_\varepsilon+\delta}_\varepsilon \cup W \setminus N) \subset J^{\bar{c}_\varepsilon-\delta}_\varepsilon \cup W. \tag{5.44}$$

Since $c_{\varepsilon,l} \to \bar{c}_\varepsilon$ as $l \to \infty$, we can choose l sufficiently large, such that $c_{\varepsilon,l} \geqslant \bar{c}_\varepsilon - \frac{1}{2}\delta$. Clearly, $c_{\varepsilon,l+\tau} \geqslant c_{\varepsilon,l} \geqslant \bar{c}_\varepsilon - \frac{1}{2}\delta$. By the definition of $c_{\varepsilon,l+\tau}$, we can find a set $A \in \Gamma_{l+\tau}$, that is $A = h(B_R \cap H_m \setminus Y)$, where $h \in G_m$, $m \geqslant l+\tau$, $\gamma(Y) \leqslant m - (l+\tau)$, such that

$$J_\varepsilon(u) \leqslant c_{\varepsilon,l+\tau} + \frac{1}{4}\delta < \bar{c}_\varepsilon + \delta, \quad \text{for any } u \in A \cap Q,$$

which implies $A \subset J^{\bar{c}_\varepsilon+\delta}_\varepsilon \cup W$. It follows from (5.44) that

$$\eta(1, A \setminus N) \subset J^{\bar{c}_\varepsilon-\delta}_\varepsilon \cup W. \tag{5.45}$$

Let $Y_1 = Y \cup h^{-1}(N)$. Then Y_1 is symmetric and open, and

$$\gamma(Y_1) \leqslant \gamma(Y) + \gamma(h^{-1}(N)) \leqslant m - (l + \tau) + \tau = m - l.$$

Then it is easy to check $\widetilde{A} := \eta(1, h(B_R \cap H_m \setminus Y_1)) \in \Gamma_l$ by (2) and (3) above. As a result, by (5.45)

$$c_{\varepsilon,l} \leqslant \sup_{\widetilde{A} \cap Q} J_\varepsilon(u) \leqslant \sup_{\eta(1, A \setminus N) \cap Q} J_\varepsilon(u) \leqslant \bar{c}_\varepsilon - \delta.$$

This is a contradiction to $c_{\varepsilon,l} \geqslant \bar{c}_\varepsilon - \dfrac{1}{2}\delta$. The proof is complete. $\qquad\square$

Lemma 5.34 *For any fixed $l \geqslant 2$, $\|u_{\varepsilon,l}\|$ is uniformly bounded with respect to ε, and then $u_{\varepsilon,l}$ converges strongly to u_l in E as $\varepsilon \to 0$.*

Proof. In deed, by using the same Γ_l above, we can also define the minimax value for the following two auxiliary function

$$J_*(u) = \frac{1}{2} \int_\Omega (|\nabla u|^2 - \frac{\mu u^2}{|y|^2} - \lambda|u|^2) dx - \frac{1}{2^*(t)} \int_\Omega \frac{|u|^\delta}{|y|^t} dx$$

and

$$J_{**}(u) = \frac{1}{2} \int_\Omega (|\nabla u|^2 - \frac{\mu u^2}{|y|^2} - \lambda|u|^2) dx - \frac{2}{2^*(t)} \int_\Omega \frac{|u|^{2^*(t)}}{|y|^t} dx,$$

where $\delta = \dfrac{1}{2}(2 + 2^*(t)) \in (2, 2^*(t))$.

$$\alpha_l := \inf_{A \in \Gamma_l} \sup_{u \in A} J_*(u), \quad l = 2, 3, \cdots$$

and

$$\beta_l := \inf_{A \in \Gamma_l} \sup_{u \in A} J_{**}(u), \quad l = 2, 3, \cdots,$$

respectively.

In the following, we will always assume that $0 < \varepsilon < \dfrac{2^*(t) - 2}{2}$ and then $\delta \in (2, \varepsilon)$. We can easily to prove that

$$\frac{|u|^\delta - 1}{2^*(t)|y|^t} \leqslant \frac{1}{2^*(t) - \varepsilon} \frac{|u|^{2^*(t) - \varepsilon}}{|y|^t} \leqslant \frac{2}{2^*(t)} \frac{|u|^{2^*(t)} + 1}{|y|^t}. \tag{5.46}$$

Therefore, we have obtain that

$$J_*(u) + d_0 \geqslant J_\varepsilon(u) \geqslant J_{**}(u) - 2d_0,$$

where

$$d_0 = \frac{1}{2^*(t)} \int_\Omega \frac{1}{|y|^t} dx.$$

By (5.46) and the definition of $\alpha_l, \beta_l, c_{\varepsilon,l}$, we have

$$\beta_l - 2d_0 \leqslant c_{\varepsilon,l} \leqslant \alpha_l + d_0. \tag{5.47}$$

Therefore, for fixed l, $c_{\varepsilon,l}$ is uniformly bounded for $\varepsilon \in (0, 2^*(t) - \delta)$. Noting that $J_\varepsilon(u_{\varepsilon,l}) = c_{\varepsilon,l}$ and $u_{\varepsilon,l}$ satisfies the equation, we obtain that

$$\int_\Omega \left(|\nabla u_{\varepsilon,l}|^2 - \frac{\mu u_{\varepsilon,l}^2}{|y|^2} - \lambda |u_{\varepsilon,l}|^2 \right) dx$$

$$= \int_\Omega \frac{|u_{\varepsilon,l}|^{2^*(t)-\varepsilon}}{|y|^t} dx = \frac{2(2^*(t) - \varepsilon)}{2^*(t) - 2 - \varepsilon} c_{\varepsilon,l} \leqslant C_1.$$

By Hölder inequality, we obtain that

$$\int_\Omega |u_{\varepsilon,l}|^2 dx \leqslant \left(\int_\Omega \frac{|u_{\varepsilon,l}|^{2^*(t)-\varepsilon}}{|y|^t} dx \right)^{\frac{2}{2^*(t)-\varepsilon}} \left(\int_\Omega |y|^{\frac{2t}{2^*(t)-2-\varepsilon}} dx \right)^{\frac{2}{2^*(t)-\varepsilon}} \leqslant C_2,$$

where C_2 depends on $|\Omega|$, N and t. So there exists a positive constant C_3 independent of n such that

$$\int_\Omega \left(|\nabla u_{\varepsilon,l}|^2 - \frac{\mu u_{\varepsilon,l}^2}{|y|^2} \right) dx \leqslant C_3.$$

By using the Hardy-Sobolev-Maz'ya inequality, we obtain that

$$\left(1 - \frac{\mu}{\bar{\mu}} \right) \int_\Omega |\nabla u_{\varepsilon,l}|^2 dx \leqslant \int_\Omega \left(|\nabla u_{\varepsilon,l}|^2 - \frac{\mu u_{\varepsilon,l}^2}{|y|^2} \right) dx \leqslant C_3,$$

where $\bar{\mu} = \dfrac{(k-2)^2}{4} > 0$. Therefore,

$$\int_\Omega |\nabla u_{\varepsilon,l}|^2 dx \leqslant C_4.$$

Therefore $\|u_{\varepsilon,l}\|$ is uniformly with respect to ε. So we can apply Proposition 5.3 and obtain a subsequence $\{u_{\varepsilon_l,l}\}_{l \in \mathbb{N}}$, such that $u_{\varepsilon_l,l} \to u_l$ strongly in E for some u_l and also $c_{\varepsilon_l,l} \to c_l$. Thus u_l is a solution of (5.37) and $J_\varepsilon(u_l) = c_l$. Moreover, since $u_{\varepsilon_l,l}$ is sign-changing, similar to Lemma 5.34, by Sobolev embedding theorem, we can prove that u_l is still sign-changing. The proof is complete. $\square$

Proof of Theorem 5.5   Now we are in a position to prove Theorem 5.5. Noting that c_l is non-decreasing with respect to l, we have the following two cases:

Case (i)   There are $2 \leqslant l_1 < \cdots < l_i < \cdots$, satisfying $c_{l_1} < \cdots < c_{l_i} < \cdots$. Obviously, in this case, equation (5.33) has infinitely many sign solutions such that $J(u_i) = c_{l_i}$.

Case (ii)   There is a positive integer L such that $c_l = c$ for all $l \geqslant L$.

From now on we assume that there exists a $\delta > 0$, such that $J(u)$ has no sign-changing critical point u with

$$J(u) \in [c - \delta, c) \cup (c, c + \delta].$$

Otherwise we are done. In this case, we claim that $\gamma(K_c^2) \geqslant 2$, where $K_c := \{u \in E : J(u) = c, J'(u) = 0\}$ and $K_c^2 = K_c \cap Q$. Then as a consequence, $J(u)$ has infinitely many sign-changing critical points.

Now we adopt a technique in the proof of Theorem 1.1 in [42]. Suppose, on the contrary, that $\gamma(K_c^2) = 1$ (note that $K_c^2 \neq \varnothing$). Moreover, we assume K_c^2 contains only finitely many critical points, otherwise we are done. Then it follows that K_c^2 is compact. Obviously, $0 \notin K_c^2$. Then there exists a open neighborhood N in E with $K_c^2 \subset N$ such that $\gamma(N) = \gamma(K_c^2)$.

Define

$$V_\varepsilon := (J_\varepsilon^{c+\delta} \setminus J_\varepsilon^{c-\delta}) \setminus N.$$

We now claim that if $\varepsilon > 0$ small, J_ε has no sign-changing critical point $u \in V_\varepsilon$. Indeed, arguing indirectly, suppose that there exist $\varepsilon_n \to 0$ and $u_n \in V_{\varepsilon_n}$ satisfying $J'_{\varepsilon_n}(u_n) = 0$, with $u_n^\pm \neq 0$, and $u_n \notin N$.

Then, by Proposition 5.3, up to a subsequence, u_n converges strongly to u in E. Therefore $J'(u) = 0$,

$$J(u) \in [c - \delta, c + \delta]$$

and $u \notin K_c^2$.

This is a contradiction to our assumption and the fact that u is still sign-changing. The following proof is similar to that of Lemma 5.32. By using Lemma 5.30, for the function J_ε, there exist a $\delta > 0$ and a map $\eta \in C([0, 1] \times E, E)$ such that $\eta(1, \cdot)$ is odd, $\eta(1, u) = u$ for $u \in J_\varepsilon^{c-2\delta}$ and

$$\eta(1, J_\varepsilon^{c+\delta} \cup W \setminus N) \subset J_\varepsilon^{c-\delta} \cup W. \tag{5.48}$$

Now fix $l > L$. Since $c_{\varepsilon,l}, c_{\varepsilon,l+1} \to c$ as $\varepsilon \to 0$, we can find an $\varepsilon > 0$ small, such that $c_{\varepsilon,l}, c_{\varepsilon,l+1} \in \left(c - \frac{1}{2}\delta, c + \frac{1}{2}\delta\right)$. By the definition of $c_{\varepsilon,l+1}$, we can find a set $A \in \Gamma_{l+1}$, that is

$$A = h(B_R \cap H_m \setminus Y),$$

where $h \in G_m$, $m \geqslant l + 1$, $\gamma(Y) \leqslant m - (l + 1)$, such that

$$J_\varepsilon(u) \leqslant c_{\varepsilon, l+1} + \frac{1}{4}\delta < c + \delta,$$

for any $u \in A \cap Q$, which implies $A \subset J_\varepsilon^{c+\delta} \cup W$. Then by (5.48), we have

$$\eta(1, A \setminus N) \subset J_\varepsilon^{c-\delta} \cup W. \tag{5.49}$$

Let $\widetilde{Y} = Y \cup h^{-1}(N)$. Then $\widetilde{Y}$ is symmetric and open, and

$$\gamma(\widetilde{Y}) \leqslant \gamma(Y) + \gamma(h^{-1}(N)) \leqslant m - (l + 1) + 1 = m - l.$$

Then it is easy to check $\widehat{A} := \eta(1, h(B_R \cap H_m \setminus \widetilde{Y})) \in \Gamma_l$ by (2) and (3) above. As a result, by (5.49)

$$c_{\varepsilon, l} \leqslant \sup_{\widehat{A} \cap Q} J_\varepsilon(u) \leqslant \sup_{\eta(1, A \setminus N) \cap Q} J_\varepsilon(u) \leqslant c - \delta.$$

This contradicts to $c_{\varepsilon, l} > c - \frac{1}{2}\delta$. Then the proof for the Case (ii) is finished. The proof is complete. $\qquad\square$

Chapter 6   Multiple Solutions for Nonhomogeneous Choquard Equations

6.1   Introduction and main results

In this Chapter, we consider the following nonhomogeneous Choquard equation

$$-\Delta u + u = \left(\frac{1}{|x|^\alpha} * |u|^p \right) |u|^{p-2}u + h(x), \quad x \in \mathbb{R}^N, \tag{6.1}$$

where $N \geqslant 3$, $0 < \alpha < N$ and $2 - \dfrac{\alpha}{N} < p \leqslant 2_\alpha^* = \dfrac{2N - \alpha}{N - 2}$.

A special case of (6.1) is the Choquard equation

$$-\Delta u + u = \left(\frac{1}{|x|^\alpha} * |u|^2 \right) u, \quad x \in \mathbb{R}^N,$$

which was proposed by Choquard in 1976, and it can be described as an approximation to Hartree-Fock theory of a one-component plasma[124, 125]. It was also proposed by Moroz, Penrose and Tod[145] as a model for the self-gravitational collapse of a quantum mechanical wave function. In this context, Choquard equation is usually called the nonlinear Schrödinger-Newton equation. For more details on the physical aspects of the problem we refer the readers to [64, 66−68, 128, 145, 150] and the references therein.

Recently, the nonlinear Choquard equations have been widely studied. When $h \equiv 0$, the existence and multiplicity results of system (6.1) have been discussed in many papers. Take for instance, Lieb[124] proved the existence and uniqueness of the ground state to (6.1) by using symmetric decreasing rearrangement inequalities. Later, Lions[128] showed the existence of infinitely many radially symmetric solutions to (6.1). Gao and Yang[94] established some existence results for the Brezis-Nirenberg type problem for the nonlinear Choquard equation with critical exponent. Further results for related problems may be found in [5−8, 71, 95, 136, 142, 144] and the references therein.

Next, we consider the nonhomogeneous case, that is $h \not\equiv 0$. In [206], Xie, Xiao and Wang proved the following Choquard equation

$$-\Delta u + V(x)u = \left(\frac{1}{|x|^\alpha} * |u|^p\right)|u|^{p-2}u + h(x), \quad x \in \mathbb{R}^N$$

had two nontrivial solutions if $2 - \dfrac{\alpha}{N} < p < \dfrac{2N-\alpha}{N-2}$ satisfies the compact condition:

(V_1) $V \in C(\mathbb{R}^N, \mathbb{R}^+)$ is coercive, that is $\lim\limits_{|x|\to+\infty} V(x) = +\infty.$

Zhang, Xu and Zhang[219] also considered the bound and ground states for nonhomogeneous Choquard equations under the condition

(V_2) $\inf\limits_{\mathbb{R}^N} V > 0$, and there exists a constant $r > 0$ such that, for any $M > 0$, meas$\{x \in \mathbb{R}^N, |x - y| \leqslant r, V(x) \leqslant M\} \to 0$ as $|y| \to \infty$, where meas stands for the Lebesgue measure.

Under condition (V_1) or (V_2), they define a new Hilbert space

$$E := \left\{ u \in H^1(\mathbb{R}^N) : \int_{\mathbb{R}^N} |\nabla u|^2 + V(x)u^2 dx < \infty \right\}$$

with the inner product

$$\langle u, v \rangle_E = \int_{\mathbb{R}^N} (\nabla u \cdot \nabla v + V(x)uv)\, dx$$

and the norm

$$\|u\|_E = \langle u, u \rangle^{1/2}.$$

Obviously, the embedding $E \hookrightarrow L^s(\mathbb{R}^N)$ is continuous, for any $s \in [2, 2^*]$. Consequently, for each $s \in [2, 2^*]$, there exists a constant $d_s > 0$ such that

$$|u|_s \leqslant d_s \|u\|_E, \quad \forall u \in E. \tag{6.2}$$

Furthermore, it follows from the condition (V_1)(or (V_2)) that the embedding $E \hookrightarrow L^s(\mathbb{R}^N)$ are compact for any $s \in [2, 2^*)$ (see [18]). Other related results about nonhomogeneous equations can be found in $[49, 55, 81, 84, 112, 153, 159, 174]$ and the references therein.

Motivated by the works above, in this chapter we study the existence of multiple solutions to the nonhomogenous Choquard equation with the critical exponent

$$-\Delta u = \left(\frac{1}{|x|^\alpha} * |u|^{2^*_\alpha}\right)|u|^{2^*_\alpha-2}u + h(x), \quad x \in \mathbb{R}^N \tag{6.3}$$

and the subcritical exponent

$$-\Delta u + u = \left(\frac{1}{|x|^\alpha} * |u|^p\right)|u|^{p-2}u + h(x), \quad x \in \mathbb{R}^N, \tag{6.4}$$

where $N \geqslant 3$, $0 < \alpha < N$ and $2 - \dfrac{\alpha}{N} < p < 2_\alpha^*$.

Before giving our main results, we give some notations. Let $H^1(\mathbb{R}^N)$ be the usual Sobolev space endowed with the standard scalar and norm

$$(u, v) = \int_{\mathbb{R}^N} (\nabla u \nabla v + uv)dx, \qquad \|u\|^2 = \int_{\mathbb{R}^N} (|\nabla u|^2 + |u|^2)dx.$$

$D^{1,2}(\mathbb{R}^N)$ is the completion of $C_0^\infty(\mathbb{R}^N)$ with respect to the norm

$$\|u\|_D^2 := \|u\|_{D^{1,2}(\mathbb{R}^N)}^2 = \int_{\mathbb{R}^N} |\nabla u|^2 dx.$$

The norm on $L^s = L^s(\mathbb{R}^N)$ with $1 < s < \infty$ is given by $|u|_s^s = \int_{\mathbb{R}^N} |u|^s dx$.

Moreover we make the following assumptions:

(H_1) $\|h\|_{H^{-1}} < C_{2_\alpha^*} S_{H,L}^{\frac{2_\alpha^*}{2(2_\alpha^*-1)}}$, where H^{-1} is the dual space of $D^{1,2}(\mathbb{R}^N)$, $S_{H,L}$ is the best constant defined by

$$S_{H,L} = \inf_{u \in D^{1,2}(\mathbb{R}^N)\setminus\{0\}} \frac{\displaystyle\int_{\mathbb{R}^N} |\nabla u|^2 dx}{\left(\displaystyle\int_{\mathbb{R}^N} \int_{\mathbb{R}^N} \frac{|u(x)|^{2_\alpha^*}|u(y)|^{2_\alpha^*}}{|x-y|^\alpha} dx dy\right)^{\frac{N-2}{2N-\alpha}}}$$

and

$$C_{2_\alpha^*} = \frac{2(2_\alpha^* - 1)}{(2 \cdot 2_\alpha^* - 1)^{\frac{2 \cdot 2_\alpha^* - 1}{2 \cdot 2_\alpha^* - 2}}}.$$

(H_2) $h \in L^{\frac{2Np}{2N(p-1)+\alpha}}(\mathbb{R}^N)$, $h(x) \geqslant 0$ and $h \not\equiv 0$.

(H_3) $|h|_{\frac{2Np}{2N(p-1)+\alpha}} < \varepsilon = \varepsilon(N, p, \alpha, d_{\frac{2Np}{2N-\alpha}})$, where ε is a positive constant, $d_{\frac{2Np}{2N-\alpha}}$ is defined in the following Lemma 6.6.

To our best knowledge, in the nonhomogeneous case, this is the first result involving critical exponent, so that we think this type of problem is worth to consider. We mentioned here that the basic idea of this section follows from that of [174]. And our main results are as follows:

Theorem 6.1 *Assume that $h \not\equiv 0$, (H_1) hold. Then (6.3) has at least two solutions. One of them is a local minimum solution with the ground state energy, and the other one has the energy which is strictly bigger than the least energy. If additionally, we assume $h > 0$ holds, then the two solutions are positive.*

Theorem 6.2 *Assume that $h \not\equiv 0$, (H_2) and (H_3) hold. Then (6.4) has a local minimum solution with the ground state energy. If additionally, we assume $h > 0$ holds, (6.4) has at least two positive solutions.*

Remark 6.1   It is well known that, in order to obtain two solutions of such a nonhomogeneous system, the method is standard. Usually it is not difficult to obtain a negative local minimum and a positive mountain-pass value of the energy function. But because of the lack of the compactness of the embedding $H^1(\mathbb{R}^N) \hookrightarrow L^p(\mathbb{R}^N)$, $p \in (2, 2^*)$, the Palais-Smale condition no longer holds. Especially, many authors avoid the lack of compactness by some coercive assumptions on the potential or by restricting the problem to the radially symmetric subspace of $H^1(\mathbb{R}^N)$. But in this section, these methods are not adopted. In order to overcome this difficulty, we use the Brezis-Nirenberg method[35, 36], which preserve the compactness except some fixed bad energy level. And then by estimating the asymptotic behavior of the local minimum solution, we obtain the second solution.

Remark 6.2   Throughout this chapter, the letters $C_0, d, c_i, i = 1, 2, 3, \cdots$ will be used to denote various positive constants which may vary from line to line and are not essential to the problem. We denote "$\rightharpoonup$" weak convergence and by "$\rightarrow$" strong convergence. Also if we take a subsequence of a sequence $\{u_n\}$, we shall denote it again $\{u_n\}$.

In Section 6.2, we will introduce the variational setting for the problem and give some related preliminaries. In Section 6.3, we manage to give the existence of the solutions for the critical case. In Section 6.4, we give the proof of Theorem 6.2.

6.2   Variational setting and compactness condition

First we give the well-known Hardy-Littlewood-Sobolev inequality.

Lemma 6.1(Hardy-Littlewood-Sobolev inequality[125])   *Assume that $f \in L^p(\mathbb{R}^N)$, $g \in L^q(\mathbb{R}^N)$. Then*

$$\int_{\mathbb{R}^N} \int_{\mathbb{R}^N} \frac{|f(x)||g(y)|}{|x-y|^\alpha} dxdy \leqslant C(p, q, \alpha)|f|_p|g|_q, \tag{6.5}$$

where $1 < p, q < \infty, 0 < \alpha < N, \dfrac{1}{p} + \dfrac{1}{q} + \dfrac{\alpha}{N} = 2$.

If $p = q = 2^*_\alpha$, then

$$C(p, q, \alpha) = C(N, \alpha) = \pi^{\frac{\alpha}{2}} \frac{\Gamma\left(\dfrac{N-\alpha}{2}\right)}{\Gamma\left(N - \dfrac{\alpha}{2}\right)} \left\{ \frac{\Gamma\left(\dfrac{N}{2}\right)}{\Gamma(N)} \right\}^{\frac{\alpha}{N}-1}.$$

The equality in (6.5) is hold if and only if f is a constant times of g and

$$g(x) = \frac{A_1}{(C + |x - a|^2)^{(2N-\alpha)/2}},$$

for some $A_1 \in \mathbb{C}, 0 \neq C \in \mathbb{R}$ and $a \in \mathbb{R}^N$.

By the Hardy-Littlewood-Sobolev inequality, the integral

$$B(u) = \int_{\mathbb{R}^N} \int_{\mathbb{R}^N} \frac{|u(x)|^p |u(y)|^q}{|x-y|^\alpha} \, dx dy$$

is well defined if $|u|^p \in L^s(\mathbb{R}^N)$ for some $s > 1$ satisfying

$$\frac{2}{s} + \frac{\alpha}{N} = 2.$$

Therefore, for $u \in H^1(\mathbb{R}^N)$, by Sobolev embedding theorem, we know that

$$2 \leqslant sp \leqslant \frac{2N}{N-2},$$

that is

$$\frac{2N - \alpha}{N} \leqslant p \leqslant \frac{2N - \alpha}{N-2}.$$

Thus, $\dfrac{2N - \alpha}{N}$ is called the lower critical exponent and $2^*_\alpha = \dfrac{2N - \alpha}{N-2}$ is the upper critical exponent in the sense of the Hardy-Littlewood-Sobolev inequality.

For all $u \in D^{1,2}(\mathbb{R}^N)$, by the Hardy-Littlewood-Sobolev inequality, we have

$$\left(\int_{\mathbb{R}^N} \int_{\mathbb{R}^N} \frac{|u(x)|^{2^*_\alpha} |u(y)|^{2^*_\alpha}}{|x-y|^\alpha} \, dx dy \right)^{\frac{N-2}{2N-\alpha}} \leqslant C(N,\alpha)^{\frac{N-2}{2N-\alpha}} |u|^2_{2^*},$$

$C(N,\alpha)$ is defined in Lemma 6.1. We use $S_{H,L}$ to denote best constant defined in (H_1).

Lemma 6.2[94]   *The constant $S_{H,L}$ defined in (H_1) is achieved if and only if*

$$U(x) = C \left(\frac{b}{b^2 + |x-a|^2} \right)^{N-2/2},$$

where $C > 0$ is a fixed constant, $a \in \mathbb{R}^N$ and $b \in (0, +\infty)$ are parameters. We can also get that

$$S_{H,L} = \frac{S}{C(N,\alpha)^{N-2/2N-\alpha}},$$

Where S is the best Sobolev constant. In particular, let

$$U(x) = \frac{[N(N-2)]^{\frac{N-2}{4}}}{(1+|x|^2)^{\frac{N-2}{2}}}$$

be a minimizer for S, S is the best Sobolev constant, then

$$W(x) = S^{\frac{(N-\alpha)(2-N)}{4(N-\alpha+2)}} C(N,\alpha)^{\frac{2-N}{2(N-\alpha+2)}} U(x)$$

is the unique minimizer for $S_{H,L}$ and satisfies

$$-\Delta u = \int_{\mathbb{R}^N} \frac{|u(y)|^{2^*_\alpha}}{|x-y|^\alpha} dy |u|^{2^*_\alpha - 2} u \quad in \quad \mathbb{R}^N.$$

Moreover,

$$\|W\|_D = \int_{\mathbb{R}^N} \frac{|W(x)|^{2^*_\alpha} |W(y)|^{2^*_\alpha}}{|x-y|^\alpha} dxdy = S_{H,L}^{\frac{2N-\alpha}{N-\alpha+2}}.$$

In order to prove the problem by variational methods, we define the energy functional associated to (6.3) by

$$I(u) = \frac{1}{2} \int_{\mathbb{R}^N} |\nabla u|^2 dx - \frac{1}{2 \cdot 2^*_\alpha} \int_{\mathbb{R}^N} \int_{\mathbb{R}^N} \frac{|u(x)|^{2^*_\alpha} |u(y)|^{2^*_\alpha}}{|x-y|^\alpha} dxdy$$

$$- \int_{\mathbb{R}^N} h(x)u dx, \quad \text{for } u \in D^{1,2}(\mathbb{R}^N). \tag{6.6}$$

By the Hardy-Littlewood-Sobolev inequality, we know $I \in C^1(D^{1,2}(\mathbb{R}^N), \mathbb{R})$ and

$$\langle I'(u), v \rangle = \int_{\mathbb{R}^N} |\nabla u||\nabla v| dx - \int_{\mathbb{R}^N} \int_{\mathbb{R}^N} \frac{|u(x)|^{2^*_\alpha} |u(y)|^{2^*_\alpha - 2} u(y) v(y)}{|x-y|^\alpha} dxdy$$

$$- \int_{\mathbb{R}^N} h(x)v dx, \quad \text{for all } v \in C_0^\infty(\mathbb{R}^N). \tag{6.7}$$

And so u is a weak solution of (6.3) if and only if u is a critical point of function I. We will constrain the functional I on the Nehari manifold

$$\Lambda = \{u \in D^{1,2}(\mathbb{R}^N), \langle I'(u), u \rangle = 0\}.$$

Denote $\Phi(u) = \langle I'(u), u \rangle$, so we know that

$$\langle I'(u), u \rangle = \|u\|_D^2 - \int_{\mathbb{R}^N} \int_{\mathbb{R}^N} \frac{|u(x)|^{2^*_\alpha} |u(y)|^{2^*_\alpha}}{|x-y|^\alpha} dxdy - \int_{\mathbb{R}^N} h(x)u dx$$

and

$$\langle \Phi'(u), u \rangle = 2\|u\|_D^2 - 2 \cdot 2^*_\alpha \int_{\mathbb{R}^N} \int_{\mathbb{R}^N} \frac{|u(x)|^{2^*_\alpha} |u(y)|^{2^*_\alpha}}{|x-y|^\alpha} dxdy - \int_{\mathbb{R}^N} h(x)u dx.$$

Notice that, when u_0 is a local minimum solution of I, there holds

$$\langle I'(u_0), u_0 \rangle = 0,$$

$$\langle \Phi'(u_0), u_0 \rangle \geqslant 0,$$

which leads us to consider the following manifolds:

$$\Lambda = \{u \in D^{1,2}(\mathbb{R}^N) : \langle I'(u), u \rangle = 0\},$$

$$\Lambda^+ = \{u \in \Lambda : \langle \Phi'(u), u \rangle > 0\},$$

$$\Lambda^- = \{u \in \Lambda : \langle \Phi'(u), u \rangle < 0\},$$

$$\Lambda^0 = \{u \in \Lambda : \langle \Phi'(u), u \rangle = 0\}.$$

Obviously, only Λ^0 contains the element 0. Furthermore, it is easy to see that $\Lambda^0 \cup \Lambda^+$ and $\Lambda^0 \cup \Lambda^-$ are both closed subsets of $D^{1,2}(\mathbb{R}^N)$.

In order to simplify the calculation, for $u \in D^{1,2}(\mathbb{R}^N)$, we denote

$$A = A(u) = \|u\|_D^2,$$

$$B = B(u) = \int_{\mathbb{R}^N} \int_{\mathbb{R}^N} \frac{|u(x)|^{2_\alpha^*}|u(y)|^{2_\alpha^*}}{|x-y|^\alpha} dxdy,$$

$$C = C(u) = \int_{\mathbb{R}^N} h(x)udx.$$

Define the fibering map

$$\varphi_u(t) = I(tu) = \frac{A}{2}t^2 - \frac{B}{2 \cdot 2_\alpha^*}t^{2 \cdot 2_\alpha^*} - Ct, \quad t > 0. \tag{6.8}$$

Therefore,

$$\varphi_u'(t) = At - Bt^{2 \cdot 2_\alpha^* - 1} - C,$$

$$\varphi_u''(t) = A - (2 \cdot 2_\alpha^* - 1)Bt^{2 \cdot 2_\alpha^* - 2}. \tag{6.9}$$

Obviously, $tu \in \Lambda$ with $t > 0$ if and only if $\varphi_u'(t) = 0$. By the sign of $\varphi_u''(t)$, the stationary points of $\varphi_u(t)$ can be classified into three types, namely local minimum, local maximum and turning point. Moreover, the set Λ is a natural constraint for the function I. This is means that if the infimum is attained by $u \in \Lambda$, then u is a solution of (6.3). However, in our case, the global maximum point of $\varphi_u(t)$ is not unique. This leads us to partition the set Λ according to the critical points of $\varphi_u(t)$. This kind of idea was first introduced by Tarantello in [174]. Later, many mathematicians apply this idea to study other problems; for instance, see [28, 153, 219] and the references therein.

Now we give some properties of $\Lambda^{\pm}$ and Λ^0.

Lemma 6.3　*Assume that $h \not\equiv 0$ for $u \in D^{1,2}(\mathbb{R}^N) \backslash \{0\}$, there is a unique $t^- = t^-(u) > 0$ such that $t^- u \in \Lambda^-$. And if additionally we assume $\int_{\mathbb{R}^N} hu dx > 0$, there exists a unique $0 < t^+ = t^+(u) < t^-$ satisfying $t^+ u \in \Lambda^+$. Moreover,*

$$I(t^- u) = \max_{t \geq 0} I(tu), \quad for \quad \int_{\mathbb{R}^N} hu dx \leq 0;$$

$$I(t^- u) = \max_{t \geq t^+} I(tu), \quad I(t^+ u) = \min_{0 \leq t \leq t^-} I(tu), \quad for \quad \int_{\mathbb{R}^N} hu dx > 0.$$

Proof. Define

$$\varphi_u(t) = \frac{A}{2}t^2 - \frac{B}{2 \cdot 2_\alpha^*}t^{2 \cdot 2_\alpha^*} - Ct, \quad \text{for all } t > 0.$$

In the case $\int_{\mathbb{R}^N} hu dx \leq 0$, there is a unique $t^- > 0$ such that $\varphi_u'(t^-) = 0$ and $\varphi_u''(t^-) < 0$. So that

$$\langle I'(t^- u), t^- u \rangle = 0,$$

$$\|t^- u\|_D^2 - (2 \cdot 2_\alpha^* - 1)B(u)(t^-)^{2_\alpha^* - 2} < 0.$$

Thus, $t^- u \in \Lambda^-$ and $I(t^- u) = \max_{t \geq 0} I(tu)$.

In the case

$$\int_{\mathbb{R}^N} hu dx > 0, \quad \text{for } t_0 = t_0(u) = \left[\frac{A}{(2 \cdot 2_\alpha^* - 1)B}\right]^{\frac{1}{2 \cdot 2_\alpha^* - 2}} > 0,$$

we have

$$\max_{t \geq 0} \varphi_u'(t) \geq A t_0 - B t_0^{2 \cdot 2_\alpha^* - 1} - C$$

$$= \left[\frac{\|u\|_D^2}{(2 \cdot 2_\alpha^* - 1)B}\right]^{\frac{1}{2 \cdot 2_\alpha^* - 2}} \cdot \frac{2 \cdot 2_\alpha^* - 2}{2 \cdot 2_\alpha^* - 1}\|u\|_D^2 - \int_{\mathbb{R}^N} hu dx$$

$$\geq S_{H,L}^{2_\alpha^*/2(2_\alpha^* - 1)} \frac{2(2_\alpha^* - 1)}{(2 \cdot 2_\alpha^* - 1)^{2 \cdot 2_\alpha^* - 1/2(2_\alpha^* - 1)}}\|u\|_D - \|h\|_{H^{-1}}\|u\|_D$$

$$= S_{H,L}^{2_\alpha^*/2(2_\alpha^* - 1)}C_{2_\alpha}^*\|u\|_D - \|h\|_{H^{-1}}\|u\|_D$$

$$> 0.$$

According to $\varphi'_u(0) = -C < 0$ and $\varphi'_u(t) \to -\infty$ as $t \to +\infty$, we know that there exist unique $0 < t^+ < t_0 < t^-$ such that

$$\varphi'_u(t^-) = \varphi'_u(t^+) = 0, \varphi''_u(t^-) < 0 < \varphi''_u(t^+).$$

Equivalently, $t^+ u \in \Lambda^+$ and $t^- u \in \Lambda^-$. Moreover, since $\dfrac{d}{dt}I(tu) = \varphi'_u(t)$, we can easily see that

$$I(t^- u) = \max_{t \geqslant t^+} I(tu) \quad \text{and} \quad I(t^+ u) = \min_{0 \leqslant t \leqslant t^-} I(tu).$$

The proof is complete. □

Lemma 6.4 *Assume that $h \not\equiv 0$, (H_1) hold, then*
(i) $\Lambda^0 = \{0\}$.
(ii) $\Lambda^{\pm} \neq \varnothing$ and Λ^- is closed.

Proof. (i) In order to prove $\Lambda^0 = \{0\}$, we need to prove that, for $u \in D^{1,2}(\mathbb{R}^N) \setminus \{0\}$, $\varphi_u(t)$ has no critical point that is a turning point. Set $\|u\|_D = 1$, define

$$\kappa(t) = At - Bt^{2 \cdot 2^*_\alpha - 1}. \tag{6.10}$$

Then

$$\varphi'_u(t) = \kappa(t) - C, \quad \kappa''(t) = -B(2 \cdot 2^*_\alpha - 1)(2 \cdot 2^*_\alpha - 2)t^{2 \cdot 2^*_\alpha - 3} < 0,$$

for $t > 0$. So $\kappa(t)$ is strictly concave. If $\kappa'(t_0) = 0$,

$$t_0 = \left(\frac{1}{(2 \cdot 2^*_\alpha - 1)B}\right)^{1/(2 \cdot 2^*_\alpha - 2)} > 0, \quad \text{for } 2^*_\alpha > 2 - \frac{\alpha}{N} > 1.$$

Moreover,

$$\lim_{t \to 0^+} \kappa(t) = 0, \quad \lim_{t \to +\infty} \kappa(t) = -\infty \quad \text{and} \quad \kappa(t) > 0, \quad \text{for } t > 0 \text{ small}.$$

Therefore, we have that $\kappa(t)$ has a unique global maximum point t_0 and

$$\kappa(t_0) = \frac{2(2^*_\alpha - 1)}{2 \cdot 2^*_\alpha - 1}\left(\frac{1}{(2 \cdot 2^*_\alpha - 1)B}\right)^{1/(2 \cdot 2^*_\alpha - 2)} := \kappa_0.$$

By (6.8) and (6.9), we infer that if $0 < C < \kappa_0$, the equation $\varphi'_u(t) = 0$ has exactly two points t_1, t_2 satisfying $t_1 < t_0 < t_2$. If $C \leqslant 0$, the equation $\varphi'_u(t) = 0$ has one root $t_3 > t_0$. Since

$$\varphi''_u(t) = A - (2 \cdot 2^*_\alpha - 1)Bt^{2 \cdot 2^*_\alpha - 2},$$

it follows that

$$\varphi''_u(t_1) > 0, \quad \varphi''_u(t_2) < 0 \quad \text{and} \quad \varphi''_u(t_3) < 0.$$

It follows that $t_1 u \in \Lambda^+, t_2 u \in \Lambda^-$ if $0 < C < \kappa_0$ and $t_3 u \in \Lambda^-$ if $C \leqslant 0$. Since $\{u \in D^{1,2}(\mathbb{R}^N) : \|u\|_D = 1, 0 < C < \kappa_0\}$ and $\{u \in D^{1,2}(\mathbb{R}^N) : \|u\|_D = 1, C \leqslant 0\}$ are nonempty, we can infer that $\Lambda^\pm$ are nonempty. This implies $\Lambda^0 = \{0\}$.

It is suffices to prove $\kappa_0 > C$. By (H_1), Lemma 6.3 and the definition of $S_{H,L}$, we have

$$\kappa_0 - C = k(t_0) - C = At_0 - Bt_0^{2 \cdot 2_\alpha^* - 1} - C$$

$$= t_0 [1 - t_0^{2 \cdot 2_\alpha^* - 2} B] - \int_{\mathbb{R}^N} hu dx$$

$$\geqslant S_{H,L}^{2_\alpha^*/2(2_\alpha^* - 1)} \frac{2(2_\alpha^* - 1)}{(2 \cdot 2_\alpha^* - 1)^{2 \cdot 2_\alpha^* - 1/2(2_\alpha^* - 1)}} - \|h\|_{H^{-1}}$$

$$> 0.$$

(ii) Let $u \in \Lambda^-$, denote $\tilde{u} = \dfrac{u}{\|u\|_D}$, then $\|\tilde{u}\|_D = 1$. By (i), we know that

$$C(\tilde{u}) < \kappa_0 = \frac{2(2_\alpha^* - 1)}{2 \cdot 2_\alpha^* - 1} \left(\frac{1}{(2 \cdot 2_\alpha^* - 1)B} \right)^{1/2(2_\alpha^* - 1)}$$

with $B := B(\tilde{u})$. Furthermore, if $0 < C(\tilde{u}) < \kappa_0$, the equation $\varphi_{\tilde{u}}'(t) = 0$ has exactly two roots $\tilde{t}_1, \tilde{t}_2$ satisfying $0 < \tilde{t}_1 < t_0 < \tilde{t}_2$ such that $\tilde{t}_1 \tilde{u} \in \Lambda^+, \tilde{t}_2 \tilde{u} \in \Lambda^-$. Then $\tilde{t}_2 \tilde{u} = u$ and so $\|u\|_D = \tilde{t}_2 > t_0$. If $C \leqslant 0$, the equation $\varphi_{\tilde{u}}'(t) = 0$ has exactly one roots $\tilde{t}_3 > t_0$. Then $\tilde{t}_3 \tilde{u} = u \in \Lambda^-$ and so $\|u\|_D = \tilde{t}_3 > t_0$. In a word,

$$\|u\|_D > t_0 > 0, \quad u \in \Lambda^-.$$

So there exists a $\tau > 0$ such that

$$\|u\|_D > \tau > 0, \quad \forall u \in \Lambda^-. \tag{6.11}$$

Therefore, $0 \notin \mathrm{cl}(\Lambda^-)$, where $\mathrm{cl}(\Lambda^-)$ is the closure of Λ^-. On the other hand, by (i),

$$\mathrm{cl}(\Lambda^-) \subset \Lambda^- \cup \Lambda^0 = \Lambda^- \cup \{0\}.$$

Hence, $\mathrm{cl}(\Lambda^-) = \Lambda^-$ and Λ^- is closed. The proof is complete. □

Lemma 6.5　*Under assumption (H_1), for $u \in \Lambda \setminus \{0\}$, there exists a $\epsilon > 0$ and a differential function $t = t(w) > 0, w \in D^{1,2}(\mathbb{R}^N), \|w\| < \epsilon$ such that*

(i) $t(0) = 1$;

(ii) $t(w)(u - w) \in \Lambda$, for all $w \in B_\epsilon(0)$;

(iii)

$$\langle t'(0), w \rangle$$

$$= \frac{2 \displaystyle\int_{\mathbb{R}^N} \nabla u \nabla w dx - 2 \cdot 2_\alpha^* \displaystyle\int_{\mathbb{R}^N} \int_{\mathbb{R}^N} \frac{|u(y)|^{2_\alpha^*} |u(x)|^{2_\alpha^* - 2} u(x) w(x)}{|x - y|^\alpha} dx dy - \displaystyle\int_{\mathbb{R}^N} hw dx}{\|u\|_D^2 - (2 \cdot 2_\alpha^* - 1)B(u)}.$$

Proof. We define $F : \mathbb{R} \times D^{1,2} \to \mathbb{R}$ by

$$F(t,w)$$
$$= t\|u-w\|_D^2 - t^{2\cdot 2^*_\alpha - 1} \int_{\mathbb{R}^N} \int_{\mathbb{R}^N} \frac{|(u-w)(x)|^{2^*_\alpha}|(u-w)(y)|^{2^*_\alpha}}{|x-y|^\alpha} dx dy - \int_{\mathbb{R}^N} h(u-w).$$

Obviously, $F(1,0) = 0$, $F'_t(1,0) = \varphi''_u(1) \neq 0$. According to the implicit function theorem at point $(1,0)$, we get that there exist $\epsilon = \epsilon(u) > 0$ and differentiable function $t : B_\epsilon(0) \to \mathbb{R}^+$ such that

    (i) $t(0) = 1$.

    (ii) $t(w)(u-w) \in \Lambda$, for all $w \in B_\epsilon(0)$.

    (iii) $\langle t'(0), w\rangle = -\dfrac{\left\langle \dfrac{\partial F}{\partial w}|_{(1,0)}, w\right\rangle}{\dfrac{\partial F}{\partial t}|_{(1,0)}}.$

The proof is complete. $\hfill\square$

6.3   Local minimum solution

Now we can consider define c_0, c_1 and c^+ by

$$c_0 = \inf_{u\in\Lambda} I(u), \quad c_1 = \inf_{u\in\Lambda^-} I(u), \quad c^+ = \inf_{u\in\Lambda^+} I(u).$$

Proposition 6.1 *Assume (H_1) holds, then (6.3) has a local minimum solution with the least energy* $c_0 = \inf_{\Lambda} I(u)$.

Proof. Firstly, we will show that $\|u\|_D$ is bounded from both above and below. For any $u \in \Lambda$,

$$I(u) = \frac{1}{2}\|u\|_D^2 - \frac{1}{2\cdot 2^*_\alpha}B(u) - C(u)$$

$$= \left(\frac{1}{2} - \frac{1}{2\cdot 2^*_\alpha}\right)\|u\|_D^2 - \left(1 - \frac{1}{2\cdot 2^*_\alpha}\right)\int_{\mathbb{R}^N} hu dx$$

$$\geqslant \frac{2^*_\alpha - 1}{2\cdot 2^*_\alpha}\|u\|_D^2 - \frac{2\cdot 2^*_\alpha - 1}{2\cdot 2^*_\alpha}\|h\|_{H^{-1}}\|u\|_D$$

$$\geqslant -\frac{(2^*_\alpha - 1)^2}{8\cdot 2^*_\alpha(2^*_\alpha - 1)}\|h\|_{H^{-1}}^2. \tag{6.12}$$

Thus,

$$c_0 \geqslant -\frac{(2\cdot 2^*_\alpha - 1)^2}{8\cdot 2^*_\alpha(2^*_\alpha - 1)}\|h\|_{H^{-1}}^2.$$

By the proof of Lemma 6.4, we have that if $u \in D^{1,2}(\mathbb{R}^N)$ and $\|u\|_D = 1$, satisfies

$$0 < C < \kappa_0 = \frac{2(2^*_\alpha - 1)}{2 \cdot 2^*_\alpha - 1} \left(\frac{1}{(2 \cdot 2^*_\alpha - 1)B} \right)^{1/2(2^*_\alpha - 1)}.$$

Then the equation $\varphi'_u(t) = 0$ has a positive solution t_1 satisfying $0 < t_1 < t_0$ and $t_1 u \in \Lambda^+$. Since $\varphi'_u(t) = t - Bt^{2^*_\alpha - 1} - C$, we know that

$$\lim_{t \to 0} \varphi'_u(t) = -C < 0, \quad \varphi''_u(t) > 0, \quad \text{for all } t \in (0, t_0).$$

From $\varphi'_u(t_1) = 0$ we have that

$$\varphi_u(t_1) < \lim_{t \to 0^+} \varphi_u(t) = 0 \quad \text{and} \quad \varphi_u(t_1) = I(t_1 u) \geqslant c^+.$$

Thus

$$c^+ < 0 \quad \text{and} \quad c_0 = \inf_\Lambda I(u) \leqslant \inf_{\Lambda^+} I(u) = c^+ < 0.$$

By using the Ekeland's Variational Principle on Λ, we get a minimizing sequence $\{u_n\} \subset \Lambda$ which satisfies

$$I(u_n) < c_0 + \frac{1}{n},$$
$$I(w) \geqslant I(u_n) - \frac{1}{n}\|u - w\|_D, \quad w \in \Lambda. \tag{6.13}$$

Since $\{u_n\} \subset \Lambda$, it follows that

$$\|u_n\|_D^2 = B(u_n) + C(u_n).$$

Furthermore, we infer from (6.13) that

$$c_0 + \frac{1}{n} \geqslant I(u_n) = \left(\frac{1}{2} - \frac{1}{2 \cdot 2^*_\alpha} \right) \|u_n\|_D^2 - \left(1 - \frac{1}{2 \cdot 2^*_\alpha} \right) \int_{\mathbb{R}^N} h(x) u_n dx$$

$$\geqslant \left(\frac{1}{2} - \frac{1}{2 \cdot 2^*_\alpha} \right) \|u_n\|_D^2 - \left(1 - \frac{1}{2 \cdot 2^*_\alpha} \right) \|h\|_{H^{-1}} \|u_n\|_D. \tag{6.14}$$

We know that $\{u_n\}$ is bounded. We claim that $\inf_n \|u_n\|_D \geqslant \sigma > 0$, which σ is a positive constant. Indeed, if not, by (6.14), $I(u_n)$ would converge to zero. We can infer that $c_0 \geqslant 0$ which is contradict with $c_0 < 0$. So we have

$$\sigma \leqslant \|u_n\|_D \leqslant \delta. \tag{6.15}$$

Secondly, we claim that, for a subsequence of $\{u_n\}$ (still denoted by $\{u_n\}$),

$$\|\nabla I(u_n)\|_D \to 0 \quad \text{as } n \to \infty.$$

In fact, if the claim is false, we could assume $\|\nabla I(u_n)\|_D \geqslant c > 0$ for n large enough. Consequently, according to Lemma 6.5, for u_n there exist ϵ_n and differentiable t_n satisfying

$$t_n(0) = 1, \quad t_n(w)(u_n - w) \in \Lambda, \quad \|w\|_D < \epsilon_n$$

and

$$\langle t'_n(0), w \rangle$$

$$= \frac{2 \displaystyle\int_{\mathbb{R}^N} \nabla u_n \nabla w dx - 2 \cdot 2^*_\alpha \displaystyle\int_{\mathbb{R}^N} \int_{\mathbb{R}^N} \frac{|u_n(y)|^{2^*_\alpha} |u_n(x)|^{2^*_\alpha - 2} u_n(x) w(x)}{|x - y|^\alpha} dx dy - \displaystyle\int_{\mathbb{R}^N} hw dx}{\|u_n\|_D^2 - (2 \cdot 2^*_\alpha - 1) B(u_n)}.$$

We choose

$$w_n = \delta_n \frac{\nabla I(u_n)}{\|\nabla I(u_n)\|_D}, \quad v_n = t_n(w_n)(u_n - w_n),$$

where $0 < \delta_n < \epsilon_n$ is sufficiently small satisfying $\delta_n \to 0$, $t_n(w_n) \to 1$ as $n \to \infty$ and

$$\frac{\left| I(v_n) - I(u_n) - \langle I'(u_n), v_n - u_n \rangle \right|}{\|u_n - v_n\|_D} < \frac{1}{n},$$

$$\frac{\left| t_n(w_n) - 1 - \langle t'_n(0), w_n \rangle \right|}{\|w_n\|_D} < 1.$$

According to (6.13), the fact that $v_n \in \Lambda$ and the above, we deduce

$$\frac{1}{n}\|v_n - u_n\|_D \geqslant I(u_n) - I(v_n) \geqslant \langle I'(u_n), u_n - v_n \rangle - \frac{1}{n}\|u_n - v_n\|_D.$$

Thus, we have

$$\frac{2}{n}\|t_n(w_n)(u_n - w_n) - u_n\|_D$$

$$\geqslant (1 - t_n(w_n))\langle I'(u_n), u_n \rangle + t_n(w_n)\delta_n \left\langle I'(u_n), \frac{\nabla I(u_n)}{\|\nabla I(u_n)\|_D} \right\rangle$$

and

$$\frac{2}{n}\left[(|\langle t'_n(0), w_n \rangle| + \|w_n\|_D)\|u_n\|_D + t_n(w_n)\|w_n\|_D \right] \geqslant t_n(w_n)\delta_n\|\nabla I(u_n)\|_D.$$

Dividing by $\delta_n > 0$ on both left and right hand of the above inequality, we get

$$\frac{2}{n}\left[(|\langle t'_n(0), \frac{\nabla I(u_n)}{\|\nabla I(u_n)\|_D} \rangle| + 1)\|u_n\|_D + t_n(w_n) \right] \geqslant t_n(w_n)\|\nabla I(u_n)\|_D. \qquad (6.16)$$

Now, if there exists $\lambda > 0$ such that

$$\left| \|u_n\|_D^2 - (2 \cdot 2_\alpha^* - 1)B(u_n) \right| \geqslant \lambda,$$

we can get the claim. In fact,

$$\left| \langle t_n'(0), h_n \rangle \right|$$

$$= \left| \frac{\displaystyle\int_{\mathbb{R}^N} (2\nabla u_n \nabla h_n - h_n u_n)dx - 2 \cdot 2_\alpha^* \int_{\mathbb{R}^N} \int_{\mathbb{R}^N} \frac{|u_n(y)|^{2_\alpha^*}|u_n(x)|^{2_\alpha^*-2}u_n(x)h_n(x)}{|x-y|^\alpha}dxdy}{\|u_n\|_D^2 - (2 \cdot 2_\alpha^* - 1)B(u_n)} \right|$$

$$\leqslant \frac{C}{\lambda}.$$

Here, $h_n = \dfrac{\nabla I(u_n)}{\|\nabla I(u_n)\|_D}$ and we have used the uniformly boundedness of $\|u_n\|_D$. Consequently, as $n \to \infty$,

$$\frac{2}{n}\left[(|\langle t_n'(0), h_n \rangle| + 1)\|u_n\|_D + t_n(w_n) \right] \to 0.$$

So that, by passing to the limit as $n \to \infty$ in (6.16), we get a contradiction which implies the claim is true.

In order to show the existence of positive lower bound of

$$\left| \|u_n\|_D^2 - (2 \cdot 2_\alpha^* - 1)B(u_n) \right|,$$

we argue indirectly again and assume

$$\|u_n\|_D^2 - (2 \cdot 2_\alpha^* - 1)B(u_n) = o(1), \quad n \to \infty.$$

Here, $\{u_n\}$ is a subsequence still denoted by itself. Combining this and (6.14), similarly to the proof of Lemma 6.4(i), we can easily get a contradiction.

So that we conclude that, for a subsequence which we still denote by $\{u_n\}$,

$$I(u_n) \to c_0,$$

$$\|\nabla I(u_n)\|_D \to 0,$$

as $n \to \infty$. By (6.14) we know that $\{u_n\}$ is bounded in $D^{1,2}(\mathbb{R}^N)$, and the weak limit of $\{u_n\}$ which we denote by u_0 is a weak solution of system (6.3). Obviously,

$u_0 \in \Lambda$ and

$$c_0 \leqslant I(u_0) = \frac{1}{2}\|u_0\|_D^2 - \frac{1}{2 \cdot 2_\alpha^*}B(u_0) - C(u_0)$$

$$= \left(\frac{1}{2} - \frac{1}{2 \cdot 2_\alpha^*}\right)\|u_0\|_D^2 - \left(1 - \frac{1}{2 \cdot 2_\alpha^*}\right)C(u_0)$$

$$\leqslant \liminf I(u_n) = c_0.$$

Therefore, u_0 is a least energy solution.

By now, we only need to show that u_0 is a local minimum solution. We apply Lemma 6.3 to u_0 and $|u_0|$. Since

$$\frac{d}{dt}I(tu_0) = \varphi'_{u_0}(t) > 0, \quad t \in (t^+(u_0), t^-(u_0)),$$

we know that $u_0 \in \Lambda^+$. Otherwise, $u_0 \in \Lambda^-$ and $c_0 \leqslant I(t^+(u_0)u_0) < I(u_0) = c_0$ which is a contradiction. By Lemma 2.3 and $u_0 \in \Lambda^+$ we know that

$$1 = t^+(u_0) < t_0(u_0) = \left[\frac{\|u_0\|_D^2}{(2 \cdot 2_\alpha^* - 1)B(u_0)}\right]^{1/(2 \cdot 2_\alpha^* - 2)}.$$

Therefore

$$1 < \left[\frac{\|u_0 - w\|_D^2}{(2 \cdot 2_\alpha^* - 1)B(u_0 - w)}\right]^{1/(2 \cdot 2_\alpha^* - 2)}, \quad \|w\|_D < \varepsilon,$$

for ε small enough. Applying Lemma 6.5, we get a $t(w) > 0$ such that $t(w)(u_0 - w) \in \Lambda$ for $\|w\| < \varepsilon$ small. Moreover, there holds $t(w) \to 1$ as $w \to 0$. Thus we can assume that, for $\|w\| < \varepsilon$ sufficiently small,

$$t(w) < \left[\frac{\|u_0 - w\|_D^2}{(2 \cdot 2_\alpha^* - 1)B(u_0 - w)}\right]^{1/(2 \cdot 2_\alpha^* - 2)}, \quad t(w)(u_0 - w) \in \Lambda^+.$$

Then by Lemma 6.3, we could conclude that

$$I(u_0) \leqslant I(t(w)(u_0 - w)) \leqslant I(t(u_0 - w)), \tag{6.17}$$

for

$$0 < t < \left[\frac{\|u_0 - w\|_D^2}{(2 \cdot 2_\alpha^* - 1)B(u_0 - w)}\right]^{1/(2 \cdot 2_\alpha^* - 2)}.$$

Taking $t = 1$ in (6.17) we have

$$I(u_0) \leqslant I(u_0 - w), \quad \|w\|_D < \varepsilon,$$

which means u_0 is a local minimum solution.

Additionally, if we assume that $h > 0$,

$$\varphi'_{|u_0|}(t) < \varphi'_{u_0}(t) < 0, \quad t \in [0, 1).$$

Hence, $t^+(|u_0|) \geq 1$ and consequently,

$$c_0 \leq I(t^+(|u_0|)|u_0|) \leq I(|u_0|) \leq I(u_0) = c_0.$$

Therefore,

$$t^+(|u_0|) = 1 \quad \text{and} \quad \int_{\mathbb{R}^N} h(x)|u_0|dx = \int_{\mathbb{R}^N} h(x)u_0 dx,$$

which yield $u_0 \geq 0$. Then by the maximum principle, we know $u_0 > 0$. The proof is complete.   □

We remark here that since $c_0 < 0$, any solution u_0 of system (6.3) with the least energy c_0 satisfies

$$c_0 = I(u_0) = \frac{1}{2}\|u_0\|_D^2 - \frac{1}{2 \cdot 2_\alpha^*}B(u_0) - \int_{\mathbb{R}^N} h(x)u_0 dx$$

$$= \left(\frac{1}{2} - \frac{1}{2 \cdot 2_\alpha^*}\right)\|u_0\|_D^2 - \left(1 - \frac{1}{2 \cdot 2_\alpha^*}\right)\int_{\mathbb{R}^N} h(x)u_0 dx$$

$$< 0.$$

Thus, $\int_{\mathbb{R}^N} h(x)u_0 dx > 0$ and consequently, $u_0 \in \Lambda^+$.

Proposition 6.2 *Let $N \geq 3$ and $0 < \alpha < N$, (H_1) holds. If $\{u_n\}$ is a $(PS)_c$ sequence of I with*

$$c < c_0 + \frac{N+2-\alpha}{4N-2\alpha}S_{H,L}^{\frac{2N-\alpha}{N+2-\alpha}}, \tag{6.18}$$

then $\{u_n\}$ has a convergent subsequence.

Proof. Obviously, $\|u_n\|_D$ is bounded. In fact,

$$c + \|u_n\|_D \geq I(u_n) - \frac{1}{2 \cdot 2_\alpha^*}\langle I'(u_n), u_n \rangle$$

$$= \frac{1}{2}\|u_n\|_D^2 - \frac{1}{2 \cdot 2_\alpha^*}B(u_n) - C(u_n)$$

$$- \frac{1}{2 \cdot 2_\alpha^*}\|u_n\|_D^2 + \frac{1}{2 \cdot 2_\alpha^*}B(u_n) + \frac{1}{2 \cdot 2_\alpha^*}C(u_n)$$

$$\geq \frac{1}{2}\left(1 - \frac{1}{2_\alpha^*}\right)\|u_n\|_D^2 - (1 - \frac{1}{2 \cdot 2_\alpha^*})\|h\|_{H^{-1}}\|u_n\|_D.$$

Thus, there exists a $w \in D^{1,2}(\mathbb{R}^N)$ which satisfies $u_n \rightharpoonup w$ weakly in $D^{1,2}(\mathbb{R}^N)$ and solves (6.3). Therefore, $w \neq 0$ and $I(w) \geqslant c_0$. Let $u_n - w = v_n$, by Brezis-Lieb lemma in [35] and Lemmas 2.1 and 2.2 in [94], we deduce

$$\|u_n\|_D^2 = \|v_n\|_D^2 + \|w\|_D^2 + o(1), \quad n \to \infty$$

and

$$\int_{\mathbb{R}^N} \int_{\mathbb{R}^N} \frac{|u_n(x)|^{2_\alpha^*} |u_n(y)|^{2_\alpha^*}}{|x-y|^\alpha} dx dy$$

$$= \int_{\mathbb{R}^N} \int_{\mathbb{R}^N} \frac{|v_n(x)|^{2_\alpha^*} |v_n(y)|^{2_\alpha^*}}{|x-y|^\alpha} dx dy + \int_{\mathbb{R}^N} \int_{\mathbb{R}^N} \frac{|w(x)|^{2_\alpha^*} |w(y)|^{2_\alpha^*}}{|x-y|^\alpha} dx dy + o_n(1)$$

as $n \to \infty$. So we obtain

$$c \leftarrow I(u_n)$$

$$= \frac{1}{2}\|u_n\|_D^2 - \frac{1}{2 \cdot 2_\alpha^*} \int_{\mathbb{R}^N} \int_{\mathbb{R}^N} \frac{|u_n(x)|^{2_\alpha^*} |u_n(y)|^{2_\alpha^*}}{|x-y|^\alpha} dx dy - \int_{\mathbb{R}^N} h(x) u_n dx$$

$$= \frac{1}{2}\|v_n\|_D^2 - \frac{1}{2 \cdot 2_\alpha^*} \int_{\mathbb{R}^N} \int_{\mathbb{R}^N} \frac{|v_n(x)|^{2_\alpha^*} |v_n(y)|^{2_\alpha^*}}{|x-y|^\alpha} dx dy - \int_{\mathbb{R}^N} h(x) v_n dx$$

$$+ \frac{1}{2}\|w\|_D^2 - \frac{1}{2 \cdot 2_\alpha^*} \int_{\mathbb{R}^N} \int_{\mathbb{R}^N} \frac{|w(x)|^{2_\alpha^*} |w(y)|^{2_\alpha^*}}{|x-y|^\alpha} dx dy - \int_{\mathbb{R}^N} h(x) w dx + o_n(1)$$

$$= I(w) + \frac{1}{2}\|v_n\|_D^2 - \frac{1}{2 \cdot 2_\alpha^*} B(v_n) + o_n(1).$$

As the result, for n large we have

$$\frac{1}{2}\|v_n\|_D^2 - \frac{1}{2 \cdot 2_\alpha^*} B(v_n) + o_n(1) < \frac{N+2-\alpha}{4N-2\alpha} S_{H,L}^{\frac{2N-\alpha}{N+2-\alpha}}. \tag{6.19}$$

On the other hand,

$$o(1) = \langle I'(u_n), u_n \rangle = \langle I'(w), w \rangle + \|v_n\|_D^2 - B(v_n) + o(1),$$

which implies

$$\|v_n\|_D^2 - B(v_n) = o(1). \tag{6.20}$$

If we can show that $\{v_n\}$ has subsequence converging strong to 0, we have done. Therefore, arguing indirectly, we assume $\|v_n\|_D \geqslant c > 0$ for n large. According to (6.20), the definition of $S_{H,L}$ and $\dfrac{2_\alpha^*}{2_\alpha^* - 1} = \dfrac{2N-\alpha}{N+2-\alpha}$, we have

$$\|v_n\|_D^2 = B(v_n) + o(1) \leqslant \frac{\|v_n\|_D^{2 \cdot 2_\alpha^*}}{S_{H,L}^{2_\alpha^*}}$$

and

$$\frac{1}{2}\frac{N+2-\alpha}{2N-\alpha}S_{H,L}^{\frac{2N-\alpha}{N+2-\alpha}} = \frac{1}{2}\frac{2^*_\alpha-1}{2^*_\alpha}S_{H,L}^{\frac{2N-\alpha}{N+2-\alpha}}$$

$$\leqslant \frac{1}{2}\frac{2^*_\alpha-1}{2^*_\alpha}\|v_n\|_D^2$$

$$= \frac{1}{2}\|v_n\|_D^2 - \frac{1}{2}\frac{1}{2^*_\alpha}B(v_n) + o_n(1)$$

$$< \frac{N+2-\alpha}{2(2N-\alpha)}S_{H,L}^{\frac{2N-\alpha}{N+2-\alpha}},$$

which is a contradiction. The proof is complete.   □

We remark again, in order to find the second solution of (6.3), the only we need to show is that

$$c_0 < c_1 = \inf_{\Lambda^-} I(u) < c_0 + \frac{N+2-\alpha}{4N-2\alpha}S_{H,L}^{\frac{2N-\alpha}{N+2-\alpha}}.$$

By the continuity of I and Lemma 6.2, we know that there exists $\delta > 0$ such that

$$I(u_0 + tW) < c_0 + \frac{N+2-\alpha}{4N-2\alpha}S_{H,L}^{\frac{2N-\alpha}{N+2-\alpha}}, \quad 0 \leqslant t < \delta,$$

u_0 is the positive local minimum solution we get in Proposition 6.1. For $t \geqslant \delta$, a directly computation shows us

$$I(u_0 + tW) = \frac{1}{2}\|u_0 + tW\|_D^2 - \frac{1}{2\cdot2^*_\alpha}B(u_0 + tW) - \int_{\mathbb{R}^N}h(u_0 + tW)dx$$

$$= \frac{1}{2}\|u_0\|_D^2 + t\int_{\mathbb{R}^N}\nabla u_0\nabla W dx + \frac{t^2}{2}\|W\|_D^2 - \frac{1}{2\cdot2^*_\alpha}B(u_0)$$

$$+ \frac{1}{2\cdot2^*_\alpha}[B(u_0) + B(tW) - B(u_0 + tW)] - \frac{1}{2\cdot2^*_\alpha}B(tW)$$

$$- \int_{\mathbb{R}^N}hu_0 dx - \int_{\mathbb{R}^N}htW dx$$

$$= I(u_0) + \frac{t^2}{2}[\|W\|_D^2 - \frac{t^{2(2^*_\alpha-1)}}{2\cdot2^*_\alpha}B(W)] + \frac{1}{2\cdot2^*_\alpha}[B(u_0) + B(tW)$$

$$- B(u_0 + tW) + 2\cdot2^*_\alpha\int_{\mathbb{R}^N}\int_{\mathbb{R}^N}\frac{|u_0(x)|^{2^*_\alpha}|u_0(y)|^{2^*_\alpha-2}u_0(y)}{|x-y|^\alpha}dxdy]$$

$$< c_0 + \frac{N+2-\alpha}{4N-2\alpha}S_{H,L}^{\frac{2N-\alpha}{N+2-\alpha}}.$$

Here, we use the fact that $\langle I'(u_0), tW\rangle = 0$ and W is a minimizer of $S_{H,L}$.

And now we can give the proof of Theorem 6.1.

Proof of Theorem 6.1   Firstly, we show

$$c_0 < c_1 = \inf_{\Lambda^-} I(u) < c_0 + \frac{N+2-\alpha}{4N-2\alpha} S_{H,L}^{\frac{2N-\alpha}{N+2-\alpha}}.$$

We observe that for every $u \in D^{1,2}(\mathbb{R}^N)$ with $\|u\|_D = 1$, there exists a unique $t^-(u) > 0$ such that (see Lemma 6.3)

$$t^-(u)u \in \Lambda^-.$$

Similar to Lemma 6.5, we know that $t^-(u)$ is a continuous function of u. And consequently the manifold Λ^- disconnects $D^{1,2}(\mathbb{R}^N)$ in exactly two connected components U_1 and U_2, where

$$U_1 = \left\{ u \in D^{1,2}(\mathbb{R}^N) : u = 0 \text{ or } \|u\|_D < t^- \left(\frac{u}{\|u\|_D} \right) \right\}$$

and

$$U_2 = \left\{ u \in D^{1,2}(\mathbb{R}^N) : \|u\|_D > t^- \left(\frac{u}{\|u\|_D} \right) \right\}.$$

Obviously, $D^{1,2}(\mathbb{R}^N) = \Lambda^- \cup U_1 \cup U_2$. In particular, $u_0 \in \Lambda^+ \subset U_1$. Since

$$t^- \left(\frac{u_0 + tW}{\|u_0 + tW\|_D} \right) \frac{u_0 + tW}{\|u_0 + tW\|_D} \in \Lambda,$$

we have

$$0 < t^- \left(\frac{u_0 + tW}{\|u_0 + tW\|_D} \right) < C_0,$$

uniformly for $t \in \mathbb{R}$.

On the other hand, there exists a $\tilde{t} > 0$ satisfies

$$\|u_0 + tW\|_D \geq t\|W\|_D - \|u_0\|_D \geq C_0, \quad t \geq \tilde{t}.$$

So we can fix a $t_0 > 0$ such that

$$\|u_0 + t_0 W\|_D > t^- \left(\frac{u_0 + t_0 W}{\|u_0 + t_0 W\|_D} \right).$$

Thus, $u_0 + t_0 W \in U_2$. Combining this and the fact $u_0 \in U_1$, we know that

$$u_0 + t_1 W \in \Lambda^-,$$

for some $0 < t_1 < t_0$. Consequently, by the remark after Proposition 6.2, we have

$$c_1 = \inf_{\Lambda^-} I(u) \leqslant \max_{0 \leqslant t \leqslant t_0} I(u_0 + tW) < c_0 + \frac{N+2-\alpha}{4N-2\alpha} S_{H,L}^{\frac{2N-\alpha}{N+2-\alpha}}.$$

Next, we show that c_1 is a critical value of I and satisfies $c_1 > c_0$. Similarly to the proof of Proposition 6.1, we apply Ekeland's Variational Principle and get a minimizing sequence $\{u_n\} \subset \Lambda^-$ such that

$$I(u_n) < c_1 + \frac{1}{n},$$

$$I(w) \geqslant I(u_n) - \frac{1}{n}\|u - w\|_D, \quad w \in \Lambda^-.$$

So we have

$$c_1 + 1 > I(u_n) = \frac{1}{2}\|u_n\|_D^2 - \frac{1}{2 \cdot 2_\alpha^*} B(u_n) - \int_{\mathbb{R}^N} h(x)u_n dx$$

$$\geqslant \left(\frac{1}{2} - \frac{1}{2 \cdot 2_\alpha^*}\right)\|u_n\|_D^2 - \left(1 - \frac{1}{2 \cdot 2_\alpha^*}\right)\|h\|_{H^{-1}}\|u_n\|_D,$$

which implies $\|u_n\|$ has a upper bound. Moreover, from $\{u_n\} \subset \Lambda^-$, we know that

$$\|u_n\|_D^2 \leqslant (2 \cdot 2_\alpha^* - 1)\frac{\|u_n\|_D^{2_\alpha^*}}{S_{H,L}^{2_\alpha^*}}.$$

Thus, $\|u_n\|_D$ has a uniform positive lower bound. Then, analogously to the proof of Proposition 6.1, we know that

$$I(u_n) \to c_1,$$

$$I'(u_n) \to 0 \quad \text{in} \quad H^{-1}.$$

According to Proposition 6.1 and $c_1 < c_0 + \dfrac{N+2-\alpha}{4N-2\alpha} S_{H,L}^{\frac{2N-\alpha}{N+2-\alpha}}$, we can conclude that there exists a subsequence of $\{u_n\}$ such that $u_n \to u_1$ strongly in $D^{1,2}(\mathbb{R}^N)$. Therefore u_1 is a critical point of I and $I(u_1) = c_1$. Noting that Λ^- is closed, we have $u_1 \in \Lambda^-$. To show $c_1 > c_0$, arguing indirectly, we assume $c_1 = c_0$. Thus by the remark after the proof of Proposition 6.1, we have

$$\int_{\mathbb{R}^N} h(x)u_1 dx > 0, \quad u_1 \in \Lambda^+,$$

which leads to a contradiction.

Finally, we consider the case $h > 0$. Apply Lemma 6.3 to u_1 and $|u_1|$, we know that there exist a $t^-(|u_1|)$ such that

$$t^-(|u_1|)|u_1| \in \Lambda^-.$$

Moreover,

$$t^-(|u_1|) \geqslant t_0(|u_1|) = t_0(u_1) = \left[\frac{A(u_1)}{(2_\alpha^* - 1)B(u_1)}\right]^{\frac{1}{2_\alpha^* - 2}}.$$

Thus both in the case $\int_{\mathbb{R}^N} h(x)u dx > 0$ and $\int_{\mathbb{R}^N} h(x)u dx \leqslant 0$, we can deduce that

$$c_1 = I(u_1) \geqslant I(t^-(u_1)u_1) \geqslant I(t^-(|u_1|)|u_1|) = t_0(u_1) \geqslant c_1.$$

Therefore,

$$\int_{\mathbb{R}^N} h(x)u_1 dx = \int_{\mathbb{R}^N} h(x)|u_1| dx,$$

which implies $u_1 \geqslant 0$. According to the maximum principle we get $u_1 > 0$. The proof is complete. □

6.4   The proof of Theorem 6.2

In order to prove Theorem 6.2, we define the energy functional associated to

$$-\Delta u + u = \left(\frac{1}{|x|^\alpha} * |u|^p\right)|u|^{p-2}u + h(x), \quad x \in \mathbb{R}^N, \tag{6.21}$$

where $N \geqslant 3$, $0 < \alpha < N$ and $2 - \dfrac{\alpha}{N} < p < 2_\alpha^*$, by

$$J(u) = \frac{1}{2}\int_{\mathbb{R}^N} |\nabla u|^2 + u^2 dx - \frac{1}{2p}\int_{\mathbb{R}^N}\int_{\mathbb{R}^N} \frac{|u(x)|^p|u(y)|^p}{|x-y|^\alpha} dx dy - \int_{\mathbb{R}^N} h(x)u dx, \tag{6.22}$$

for $u \in H^1(\mathbb{R}^N)$.

By the Hardy-Littlewood-Sobolev inequality of Lemma 6.1, we know $J \in C^1(H^1(\mathbb{R}^N), \mathbb{R})$ and

$$\langle J'(u), v\rangle = \int_{\mathbb{R}^N} (|\nabla u||\nabla v| + uv)dx - \int_{\mathbb{R}^N}\int_{\mathbb{R}^N} \frac{|u(x)|^p|u(y)|^{p-2}u(y)v(y)}{|x-y|^\alpha}dx dy$$

$$- \int_{\mathbb{R}^N} h(x)v dx.$$

We will constrain the function J on the Nehari manifold

$$\mathcal{N} = \{u \in H^1(\mathbb{R}^N), \langle J'(u), u\rangle = 0\}. \tag{6.23}$$

Denote $\Psi(u) = \langle J'(u), u \rangle$, so we know that

$$\langle J'(u), u \rangle = \|u\|^2 - \int_{\mathbb{R}^N} \int_{\mathbb{R}^N} \frac{|u(x)|^p |u(y)|^p}{|x - y|^\alpha} \, dx dy - \int_{\mathbb{R}^N} h(x) u \, dx$$

and

$$\langle \Psi'(u), u \rangle = 2\|u\|^2 - 2p \int_{\mathbb{R}^N} \int_{\mathbb{R}^N} \frac{|u(x)|^p |u(y)|^p}{|x - y|^\alpha} \, dx dy - \int_{\mathbb{R}^N} h(x) u \, dx.$$

Notice that, when u_0 is a local minimum solution of J, there holds

$$\langle J'(u), u \rangle = 0,$$

$$\langle \Psi'(u), u \rangle \geqslant 0,$$

which leads us to consider the following manifolds:

$$\mathcal{N} = \{u \in H^1(\mathbb{R}^N) : \langle J'(u), u \rangle = 0\},$$

$$\mathcal{N}^+ = \{u \in \mathcal{N} : \langle \Psi'(u), u \rangle > 0\},$$

$$\mathcal{N}^- = \{u \in \mathcal{N} : \langle \Psi'(u), u \rangle < 0\},$$

$$\mathcal{N}^0 = \{u \in \mathcal{N} : \langle \Psi'(u), u \rangle = 0\}.$$

Moreover, we define j_0, j_1 and j^+ by

$$j_0 = \inf_{\mathcal{N}} J(u), \quad j_1 = \inf_{\mathcal{N}^-} J(u), \quad j^+ = \inf_{\mathcal{N}^+} J(u).$$

Obviously, only $\mathcal{N}^0$ contains the element 0. Furthermore, it is easy to see that $\mathcal{N}^0 \cup \mathcal{N}^+$ and $\mathcal{N}^0 \cup \mathcal{N}^-$ are both closed subsets of $H^1(\mathbb{R}^N)$.

In order to simplify the calculation, for $u \in H^1(\mathbb{R}^N)$, we denote

$$\tilde{A} = \tilde{A}(u) = \|u\|^2,$$

$$\tilde{B} = \tilde{B}(u) = \int_{\mathbb{R}^N} \int_{\mathbb{R}^N} \frac{|u(x)|^p |u(y)|^p}{|x - y|^\alpha} \, dx dy,$$

$$\tilde{C} = \tilde{C}(u) = \int_{\mathbb{R}^N} h(x) u \, dx.$$

Define the fibering map

$$\psi(t) = \psi_u(t) := J(tu) = \frac{\tilde{A}}{2} t^2 - \frac{\tilde{B}}{2p} t^{2p} - \tilde{C} t, \quad t > 0. \tag{6.24}$$

Therefore,

$$\psi'(t) = \tilde{A}t - \tilde{B}t^{2p-1} - \tilde{C},$$

$$\psi''(t) = \tilde{A} - (2p-1)\tilde{B}t^{2p-2}. \tag{6.25}$$

Obviously, $tu \in \mathcal{N}$ with $t > 0$ if and only if $\psi'(t) = 0$. By the sign of $\psi''(t)$, the stationary points of $\psi(t)$ can be classified into three types, namely local minimum, local maximum and turning point. Moreover, the set $\mathcal{N}$ is a natural constraint for the functional J. This means that if the infimum is attained by $u \in \mathcal{N}$, then u is a solution of (6.4). However, in our case, the global maximum point of $\psi(t)$ is not unique. This leads us to partition the set $\mathcal{N}$ according to the critical points of $\psi(t)$.

Now we give some properties of $\mathcal{N}^{\pm}$ and $\mathcal{N}^0$.

Lemma 6.6   *Assume that $h \not\equiv 0$ for $u \in H^1(\mathbb{R}^N)\backslash\{0\}$, there is a unique $\tilde{t}^- = \tilde{t}^-(u) > 0$ such that $\tilde{t}^- u \in \mathcal{N}^-$. And if additionally we assume $\int_{\mathbb{R}^N} hu\, dx > 0$ and (H_3), there exists $\varepsilon = \varepsilon(N, p, \alpha, d_{\frac{2Np}{2N-\alpha}})$ and a unique $0 < \tilde{t}^+ = \tilde{t}^+(u) < \tilde{t}^-$ satisfying $\tilde{t}^+ u \in \mathcal{N}^+$. Moreover,*

$$J(\tilde{t}^- u) = \max_{t \geqslant 0} J(tu), \quad for \int_{\mathbb{R}^N} hu\, dx \leqslant 0;$$

$$J(\tilde{t}^- u) = \max_{t \geqslant \tilde{t}^+} J(tu), \quad J(\tilde{t}^+ u) = \min_{0 \leqslant t \leqslant \tilde{t}^-} J(tu), \quad for \int_{\mathbb{R}^N} hu\, dx > 0.$$

Proof. Define

$$\psi(t) = \frac{\tilde{A}}{2}t^2 - \frac{\tilde{B}}{2 \cdot p}t^{2p} - \tilde{C}t, \quad \text{for all } t > 0.$$

In the case $\int_{\mathbb{R}^N} hu\, dx \leqslant 0$, there is a unique $\tilde{t}^- > 0$ such that $\psi'(\tilde{t}^-) = 0$ and $\psi''(\tilde{t}^-) < 0$. So that

$$\langle J'(\tilde{t}^- u), \tilde{t}^- u \rangle = 0,$$

$$\|\tilde{t}^- u\|^2 - (2p-1)\tilde{B}(u)(\tilde{t}^-)^{2p-2} < 0.$$

Thus, $\tilde{t}^- u \in \mathcal{N}^-$ and $J(\tilde{t}^- u) = \max_{t \geqslant 0} J(tu)$.

In the case $\int_{\mathbb{R}^N} hu\, dx > 0$, for $\|u\| = 1, \tilde{t}_0 = \tilde{t}_0(u) = \left[\frac{1}{(2p-1)\tilde{B}}\right]^{\frac{1}{2p-2}} > 0$ and

(H_3), we have

$$\max_{t \geqslant 0} \psi'(t) \geqslant t_0 - \tilde{B}t_0^{2p-1} - \tilde{C}$$

$$= \left[\frac{1}{(2p-1)\tilde{B}}\right]^{\frac{1}{2p-2}} \cdot \frac{2p-2}{2p-1} - \int_{\mathbb{R}^N} hu dx$$

$$\geqslant \left[\frac{2p-2}{(2p-1)^{2p-1/(2p-2)}B_0^{1/2p-2}} - |h|_{\frac{2Np}{2N(p-1)+\alpha}} d_{\frac{2Np}{2N-\alpha}}\right]$$

$$> 0.$$

Here

$$\varepsilon(N, p, \alpha, d_{\frac{2Np}{2N-\alpha}}) = \frac{2p-2}{(2p-1)^{2p-1/(2p-2)}B_0^{1/2p-2}} d_{\frac{2Np}{2N-\alpha}}$$

and

$$B_0 = \sup_{\|u\|=1} \int_{\mathbb{R}^N} \int_{\mathbb{R}^N} \frac{|u(x)|^p|u(y)|^p}{|x-y|^\alpha} dx dy.$$

According to $\psi'(0) = -\tilde{C} < 0$ and $\psi'(t) \to -\infty$ as $t \to +\infty$, we know that there exist unique $0 < \tilde{t}^+ < \tilde{t}_0 < \tilde{t}^-$ such that

$$\psi'(\tilde{t}^-) = \psi'(\tilde{t}^+) = 0, \quad \psi''(\tilde{t}^-) < 0 < \psi''(\tilde{t}^+).$$

Equivalently, $\tilde{t}^+u \in \mathcal{N}^+$ and $\tilde{t}^-u \in \mathcal{N}^-$.

Moreover, since $\dfrac{d}{dt}J(tu) = \psi'(t)$, we can easily see that $J(\tilde{t}^-u) = \max_{t \geqslant \tilde{t}^+} J(tu)$ and $J(\tilde{t}^+u) = \min_{0 \leqslant t \leqslant \tilde{t}^-} J(tu)$. The proof is complete. □

Lemma 6.7　Assume that $h \not\equiv 0$, (H_2) and (H_3) hold, then
(i) $\mathcal{N}^0 = \{0\}$;
(ii) $\mathcal{N}^\pm \neq \varnothing, \mathcal{N}^-$ is closed.

Proof. (i) In order to prove $\mathcal{N}^0 = \{0\}$, we need to prove that, for $u \in H^1(\mathbb{R}^N) \setminus \{0\}$, $\tilde{\varphi}(t)$ has no critical point that is a turning point. Set $\|u\| = 1$, define

$$k(t) = \tilde{A}t - \tilde{B}t^{2p-1}. \tag{6.26}$$

Then

$$\psi'(t) = k(t) - \tilde{C}, \quad k''(t) = -\tilde{B}(2p-1)(2p-2)t^{2p-3} < 0, \quad \text{for } t > 0.$$

So $k(t)$ is strictly concave. If

$$k''(\tilde{t}_0) = 0, \quad \tilde{t}_0 = \left(\frac{\tilde{A}}{(2p-1)\tilde{B}}\right)^{1/(2p-2)} > 0, \quad \text{for } p > 2 - \frac{\alpha}{N} > 1.$$

Moreover, $\lim\limits_{t\to 0^+} k(t) = 0$, $\lim\limits_{t\to +\infty} k(t) = -\infty$ and $k(t) > 0$ for $t > 0$ small. Therefore, we have that $k(t)$ has a unique global maximum points t_0 and

$$k(t_0) = \frac{2\tilde{A}(2p-1)}{2p-1}\left(\frac{\tilde{A}}{(2p-1)\tilde{B}}\right)^{1/(2p-2)} := k_0.$$

By (6.24) and (6.25), we infer that if $0 < \tilde{C} < k_0$, the equation $\psi'(t) = 0$ has exactly two points $\tilde{t}_1, \tilde{t}_2$ satisfying $\tilde{t}_1 < \tilde{t}_0 < \tilde{t}_2$. If $\tilde{C} \leqslant 0$, the equation $\psi'(t) = 0$ has one root $\tilde{t}_3 > \tilde{t}_0$. Since

$$\psi''(t) = \tilde{A} - (2p-1)\tilde{B}t^{2p-2},$$

it follows that $\psi''(\tilde{t}_1) > 0, \psi''(\tilde{t}_2) < 0$ and $\psi''(\tilde{t}_3) < 0$. It follows that $\tilde{t}_1 u \in \mathcal{N}^+, \tilde{t}_2 u \in \mathcal{N}^-$ if $0 < \tilde{C} < k_0$ and $\tilde{t}_3 u \in \mathcal{N}^-$ if $\tilde{C} \leqslant 0$. Since

$$\{u \in H^1(\mathbb{R}^N) : \|u\| = 1, 0 < \tilde{C} < k_0\}$$

and

$$\{u \in H^1(\mathbb{R}^N) : \|u\| = 1, \tilde{C} \leqslant 0\}$$

are nonempty, we can infer that $\mathcal{N}^\pm$ are nonempty. This implies $\mathcal{N}^0 = \{0\}$.

It is suffices to prove $k_0 > \tilde{C}$. By (H_2), (H_3) and Lemma 6.6 we have

$$k_0 - \tilde{C} = k(t_0) - \tilde{C} = \tilde{A}t_0 - \tilde{B}t_0^{2p-1} - \tilde{C} > 0.$$

(ii) Let $u \in \mathcal{N}^-$, denote $\tilde{u} = \dfrac{u}{\|u\|}$, then $\|\tilde{u}\| = 1$. By (i), we know that

$$\tilde{C}(\tilde{u}) < k_0 = \frac{2(p-1)}{2p-1}\left(\frac{1}{(2p-1)\tilde{B}}\right)^{1/(2p-1)}$$

with $\tilde{B} := B(\tilde{u})$. Furthermore, if $0 < \tilde{C}(\tilde{u}) < \kappa_0$, the equation $\psi'(t) = 0$ has exactly two roots $\tilde{t}_1, \tilde{t}_2$ satisfying $0 < \tilde{t}_1 < t_0 < \tilde{t}_2$ such that $\tilde{t}_1 u \in \mathcal{N}^+, \tilde{t}_2 u \in \mathcal{N}^-$. Then $\tilde{t}_2\tilde{u} = u$ and so $\|u\| = \tilde{t}_2 > \tilde{t}_0$. If $\tilde{C} \leqslant 0$, the equation $\psi'(t) = 0$ has exactly one root $\tilde{t}_3 > \tilde{t}_0$. Then $\tilde{t}_3\tilde{u} = u \in \mathcal{N}^-$ and so $\|u\| = \tilde{t}_3 > \tilde{t}_0$. In a word,

$$\|u\| > \tilde{t}_0 > 0, \quad u \in \mathcal{N}^-.$$

So there exists a $\tau > 0$ such that

$$\|u\| > \tau > 0, \quad \forall u \in \mathcal{N}^-. \tag{6.27}$$

Therefore, $0 \notin \mathrm{cl}(\mathcal{N}^-)$, where $\mathrm{cl}(\mathcal{N}^-)$ is the closure of $\mathcal{N}^-$. On the other hand, by (i),

$$\mathrm{cl}(\mathcal{N}^-) \subset \mathcal{N}^- \cup \mathcal{N}^0 = \mathcal{N}^- \cup \{0\}.$$

Hence, $\mathrm{cl}(\mathcal{N}^-) = \mathcal{N}^-$ and $\mathcal{N}^-$ is closed. The proof is complete.   □

Lemma 6.8   *Under assumption (H_2) and (H_3), for $u \in \mathcal{N} \setminus \{0\}$, there exists a $\epsilon > 0$ and a differential function $\eta = \eta(w) > 0, w \in H^1(\mathbb{R}^N), \|w\| < \epsilon$ such that*

(i) $\eta(0) = 1$;

(ii) $\eta(w)(u - w) \in \mathcal{N}$, *for all* $w \in B_\epsilon(0)$;

(iii)

$$\langle \eta'(0), w \rangle$$

$$= \frac{2 \int_{\mathbb{R}^N} (\nabla u \nabla w + uw) dx - 2p \int_{\mathbb{R}^N} \int_{\mathbb{R}^N} \frac{|u(y)|^{2p} |u(x)|^{p-2} u(x) w(x)}{|x - y|^\alpha} dx dy - \int_{\mathbb{R}^N} hw dx}{\|u\|^2 - (2p - 1)\tilde{B}(u)}.$$

Proposition 6.3   *Assume (H_2) and (H_3) hold, then (6.4) has a local minimum solution with the least energy $j_0 = \inf_{\mathcal{N}} J(u)$.*

Proof. Firstly, we will show that $\|u\|$ is bounded from both above and below. For any $u \in \mathcal{N}$,

$$J(u) = \frac{1}{2}\|u\|^2 - \frac{1}{2p}\tilde{B}(u) - \tilde{C}(u)$$

$$= \left(\frac{1}{2} - \frac{1}{2p}\right)\|u\|^2 - \left(1 - \frac{1}{2p}\right)\int_{\mathbb{R}^N} h(x)u dx$$

$$\geqslant \frac{p-1}{2p}\|u\|^2 - \frac{2p-1}{2p}|h|_{\frac{2Np}{2N(p-1)+\alpha}} d_{\frac{2Np}{2N-\alpha}}\|u\|$$

$$\geqslant -\frac{(2p-1)^2}{8p(p-1)}\|h\|^2_{\frac{2Np}{2N-\alpha}}. \tag{6.28}$$

Thus,

$$j_0 \geqslant -\frac{(2p-1)^2}{8p(p-1)}\|h\|^2_{\frac{2Np}{2N-\alpha}}.$$

Similar to the proof of Proposition 6.1, we can prove $j_0 < 0$. By using the Ekeland's Variational Principle on $\mathcal{N}$, we get a minimizing sequence $\{u_n\} \subset \mathcal{N}$ which satisfies

$$J(u_n) < j_0 + \frac{1}{n},$$

$$\tag{6.29}$$

$$J(w) \geqslant J(u_n) - \frac{1}{n}\|u - w\|, \quad w \in \mathcal{N}.$$

Since $\{u_n\} \subset \mathcal{N}$, it follows that $\|u_n\|^2 = \tilde{B}(u_n) + \tilde{C}(u_n)$. Furthermore, we infer from (6.29) that

$$j_0 + \frac{1}{n} \geqslant J(u_n) = \left(\frac{1}{2} - \frac{1}{2p}\right)\|u_n\|^2 - \left(1 - \frac{1}{2p}\right)\int_{\mathbb{R}^N} h(x)u_n dx$$

$$\geqslant \left(\frac{1}{2} - \frac{1}{2p}\right)\|u_n\|^2 - \left(1 - \frac{1}{2p}\right)|h|_{\frac{2Np}{2N(p-1)+\alpha}} d_{\frac{2Np}{2N-\alpha}}\|u_n\|. \tag{6.30}$$

We know that $\{u_n\}$ is bounded. We claim that $\inf_n \|u_n\| \geqslant \sigma_1 > 0$, which σ_1 is a positive constant. Indeed, if not, by (6.30), $J(u_n)$ would converge to zero. We can infer that $j_0 \geqslant 0$ which is contradict with $j_0 < 0$. So we have

$$\sigma_1 \leqslant \|u_n\| \leqslant \delta_1. \tag{6.31}$$

Secondly, we claim that, for a subsequence of $\{u_n\}$ (still denoted by $\{u_n\}$), $\|\nabla J(u_n)\| \to 0$ as $n \to \infty$.

In fact, if the claim is false, we could assume

$$\|\nabla J(u_n)\| \geqslant d > 0, \text{ for } n \text{ large enough.}$$

Consequently, according to Lemma 6.8, for u_n there exist ϵ_n and differentiable η_n satisfying

$$\eta_n(0) = 1, \quad \eta_n(w)(u_n - w) \in \mathcal{N}, \quad \|w\| < \epsilon_n$$

and

$$\langle \eta_n'(0), w \rangle$$

$$= \frac{2\int_{\mathbb{R}^N}(\nabla u_n \nabla w + u_n w)dx - 2p\int_{\mathbb{R}^N}\int_{\mathbb{R}^N}\frac{|u_n(y)|^p|u_n(x)|^{p-2}u_n(x)w(x)}{|x-y|^\alpha}dxdy - \int_{\mathbb{R}^N} hwdx}{\|u_n\|^2 - (2p-1)\tilde{B}(u_n)}.$$

We choose

$$w_n = \delta_n \frac{\nabla J(u_n)}{\|\nabla J(u_n)\|}, \quad v_n = \eta_n(w_n)(u_n - w_n),$$

where $0 < \delta_n < \epsilon_n$ is sufficiently small satisfying $\delta_n \to 0$, $\eta_n(w_n) \to 1$ as $n \to \infty$ and

$$\frac{\left|J(v_n) - J(u_n) - \langle J'(u_n), v_n - u_n \rangle\right|}{\|u_n - v_n\|} < \frac{1}{n},$$

$$\frac{\left|\eta(w_n) - 1 - \langle \eta_n'(0), w_n \rangle\right|}{\|w_n\|} < 1.$$

According to (6.28), the fact that $v_n \in \mathcal{N}$ and the above, we deduce

$$\frac{1}{n}\|v_n - u_n\| \geqslant J(u_n) - J(v_n) \geqslant \langle J'(u_n), u_n - v_n \rangle - \frac{1}{n}\|u_n - v_n\|.$$

Thus, we have

$$\frac{2}{n}\|\eta_n(w_n)(u_n - w_n) - u_n\|$$

$$\geqslant (1 - \eta_n(w_n))\langle J'(u_n), u_n\rangle + \eta_n(w_n)\delta_n\left\langle J'(u_n), \frac{\nabla J(u_n)}{\|\nabla J(u_n)\|}\right\rangle,$$

and

$$\frac{2}{n}\left[(|\langle \eta_n'(0), w_n\rangle| + \|w_n\|)\|u_n\| + \eta_n(w_n)\|w_n\|\right] \geqslant \eta_n(w_n)\delta_n\|\nabla J(u_n)\|.$$

Dividing by $\delta_n > 0$ on both left and right hand of the above inequality, we get

$$\frac{2}{n}\left[(|\langle \eta_n'(0), \frac{\nabla J(u_n)}{\|\nabla J(u_n)\|}\rangle| + 1)\|u_n\| + \eta_n(w_n)\right] \geqslant \eta_n(w_n)\|\nabla J(u_n)\|. \tag{6.32}$$

Now, if there exists $\lambda > 0$ such that

$$\left|\|u_n\|^2 - (2p - 1)\tilde{B}(u_n)\right| \geqslant \lambda,$$

we can get the claim. In fact,

$$\left|\langle \eta_n'(0), h_n\rangle\right|$$

$$= \left|\frac{2(u_n, h_n) - \int_{\mathbb{R}^N} h_n u_n - 2p\int_{\mathbb{R}^N}\int_{\mathbb{R}^N}\dfrac{|u_n(y)|^p|u_n(x)|^{p-2}u_n(x)h_n(x)}{|x - y|^\alpha}dxdy}{\|u_n\|^2 - (2p - 1)\tilde{B}(u_n)}\right|$$

$$\leqslant \frac{\tilde{C}}{\lambda}.$$

Here, $h_n = \dfrac{\nabla J(u_n)}{\|\nabla J(u_n)\|}$ and we have used the uniformly boundedness of $\|u_n\|$.

Consequently, as $n \to \infty$,

$$\frac{2}{n}\left[(|\langle \eta_n'(0), h_n\rangle| + 1)\|u_n\| + \eta_n(w_n)\right] \to 0.$$

So that, by passing to the limit as $n \to \infty$ in (6.32), we get a contradiction which implies the claim is true.

In order to show the existence of positive lower bound of $\left|\|u_n\|^2 - (2p-1)\tilde{B}(u_n)\right|$, we argue indirectly again and assume

$$\|u_n\|^2 - (2p - 1)\tilde{B}(u_n) = o(1), \quad n \to \infty.$$

Here, $\{u_n\}$ is a subsequence still denoted by itself. Combining this and (6.30), similarly to the proof of Lemma 6.7 (ii), we can easily get a contradiction.

So that we conclude that, for a subsequence which we still denote by $\{u_n\}$,

$$I(u_n) \to j_0,$$

$$\|\nabla J(u_n)\| \to 0,$$

as $n \to \infty$. By (6.30) we know that $\{u_n\}$ is bounded in $H^1(\mathbb{R}^N)$, and the weak limit of $\{u_n\}$ which we denote by u_0 is a weak solution of system (6.4). Obviously, $u_0 \in \mathcal{N}$ and

$$j_0 \leqslant J(u_0) = \frac{1}{2}\|u_0\|^2 - \frac{1}{2p}\tilde{B}(u_0) - \tilde{C}(u_0)$$

$$= \left(\frac{1}{2} - \frac{1}{2p}\right)\|u_0\|^2 - \left(1 - \frac{1}{2p}\right)\tilde{C}(u_0)$$

$$\leqslant \liminf J(u_n) = j_0.$$

Therefore, u_0 is a least energy solution.

By now, we only need to show that u_0 is a local minimum solution. We apply Lemma 6.6 to u_0 and $|u_0|$. Since

$$\frac{d}{dt}J(tu_0) = \psi'(t) > 0, \quad t \in (\tilde{t}^+(u_0), \tilde{t}^-(u_0)),$$

we know that $u_0 \in \mathcal{N}^+$. Otherwise, $u_0 \in \mathcal{N}^-$ and $j_0 \leqslant J(\tilde{t}^+(u_0)u_0) < J(u_0) = j_0$ which is a contradiction. By Lemma 6.6 and $u_0 \in \mathcal{N}^+$ we know that

$$1 = \tilde{t}^+(u_0) < \tilde{t}_0(u_0) = \left[\frac{\|u_0\|^2}{(2p-1)\tilde{B}(u_0)}\right]^{1/(2p-2)}.$$

Therefore,

$$1 < \left[\frac{\|u_0 - w\|^2}{(2p-1)\tilde{B}(u_0 - w)}\right]^{1/(2p-2)}, \quad \|w\| < \varepsilon,$$

for ε small enough. Applying Lemma 6.8, we get a $\eta(w) > 0$ such that $\eta(w)(u_0 - w) \in \mathcal{N}$ for $\|w\| < \varepsilon$ small. Moreover, there holds $\eta(w) \to 1$ as $w \to 0$. Thus we can assume that, for $\|w\| < \varepsilon$ sufficiently small,

$$\eta(w) < \left[\frac{\|u_0 - w\|^2}{(2p-1)\tilde{B}(u_0 - w)}\right]^{1/(2p-2)}, \quad \eta(w)(u_0 - w) \in \mathcal{N}^+.$$

Then by Lemma 6.6, we could conclude that

$$J(u_0) \leqslant J(\eta(w)(u_0 - w)) \leqslant J(t(u_0 - w)), \tag{6.33}$$

for

$$0 < \eta < \left[\frac{\|u_0 - w\|^2}{(2p-1)\tilde{B}(u_0 - w)} \right]^{1/(2p-2)}.$$

Taking $\eta = 1$ in (6.33) we have

$$J(u_0) \leqslant J(u_0 - w), \quad \|w\| < \varepsilon,$$

which means u_0 is a local minimum solution.

Additionally, if we assume that $h > 0$,

$$\psi'_{|u_0|}(t) < \psi'_{u_0}(t) < 0, \quad \iota \in [0, 1).$$

Hence, $\tilde{t}^+(|u_0|) \geqslant 1$ and consequently,

$$j_0 \leqslant J(\tilde{t}^+(|u_0|)|u_0|) \leqslant J(|u_0|) \leqslant J(u_0) = j_0.$$

Therefore,

$$\tilde{t}^+(|u_0|) = 1 \quad \text{and} \quad \int_{\mathbb{R}^N} h(x)|u_0| dx = \int_{\mathbb{R}^N} h(x)u_0 dx,$$

which yield $u_0 \geqslant 0$. Then by the maximum principle, we know $u_0 > 0$. The proof is complete.   □

Consider the following nonlinear Schrödinger equation

$$-\Delta u + u = \left(\frac{1}{|x|^\alpha} * |u|^p \right) |u|^{p-2} u \quad \text{in} \quad \mathbb{R}^N. \tag{6.34}$$

By Proposition 2.2 of [143], we know that (6.34) has positive smooth solution $V(x)$, which is also a minimizer of

$$S_{\alpha,p} = \inf_{u \in H^1(\mathbb{R}^N) \setminus \{0\}} \frac{\displaystyle\int_{\mathbb{R}^N} |\nabla u|^2 + u^2 dx}{\left(\displaystyle\int_{\mathbb{R}^N} \int_{\mathbb{R}^N} \frac{|u(x)|^p |u(y)|^p}{|x-y|^\alpha} dx dy \right)^{\frac{1}{p}}}.$$

If V is a positive solution of (6.34) if and only if V is a critical point of the energy functional

$$J(u) = \frac{1}{2} \int_{\mathbb{R}^N} (|\nabla u|^2 + u^2) dx - \frac{1}{2p} \int_{\mathbb{R}^N} \int_{\mathbb{R}^N} \frac{|u(x)|^p |u(y)|^p}{|x-y|^\alpha} dx dy.$$

We know that
$$\|V\| = \tilde{B}(V) = S_{\alpha,p}^{\frac{p}{p-1}}.$$

According to the fact that the Sobolev embedding

$$H^1(\mathbb{R}^N) \hookrightarrow L^q(\mathbb{R}^N) \quad (2 \leqslant q \leqslant 2^*)$$

is not compact, the variational functional $J(u)$ fails to satisfy the (PS) condition. Such a failure brings us some difficulties in applying the variational approach. In order to overcome the lack of compactness, we introduce the following proposition which plays a key role in our argument. We remark here that since $j_0 < 0$, any solution u_0 of system (6.4) with the least energy j_0 satisfies

$$j_0 = J(u_0) = \frac{1}{2}\|u_0\|^2 - \frac{1}{2p}\tilde{B}(u_0) - \int_{\mathbb{R}^N} h(x)u_0 dx$$

$$= \left(\frac{1}{2} - \frac{1}{2p}\right)\|u_0\|^2 - \left(1 - \frac{1}{2p}\right)\int_{\mathbb{R}^N} h(x)u_0 dx$$

$$< 0.$$

Thus, $\int_{\mathbb{R}^N} h(x)u_0 dx > 0$ and consequently, $u_0 \in \mathcal{N}^+$.

Proposition 6.4   Let $N \geqslant 3$ and $0 < \alpha < N$, (H_2) and (H_3) hold. If $\{u_n\}$ be a $(PS)_c$ sequence of J with

$$c < j_0 + \frac{p-1}{2p}S_{\alpha,p}^{\frac{p}{p-1}}, \tag{6.35}$$

then $\{u_n\}$ has a convergent subsequence.

Proof. Obviously, $\|u_n\|$ is bounded. Thus, there exists a $w \in H^1(\mathbb{R}^N)$ which satisfies $u_n \rightharpoonup v$ weakly in $H^1(\mathbb{R}^N)$ and solves (6.4). Therefore, $v \neq 0$ and $J(v) \geqslant j_0$. Let $u_n - v = w_n$, by Brezis-Lieb lemma and Lemmas 2.1 and 2.2 in [94], we deduce

$$\|u_n\|^2 = \|w_n\|^2 + \|v\|^2 + o(1), \quad n \to \infty$$

and

$$\int_{\mathbb{R}^N}\int_{\mathbb{R}^N} \frac{|u_n(x)|^p |u_n(y)|^p}{|x-y|^\alpha} dx dy$$

$$= \int_{\mathbb{R}^N}\int_{\mathbb{R}^N} \frac{|w_n(x)|^p |w_n(y)|^p}{|x-y|^\alpha} dx dy + \int_{\mathbb{R}^N}\int_{\mathbb{R}^N} \frac{|w(x)|^p |w(y)|^p}{|x-y|^\alpha} dx dy + o_n(1)$$

as $n \to \infty$.

So we obtain

$$
\begin{aligned}
c \leftarrow J(u_n) &= \frac{1}{2}\|u_n\|^2 - \frac{1}{2p}\int_{\mathbb{R}^N}\int_{\mathbb{R}^N}\frac{|u_n(x)|^p|u_n(y)|^p}{|x-y|^\alpha}\,dxdy - \int_{\mathbb{R}^N}h(x)u_n dx \\
&= \frac{1}{2}\|w_n\|^2 - \frac{1}{2p}\int_{\mathbb{R}^N}\int_{\mathbb{R}^N}\frac{|w_n(x)|^p|w_n(y)|^p}{|x-y|^\alpha}\,dxdy - \int_{\mathbb{R}^N}h(x)w_n dx \\
&\quad + \frac{1}{2}\|v\|^2 - \frac{1}{2p}\int_{\mathbb{R}^N}\int_{\mathbb{R}^N}\frac{|v(x)|^p|v(y)|^p}{|x-y|^\alpha}\,dxdy - \int_{\mathbb{R}^N}h(x)v dx + o_n(1) \\
&= J(v) + \frac{1}{2}\|w_n\|^2 - \frac{1}{2p}\tilde{B}(w_n) + o_n(1).
\end{aligned}
$$

As the result, for n large we have

$$
\frac{1}{2}\|w_n\|^2 - \frac{1}{2p}\tilde{B}(w_n) + o_n(1) < \frac{p-1}{2p}S_{\alpha,p}^{\frac{p}{p-1}}. \tag{6.36}
$$

On the other hand,

$$
o(1) = \langle J'(u_n), u_n\rangle = \langle J'(v), v\rangle + \|w_n\|^2 - \tilde{B}(w_n) + o(1),
$$

which implies

$$
\|w_n\|^2 - \tilde{B}(w_n) = o(1). \tag{6.37}
$$

If we can show that $\{w_n\}$ has subsequence converging strong to 0, we have done. Therefore, arguing indirectly, we assume $\|w_n\| \geqslant C > 0$ for n large. According to (6.37), we have

$$
\|w_n\|^2 = \tilde{B}(w_n) \leqslant \frac{\|w_n\|^{2p}}{S_{\alpha,p}^p}
$$

and

$$
\begin{aligned}
\frac{1}{2}\frac{p-1}{p}S_{\alpha,p}^{\frac{p}{p-1}} &= \frac{1}{2}\left(1-\frac{1}{p}\right)S^{\frac{p}{p-1}} \\
&\leqslant \frac{1}{2}\left(1-\frac{1}{p}\right)\|w_n\|^2 \\
&= \frac{1}{2}\|w_n\|^2 - \frac{1}{2p}\tilde{B}(w_n) + o_n(1) \\
&< \frac{p-1}{2p}S_{\alpha,p}^{\frac{p}{p-1}},
\end{aligned}
$$

which is a contradiction. The proof is complete. $\qquad\square$

We remark again, in order to prove Theorem 6.2, the only we need to show

$$
j_0 < j_1 = \inf_{\mathcal{N}^-} J(u) < j_0 + \frac{p-1}{2p}S_{\alpha,p}^{\frac{p}{p-1}}.
$$

Consider $V(x)$ is a minimizer for both $S_{\alpha,p}$. Let u_0 be the positive local minimum solution we get above. By the continuity of J, we know that there exists $\gamma > 0$ such that

$$J(u_0 + tV) < j_0 + \frac{p-1}{2p}S_{\alpha,p}^{\frac{p}{p-1}}, \quad 0 \leqslant t < \gamma,$$

$$J(u_0 + tV) = \frac{1}{2}\|u_0 + tV\|^2 - \frac{1}{2p}\tilde{B}(u_0 + tV) - \int_{\mathbb{R}^N} h(u_0 + tV)dx$$

$$= J(u_0) + \frac{t^2}{2}\left[\|V\|^2 - \frac{t^{p-2}}{p}\tilde{B}(V)\right] + \tilde{B}(u_0) + \tilde{B}(tV) - \tilde{B}(u_0 + tV)$$

$$< j_0 + \frac{p-1}{2p}S_{\alpha,p}^{\frac{p}{p-1}}.$$

For $t \geqslant \gamma$, a directly computation shows us

$$J(u_0 + tV) = \frac{1}{2}\|u_0 + tV\|^2 - \frac{1}{2p}\tilde{B}(u_0 + tV) - \int_{\mathbb{R}^N} h(u_0 + tV)dx$$

$$= \frac{1}{2}\|u_0\|^2 + t\int_{\mathbb{R}^N} \nabla u_0 \nabla V + u_0 V dx + \frac{t^2}{2}\|V\|^2 - \frac{1}{2p}\tilde{B}(u_0)$$

$$+ \frac{1}{2p}[\tilde{B}(u_0) + \tilde{B}(tV) - \tilde{B}(u_0 + tV)] - \frac{1}{2p}\tilde{B}(tV)$$

$$- \int_{\mathbb{R}^N} hu_0 dx - \int_{\mathbb{R}^N} htV dx$$

$$= J(u_0) + \frac{t^2}{2}[\|V\|^2 - \frac{t^{2(p-1)}}{2p}\tilde{B}(V)] + \frac{1}{2p}\left[\tilde{B}(u_0) + \tilde{B}(tV)\right.$$

$$- \tilde{B}(u_0 + tV) + 2p\int_{\mathbb{R}^N}\int_{\mathbb{R}^N} \frac{|u_0(x)|^p|u_0(y)|^{p-2}u_0(y)}{|x-y|^\alpha}dxdy\bigg]$$

$$< j_0 + \frac{p-1}{2p}S_{\alpha,p}^{\frac{p}{p-1}}.$$

Here, we use the fact that $\langle J'(u_0), tV \rangle = 0$ and $V(x)$ is a solution of (6.34).

And now we can give the proof of Theorem 6.2.

Proof of Theorem 6.2 In order to show

$$j_0 < j_1 = \inf_{\mathcal{N}^-} J(u) < j_0 + \frac{p-1}{2p}S_{\alpha,p}^{\frac{p}{p-1}}.$$

Firstly, we observe that for every $u \in H^1(\mathbb{R}^N)$ with $\|u\| = 1$, there exists a unique $\eta^-(u) > 0$ such that (see Lemma 6.8)

$$t^-(u) \in \mathcal{N}^-.$$

By Lemma 6.8, we know that $\eta^-(u)$ is a continuous function of u. And consequently the manifold $\mathcal{N}^-$ disconnects $H^1(\mathbb{R}^N)$ in exactly two connected components U_1 and U_2, where

$$U_1 = \left\{ u \in H^1(\mathbb{R}^N) : u = 0 \text{ or } \|u\| < t^- \left(\frac{u}{\|u\|} \right) \right\}$$

and

$$U_2 = \left\{ u \in H^1(\mathbb{R}^N) : \|u\| > t^- \left(\frac{u}{\|u\|} \right) \right\}.$$

Obviously, $H^1(\mathbb{R}^N) = \mathcal{N}^- \cup U_1 \cup U_2$. In particular, $u_0 \in \mathcal{N}^+ \subset U_2$. Since

$$t^- \left(\frac{u_0 + tV}{\|u_0 + tV\|} \right) \frac{u_0 + tV}{\|u_0 + tV\|} \in \mathcal{N},$$

we have

$$0 < t^- \left(\frac{u_0 + tV}{\|u_0 + tV\|} \right) < C_0,$$

uniformly for $t \in \mathbb{R}$.

On the other hand, there exists $\tilde{t} > 0$ satisfies

$$\|u_0 + tU\| \geqslant t\|V\| - \|u_0\| \geqslant C_0, \quad t \geqslant \tilde{t}.$$

So we can fix a $t_0 > 0$ such that

$$\|u_0 + t_0 V\| > t^- \left(\frac{u_0 + t_0 V}{\|u_0 + t_0 V\|} \right).$$

Thus, $u_0 + t_0 V \in U_2$. Combining this and the fact $u_0 \in U_1$, we know that

$$u_0 + t_1 V \in \Lambda^-,$$

for some $0 < t_1 < t_0$. Consequently, by the remark after Proposition 6.4, we have

$$j_1 = \inf_{\Lambda^-} J(u) \leqslant \max_{0 \leqslant t \leqslant t_0} J(u_0 + tV) < j_0 + \frac{p-1}{2p} S_{\alpha,p}^{\frac{p}{p-1}}.$$

Next, we show that j_1 is a critical value of J and satisfies $j_1 > j_0$.

Similarly to the proof of Proposition 6.3, we apply Ekeland's Variational Principle and get a minimizing sequence $\{u_n\} \subset \mathcal{N}^-$ such that

$$J(u_n) < j_1 + \frac{1}{n},$$

$$J(w) \geqslant J(u_n) - \frac{1}{n}\|u - w\|, \quad w \in \mathcal{N}^-.$$

So that we have

$$j_1 + 1 > J(u_n) = \frac{1}{2}\|u_n\|^2 - \frac{1}{2p}\tilde{B}(u_n) - \int_{\mathbb{R}^N} h(x)u_n dx$$

$$\geqslant \left(\frac{1}{2} - \frac{1}{2p}\right)\|u_n\|^2 - \left(1 - \frac{1}{2p}\right)|h|_{\frac{2Np}{2N(p-1)+\alpha}} d_{\frac{2Np}{2N-\alpha}}\|u_n\|,$$

which implies $\|u_n\|$ has a upper bound. Moreover, from $\{u_n\} \subset \mathcal{N}^-$, we know that

$$\|u_n\|^2 \leqslant (2p - 1)\frac{\|u_n\|^p}{S_{\alpha,p}^p}.$$

Thus, $\|u_n\|$ has a uniform positive lower bound. Then, analogously to the proof of Proposition 6.3, we know that

$$J(u_n) \to j_1,$$

$$J'(u_n) \to 0 \quad \text{in} \quad H^{-1}.$$

According to Proposition 6.4 and $j_1 < j_0 + \dfrac{p-1}{2p}S_{\alpha,p}^{\frac{p}{p-1}}$, we can conclude that there exists a subsequence of $\{u_n\}$ such that $u_n \to u_1$ strongly in $H^1(\mathbb{R}^N)$. Therefore u_1 is a critical point of J and $J(u_1) = j_1$. Noting that $\mathcal{N}^-$ is closed, we have $u_1 \in \mathcal{N}^-$. To show $j_1 > j_0$, arguing indirectly, we assume $j_1 = j_0$. Thus by the remark after the proof of Proposition 6.3, we have

$$\int_{\mathbb{R}^N} h(x)u_1 dx > 0, \quad u_1 \in \mathcal{N}^+,$$

which leads to a contradiction.

Finally, we consider the case $h > 0$. Appling Lemma 6.8 to u_1 and $|u_1|$, we know that there exists a $\eta^-(|u_1|)$ such that

$$\eta^-(|u_1|)|u_1| \in \mathcal{N}^-.$$

Moreover,

$$\eta^-(|u_1|) \geqslant \eta_0(|u_1|) = \eta_0(u_1) = \left[\frac{\tilde{A}(u_1)}{(p-1)\tilde{B}(u_1)}\right]^{\frac{1}{p-2}}.$$

Thus both in the case $\displaystyle\int_{\mathbb{R}^N} h(x)u dx > 0$ and $\displaystyle\int_{\mathbb{R}^N} h(x)u dx \leqslant 0$, we can deduce that

$$j_1 = J(u_1) \geqslant J(\eta^-(u_1)u_1) \geqslant J(\eta^-(|u_1|)|u_1|) = \eta_0(u_1) \geqslant j_1.$$

Therefore,

$$\int_{\mathbb{R}^N} h(x)u_1 dx = \int_{\mathbb{R}^N} h(x)|u_1| dx,$$

which implies $u_1 \geqslant 0$. According to the maximum principle we get $u_1 > 0$. The proof is complete. $\qquad\square$

References

[1] Ackermann N. A nonlinear superposition principle and multibump solutions of periodic Schrödinger equations. Journal of Functional Analysis, 2006, 234: 277-320.

[2] Albuquerque F S B, Chen S J, Li L. Solitary wave of ground state type for a nonlinear Klein-Gordon equation coupled with Born-Infeld theory in $\mathbb{R}^2$. Electronic Journal of Qualitative Theory of Differential Equations, 2020, 12: 1-18.

[3] Alves C O, Carrião P C, Medeiros E S. Multiplicity of solutions for a class of quasilinear problem in exterior domains with Neumann conditions. Abstract and Applied Analysis, 2004, 3: 251-268.

[4] Alves C O, Souto M A S, Soares S H M. Schrödinger-Poisson equations without Ambrosetti-Rabinowitz condition. Journal of Mathematical Analysis and Applications, 2011, 377: 584-592.

[5] Alves C O, Yang M B. Investigating the multiplicity and concentration behavior of solutions for a quasilinear Choquard equation via penalization method. Proceedings of the Royal Society of Edinburgh Section A, 2016, 146(1): 23-58.

[6] Alves C O, Cassani D, Daniele, Tarsi C, Yang M B. Existence and concentration of ground state solutions for a critical nonlocal Schrödinger equation in $\mathbb{R}^2$. Journal of Differential Equations, 2016, 261(3): 1933-1972.

[7] Alves C O, Gao F S, Squassina M, Yang M B. Singularly perturbed critical Choquard equations. Journal of Differential Equations, 2017, 263(7): 3943-3988.

[8] Alves C O, Yang M B. Existence of semiclassical ground state solutions for a generalized Choquard equation. Journal of Differential Equations, 2014, 257: 4133-4164.

[9] Ambrosetti A, Rabinowitz P H. Dual variational methods in critical point theory and applications. Journal of Functional Analysis, 1973, 14: 349-381.

[10] Ambrosetti A. On Schrödinger-Poisson systems. Milan Journal of Mathematics, 2008, 76: 257-274.

[11] Ambrosetti A, Ruiz D. Multiple bound states for the Schrödinger-Poisson equation. Communications in Contemporary Mathematics, 2008, 10: 391-404.

[12] Arioli G, Gazzola F, Grunau H C, et al. The second bifurcation branch for radial solutions of the Brézis-Nirenberg problem in dimension four. Nonlinear Differential Equations Applications, 2008, 15: 69-90.

[13] Atkinson F V, Brézis H, Peletier L A. Nodal solutions of elliptic equations with critical Sobolev exponents. Journal of Differential Equations, 1990, 85: 151-170.

[14] Azzollini A, Pomponio A. Ground state solutions for the nonlinear Schrödinger-Maxwell equations. Journal of Mathematical Analysis and Applications, 2008, 345: 90-108.

[15] Azzollini A, Pisani L, Pomponio A. Improved estimates and a limit case for the electrostatic Klein-Gordon-Maxwell system. Proceedings of the Royal Society of Edinburgh Section A, 2011, 141: 449-463.

[16] Badiale M, Tarantello G. A Sobolev Hardy inequality with applications to a nonlinear elliptic equation arising in astrophysics. Archive for Rational Mechanics and Analysis, 2002, 163: 259-293.

[17] Bahrouni A, Ounaies H, Radulescu V. Infinitely many solutions for a class of sublinear Schrödinger equations with indefinite potentials. Proceedings of the Royal Society of Edinburgh Section A, 2015, 145: 445-465.

[18] Bartsch T, Wang Z Q. Existence and multiplicity results for some superlinear elliptic problem on $\mathbb{R}^N$. Communications in Partial Differential Equations, 1995, 20: 1725-1741.

[19] Bartsch T, Peng S J, Zhang Z T. Existence and non-existence of solutions to elliptic equations related to the Caffarelli-Kohn-Nirenberg inequalities. Calculus of Variations and Partial Differential Equations, 2007, 30: 113-136.

[20] Bartsch T, Liu Z L, Weth T. Nodal solutions of a p-Laplacian equation. Proc. Lond. Soc., 2005, 91(3): 129-152.

[21] Bartsch T, Liu Z L, Weth T. Sign changing solutions of superlinear Schrödinger equations. Communications in Partial Differential Equations, 2004, 29: 25-42.

[22] Batt J, Faltenbacher W, Horst E. Stationary spherically symmetric models in stellar dynamics. Archive for Rational Mechanics and Analysis, 1986, 93: 159-183.

[23] Benci V, Fortunato D. An eigenvalue problem for the Schrödinger-Maxwell equations. Topol. Methods Nonlinear Analysis, 1998, 11(2): 283-293.

[24] Benci V, Fortunato D. The nonlinear Klein-Gordon equation coupled with the Maxwell equations. Nonlinear Analysis, 2001, 47: 6065-6072.

[25] Benci V, Fortunato D. Solitary waves of the nonlinear Klein-Gordon equation coupled with the Maxwell equations. Rev. Math. Phys., 2002, 14: 409-420.

[26] Benci V, Fortunato D, Masiello A, Pisani L. Solitons and the electromagnetic field. Math. Z., 1999, 232(1): 73-102.

[27] Benguria R, Brezis H, Lieb E. The Thomas-Fermi-Von Weizsäcker theory of atoms and molecules. Comm. Math. Phys., 1981, 79: 167-180.

[28] Benmansour S, Bouchekif M. Nonhomogeneous elliptic problems of Kirchoff type involving critical Sobolev exponent. Electronic Journal of Differential Equations, 2015, 69: 1-11.

[29] Bhakta M. Infinitely many sign-changing solutions of an elliptic problem involving critical Sobolev and Hardy-Sobolev exponent. Proceedings of the Indian Academy of Sciences, Mathematical sciences, 2017, 127(2): 337-347.

[30] Bhakta M, Sandeep K. Poincaré-Sobolev equations in the hyperbolic space. Calculus of Variations and Partial Differential Equations, 2012, 44 (1-2): 247-269.

[31] Bonheure D, Mercuri C. Embedding theorems and existence results for nonlinear Schrödinger-Poisson systems with unbounded and vanishing potentials. Journal of Differential Equations, 2011, 251(4-5): 1056-1085.

[32] Born M. Modified field equations with a finite radius of the electron. Nature, 1933, 132: 282.

[33] Born M. On the quantum theory of the electromagnetic field. Proceedings of the Royal Society A, 1934, 143: 410-437.

[34] Born M, Infeld L. Foundations of the new field theory. Proceedings of the Royal Society of London, 1934, 425-451.

[35] Brézis H, Lieb E H. A relation between pointwise convergence of functions and convergence functionals. Proceedings of the American Mathematical Society, 1983, 8: 486-490.

[36] Brézis H, Nirenberg L. Positive solutions of nonlinear elliptic problems involving critical Sobolev exponent. Communications on Pure and Applied Mathematics, 1983, 36: 437-477.

[37] Byeon J, Wang Z Q. Standing waves with a critical frequency for nonlinear Schrödinger equations. Archive for Rational Mechanics and Analysis, 2002, 165(4): 295-316.

[38] Caffarelli L, Kohn R, Nirenberg L. First order interpolation inequalities with weights. Compositio Mathematica, 1984, 53: 259-275.

[39] Cao D M, Han P G. Solutions for semilinear elliptic equations with critical exponents and Hardy potential. Journal of Differential Equations, 2004, 205: 521-537.

[40] Cao D M, Han P G. Solutions to critical equation with multi-singular inverse square potentials. Journal of Differential Equations, 2006, 224: 332-372.

[41] Cao D M, Peng S J, Yan S S. Infinitely many solutions for p-Laplacian equation involving critical Sobolev growth. Journal of Functional Analysis, 2012, 262: 2861-2902.

[42] Cao D M, Yan S S. Infinitely many solutions for an elliptic problem involving critical Sobolev growth and Hardy potential. Calculus of Variations and Partial Differential Equations, 2010, 38: 471-501.

[43] Capozzi A, Fortunato D, Palmieri G. An existence result for nonlinear elliptic problems involving critical Sobolev exponent. Ann. Inst. H. Poincaré Anal. Non Linéarier, 1985, 2: 463-470.

[44] Carmeli M. Field theory on $R \times S$ 3 topology I: The Klein-Gordon and Schrödinger equations. Foundations of Physics, 1985, 15: 175-184.

[45] Carrião P C, Cunha P L, Miyagaki O H. Existence results for the Klein-Gordon-Maxwell equations in higher dimensions with critical exponents. Communications on Pure and Applied Analysis, 2011, 10(2): 709-718.

[46] Carrião P C, Cunha P L, Miyagaki O H. Positive ground state solutions for the critical Klein-Gordon-Maxwell system with potentials. Nonlinear Analysis, 2012, 75(10) : 4068-4078.

[47] Cassani D. Existence and non-existence of solitary waves for the critical Klein-Gordon equation coupled with Maxwell's equations. Nonlinear Analysis, 2004, 58: 733-747.

[48] Castorina D, Fabbri I, Mancini G, Sandeep K. Hardy-Sobolev extremals, hyperbolic symmetry and scalar curvature equations. Journal of Differential Equations, 2009, 246: 1187-1206.

[49] Cerami G, Vaira G. Positive solution for some non-autonomous Schrödinger-Poisson systems. Journal of Differential Equations, 2010, 248: 521-543.

[50] Cerami G, Fortunato D, Struwe M. Bifurcation and multiplicity results for nonlinear elliptic problems involving critical Sobolev exponents. Ann. Inst. H. Poincaré Anal. Non Linéarier, 1984, 1: 341-350.

[51] Cerami G, Solimini S, Struwe M. Some existence results for superlinear elliptic boundary value problems involving critical exponents. Journal of Functional Analysis, 1986, 69: 289-306.

[52] Cerami G, Vaira G. Multiple solutions for nonhomogeneous Schrödinger-Maxwell and Klein-Gordon-Maxwell equations on $\mathbb{R}^3$. Journal of Differential Equations, 2010, 248: 521-543.

[53] Chen S W, Wang Z Q. Localized nodal solutions of higher topological type for semiclassical nonlinear Schrödinger equations. Calculus of Variations and Partial Differential Equations, 2017, 56(1): 1-26.

[54] Chen S J, Tang C L. High energy solutions for the superlinear Schrödinger-Maxwell equations. Nonlinear Analysis, 2009, 71: 4927-4934.

[55] Chen S J, Tang C L. Multiple solutions for a non-homogeneous Schrödinger-Maxwell and Klein-Gordon-Maxwell equations on $\mathbb{R}^3$. Nonlinear Differential Equations and Applications, 2010, 17: 559-574.

[56] Chen S J, Li L. Multiple solutions for the nonhomogeneous Klein-Gordon equation coupled with Born-Infeld theory on $\mathbb{R}^3$. Journal of Mathematical Analysis and Applications, 2013, 400: 517-524.

[57] Chen S J, Li L. Infinitely many solutions for Klein-Gordon-Maxwell system with potentials vanishing at infinity. Zeitschrift fur Analysis und ihre Anwendungen, 2018, 37: 39-50.

[58] Chen H Y, Liu S B. Standing waves with large frequency for 4-superlinear Schrödinger-Poisson systems. Annali di Matematica, 2015, 194: 43-53.

[59] Chen S J, Song S Z. Multiple solutions for nonhomogeneous Klein-Gordon-Maxwell equations on $\mathbb{R}^3$. Nonlinear Analysis: Real World Applications, 2015, 22: 259-271.

[60] Chen S J, Song S Z. The existence of multiple solutions for the Klein-Gordon equation with concave and convex nonlinearities coupled with Born-Infeld theory on $\mathbb{R}^3$. Nonlinear Analysis, 2017, 38: 78-95.

[61] Chen Z J, Zou W M. On an elliptic problem with critical exponent and Hardy potential. Journal of Differential Equations, 2012, 252: 969-987.

[62] Chern J L, Lin C S. Minimizers of Caffarelli-Kohn-Nirenberg inequalities with the singularity on the boundary. Archive for Rational Mechanics and Analysis, 2010, 197: 401-432.

[63] Chipot M, Lovat B. Some remarks on nonlocal elliptic and parabolic problems. Nonlinear Analysis, 1997, 30(7): 4619-4627.

[64] Choquard P, Stubbe J, Vuffray M. Stationary solutions of the Schröinger-Newton model—an ODE approach. Differential Integral Equations, 2008, 21(7-8): 665-679.

[65] Cingolani S, Lazzo N. Multiple semiclassical standing waves for a class of nonlinear Schrödinger equations. Topological Methods in Nonlinear Analysis, 1997, 10: 1-13.

[66] Cingolani S, Secchi S. Ground states for the pseudorelativistic Hartree equation with external potential. Proceedings of the Royal Society of Edinburgh Section A, 2015, 145(1): 73-90.

[67] Cingolani S, Clapp M, Secchi S. Intertwining semiclassical solutions to a Schrödinger-Newton system. Discrete and Continuous Dynamical Systems S, 2013, 6(4): 891-908.

[68] Cingolani S, Clapp M, Secchi S. Multiple solutions to a magnetic nonlinear Choquard equation. Zeitschrift für Angewandte Mathematik und Physik, 2012, 63: 233-248.

[69] Coclite G M. A multiplicity result for the nonlinear Schrödinger-Maxwell equations. Communications on Pure and Applied Analysis, 2003, 7(2-3): 417-423.

[70] Coclite G M. A multiplicity result for the Schrödinger-Maxwell equations with negative potential. Annales Polonici Mathematici, 2002, 79(1): 21-30.

[71] Clapp M, Weth T. Multiple solutions for the Brézis-Nirenberg problem. Advances in Differential Equations, 2005, 10: 463-480.

[72] Clapp M, Salazar D. Positive and sign changing solutions to a nonlinear Choquard equation. Journal of Mathematical Analysis and Applications, 2013, 407: 1-15.

[73] Cunha P. Subcritical and supercritical Klein-Gordon-Maxwell equtions without Ambrosetti-Rabinowitz condition. Differential Integral Equations, 2014, 27(3/4): 387-399.

[74] DAprile T, Mugnai D. Non-existence results for the coupled Klein-Gordon-Maxwell equations. Advanced Nonlinear Studies, 2004, 4(3): 307-322.

[75] DAprile T, Mugnai D. Solitary waves for nonlinear Klein-Gordon-Maxwell and Schrödinger-Maxwell equations. Proceedings of the Royal Society of Edinburgh Section A, 2004, 134: 893-906.

[76] D'Avenia P, Pisani L. Nonlinear Klein-Gordon equations coupled with Born-Infeld type equations. Electronic Journal of Differential Equations, 2002, 26: 1-13.

[77] D'Avenia P, Pisani L, Siciliano G. Dirichlet and Neumann problems for Klein-Gordon-Maxwell systems. Nonlinear Analysis, 2009, 71(12): 1985-1995.

[78] d'Avenia P, Pisani L, Siciliano G. Klein-Gordon-Maxwell system in a bounded domain. Discrete and Continuous Dynamical Systems, 2010, 26(1): 135-159.

[79] Devillanova G, Solimini S. Concentration estimates and multiple solutions to elliptic problems at critical growth. Advances in Differential Equations, 2002, 7: 1257-1280.

[80] Devillanova G, Solimini S. A multiplicity result for elliptic equations at critical growth in low dimension. Communications in Contemporary Mathematics, 2003, 15: 171-177.

[81] Ding L, Li L, Zhang J L. Mulltiple solutions for nonhomogeneous Schrödinger-Poisson system with asymptotical nonlinearity in $\mathbb{R}^3$. Taiwanese Journal of Mathematics, 2013, 17(5): 1627-1650.

[82] Ding Y H, Szulkin A. Bound states for semilinear Schröinger equations with sign-changing potential. Calculus of Variations and Partial Differential Equations, 2007, 29: 397-419.

[83] Du M, Zhang F B. Existence of positive solutions for a nonhomogeneous Schrödinger-Poisson system in $\mathbb{R}^3$. International Journal of Nonlinear Science, 2013, 16(2): 185-192.

[84] Du M, Zhang F B. Multiple solutions for nonhomogeneous Schrödinger-Poisson systems with asymptotical nonlinearity in $\mathbb{R}^3$. International Journal of Nonlinear Sciences, 2013, 16: 185-192.

[85] Ekeland I. Convexity Methods in Hamiltonian Mechanics. Berlin: Springer-Verlag, 1990.

[86] Estaban M J, Lions P L. Existence and nonexistence results for semilinear elliptic problem in unbounded domains. Proceedings of the Royal Society of Edinburgh Section A, 1982/83, 93: 1-14.

[87] Felsager B. Geometry, Particles and Fields. Odense: Odense University Press, 1981.

[88] Figueiredo G M, Ikoma N, Santos Junior J R. Existence and concentration result for the Kirchhoff type equations with general nonlinearities. Archive for Rational Mechanics and Analysis, 2014, 213: 931-979.

[89] Filippucci R, Pucci P, Robert F. On a p-Laplace equation with multiple critical nonlinearities. Journal of Math. Pures Appl., 2009, 91(2): 156-177.

[90] Floer A, Weistein A. Nonspreading wave packets for the cubi Schrödinger equation with a bounded potential. Journal of Functional Analysis, 1986, 69: 397-408.

[91] Fortunato D, Orsani L, Pisina L. Born-Infeld type equations for electrostatic fields. Journal of Mathematical Physics, 2002, 11: 5698-5706.

[92] Fortunato D, Jannelli E. Infinitely many solutions for some nonlinear elliptic problems in symmetrical domains. Proceedings of the Royal Society of Edinburgh Section A, 1987, 105: 205-213.

[93] Ganguly D. Sign changing solutions of the Hardy-Sobolev-Maz'ya equation. Advanced Nonlinear Analysis, 2014, 3(3): 187-196.

[94] Gao F S, Yang M B. On the Brezis-Nirenberg type critical problem for nonlinear Choquard equation. Science China Mathematics, 2018, 61(7): 1219-1242.

[95] Gao F S, Yang M B. A strongly indefinite Choquard equation with critical exponent due to the Hardy-Littlewood-Sobolev inequality. Communications in Contemporary Mathematics, 2017: 1750037.

[96] Gazzini M, Musina R. Hardy-Sobolev-Maz'ya inequalities: symmetry and breaking symmetry of extremals. Communications in Contemporary Mathematics, 2009, 11(6): 993-1007.

[97] Georgiev V, Visciglia N. Solitary waves for Klein-Gordon-Maxwell system with external Coulomb potential. J. Math. Pures Appl., 2005, 9: 957-983.

[98] Ghanmi A, Maagli H, Radulescu V, Zeddini N. Large and bounded solutions for a class of nonlinear Schrödinger stationary systems. Analysis and Applications, 2009, 7: 391-404.

[99] Ghoussoub N, Kang X S. Hardy-Sobolev critical elliptic equations with boundary singularities. Ann. Inst. H. Poincaré Anal. Non Linéarier, 2004, 21: 767-793.

[100] Ghoussoub N, Robert F. The effect of curvature on the best constant in the Hardy-Sobolev inequalities. Geometric and Functional Analysis, 2006, 16: 1201-1245.

[101] Ghoussoub N, Yuan N C. Multiple solutions for quasilinear PDEs involving critical Sobolev and Hardy exponents. Transactions of the American Mathematical Society, 2000, 352: 5703-5743.

[102] Gidas B, Ni W M, Nirenberg L. Symmetry of positive solutions of nonlinear elliptic equations in $\mathbb{R}^3$. Adv. Math. Suppl. Stud., 1981, 7: 369-402.

[103] He X M, Zou W M. Existence and concentration behavior of positive solutions for Kirchhoff equation in $\mathbb{R}^3$. Journal of Differential Equations, 2012, 2: 1813-1834.

[104] He X M. Multiplicity of solutions for a nonlinear Klein-Gordon-Maxwell system. Acta Applicandae Mathematicae, 2014, 130: 237-250.

[105] He Y. Concentrating bounded states for a class of singularly perturbed Kirchhoff type equations with a general nonlinearity. Journal of Differential Equations, 2016, 261: 6178-6220.

[106] Hsia C H, Lin C S, Wadade H. Revisiting an idea of Brezis and Nirenberg. Journal of Functional Analysis, 2010, 259: 1816-1849.

[107] Huang L R, Rocha E M, Chen J Q. Two positive solutions of a class of Schrödinger-Poisson system with indefinite nonlinearity. Journal of Differential Equations, 2013, 255: 2463-2483.

[108] Huang L R, Rocha E M. A positive solution of a Schrödinger-Poisson system with critical exponent. Communications in Mathematical Analysis, 2013, 15: 29-43.

[109] Huang L R, Rocha E M, Chen J Q. Positive and sign-changing solutions of a Schrödinger-Poisson system involving a critical nonlinearity. Journal of Mathematical Analysis and Applications, 2013, 408: 55-69.

[110] Jannelli E. The role played by space dimension in elliptic critical problems. Journal of Differential Equations, 1999, 156: 407-426.

[111] Jeanjean L. On the existence of bounded Palais-Smale sequences and application to a Landesman-Lazer-type problem set on $\mathbb{R}^N$. Proceedings of the Royal Society of Edinburgh Section A, 1999, 129: 787-809.

[112] Jiang Y S, Wang Z P, Zhou H S. Multiple solutions for a nonhomogeneous Schrödinger-Maxwell system in $\mathbb{R}^3$. Nonlinear Analysis, 2013, 83: 50-57.

[113] Kikuchi H. On the existence of a solution for elliptic system related to the Maxwell-Schrödinger equations. Nonlinear Analysis, 2007, 67(5): 1445-1456.

[114] Kirchhoff G. Mechanik. Leipzig: Teubner, 1883.

[115] Li Y Y. On the positive solutions of the Matukuma equation. Duke Mathematical Journal, 1993, 70: 575-589.

[116] Li Y Y, Ni W N. On conformal scalar curvature equations in $\mathbb{R}^N$. Duke Mathematical Journal, 1988, 57: 895-924.

[117] Li Y Y. On the existence and symmetry properties of finite total mass solutions on Matukuma equation, the Eddington equation and their generalization. Archive for Rational Mechanics and Analysis, 1989, 108: 175-194.

[118] Li L, Tang C L. Infinitely many solutions for a nonlinear Klein-Gordon-Maxwell system. Nonlinear Analysis, 2014, 110: 157-169.

[119] Li G B, Ye H Y. Existence of positive ground state solutions for the nonlinear Kirchhoff type equations in $\mathbb{R}^3$. Journal of Differential Equations, 2014, 257: 566-600.

[120] Li L, Boucherif A, Merzagui N D. Multiple solutions for 4-superlinear Klein-Gordon-Maxwell system without odd nonlinearity. Taiwanese Journal of Mathematics, 2017, 21(1): 151-165.

[121] Li L, Sun J J, Tersian S. Infinitely many sign-changing solutions for the Brézis-Nirenberg problem involving the fractional Laplacian. Fractional Calculus and Applied Analysis, 2017, 20(5): 1146-1164.

[122] Li S J, Wang Z Q. Ljusternik-Schnirelman theory in partially ordered Hilbert spaces. Transactions of the American Mathematical Society, 2002, 354: 3207-3227.

[123] Lieb E H. Thomas-Fermi and related theories and molecules. Reviews of Modern Physics, 1981, 53: 603-641.

[124] Lieb E H. Existence and uniqueness of the minimizing solution of Choquard's nonlinear equation. Studies in Applied Mathematics, 1976/77, 57(2): 93-105.

[125] Lieb E H, Loss M. Analysis. Graduate Studies in Mathematics. Am. Math. Soc., Provience 2001.

[126] Lions P L. The Choquard equation and related questions. Nonlinear Analysis, 1980, 4(6): 1063-1072.

[127] Li Y Y, Lin C S. A nonlinear elliptic PDE with two Sobolev-Hardy critical exponents. Archive for Rational Mechanics and Analysis, 2012, 203: 943-968.

[128] Lions P L. The concentration-compactness principle in the calculus of variations: the limit case. Rev. Mat. Iberoamericana, 1985, 1: 45-121, 145-201.

[129] Lions P L. Solutions of Hartree-Fock equations for Coulomb systems. Communications in Mathematical Physics, 1984, 109: 33-97.

[130] Liu Z L, van Heerden F A, Wang Z Q. Nodal type bound states of Schrödinger equations via invariant set and minimax methods. Journal of Differential Equations, 2005, 214: 358-390.

[131] Liu J Q, Liu X Q, Wang Z Q. Multiple mixed states of nodal solutions for nonlinear Schrödinger systems. Calculus of Variations and Partial Differential Equations, 2015, 52: 565-586.

[132] Liu X Q, Chen S J, Tang C L. Ground state solutions for Klein-Gordon-Maxwell system with steep potential well. Applied Mathematics Letters, 2019, 90: 175-180.

[133] Liu X Q, Tang C L. Infinitely many solutions and concentration of ground state solutions for the Klein-Gordon-Maxwell system. Journal of Mathematical Analysis and Applications, 2022, 505: 1-18.

[134] Liu X Q, Li G D, Tang C L. Existence of nontrivial solutions for the Klein-Gordon-Maxwell system with Berestycki-Lions conditions. Advances in Nonlinear Analysis, 2023, 12: 1-30.

[135] Li S J, Zhang Z T. Topology and Variational Methods and Their Applications (Chinese). Beijing: Science Press, 2021.

[136] Ma L, Zhao L. Classification of positive solitary solutions of the nonlinear Choquard equation. Archive for Rational Mechanics and Analysis, 2010, 195: 455-467.

[137] Mancini G, Sandeep K. On a semilinear elliptic equation in H^n. Ann. Soc. Norm. Super. Pisa CI. Sci., 2008, 7(4): 635-671.

[138] Mancini G, Fabbri I, Sandeep K. Classification of solutions of a critical Hardy Sobolev Operator. Journal of Differential Equations, 2006, 224: 258-276.

[139] Markowich P, Ringhofer C, Schmeiser C. Semiconductor Equations. New York: Springer-Verlag, 1990.

[140] Mawhin J, Willem M. Critical Point Theory and Hamiltonian Systems. New York: Springer, 1989.

[141] Mercuri C. Positive solutions of nonlinear Schrödinger-Poisson systems with radial potentials vanishing at infinity. (English summary) Atti Accad. Naz. Lincei Cl. Sci. Fis. Mat. Natur. Rend. Lincei Mat. Appl., 2008, 19(3): 211-227.

[142] Moroz V, van Schaftingen J. Existence of groundstates for a class of nonlinear choquard equations. Transactions of the American Mathematical Society, 2015, 367(9): 6557-6579.

[143] Moroz V, van Schaftingen J. Groundstates of nonlinear Choquard equations: existence, qualitative properties and decay asymptotics. Journal of Functional Analysis, 2013, 265(2): 153-184.

[144] Moroz V, van Schaftingen J. Nonexistence and optimal decay of supersolutions to Choquard equations in exterior domains. Journal of Differential Equations, 2013, 254(8): 3089-3145.

[145] Moroz I M, Penrose R, Tod P. Spherically-symmetric solutions of the Schröinger-Newton equations. Classical Quantum Gravity, 1998, 15(9): 2733-2742.

[146] Mugnai D. Coupled Klein-Gorndon and Born-Infeld type equations: looking for solitary waves. Proceedings of the Royal Society of London, 2004, 460: 1519-1527.

[147] Musina R. Ground state solutions of a critical problem involving cylindrical weights. Nonlinear Analysis, 2008, 68: 3927-3986.

[148] Nieto J J, ORegan D. Variational approach to impulsive differential equations. Nonlinear Analysis: Real World Appllications, 2009, 10: 680-690.

[149] Oh Y G. Corrections to existence of semi-classical bounded states of nonlinear Schrödinger equations with potential on the class $(V)_a$. Communications in Partial Differential Equations, 1989, 14: 833-834.

[150] Pekar S I. Untersuchungen über die Elektronentheorie der Kristalle. Berlin: Akademie Verlag, 1954.

[151] Perera Kanishka K, Zhang Z T. Nontrivial solutions of Kirchhoff-type problems via the Yang index. Journal of Differential Equations, 2006, 221(1): 246-255.

[152] del Pino M, Felmer P. Local mountain passes for semilnear elliptic problems in unbounded domains. Calculus of Variations and Partial Differential Equations, 1996, 4: 121 137.

[153] Qi Z X, Zhang Z T. Existence of multiple solutions to a class of nonlinear Schrödinger system with external sources terms. Journal of Mathematical Analysis and Applications, 2014, 420(2): 972-986.

[154] Rabinowitz P H. Minimax Methods in Critical Point Theory with Applications to Differential Equations. CBMS Reg. Conf. Ser. Math., vol. 65, Amer. Math. Soc., Providence, RI, 1986.

[155] Ruiz D. The Schrödinger-Poisson equation under the effect of a nonlinear local term. Journal of Functional Analysis, 2006, 237(2): 655-674.

[156] Sato Y, Tanaka K. Sign-changing multi-bump solutions for nonlinear Schrödinger equations with steep potential wells. Transactions of the American Mathematical Society, 2009, 361: 6205-6253.

[157] Shen Z P, Han Z Q. Multiple solutions for a class of Schrödinger-Poisson systems with indefinite nonlinearity. Journal of Mathematical Analysis and Applications, 2015, 426(2): 839-854.

[158] Schechter M, Zou W M. On the Brézis-Nirenberg problem. Archive for Rational Mechanics and Analysis, 2010, 197: 337-356.

[159] Salvatore A. Multiple solitary waves for a non-homogeneous Schrödinger-Maxwell system in $\mathbb{R}^3$. Advanced Nonlinear Studies, 2006, 6(2): 157-169.

[160] Seok J. On nonlinear Schrödinger-Poisson equations with general potentials. Journal of Mathematical Analysis and Applications, 2013, 401: 672-681.

[161] Shi H X, Chen H B. Multiple positive solutions for nonhomogeneous Klein-Gordon-Maxwell equations. Applied Mathematics and Computation, 2018, 337: 504-513.

[162] Solimini S. A note on compactness-type properties with respect to Lorentz norms of bounded subsets of a Sovolev space. Ann. Inst. H. Poincaré Anal. Non Linéarier, 1995, 12: 319-337.

[163] Strauss W A. Existence of solitary waves in higher dimensions. Communications in Mathematical Physics, 1977, 55: 149-162.

[164] Struwe M. Variational Methods. Applications to Nonlinear Partial Differential Equations and Hamiltonian Systems. 3rd Edition. Berlin: Springer-Verlag, 2000.

[165] Struwe M. A global compactness result for elliptic boundary value problems involving limiting nonlinearities. Mathematische Zeitschrift, 1984, 187: 511-517.

[166] Sun J J, Ma S W. Infinitely many sign-changing solutions for the Brézis-Nirenberg problem. Communication on Pure and Applied Ananlysis, 2014, 13(6): 2317-2330.

[167] Sun J T, Chen H B, Nieto J J. Homoclinic solutions for a class of subquadratic second-order Hamiltonian systems. Journal of Mathematical Analysis and Applications, 2011, 373: 20-29.

[168] Sun J T, Chen H B, Nieto J J. Homoclinic orbits for a class of first-order nonperiodic asymptotically quadratic Hamiltonian systems with spectrum point zero. Journal of Mathematical Analysis and Applications, 2011, 378: 117-127.

[169] Sun J T. Infinitely many solutions for a class of sublinear Schrödinger-Maxwell equations. Journal of Mathematical Analysis and Applications, 2012, 390: 514-522.

[170] Sun M Z, Su J B, Zhao L G. Infinitely many solutions for a Schrödinger-Poisson system with concave and convex nonlinearities. Discrete and Continuous Dynamical Systems, 2015, 35: 427-440.

[171] Sun J T, Wu T F. On the nonlinear Schrödinger-Poisson system with sign-changing potential. Zeitschrift für angewandte Mathematik und Physik, 2015, 66(4): 1-21.

[172] Sun J T, Chen H B, Nieto J J. On ground state solutions for some non-autonomous Schrödinger-Poisson systems. Journal of Differential Equations 2012, 252: 3365-3380.

[173] Szulkin A, Weth T, Willem M. Ground state solutions for a semilinear problem with critical exponent. Differential Integral Equations, 2009, 22: 913-926.

[174] Tarantello G. On nonhomogeneous elliptic equations involving critical Sobolev exponent. Ann. Inst. H. Poincaré Anal. Non Linéarier, 1991, 9(3): 281-304.

[175] Teng K M, Zhang K. Existence of solitary wave solutions for the nonlinear Klein-Gordon equation coupled with Born-Infeld theory with critical Sobolev exponent. Nonlinear Analysis, 2011, 74(12): 4241-4251.

[176] Teng K M. Existence and multiple of the solutions for the nonlinear Klein-Gordon equation coupled with Born-Infeld theory on boundary domain. Differential Equations and Applications, 2012, 4(3): 445-457.

[177] Tertikas A K, Tintarev K. On the existence of minimizers for the Hardy-Sobolev-Maz'ya inequality. Ann. Mat. Pura Appl., 2007, 186(1): 645-662.

[178] Vaira G. Semiclassical states for the nonlinear Klein-Gordon-Maxwell system. J. Pure and Applied Mathematics: Advances and Aplications, 2010, 4(1): 59-95.

[179] Maz'ja V G. Sobolev Spaces. Springer Ser. in Soviet Math. Berlin: Springer-Verlag, 1985.

[180] Wang C H, Wang T J. Infinitely many solutions for Hardy-Sobolev-Maz'ya equation involving critical growth. Communications in Contemporary Mathematics, 2012, 14(6): 1-38.

[181] Wang F Z. Solitary waves for the coupled nonlinear Klein-Gordon and Born-Infeld type equations. Electronic Journal of Differential Equations, 2012, 82: 1-12.

[182] Wang F Z. Solitary waves for the Klein-Gordon-Maxwell system with critical exponent. Nonlinear Analysis, 2011, 74: 827-835.

[183] Wang F Z. Ground-state solutions for the electrostatic nonlinear Klein-Gordon-Maxwell system. Nonlinear Analysis, 2011, 74(14): 4796-4803.

[184] Wang C H, Yang J. Infinitely many solutions for an elliptic problem with double Hardy-Sobolev-Maz'ya terms. Discrete and Continuous Dynamical Systems, 2016, 36(3): 1603-1628.

[185] Wang Z P, Zhou H S. Positive solutions for a nonlinear stationary Schrödinger-Poisson system in $\mathbb{R}^3$. Discrete and Continuous Dynamical Systems, 2007, 18: 809-816.

[186] Wang L X, Wang X M, Zhang L Y. Ground state solutions for the critical Klein-Gordon-Maxwell system. Acta Mathematica Scientia, 2019, 39B(5): 1451-1460.

[187] Wang L X, Xiong C L, Zhao P P. On the existence and multiplicity of solutions for nonlinear Klein-Gordon-Maxwell systems. Electronic Journal of Qualitative Theory of Differential Equations, 2023, 19: 1-18.

[188] Wang L X, Ma S W. Multiple solutions for a nonhomogeneous Schrödinger-Poisson system with concave and convex nonlinearities. Journal of Applied Analysis and Computation, 2019, 9(2): 628-637.

[189] Wang L X. Infinitely many sign-changing solutions for Hardy-Sobolev-Maz'ya equation involving critical growth. Rocky Mountain Journal of Mathmatics, 2019, 49(4): 1371-1390.

[190] Wang L X, Chen S J. Two solutions for nonhomogeneous Klein-Gordon-Maxwell system with sign-changing potential. Electronic Journal of Differential Equations, 2018, 2018(124): 1-21.

[191] Wang L X, Ma S W, Xu N. Multiple solutions for nonhomogeneous Schrödinger-Poisson equations with sign-changing potential. Acta Mathematica Scientia, 2017, 37B(2): 555-572.

[192] Wang L X, Ma S W, Wang X M. On the existence of solutions for nonhomogeneous Schrödinger-Poisson system. Boundary Value Problems, 2016, 76: 1-11.

[193] Wang L X. Two solutions for nonhomogeneous klein-Gordon-Maxwell system. Electronic Journal of Qualitative Theory of Differential Equations, 2019, 40: 1-12.

[194] Wang L X, Xiong C L, Zhao P P. Two solutions for the nonhomogeneous Klein-Gordon equation coupled with Born-Infeld theory on R^3. Electronic Journal of Diffferential Equations, 2022, 74: 1-11.

[195] Wang L X. Localized nodal solutions for semiclassical nonlinear Kirchhoff equations. Electronic Journal of Diffferential Equations, 2022, 57: 1-23.

[196] Wang L X, Zhao P P. Sign-changing solutions for an elliptic equation involving critical Sobolev and Hardy-Sobolev exponent. Acta Scientiarum Naturalium Universitatis Nankaiensis, 2023, 56: 61-70.

[197] Wang L X, Zhao P P, Zhang D. Infinitely many sign-changing solutions for an elliptic equation involving double critical Hardy-Sobolev-Maz'ya terms. Nonlinear Analysis: Modelling and Control, 2022, 5: 1-16.

[198] Wang J, Tian L X, Xu J X, Zhang F B. Existence and concentration of positive solutions for semilinear Schrödinger-Poisson systems in $\mathbb{R}^3$. Calculus of Variations and Partial Differential Equations, 2013, 48: 243-273.

[199] Wen L X, Tang X H, Chen S T. Infinitely many solutions and least energy solutions for Klein-Gordon equation coupled with Born-Infeld theory. Complex Variables and Elliptic Equations, 2019, 1-14.

[200] Willem M. Minimax Theorems. Progress in Nonlinear Differential Equations and their Applications, 24. Boston: Birkhäuser Boston Inc., 1996.

[201] Willem M. Analyse Harmonique Réelle. Paris: Hermann, 1995.

[202] Wu T F. Multiplicity results for a semi-linear elliptic equation involving sign-changing weigh function. Rocky Mountain Journal of Mathematics, 2009, 39(3): 995-1011.

[203] Wu T F. Four positive solutions for a semilinear elliptic equation involving concave and convex nonlinearities. Nonlinear Analysis, 2009, 70: 1377-1392.

[204] Wu T F. The Nehari manifold for a semilinear elliptic system involving sign-changing weight functions. Nonlinear Analysis, 2008, 68: 1733-1745.

[205] Wu Y Z, Huang Y S. Infinitely many sign-changing solutions for p-Laplacian equation involving the critical Sobolev exponent. Boundary Value Problems, 2013, 2013: 1-10.

[206] Xie T, Xiao L, Wang J. Existence of multiple positive solutions for choquard equation with perturbation. Advances in Mathematical Physics, 2015, 2015: 1-10.

[207] Xu L P, Chen H B. Existence and multiplicity of solutions for nonhomogenous Klein-Gordon-Maxwell equations. Electronic Journal of Diffferential Equations, 2015, 102: 1-12.

[208] Xu L P, Chen H B. Existence of positive ground state solutions of critical nonlinear Klein – Gordon – Maxwell systems. Electronic Journal of Qualitative Theory of Differential Equations, 2022, 44: 1-19.

[209] Yan S S, Yang J F. Infinitely many solutions for an elliptic problem involving critical Sobolev and Hardy-Sobolev exponents. Calculus of Variations and Partial Differential Equations, 2013, 48: 587-610.

[210] Yang M B, Li B R. Solitary waves for non-homogeneous Schrödinger-Maxwell system. Appl. Math. Comput., 2009, 215: 66-70.

[211] Yang Y. Classical solutions in the Born-Infeld theory. R. Soc. Lond. Proc. Ser. A Math. Phys. Eng. Sci., 1995, 456: 615-640.

[212] Ye Y W, Tang C L. Existence and multiplicity of solutions for Schrödinger-Poisson equations with sign-changing potential. Calculus of Variations and Partial Differential Equations, 2015, 53: 383-411.

[213] Yu Y. Solitary waves for nonlinear Klein-Gordon equations coupled with Born-Infeld theory. Ann. Inst. H. Poincaré Anal. Non Linéarier, 2010, 27(1): 351-376.

[214] Zhao L G, Zhao F K. Positive solutions for Schrödinger-Poisson equations with a critical exponent. Nonlinear Analysis, 2009, 70: 2150-2164.

[215] Zhao L G, Zhao F K. On the existence of solutions for the Schrödinger-Poisson equations. Journal of Mathematical Analysis and Applications, 2008, 346(1): 155-169.

[216] Zhao L G, Liu H D, Zhao F K. Existence and concentration of solutions for the Schröinger-Poisson equations with steep well potential. Journal of Differential Equations, 2013, 255: 1-23.

[217] Zhang J J, Liu Z S, Squassina M. Modulational stability of ground states to nonlinear Kirchhoff equations. Journal of Mathematical Analysis and Applications, 2019, 477: 844-859.

[218] Zhang Z H, Liu J L. Existence and multiplicity of sign-changing solutions for Klein-Gordon equation coupled with Born-Infeld theory with subcritical exponent. Qualitative Theory of Dynamical Systems, 2023: 22(7), 1-29.

[219] Zhang H, Xu J X, Zhang F B. Bound and Ground states for a concave-convex generaliezed Choquard equation. Acta Applicandae Mathematicae, 2017, 147: 81-93.

[220] Zhang J, Ma S W. Infinitely many sign-changing solutions for the Brézis-Nirenberg problem involving Hardy potential. Acta Mathematica Scientia, 2016, 36B (2): 527-536.

[221] Zhang Z T, Perera K. Sign changing solutions of Kirchhoff type problems via invariant sets of descent flow. Journal of Mathematical Analysis and Applications, 2006, 317(2): 456-463.

[222] Zhang Z T. Variational, topological, and partial order methods with their applications. Developments in Mathematics, 29. Heidelberg: Springer, 2013.

[223] Zhang J J, Zou W M. Solutions concentrating around the saddle points of the potential for critical Schrödinger equations. Calculus of Variations and Partial Differential Equations, 2015, 54: 4119-4142.

[224] Zou W M, Schechter M. Critical Point Theory and its Applications. New York: Springer, 2006.

Index

编 后 记

　　《博士后文库》是汇集自然科学领域博士后研究人员优秀学术成果的系列丛书.《博士后文库》致力于打造专属于博士后学术创新的旗舰品牌，营造博士后百花齐放的学术氛围，提升博士后优秀成果的学术和社会影响力.

　　《博士后文库》出版资助工作开展以来，得到了全国博士后管委会办公室、中国博士后科学基金会、中国科学院、科学出版社等有关单位领导的大力支持，众多热心博士后事业的专家学者给予积极的建议，工作人员做了大量艰苦细致的工作.在此，我们一并表示感谢！

《博士后文库》编委会